OSTEND

MAXSENSE MAXIMUS

Printed on-demand at various locations.

For more information: www.maxsensemaximus.com

Book design by Euraus Developments Pty Ltd
Cover design by Euraus Developments Pty Ltd

ISBN - Paperback: 978-0-6488470-4-5
ISBN - Ebook : 978-0-6488470-5-2

First Edition: November 2024
Second Edition: April 2025

DEDICATED

To L.N.L.L.

TABLE OF CONTENTS

Preface

OSTEND

Noun: A port and resort town in North West Belgium
Verb: To exhibit; to reveal; to manifest

Chapter one

I will drink to your tits!

Eight thousand companies and organisations worldwide have secretly entered one of their undesired employees to participate in the 'Swap Your Job with a Stranger' lottery. The insane and provocative inaugural corporate event is held in Las Vegas. Two strangers are forced to swap jobs for ninety days. The swapping and matching process is simple; some matches have been organised for compatibility reasons, and names are picked from a hat for the less fortunate. Participants have no idea what is coming their way and believe they are rocking up to a special 'Cirque du Soleil' event courtesy of their employers. Inside the Convention Centre, a circus of emotions explodes when the master of ceremony exposes the corporate trickery.

Armed with a fluffy mini-designer dress and sleek high heels, a female partaker marches like a paratrooper through the disgruntled crowd. She squeezes and rubs her physical assets uncannily against all human barricades as she is determined to catch up with her lottery match, who tries to escape his new corporate fate. Acting like a cheated wife seeking revenge, she navigates fearlessly through the corridors of the venue. Her elegance-less tracking pace swallows kilometres of luring carpet in no time. In the foyer area and metres away from the exit doors, she physically blocks her target and confronts him.

— 'Are you Jay Smith?'

— 'Leave me alone!'

— 'I'm Juliana Susas and guess what? You are not going anywhere because you and I are swapping jobs for ninety days!'

— 'Move out of my way, I've no time or humour for you. This whole thing makes me insanely angry!'

— 'I'm over the moon!' replies Juliana, holding her stance while performing a few sensual moves.

— 'I'm disgusted and gutted. How can someone treat me with such a lack of respect?' snaps back Jay.

— 'I'm so delighted!' laughs Juliana, now moving around in excitement and squeezing her breasts.

— 'Everyone calls me 'Captain'; keep that in mind!'

— 'Hey, Captain, I can't wait to see the Midwest. I always dreamed of going to Nebraska. Just like Bruce Springsteen's album! I can't wait!'

— 'I wish I could say the same. Where are you based? Let me guess! New York! You look like a fucking New Yorker and sound like one too. I fucking hate New York. Nothing good comes from there. Do you understand?'

— 'Sorry, Captain! No fucking New York for you! By the way, what's your occupation? Your deflated look and superior attitude tell me you're a Financial Analyst in a poultry processing facility! You look like a headless chicken. You're so agitated!'

— 'What's your name again?'

— 'Juliana Susas, I'm a journalist for The New York World News and a great babe from South America, as you can see. No New York for you! Trust me on that one; always on the road, Captain! Get ready to put some miles on your chicken legs.'

— 'Juliana, I don't think you're the right candidate for my job. I don't believe a bimbo from New York can write user manuals for lawnmowers and garden trimmers. Fifteen years doing the same thing. I know everything about bolts, grease, springs, switches, power cords, fuel mixes and lubricants.'

— 'Lubes, I like lubricant! Lube is my life!' laughs Juliana, feeling her crotch, a smile tugging on her lips.

— 'I invite you to pack your plastic tits away when you're in Lincoln if you don't want your cherry to be popped against your will. Meat like you won't last till dinner time,' replies Jay before adding, 'What do you mean no New York for me?'

— 'Captain, don't worry about Baby Babe here. I know how to handle country folks like you who dream of popping my cherry. A lot of talking and little action. I'm happy to bet you're a one-minute man – on your lucky day!'

— 'You don't need to worry about my performance; it would never happen with you! You're not my type! I stay clear of women with big boobs! One was more than enough for me!'

— 'Why are you so bitter? This is a great opportunity to put some miles onto your passport. Living the dream, Captain! I'm ecstatic!' laughs Juliana, rubbing the curve of her body shape.

— 'Passport; I don't have a passport! Americans don't have passports! We own the world; we are the world! Only people who hate their homeland have a passport.'

— 'Time to move on, Jay! I'm going for a drink! You should come along to distil your bitterness! A Nebraska celebration!'

— 'Fuck you, bitch! I'll drink to your tits!'

Chapter two

Bruno Lefevre

— 'I'm Jay Smith.'

— 'Welcome to The New York World News Headquarters, Mr Smith! How was your trip? How was Las Vegas? Let me call HR; they'll take care of you. This is your one-hour pass, and the lift is around the corner. Level 17,' says the receptionist.

— 'Level 17. One-hour pass, is that correct?' replies Jay sheepishly, with a dry, hangover voice.

— 'Yes, they're waiting for you! Are you ready, Mr Smith? Good luck!'

The sound of a pronounced theatrical French accent welcomes Jay,

— 'Welcome to The New York World News, Mr Smith! I'm Bruno Charles Henri Lefevre. I'll be your boss for the next ninety days. Welcome on board! I have three envelopes in my hand, and I invite you to pick one of them and read the message's content out loud.'

— 'I'm sorry! I didn't sign up for the lottery. I don't want to swap my job. This is a stupid idea. This is a fucking stupid idea! I want to go back to Lincoln. I'm the 'Captain'; I'm in charge!' presses Jay.

— 'I'm sorry to hear your self-pitying story, Captain, but let me explain your situation. If you return to Lincoln and don't commit to the assignment as directed in one of these envelopes, your job is gone! You'll be terminated on the spot as you fail the lottery! Goodbye, Captain! Au revoir! Bon voyage!'

— 'That can't be true! This is bullshit! This is fucking bullshit! Do you understand? Do you fucking understand?'

— 'You're so funny, Mr Smith!'

— 'I want to speak to the low-life who put me in this misery. I'm not going anywhere! Fucking New York! I hate this place. I hate this building. I hate the colour of the walls. Who had the fucking idea to paint the fucking wall in fucking yellow? That's terrible. It should be white. All walls should be white, for God's sake. Just fucking plain white.'

— 'Mr Smith, if I may, I'm sorry that New York is not to your taste; I'm deeply sorry that the colours of our walls are not up to your expectations. But I'm not here to apologise for your likes or dislikes. I'll get straight to the point with you, Mr Smith. You're a cheat! You're not a captain, and you're far from being one! You're currently under investigation by your Human Resources Manager, Miss Pinballs, and her conclusions about you are simple. You're a fraud! You haven't written a single user manual in the last five years. Your virtual and personal assistants are doing the hard work on your behalf. Your daily occupation is watching kinky videos on Pornhub and buying spare parts for your Dodge Challenger! Mr Smith, with all due respect, would you prefer to talk to Miss Pinballs or to pick an envelope?'

— 'I can't understand what you're saying. What is your accent?' Jay says bluntly.

— 'I'm French, Mr Smith. I come from France, the country of love, passion, refinement, grace, elegance, sexy lingerie, haute couture, glamorous ladies, delicious cuisine, outstanding wines, cheeses to die for, and so much more.'

— 'Where is Frennnss? How do you pronounce it?'

— 'La France, Mr Smith! The capital of the world! Mr Smith, France is the best. French people are the best. Just look at me!'

— 'You make me sick! Nothing can beat Nebraska,' angrily replies Jay before asking with a voice full of concern, 'What about my family?'

— 'Speaking of your family, it's now time to say goodbye to them. I've organised a video call with your loved ones on your behalf.'

— 'Does Judy, my wife, know about this fucking shit?'

— 'Pornhub? I don't know. Let's ask her!'

— 'No, the lottery! This 'swap your job with a stranger' bullshit.'

— 'Miss Pinballs had conversations with your wife about organising your passport. The underline of their conversations was that you've been awarded a trip overseas as part of your duty at Nebraska Mowers and Chainsaws.'

— 'Nothing else! Does she know about the Dodge and the rest?'

— 'Let's ask her! She's online in the boardroom. Please follow me!'

— 'Hi Judy!' says Jay.

— 'Jay! Give me a moment!' she replies.

— 'What's up? The captain is not there, and now you need a moment,' Jay comments with a sarcastic voice as the tone of the conversation escalates in no time.

— 'Jay, no! It's not that! I'm using your computer while waiting for the video call to come live. Your Google Drive updated your pictures in Vegas. Who is the woman stroking your cock in the photos? Did you pay for sex? What were you thinking?' explodes Judy verbally.

— 'I don't understand. I don't remember a thing; I was angry and went for a drink and drank my head off. Give me a chance; let me check Google!' he adds while reaching for his mobile phone.

— 'You're a son of a bitch! It's over, Jay! We're over! I want a divorce! Go to hell!' screams Judy.

— 'Give me a second! Let me check! I don't know what you're talking about. Just calm down for a second,' says Jay, typing erratically on his phone keyboard.

— 'Oops. Time to go!' says Bruno while logging off the video platform.

— 'Wait! Oh no! That can't be true! No! Juliana, you fucking bitch!'

— 'Can I see? I'm happy to bet she told you that you

wouldn't last two minutes, and you couldn't resist proving her wrong. Every man has two heads but not enough blood to run the two simultaneously,' says Bruno, exuding a fair amount of arrogance.

Jay receives a phone notification.

— 'No! My bank account is empty. Judy's emptied my bank account! I must talk to Judy. I'm the fucking Captain. Let me talk to Judy!' yells Jay.

— 'Mr Smith, I'm sorry for your losses, but I now give you three seconds to decide and pick an envelope. Three seconds, Mr Smith, or you're jobless. You're already homeless and penniless. The choice is yours!'

— 'The middle one!' says Jay with a deflated voice, slowly catching up with his reality.

— 'Juliana is right! No New York for you, Mr Smith. You're going for a trip around the world as a journalist for The New York World News.'

— 'Journalist for The New York World News! You're fucking kidding!'

— 'Mr Smith, I do have expectations! Do you understand? Did I make myself clear? I want the best, just like my beautiful France. I want grace, emotions, sophistication, glamour, humour, and the joy of life to be portrayed. Your first flight is leaving in six hours. All information about your assignment is in this envelope and on your laptop. Time to go, Mr Smith. Bon voyage. This is your credit card to pay for your expenses abroad. Bonne chance, Mr Smith!'

— 'What is the content of the other envelopes?'

— 'A trip around the world and a trip around the world.

I've selected your assignment. Your life needs a reality check, Mr Smith. You're so unpleasant. You're so un-French! Time to go, Mr Smith. We'll be in touch!'

— 'What about my children?'

— 'Mr Smith, you'll have time to deal with your family matters at the airport. As mentioned earlier, I apologise for your losses, but I'm not running a childcare service or a marital counselling agency. Your assignment has already started; any fallout and you'll be jobless. Is that clear?'

Chapter three

La Guarda Airport

Jay Smith can't contact his wife, Judy, or his kids at La Guardia Airport. Nebraska Bank has confirmed that Jay's account balance is below zero. Jay rushes to contact his foster brother, Lenny, and orders him to find Judy. Jay must dispose of his gun before crossing airport security. His Human Resources Manager, Natalia Pinballs, catches up with him as he tries to find a locker to store his weapon.

Their encounter is awkward, bringing back old memories — ones of their high school and platonic romances. Jay had offered to take her to prom night, but on the bus trip towards Natalia's house, Jay was approached by Judy Dicksmith and her massive cleavage. Being filled with teenage hormones, she had Jay's full and instant attention. Judy's plan for the evening was to get laid by the entire school, but during her raunchy encounter with Jay, the back of her dress gave up.

She was forced to go home half-naked and dissatisfied. Judy was pregnant within seventeen seconds and gave birth to twin boys. Under pressure and forced by their respective parents, Jay married Judy and never had another sexual encounter with her since their bus trip. On prom night, Natalia's doorbell never rang, and she has had a broken heart ever since. Miss Pinballs' virginity is still on offer to Jay.

In the busyness of the airport, both are emotional and look washed out. They hug passionately and silently — a hug that is over fifteen years overdue. Natalia takes possession of Jay's gun as his flight to Amsterdam is ready to board. She tells him to run and to enjoy the opportunity on offer.

Jay doesn't understand why the same place is called 'Holland' and 'The Netherlands', and why their nationals and citizens are called 'Dutch'. Jay's anger is unextinguishable, and the identity photo on his first passport doesn't improve his mood. His frustration rises when he reads his first journalist assignment. He must report on a hypnotherapy medical trial on long-term coma patients. The experiment will be conducted by two Australian hypnotherapists, Andrea Fallusio and Ed Michel, who've teamed up with Dr Braam Van Der Steel, a neuroscientist and head of the Amsterdam Neuroscience Clinical Research Unit.

Chapter four

Stop your fairy shit talk with me

Andrea Fallusio's favourite place to meet in Amsterdam is Barney's Coffeeshop. Barney's is listed as the temple of Dutch weed culture. The local reviews on the business state that their quality cannabis is slightly above the market price. The old-fashioned apothecary décor makes the place appear like a cosy bird's nest, opening its doors at seven o'clock in the morning. Someone here said that you need to start the day the right way. The house rules sign welcomes you, boldly stating that the place can't be yours if you're under eighteen.

Andrea likes to come there to observe the behaviours of the surrounding patrons and the before-and-after effects of their marijuana practices. Andrea's not the only one fascinated by human behaviour. Ed, his business associate and the creator of the 'Soul to Soul' therapy, is there too. They met through hypnosis training and developed a long-term friendship. Their connection is linked to hypnosis, emotional cleaning therapy, Andrea's love affairs, and life's lightness. Ed Michel is also a club DJ with a profound love for techno and electronica music, which he calls mathematical poetry. After hours, he'll most likely be inside some random nightclub that's accepted his request to perform.

Jay is late for the first meeting with Andrea and Ed. When he finally arrives, no formal welcomes or gestures occur. His frustration and anger get the best of him, and a verbal rampage ensues in no time. His loudness and disruptiveness take over the establishment. Jay's outburst is interrupted by the waitress, who invites him to calm down or leave the premises. With his legendary smile plastered across his face, Andrea invites Jay to join them and take it easy.

— 'Come on, man, breathe and relax a bit. Today, it's not about you, me, us! In Holland alone, there are up to three thousand people a year in a coma. Could you imagine three thousand beds side by side, filled with unconscious people? This is why we're here,' Andrea calmly explains.

— 'Sorry guys, but this shit is not my passion. I didn't ask for a sea change or to be part of your spooky adventure. I can't take much more of your so-called life purpose. I just want to fucking go home,' answers Jay.

— 'Settle down, man! Come on, there's nothing to get angry about. Life gives you a new direction; embrace it. Please grab a drink; it's on us!' says Andrea with a welcoming voice.

Ed intervenes,

— 'Bruno Lefevre told us about your circumstance, which has nothing to do with us. We're here to have a good time, help people along the way, and, if we're lucky, maybe change how coma patients are treated. I understand your situation is challenging, but someone's looking after you. You're not here by accident. Trust me on that one. Let's enjoy ourselves and be the best version of ourselves!'

— 'Boys, you don't understand the depth of my problems! A foolish woman just took over my job, my wife emptied my bank account and asked for a divorce, and most importantly, I need to know if FedEx delivered my new exhaust line for my Dodge Challenger.'

— 'We're all in love with our life story, Jay. Our sad little story is our identity. We all do it until we aim for something bigger, more truthful, and more palatable. I can guarantee that when you enter a ward filled with unconscious human beings, your story will look like an ice cream in the sun. It'll melt without you knowing. Anger is one of the biggest contributing factors in developing illnesses. When you're angry, your body secretes chemicals and toxins that can kill you in the long run. Repetitive anger is a recipe for disaster,' warns Andrea.

Ed again supports Andrea's message of care,

— 'You're not alone, Jay! We'll support you. We understand your challenge and promise that we'll be there for you. Whatever you think of us, whatever you report on us, whether you believe in us and whatever happens during our medical trial — it would be best not to be angry for the next few weeks. Living with anger is like living with a closed fist; nothing can land into it. A closed fist is a sign of isolation from the world and a way to say 'No' to the blessings of life. We're not preachers; we talk through our life experiences and don't want you to waste precious days of your life guided by outdated emotional patterns. Are you ready to give your best?'

— 'Boys, you sound like con artists. Stop your fairy shit talk with me! I'm the 'Captain', for God's sake,' shouts Jay while standing in the middle of the establishment.

— 'What you'll see in the coming weeks may not be easy for you, me, or Ed. Keep this in mind, Captain! We're not here to play with people's lives; we're not clowns,' clarifies Andrea with a soft voice.

— 'I'll be the clown! I'll be the fucking clown! I'll be Amsterdam's biggest phobia!' screams Jay before being pushed out of the premises by the waitress.

As soon as Jay is out in the street, he performs an online search on his mobile phone and walks towards a party supplies shop.

Chapter five

11th February

The next day, early morning, Jay crosses Amsterdam dressed as a clown. He makes his way towards the train station through the red-light district. Everyone who crosses his path is shocked by the scariness of his big blue and black bat-shaped painted eyes, fat red nose, and sharp set of evil teeth. His curly orange wig is squashed under a thick white veil neatly pinned under his chin. An oversized cape covers his backpack and the rest of his outfit. He looks like the Hunchback of Notre Dame.

As he cuts through the alleyways, he notices two tall women wearing bright gym outfits and camouflage puffer jackets exiting an adult entertainment centre. As they walk in front of him, their pantyless bums dance joyfully to the rhythm of the cobble street pavers. One of them lifts the back of her jacket to adjust the position of a concealed weapon. The squarish end of the small calibre barrel is now in the middle of her athletic buttocks and moulded into the polyester fabric of her pants. Jay enjoys the erotic scene from behind.

As the pair reach the corner of the street, a man wearing a square-shouldered leather jacket jumps out of a mid-nineties classic black Mercedes-Benz, confronting the women verbally while brandishing a knife savagely in their direction. In no time, one of the women is stabbed in the arm, and the other punches and kicks their aggressor with great force. As retribution, he pulls out a gun and presses it on the bleeding victim's chest. The two women are pinned against a wall.

Assessing the situation, Jay stops and pretends to check his outfit in the reflection on the tinted window of a nearby parked Volvo. The grey window rolls slightly down; he is the receiver of an instant hard middle-finger benediction, elegantly cushioned by a thick cloud of marijuana smoke escaping the vehicle.

Jay walks towards the women and their aggressor, angrily forcing his clown appearance to divert the situation. Three accomplices, wearing the same leather jackets, come out and position themselves around the car's bonnet. In no time and without much movement, the four men lay on the ground. Each of them has a bullet in their forehead. The noise of gunfire is quickly muffled when Jay yells to the women to jump in the Mercedes, which is now sprayed with blood and human flesh.

As they comply with his order to drive them to the nearest hospital, Jay runs back to the Volvo and fires twice the gun that belongs to one of the women wearing flashy gym gear.

Opening the back door, he retrieves a near-naked, trembling young Japanese girl from the car. Her swimwear is pulled to her knees. An odour of urine emanates off her, the smell mingling with her molester's fresh blood and warm flesh particles. Her body is covered with glass shards. He offers her safety in the back seat of the Benz, sitting alongside the stabbed victim.

Jay hears violent and erratic kicking and muffled screaming noise coming from the Volvo's boot. Returning to the car, he opens the door; a strong ammonia smell engulfs his respiratory system. Coughing, Jay faces the challenge of freeing a woman from her restrained position. She wears an extremely dirty, torn-up, glittery one-piece swimsuit; both her face and body are bruised, with her wrists and ankles carved by rope marks. Jay helps her out and carries her safely inside their stolen emergency vehicle.

The Japanese mother and daughter reunite and cry in each other's arms. Jumping behind the wheel, Jay drives erratically, weaving through the centre of Amsterdam. One of the victims assists him with navigating. Dropping everyone at the UMC hospital, they rush to disembark from the car and into the emergency department. Jay is halted as the Japanese lady grabs his wrist and forces her luxury watch into the palm of his hand.

Jay drives away, seeking refuge in an underground car park for safety. He undresses himself as quickly as he can, battling with his clown mask, pulls clothes out of his backpack and dresses himself back in a flash. His heart is racing mad, and like in a movie, he cleans the steering wheel, the shifter and the door handles.

In the process, he discovers a diary tacked under the passenger floor mat; each page to date is filled with names and glued Polaroid pictures next to them. Each photo has captured either an execution or a funeral. The central figures in all photographic compositions are women who are either beaten or dead. On today's page, Kora and Tia Tanganyika's names appear, along with others. Jay realises that the women he dropped at the hospital were due for execution today.

He searches the rest of the car; the trunk is packed with travel bags full of €500 notes, credit cards, firearms and ammunition of all sorts.

His anguish and adrenaline rush take over his reasoning. Calling for assistance doesn't cross his mind at all; his only focus is to bring the car's contents back to his hotel room by booking a rental car. As time is against him, he searches the net on his mobile phone and secures a Volkswagen Caddy on the Greenwheels app.

He rushes to the rental car pick-up location by taking an Uber. Returning to the car park, he frantically transfers the contents of the Mercedes to the safety of the Volkswagen. As he notices the heavy police presence in the city centre while driving back to Hotel Lucius, his nerves are on overdrive. His body can't stop trembling as reality catches up with him.

At the hotel, Jay is welcomed by Ozzie, a thirty-year-old computer nerd working part-time as a receptionist. He's a chubby guy wearing thick glasses and hiding behind a rough moustache. He has a scholarship to study cybercrime security in Amsterdam, and he's delighted to share with

Jay that he's also from Nebraska and that his grandparents own Lea's Chicken in Lincoln. An instant bond is formed between the pair.

After painfully hiding the bags and the diary in his bedroom, Jay returns the rental van and invites Ozzie out for dinner to celebrate their newfound friendship. Korean fried chicken and Heineken beers await them at the Gangnam Chicken Restaurant.

With the help of a few cold beers, Ozzie happily shares his hacking skills and how he satisfies his stalking addiction by hijacking the surveillance cameras inside Amsterdam's brothels and around the red-light district.

Every news channel shows images and footage of this morning's shooting. Jay spends the rest of the evening watching the picture of himself on his television set. Some locals brand the 'Clown of Amsterdam' a hero; a Japanese businessman offers a reward to the person who can return his wife's watch. The two women are identified as Tia and Kora Tanganyika. They are well-known public figures in Amsterdam called the 'Haka Girls.' The news updates confirm the information contained in the diary.

All evening, Jay browses and analyses the extent of the diary's content. He realises that the Tanganyika sisters were part of a six-person hit list; all of them are women. He jumps onto his computer and types the names of the dead victims recorded in the diary; most of them appear on different missing persons websites. He is counting the number of victims contained in the nightmarish book.

His arithmetic skills are interrupted when he receives a

text message from Bruno Lefevre ordering him to report on the 'Clown of Amsterdam' incident. Jay tries to gather his thoughts on how to report on something already going wild on many news platforms. He acknowledges that he needs to be innovative as he can't compromise his identity. His biggest worry is his ability to write a worthy newspaper article.

While looking for inspiration in the Amsterdam crime diary now in his possession, he discovers a set of credit cards and four 'Lockbox Luggage Storage' dockets hidden inside the back sleeve.

Jay spends the rest of the night roaming the red-light district, attempting to secure vital information on the 'Haka Girls.' His investigative actions are unsuccessful, and he only receives generous sexual offers of all natures. The Amsterdam sex workers would be delighted to add Jay to their trophy boards in exchange for a fifty-euro note or more.

Chapter six

Six well-dressed women

At his hotel in the early morning hours, Jay is welcomed by Ozzie, who's just started his morning shift. The Nebraskan pair share a few jokes and some great laughter. Jay seeks assistance from his new pal to help him track down the Tanganyika duo. Within no time, Ozzie becomes a search engine, hacker, and information gatherer for The New York World News. To keep Ozzie's motivation alive, Jay gives him a bundle of cash as payment for his services.

They meet for a brainstorming session mid-morning, with Ozzie providing an address for the 'Haka Girls'. They own a fitness centre, and Jay decides to visit them.

The greeting reception at the centre could be better, while the building has plenty of security. The gym receptionist is unaccommodating, as dozens of journalists queue trying to interview the duo. After waiting over an hour, Jay types a note on his mobile phone and shows it to the receptionist. The note reads:

— 'Ronald McDonald's cousin would like to know where he can drop the P365?'

The unusual request takes the receptionist aback, who excuses herself and reappears a few minutes later. She apologises for the delay and discreetly gives Jay a folded note while walking him back to the front door, where she whispers:

— 'Thank you for coming; sorry we can't help today, and see you next time.'

Back in the street, the message reads:

— 'De Schatkamer, Hotel L'Europa, 3:00 p.m. today.'

A quick online search delivers the rendezvous address.

On his way to the hotel, Jay stops at a grocery store where he buys a set of plastic gloves, a bottle of olive oil, a pack of flour, and large-size envelopes. Back in his hotel room, Jay proceeds to his bathroom, where he pours the flour into an envelope, tears the gun apart, and meticulously rubs the white organic powder on each part of the gun to remove all fingerprints. The tension in the air is palpable as he rinses all metallic parts under hot water and uses the bathroom blow dryer to tackle the surface water. Olive oil is used to lubricate and polish the weapon parts. He repeats the process three times before reassembling and dropping the gun in a clean envelope.

Jay receives a phone call from Bruno Lefevre; the French guy is furious, and his screams blurt out of the phone speaker. He saw Jay walking out of the convenience store during a CNN livestream, while The New York World News is impatiently waiting for an update on the Amsterdam shooting.

As a matter of urgency, Jay runs down to the reception desk and asks Ozzie if he can access the red-light district CCTV network, as he needs help with his news article. The cybersecurity student confirms that accessing and downloading the event footage related to the 'Clown of Amsterdam' will take little time. After reviewing all evidence, potential abnormalities, and police activities — and knowing that Jay has little news reporting experience — Ozzie surprises his Nebraskan comrade by using artificial intelligence to draft The New York World News assignment. As a good cheater, he tweaks the article to make it original, and Jay's first article is submitted for publishing in no time.

Ozzie then encourages Jay to upgrade his mobile and computer security, use a VPN, and install non-identity software to access the depths of the dark web.

Realising that his stay in Amsterdam will be longer than expected, Jay needs more to wear than what was thrown together in his suitcase and decides to overhaul his look using The New York World News credit card. He decides on a fancy, sleek haircut, and based on Ozzie's recommendation, he visits 'Smoked Barbers', located two blocks down from his hotel. One of many five-star online reviews reads:

— 'Cannabis and haircuts balanced with some rough garage reggae electronica DJ mixes.'

With no second thoughts, Jay proceeds. The owner of the joint is Lucy Wang, a vision-impaired Chinese lady who wears a pink fluorescent tube dress and a pair of designer sunglasses. Hearing Jay's accent, she invites him to the blue neon backroom. Jay notices other male customers making provocative hand gestures as he follows the hairdresser into the room.

Not everyone is invited to Lucy's exclusive altar; the sound and richness of your accent will guide you into the most sensual nude haircut session that Amsterdam offers.

Lucy knows how to undress herself and a man in erotic, perfect synchronicity. She invites Jay to sit on an old steel stool and positions herself to keep his legs open and his manhood exposed and accessible. She means business and slowly rubs her naked body all over Jay. Her breasts have a prepubescent flatness that visually interrupts the wavy rhythm of her carved ribcage. Only a pair of stiff and unusually long nipples emerge from her bluish-pale anorexic figure.

Her bony body moves, following the snipping sounds of her scissors, and from time to time, she runs the edge of her fingers along Jay's ball seam, anatomically called the raphe, to stimulate his blood flow. Jay's cock is hard, and every millimetre of his penis skin is stretched well beyond his belief. In a subtle move, Lucy reaches for her hairdressing tool trolley located on her right side and grabs a condom along with lubricants. With trained skill, she opens the packaging with her teeth and rolls the condom onto Jay's cock. She fills her arse with the jelly lube, turns around and pushes herself with ease onto her newly made joystick. She orders Jay to fuck her hard. Jay's cock has no time for a second thought as she bounces her bottom with a significant amount of energy.

In her mixed Chinese, Dutch and English accent, the

phrase 'fuck me, fuck my arse' fills the tiny, blue-lit space. Jay notices the change in her pitch, subject to how deep his inflated, hard cock is within her — her words beginning to slur. As her climax nears the peak of its implosive explosion, she grabs Jay's knees to gain crazy momentum, then suddenly stops her bouncing act, spreads her legs as far as she can, and slaps the lips of her genitalia in a fast, repetitive way with a heavy hand. She squirts like a broken garden hose, and the spray coming out of her juicy pussy splashes the room in uncontrolled directions as she massages and rubs herself with her pressured liquid flow. She slides on Jay's cock for a little bit longer. Jay cums loudly as he grabs Lucy's intriguing twenty-millimetre-long, thimble-shaped nipples.

The floor of the tiny altar is now a multitude of mini waterways making their way around the geometric pattern of the dark tile grout and disappearing into the floor waste. Lucy's intimacy will soon flavour Amsterdam's canals.

In the blue halo darkness of the room, she pushes her trolley away into a corner, removes Jay's condom, and cleans his genitalia with an expert hand. In a subtle move, she climbs the steel stool and squeezes the edge of her toes under Jay's bottom. As she rises, she forces him to suck, lick and vacuum her clitoris. She moans madly while both of them try to maintain their acrobatic posture. Without warning, she ejaculates a high-pressure, warm, salty spray onto Jay's face.

While still standing, she frees up one of her feet and turns on the shower taps. Most of the water cascades from her belly onto Jay's body, automatically creating other waterways that make their way to the Dutch capital city centre. Lucy stops the shower, sits on Jay's lap, grabs her trolley back and resumes his haircut.

The same scenario starts again when the scissors and the battery-operated clippers reach a state of rest. She pushes the trolley into the corner, turns the shower taps on, rinses Jay's hair and strokes his deflated manhood. She helps him dry himself, putting on his clothes and wet shoes. Without much affection, she taps his credit card and grabs the functional mop to erase and dry any traces of their business encounter.

As Jay leaves the room, he gets cheered on by the other patrons. The Bangladeshi barber on duty invites Jay to have a bong. Jay declines politely before making his way to the menswear store.

Back at his hotel, he looks in a mirror to check his haircut and sees a younger version of himself. A smile grows on his face. He removes the tags and labels from his newly purchased clothes, dresses sharply, and goes to Hotel L'Europa. His empty testicles ache as he walks.

At De Schatkamer, Jay sits on a curved sofa. He admires the lavish green décor, stylish furniture, and contemporary artworks adorning the walls. He looks around, and the place is empty. No one is to be seen.

— 'Maybe it's a trap,' he thinks, checking the time on his phone and noticing his body's unease with the situation as he feels watched.

As he decides to leave, the noise of a street performance brings him to the window. Over two hundred female MMA fighters have interrupted the traffic to perform a Haka; four hundred eyes are locked on him. Some of the participants have black eyes, skin cuts and swollen lips. Their raw power makes Jay feel terrified. As the ceremony ends, Jay takes a step back from the window. A voice behind him says:

— 'This dance ceremony represents our tribe's pride, strength, and unity. I want to warn you that today, you have no choice; you will be a part of us or alone against us. The outcome of our meeting will be the decider. I am Kora Tanganyika; please follow me!'

Jay turns around, recognising the woman who tucked her gun in her butt crack.

Jay follows Kora, the Haka girl. They enter a service staircase and climb the stairs at a military pace. Jay is puffed out as they arrive on the top floor and enter a corridor; he's greeted by dozens of MMA female fighters who form a line of terror. Taken aside, Jay is invited into a small room. Two chairs and the smell of freshly pressed linen will be the only witnesses of his determining fate. Needing to keep his composure, Jay feels the soft fabric of the professionally folded pillowcases. They sit opposite each other.

Performing an over-choreographed preventive gesture, Jay reaches the inner pocket of his jacket, grabs the envelope and presents it to Kora,

— 'Here is your P365,' he says.

— 'How much ammunition is left?' she asks.

— 'Four!' replies Jay. 'Six bullets were used yesterday.'

It's Kora's turn to put her hand into the pocket of her sports jacket. She grabs a handful of ammunition and hands it to Jay.

— 'All yours!' she says. 'Maybe you'll need it more than I do.'

— 'Who are you?' asks Jay.

— 'Who are you?' replies Kora snarkily.

— 'Jay Smith. I'm Jay Smith, and I didn't expect to meet you or what happened yesterday. My name is Jay Smith!' he repeats nervously with a shaky voice.

Kora is now tight-lipped; discomfort envelopes the pair and forces Jay to enter a monologue as a way to kill the silence.

— 'I was going to the train station, looking to go to a carnival. This explains my colourful, scary clown outfit. After dropping your sister and others at the hospital, I found a diary with many other things in the car. By the way, I hope everyone is safe and okay, especially the little girl.'

Kora knows how to negotiate; she maintains her silence, yet Jay can tell she's intrigued by their conversation.

— 'The diary is filled with photos of executions. The bodies are mostly women, and most of them appear, due to their revealing and erotic outfits, to be sex workers. There's also a hit list. Yesterday was your day to be executed. Same for your sister. Time is against some people in this town,' states Jay quietly.

Again, with robotised safety gestures, he stands up, grabs his phone out of his pants pocket, and shows Kora a few photos from the diary. Flicking through them, he says:

— 'This is yesterday! You and your sister's names are on the page. This is today and the days to come.'

Kora checks the time and yells something in Dutch loudly, and the MMA crew vanishes from the corridor with little elegance.

Kora looks at Jay, tears rolling down her cheeks. Her steel

stature is vulnerable.

— 'Please, tell me it won't happen! My best friend must not die today,' begs Kora.

Jay is silent. He double-checks the photo and realises that an execution is planned for 3:30 p.m. this afternoon.

Kora's phone rings. It's terrible news. Her friend has been executed on her way to pick up her children from school. Kora's anger is now on full display. She punches the linen, kicks the shelving, and smashes the chairs, screaming her frustrations. Jay, expressing his empathy with a few sad words, silently leaves the room. Not long after, she catches up with him in the corridor, bluntly stating:

— 'Go on your phone, go on maps! Here is the address: Van Ostadestraat 147 H, 1072 SW Amsterdam. Stay in proximity, and don't make yourself noticeable. One of my crew will pick you up there around 8:00 p.m. I know the next five victims,' she adds. 'You'll meet them tonight. Bring the diary along.'

— 'How is your sister?' replies Jay.

— 'She'll be there tonight too,' Kora adds, drying her eyes.

Jay realises that Amsterdam is no longer a laughing matter. He makes his way back to his hotel, and Ozzie is impatient to see him.

— 'The hotel owner had an emergency and must go abroad. He asked me to take care of the business during his absence,' tells Ozzie.

— 'I'm your only client, and I'm not hard to manage,' jokes Jay.

— 'We'll have time for fried chicken!' says Ozzie, high-fiving Jay.

— 'Cancel all bookings! The place is ours for the next three months,' Jay replies, tendering his credit card.

Ozzie processes the payment. The New York World News now has an office in Amsterdam. Within a matter of seconds, Jay and Ozzie's phones ring. Bruno Lefevre loses his cool about the hotel bill, and Ozzie's boss is delighted with a surge in income. Jay invites Ozzie to take up residency in the hotel for the next ninety days and to offer the entire team a three-month holiday package courtesy of The New York World News.

— 'Let's set up our workstations on the first floor next to the bay window. All the beds can go out. We've got some urgent business to go through,' tells Jay to Ozzie, who's excited by the prospect of having a lifestyle change for the next three months.

Jay thanks him for the hairdresser recommendation. Ozzie jokes:

— 'There's a rumour that a blind girl fucks customers like a machine. I'm too chicken to check her out.'

— 'Sounds like she's too hot for you, Ozzie,' replies Jay. 'If you go there, you'll be a fried chicken in no time!'

As directed by Ozzie, Jay calls Bruno Lefevre and requests FTP access to one of The New York World News' servers, where he can drop some confidential information. He also demands that Bruno and The New York World News not use the confidential material without his permission, as his life, and the lives of others, are at stake. Bruno Lefevre is confused but concedes to the request.

Jay gives Ozzie a pep talk on journalism, confidentiality, and the kind of information a news article can uncover. Ozzie nods, approving whatever is coming out of Jay's mouth. Their friendship turns into a Nebraskan bromance until Jay asks Ozzie to scan the diary and organise a few copies onto USB sticks. Just going through the pages to evaluate the content, Ozzie feels nauseous, looks yellowish, and faints. Jay takes care of him, brings some ice, and asks him to rest.

Finding a scanner in the hotel office, Jay unplugs it and checks on Ozzie before moving to his computer, where he downloads the scanner driver, connects the hardware, and silently scans the diary. His next search is for empty USB sticks.

Jay arrives at the last page. He cuts the credit cards into pieces and hides the locker dockets above his wardrobe. He plans to find and check the locker's location soon. Ozzie is still in shock. He doesn't want to go out for dinner. After uploading the scanned diary to The New York World News FTP server, Jay leaves him on the couch and proceeds to the meeting point.

Jay is spotted by one of the MMA fighters close to the meeting point. She monitors his moves for a while before inviting him to a car ride down to the outskirts of Amsterdam. She doesn't speak as they drive, and not before long, they arrive at a rural-looking cottage where two luxury cars and a small van are already parked in the driveway. In the darkness of the driveway, the driver invites him to proceed inside the cottage.

Six well-dressed women sit around the dining table. Their

computers are out, and their body language is taut and formal.

— 'Hi, my name is Jay!' he says, going around the table and sheepishly shaking everyone's hands.

Tia stands up, facing him, and wraps her unharmed hand around Jay's back affectionately, thanking him for yesterday.

— 'I'm glad you made it. I'm sorry for your loss this afternoon,' he adds in a low, gentle voice, placing a USB stick on the table's edge.

— 'What's your common denominator for being on a hit list? You don't look like outlaws or criminals!' he adds.

— 'Who are you?' asks one of the women with a powerful Dutch accent and a bully voice.

— 'Should I assume that you're the head of the pack?' replies Jay. 'Why don't we introduce ourselves more candidly? It's not just about me; it's about us. So, please take the lead and tell me who you are,' he adds, slightly mimicking her strong Dutch intonation.

The first lady to talk has drooped, flappy jaws, a podgy neck, and an oversized torso. She looks like a cylindrical drum or an unhealthy, obese mastiff sitting on a small chair. With a very affirmative and controlling voice, she says:

— 'I'm Ingrid de Rooy, Amsterdam's police commissioner. As a former undercover cop, I work closely with these ladies to fight crime — largely sex slavery, human trafficking, and money laundering. I also supervise the operation of a legal aid service dedicated to the sex workers' industry. As for now, my role here is to keep you safe and under the radar.'

The following persons to introduce themselves are the 'Haka Girls'. With correct athletic body posture, Kora is their spokesperson:

— 'We are Tia and Kora Tanganyika. We're twins and UFC pro fighters. We own a gym and a security company that offers self-defence classes to the sex worker industry and protective services to the A-listers, celebrities, and government agencies. We support the sex worker industry because of our mother.'

— 'Why your mum?' queries Jay.

— 'We migrated from New Zealand a while ago, and upon arrival, our father became a wild party boy. Amsterdam became his adult playground, and we were quickly left behind. Due to the financial pressure, Mum, who had only housewife skills, became a sex worker to avoid eviction. On her first night out, she was knocked out cold for refusing to perform a free blowjob,' clarifies Tia, with tears pearling from the corners of her eyes.

— 'Why do people call you the 'Haka Girls'?' queries Jay.

— 'As UFC pro fighters, and as part of our fight warm-up tradition, we perform a Haka to warn our opponents that our families, tribes, ancestors, and traditions are with us and within us. Our message to the opposition is clear: they won't fight a Haka Girl or the Haka Girls; they'll fight the entire Haka Army.'

Next is Abigail Ashton to introduce herself. She's a stunning Irish redhead with a freckly face who can confidently, with her lovely accent, invite any man living on this planet to drink a Guinness or two at the pub in her company on Saint Patrick's Day. Without hesitation, she fires:

— 'I'm a private escort and a well-paid creator on OnlyFans.

I've no mobility in my legs, and my physical disability bounds me to a wheelchair. Recently, I was awarded Dutch Woman of the Year and Dutch Woman Entrepreneur of the Year. I'm the co-founder of the Shelter for Sex Workers Foundation. We're in the process of finalising the acquisition of Hotel L'Europa. With Coco' — pointing to another woman across the table — 'we train and educate sex workers to become financially independent and teach them how to make the most of their efforts, life sacrifices, and money. My disability and my black eye are results of poor life choices,' concludes Abigail proudly.

— 'I'm Zoetje Saar,' proceeds the next woman with a deep, scratchy Dutch accent that can only be achieved by avid smoking. 'I'm a former prostitute and a Sex Worker Protection Union member. I fight for the rights of our industry in Dutch society. Banks and health funds penalise our members; we can't access home loans and health insurance. Together — showing the other ladies around the table — we've changed the laws and invited our government to create a sex worker register for the members of our community. We try our best to ban and combat any form of illegal activities, such as slavery and human trafficking. The Dutch public well receives our ideas and initiatives — except for the sex cartels from here and abroad. We're in a constant war to save, protect, and care for the members of our industry. Illegal brothels are discovered and closed by police daily but reopen somewhere else within hours. We also try to control unsafe web applications, where prostitutes are available on demand and to be ordered like pizza. I've a logistical role in the foundation, and we,' — pointing again in a circular motion with her finger around the table — 'have something to do with it. Time is currently of the essence.'

— 'Could you elaborate on that for me?' asks Jay.

— 'Sorry to interrupt, I'll answer your question. I'm Coco Carajuca. I'm the Chief Executive Officer of the largest ice cream company in Holland and the third-largest one in Europe. I'm also a professional ballet dancer and choreographer. At the peak of my dancing career, I was the principal dancer of the Royal Ballet and the lead principal of the English National Ballet. As a child, I was sexually molested and placed for adoption. Today, I work around the clock to finalise the funding for the sex worker shelter. I've a couple of days to find and secure €35 million. I've a buyer for the ice cream business, but as the Eastern European mafia targets my products, the value of my business is now next to nothing. I've a matter of days to finalise the purchase of Hotel L'Europa, or they'll take it over and convert it into a mega-size brothel. If this happens, all our efforts to make Amsterdam safer and better can be reduced to nothing.'

Jay can't keep his eyes away from Coco, who reciprocates his gaze. Jay can feel her radiating energy, and with a shy, distracted voice, he asks:

— 'Is yesterday's attack on Tia and Kora linked to all that? Is your arm okay?'

— 'It's just a surface cut. Nothing serious,' replies Tia.

— 'What happened to Hotel L'Europa? The online pictures look amazing, but it seemed sad and empty this afternoon,' queries Jay.

— 'The property was never for sale or on the market. The mafia sabotaged and destroyed their business to acquire the building. The hotel had just survived the pandemic crisis and is now fighting for survival. My legal team informed me of the situation, as I own the sole apartment within the building. Having a shelter at that location doesn't make much sense, but it prevents the establishment of a monumental brothel on our doorstep. I wish I could rewind time and enjoy once again the splendour of our refined gastronomy and our beautiful national heritage without fear,' says Coco with a melancholic voice.

As Jay locks eye contact with her, she feels the urge to clarify her statement:

— 'Trust me, it's the best. It's my home, and it's my calling to save it — and so far, I'm failing.'

— 'Something great will happen soon,' says Jay with a charming voice that catches the Haka Girls' attention.

— 'I'm confident. I don't know how it'll happen,' says Coco, wearing a smiling glow on her face.

Jay is the last one to introduce himself. With a nervous voice, he starts:

— 'I'm Jay Smith, and I'm from Lincoln, Nebraska. Long story short, against my will, I swapped my job with a stranger at a Las Vegas convention, and for the next three months, I'm a journalist for The New York World News. Amsterdam wasn't my choice. My first assignment is to report on a medical trial for people in a coma. I met with the organisers the day before the attack. They're hypnotherapists, and my anger got the best of me. I told them I'd be a clown to test their abilities on phobias. On my way back to my hotel, I bought my clown outfit at a fancy dress shop. The lady at the shop told me about your carnival season. She mentioned that the city of Maastricht had one the next day. I checked it out and decided to go. I needed something to escape my foul mood. On my way to the train station, dressed as the 'Clown of Amsterdam', I walked behind Tia and Kora, and now I'm in the Dutch countryside alongside some interesting and intriguing women.'

After a short silence:

— 'Am I in trouble? Are you looking to arrest me?' Jay asks Ingrid.

Ingrid starts laughing and snorting out loud. From her waistline to the top of her head, she appears welded as one piece; she must turn her whole frame to make visual contact. She apologises but can't stop snorting. With watery eyes, she finally answers Jay's question:

— 'Yes, you're in trouble, no doubt about that — but it's not with me,' she adds. 'At some stage, the Eastern European mafia will look for you. I've already organised protection for you around the clock. For our benefit, I've got my eyes on you.'

— 'Our benefits? I don't understand,' questions Jay.

— 'Don't worry too much about that. It's none of your business anyway,' cuts back Ingrid.

The last sentence introduces awkwardness around the table, but Ingrid is far from over.

— 'I've a burning question for you, Jay,' continues Ingrid. 'How did you know about the Japanese girl and her mother?

They were missing for a good three weeks.'

Feeling the pressure, Jay's face suddenly turns pale, and his body language is far from comfortable.

— 'Could I have something to drink?' he asks. 'I froze when I noticed Tia and Kora's violent interaction with their aggressor. It was a little too much for me; I panicked due to a bad memory of a painful past life event. So, I stopped beside a car to compose myself and assess the situation. I didn't know what to do. The back window of the car went down for a few seconds. A man gave me the finger, but through the smoke cloud, I saw a glimpse of the little girl getting sexually assaulted in the back seat. Her chest was exposed, and she was trying to resist her molester. With that vision in my mind, I walked to Tia and Kora to secure a gun to shoot the two fuckers in the car. As I came closer, I knew that Kora had a concealed weapon in the back of her pants, but she couldn't — or wasn't in a position to — access it. With no hesitation, I retrieved it, and when I realised their attacker wasn't alone, as three accomplices made their way out of the car, I delivered four deadly bullseye rounds and yelled things before making my way to save the little girl. Knowing her position, I fired on the right side of the car first, opened the door and shot the second guy. His pants were down. I threw the first guy out and grabbed the girl from the car. She was screaming madly; she had blood and pieces of flesh and glass over her naked body. I gave her to Kora and returned to free her mother.'

As Jay looks disturbed and shaking, Coco, sitting next to him, moves slightly closer and rubs her hand on his right knee under the table. Their eyes meet again with great intensity. Her facial expression radiates a humble and genuine thank you.

Jay pushes the USB stick to the middle of the table and mentions the diary found in the car.

— 'I traced back to Tia and Kora to warn them about the hit list, and I'm sorry I wasn't quick enough to find you. I could've spared your friend's life.'

Kora sobs silently at the table. Tia interrupts Jay, demanding more information about the coma treatment therapy.

— 'Our mum is in a coma. Could you help us? She needs help. We need your help!'

— 'I'll ask and do my best, I promise,' replies Jay.

The twins visually thank Jay with a head nod and charismatically express their gratitude by holding their hands proudly together against their chests. Everyone at the table acknowledges their pain.

— 'The content of the USB stick will be published soon. I don't know when yet. Everything inside the diary is disturbing, which will probably create grief, anger, fear, and most likely revenge — while hopefully producing closure for some people. I don't want to keep the diary; it's not my responsibility. After meeting all of you, I believe that Ingrid is the best person around the table to keep it safe and has the best network and capabilities to identify all victims,' he adds with a firmer and slightly louder voice.

Receiving no reaction from the Police Commissioner, Jay enters a monologue in a more controlled voice and seeks clarification on the €35 million required for the acquisition.

— 'Is anything needed after that? I'm no businessman and

have never talked about this sum of money before. Could you explain the full picture? What's the business model? What's your exit plan? Do you have any alternative scenario?'

Directing his hand towards Coco's knee and stopping halfway through, he gently confronts her:

— 'What are the alternatives for your business? Do you need to sell it? Your body language was aching early on. Have you brainstormed your options? Or are all of you ready to lose or sacrifice your life and livelihood for a shelter? Did you consider resurrecting Hotel L'Europa? With your skills, you can turn a positive cash flow in no time and invest your profit into small-size shelters. They're cheaper to buy, maintain, and secure — and are smaller targets against your enemy. It sounds like you're putting all your eggs in the same basket,' Jay rambles.

Everyone around the table, except Ingrid, nods their heads as a form of participation in the conversation.

— 'I need protection for another person. I've met him here, and he's helping me with my work assignments. He doesn't know I'm the 'Clown of Amsterdam', but he's aware of the diary. Is that okay, Ingrid?' Jay asks fearlessly, realising her disinterest in the conversation.

— 'It's getting late! Let's catch up tomorrow!' Ingrid replies harshly, grabbing the USB from the table.

Putting a hand on Jay's leg for a second time, Coco invites him to return to Amsterdam together. Everyone at the table feels their electric connection as Jay accepts the offer.

Back in town, Coco invites Jay out for breakfast the following day.

— 'I have a gift for you,' she says, tendering her business card, on which she adds her personal phone number and email address on the back. Coco requests Jay to keep it safe too, and not to share it.

— 'I have something for you too,' replies Jay, giving her a copy of the USB drive. 'Keep it safe! There's always a weak link in all associations,' he adds.

On his return to his hotel, Jay checks on Ozzie. He looks better and has many questions for Jay — all related to the diary's content and his reporting status on the 'Clown of Amsterdam'.

— 'I'll answer all questions, but first, we must secure the hotel. All existing access cards must be cancelled. The hotel must be locked 24/7 and the content of the CCTV network must be backed up on the server,' Jay instructs Ozzie.

The pair regroup in Jay's room once the logistical matters are over. Both men are sitting at the bay window.

— 'We, maybe, are in danger. I want you to see Lincoln, Nebraska, one more time — and not in a coffin,' says Jay.

Ozzie laughs; he thinks Jay is joking.

— 'We've got police protection and other things. You and I need to stay under the radar, and your genius brain can help us to do so.'

Ozzie's attention becomes sharper.

— 'To my knowledge, we did nothing wrong. We're simply aware of the diary and its atrocious content,' adds Jay.

— 'It's just plain sick,' comments Ozzie.

— 'The diary most likely belongs to an organised crime syndicate. They don't want or need free advertising. Due to the seriousness of the situation, I've got a gun under my mattress for you. Let me grab it.'

Jay opens the envelope containing Kora's gun and gives Ozzie the P365 and a handful of spare ammunition.

— 'Do you know how to use it?' asks Jay while loading the bullets into the magazine.

— 'Yes,' replies Ozzie. 'But not on people. I once went to a shooting range in Lincoln and disliked it. I don't like violence.' He shudders.

— 'I understand, Ozzie,' replies Jay. 'We've got no choice. I need to protect you, and you've got no choice but to protect yourself. Are we clear? It's not negotiable. Let's catch up on sleep and see what tomorrow brings,' concludes Jay.

While leaving the room with a heavy envelope in his hand, Ozzie grimaces, disagreeing with the situation.

Chapter seven

A bad-flavoured ice cream tub

Early morning, Jay walks fast and fearfully with Hotel L'Europa in sight. While waiting to cross the road, Tia and Kora catch up with him. They've been patiently waiting for him to appear, hiding inside a shopfront alcove and protecting themselves from the cold wind and the light rain. At first, Jay didn't recognise them. Both looked like K-pop anime characters dressed in elegant Tomb Raider-inspired outfits and wearing outrageous fluorescent manga makeup. Jay's surprise matches his nervousness.

— 'We wanted to catch up with you one-on-one,' says Tia.

— 'We want to receive a copy of the USB stick too. We doubt that Ingrid will share the diary's content with us. We love her, but she plays by the rules of the police book. We are the weakest link without this information,' adds Kora.

Jay puts his hands in his jacket pockets, listens carefully to the message conveyed by the twins and asks bluntly,

— 'Did you have bad business with the guys I killed two days ago?'

— 'Bad business can be resolved, war not!' comments Tia.

— 'You are at war as much as we are now, except that you have police protection and, as a bonus, the 'Haka Army' will take care of you,' clarifies Kora.

— 'You are so intriguing!' Tia says, looking at Jay.

— 'As much as you are! You both look great in your outfits; I like the crazy makeup. I wish I could reinvent myself like you do. I don't want to be rude, but Coco is waiting for me, and I don't like to be late,' Jay tells the pair.

He puts his hands out of his jacket and offers Tia a handshake.

— 'What the fuck?' she tells Jay, shaking her fighter's head Turning to Kora, he does the same and says,

— 'What you've asked for is in my hand. So, please shake my hand and take the USB stick. Let's meet again at lunchtime. I need help with my next news articles. 1:00 p.m. at the Oude Kerk.'

— 'At Coco's place, you can avoid the hotel's main entry by using the now-closed Native Dutch Society door. The four-digit entry code is '2704', which is easy to remember as it symbolises Koningsdag or King's Day here in Holland. Take the lift to the top floor. The first door on the left is Coco's Amsterdam pied-à-terre,' Kora informs.

— 'I'm sorry for the missed handshake!' says Tia.

— 'It's all good! I've no hard feelings. I'm scared, tense, tired, and all out of sorts too. It's better if we work as a team.

It'll benefit all of us,' says Jay, acknowledging his scariness, tenseness and tiredness.

As he crosses the road, he calls the hypnotherapists and invites them for lunch. They both accept. He realises Ozzie's numerous missed calls and gives him some attention. When Ozzie picks up, he's pumped and has verbal diarrhoea as a hood of words fills Jay's ear. Jay thanks him for his support and spirit and tells him he'll return after breakfast. Their Nebraskan friendship takes on new heights.

Arriving at Coco's door, Jay knocks gently. Coco opens the door and appears in a high-cut white see-through leotard. Her athletic body is perfectly moulded to her garment, acting as a second thin skin.

— 'I'm all sweaty, just doing my morning stretches,' she says, an athletic glow on her face.

Coco's body is on display, and Jay tries not to look. She hugs him firmly, and he can feel her tiny, firm breast squeezed up against his chest. She kisses him on both cheeks, strategically placed close to Jay's lips.

— 'Get used to it!' she says with a big smile as she pushes Jay's coat away. 'Hug me closer to you; I want to feel you. Let your hands run on my body, feel my back, touch my hips, squish my ass,' she adds while she moves Jay's hand where she wants to be touched. She empowers Jay verbally, 'I'm so turned on; I masturbated last night thinking about how you'll touch my belly, feel my chest, tweak my nipples or enter my pussy. It's wet, you made it wet, and it's wild for you.'

She forces Jay's hand onto her genitalia. He feels the tight leotard fabric beautifully embracing Coco's shaved pussy.

'She is a cameltoe girl,' he thinks, referencing his Pornhub education.

She moves Jay's hand backwards and forwards. Her pelvis embraces the rhythm of his forced hand. Jay can feel her wetness going through the fabric of her clothing; she moves her leotard over the side of her vulva to facilitate his touch on her well-groomed pussy. Jay acknowledges, through a deeper breathing pattern, the smoothness and softness of her pubic skin. As she moves her hips backwards and forwards, she tells Jay that she's a two-finger girl. Jay moves in unison while kissing her neck and shoulders and licking her nipples over her bodysuit material. He truly enjoys the salted taste of her smooth skin. She knows her desired outcome as she selects two of his fingers and directs them into her drenched vagina. She helps him to locate her G-spot and instructs him how to pleasure it the right way. She tiptoes to benefit fully from the experience and kisses her lover with passion. Jay grabs the back of her leotard to keep his balance, which passes beautifully into her rounded, muscular bum cheeks. The fabric buffs her anal rose in linear motion, which induces numerous pleasure noises out of Coco. As the steam between the pair builds up, Coco opens Jay's zip trousers and undoes the button on his jeans. While performing some contortion moves, she grabs his cock and strokes him vigorously. Jay is hard, his cock head is blood-inflated. She takes his vibrating fingers out of her pussy and pushes his pants downward. Jay lifts her and effortlessly slides his hard knob into the wetness and warmth of her vagina. He lays his back and shoulders on the entry door to maintain his position. Coco's legs are around his lower back, and her arms and hands are around his neck. She looks like a koala pleasuring a tree. He can't move or open his legs as his trousers are only halfway down. Jay feels his sperm leaving his body to embrace Coco's tightness and wetness.

— 'I feel your warmth,' she says. 'Keep on going, I'm coming too,' she adds.

Her sentence wasn't finished yet, and a loud orgasmic noise echoed in the hallway.

— 'Don't stop, don't stop,' she repeats, 'Stroke me. Stroke me more, yes, yes, now, keep on going; I'm coming; I'm coming,' she begs with an out-of-breath voice.

To Jay's surprise, his cock is still hard. He can feel their combined juicy wetness running along his testicles and down his thighs. His breathing is heavy. His hand holds Coco's bums firmly, helping her to thrust his cock at a quicker speed for an extra few seconds. Coco lets out more pleasurable sounds and squeezes as hard as she can Jay's penis by contracting her pelvic muscles. It's Jay's turn to be loud. His body has numerous spasms, and his unwinding nerves turn him into a shaking skeleton. Coco releases Jay's cock, kisses him and elegantly knees down, licking and sucking his balls. As Jay maintains his erection, she places her hands on his bum cheeks, stretching his ass wide open and pushing forwards and backwards his hips while worshipping his manhood. Jay holds Coco's head; he gently moves her hair out of her face. As he comes closer to ejaculating for the second time, he presses Coco's head as close as possible to his belly. As he climaxes, his body is an entire pleasure twitch; he has no control over the situation and himself. His mouth lets out words, making no sense between orgasmic noises and short, stuttered breaths. The doorbell rings, and an unusual but repetitive doorknock abruptly stops Jay's wild sexual encounter. Coco effortlessly stands up and shares the taste of the warm semen by passionately kissing her morning lover. Acknowledging Jay's pleasurable reaction to his cum, she pushes two of her fingers into her vagina and forces them into his mouth, and without much hesitation, opens the door. Her face is wet, her hair looks like a battlefield, and her body is to die for. With no second thought, she helps Abigail to enter her place in her wheelchair. Jay tries his best to cover himself by pulling up his pair of jeans. While doing it, he realises that Abigail has received another beating, her face needing some medical attention.

— 'Let us have a quick shower,' says Coco to Abigail. 'We won't be long; please make yourself at home. There are some frozen peas in the freezer,' she adds.

Making his way towards the bathroom, Jay discovers Coco's place; his attention is drawn directly to the century-old outstanding carpentry work that defines the double-height attic space. All the timber beams are painted in light aqua green, and the ceiling infills and walls are warm light grey. The paint contrast is unusual, and the white oak limewash timber floor supports and brings unity to the drama of its spatial magnificence. The well-crafted furniture and the content of the display cabinets offer hundreds of unfinished life stories. Intriguing fine art hanging on the walls is another world, and Jay's curiosity is alive like a kid walking for the first time through an art gallery. His eyes are greedy, and he wants more of this unique sensory language. Every artwork makes him walk slower. Coco invites and guides him to the bathroom located on the lower floor. The space is ample, modern and sleek; from the natural light blessing to the tapware selection, the whole room is a piece of jewellery to be appreciated by the senses. The detailing of the vanity unit catches Jay's eye.

— 'It's beautiful and well-crafted,' he says.

Coco replies,

— 'It'll be magical under the water,' as she undresses him and removes her leotard.

Looking into Jay's eyes, she confesses with an open heart,

— 'It's the first time in my entire life that I feel attracted to a man. It's the first time I want to be with someone. You triggered me when you entered the cottage last night; your presence, energy, and weakness seduced me, and to top it up, your kindness and actions towards strangers who are my loved ones.'

A shy, naked Jay stands in the middle of the gigantic bathroom with no words coming out of his mouth. It's the first time Jay experiences kind, warm, and loving words towards himself, which he's long wanted. Embarrassed and trying to avoid his awkwardness, he opens his arms and invites Coco to seek his connection in the present moment. Under a dry showerhead, Jay and Coco are physically one. Sheepishly, after a few long seconds of silence, Jay says quietly,

— 'I have the money for you to purchase the hotel. I've got it here in Amsterdam, and I've got it in cash. The money is not mine; it belongs to the guys I killed. It was in their car. I found it after I dropped everyone off at the hospital. My life has no plans for this type of money, so take it, but do me a favour. Don't turn this place into a dormitory. Putting all your eggs in one basket won't bring you the desired outcome.'

As Jay stops talking, he feels Coco's tears running down his chest.

— 'Thank you from me and everyone,' says Coco timidly.

— 'There's no need to thank me; it's not my money. Let's make it work for all of you,' replies Jay. 'I don't want anyone or anybody to know about the money and our deal. Just take it as an anonymous gift from the universe,' Jay adds.

Coco melts into Jay's arms and holds him tight like a baby to his mother. Her skin is silky soft, and a wave of goosebumps covers her nude body. She's very thankful, and by the same token, she's well aware that she won't be able to keep their deal a secret. She prefers not to address this matter now, as Jay's warmth is the only thing that matters. Holding Jay tightly against her body, she asks him to have dinner together. Without great movement, Jay kisses her on her forehead and smiles as a sign of acceptance.

Jay is the first one to leave the bathroom and check on Abigail. Her face is swollen. She has pain keeping her eyes open as another layer of purple bruises is added to yesterday's blackness.

— 'Did you find the ice in the freezer?' Jay asks.

— 'No! I can't reach it. I'm too sore.'

— 'Let me help you,' he replies, crossing the kitchen floor and opening the freezer door.

— 'I need help, Jay!' she adds with a struggling voice. 'I'm scared. He's coming to kill me, but first, he wants me to suffer a little bit more every day. I'm scared to die. We all are scared to die.'

Abigail is cut short in her lamentations.

— 'I'm here, Abi,' says Coco, entering the room joyfully and with a very affirmative voice. She repeats, 'I'm here, and we all are here for you. No one is going to kill you, or me, or anyone. No one will take away our freedom, great hearts, smiles, and love. I'm with you, and Jay is with us. Let me take care of you now. It's time for Jay to go!' she quickly adds, visually pushing Jay towards the hallway while placing her two hands on Abigail's shoulders and drying her eyes with her stretched pullover sleeves.

At the Hotel Lucius, Ozzie is pumped and jumping out of his skin like a young, enlightened puppy when he sees Jay's arrival. Ozzie has worked all night, and his ingenuity is displayed in their makeshift office.

— 'Jay, Jay, come here!' he yells out. 'I secured access to all Amsterdam CCTV networks, look!' as he shows his desk full of computer screens. 'Through a few applications that I borrowed,' he laughs simultaneously, 'I run all live streams through a number plate decoder, and I can detect a car, or any vehicle, by country of origin, vehicle brand, colour and so on. The cool feature is that I can track cars with no registration number as I pick other attributes in the pictures to create a virtual identity.'

Moving over to the next set of screens, Ozzie points out that this computer processes all number plates and validates their authenticity and feedback to the CCTV scanner data. The next three screens are a second layer of scanning in the red-light district and a kilometre radius around it. Every moving object and its driver are photographed and run through another borrowed face recognition software linked to numerous police databases.

— 'This last screen does the same thing, except it can track activity from now back into the past—as far back as we want, as long as the monitoring data are available. On a test run, it gave me the names of all six men killed by the 'Clown of Amsterdam'. And that's not all!' Ozzie rejoices. 'I've also got their entire movements for that day, and by lunchtime, I should have a full week's worth of data from their time in the Netherlands. I can dig even deeper, but I'll need more computing power.'

— 'How do you do that so quickly?' questions Jay. 'You are a freak! You're a fucking freak!'

Jay grabs Ozzie by the shoulder and invites him for a high-five. Ozzie's answer is blunt and easy to digest,

— 'See, this computer is set up as Lego blocks; you just connect them. The hardest part is to anonymously borrow software, AI platforms, server access, and a few broken mobile phones to secure multiple and unlimited internet connections. I hijacked some of The New York World News' server spaces and created secured vaults to store our priceless data. The mobile phones set up hotspots automatically on all open networks available through this box, which is connected to the roof antenna. It's all illegal, and the tourists of Amsterdam are the best target.'

Changing abruptly the direction of the conversation, Jay asks,

— 'How can we go under the radar physically?'

The tone of his voice is sombre.

— 'I'd prefer if no one could recognise us. Any thoughts on that?' adds Jay.

— 'Yes, I do!' replies quickly Ozzie. 'Two options. Like the 'Clown of Amsterdam', we wear masks to walk through the city, or I can develop an app that diverts the CCTV livestream onto a remote server, edits each frame that we appear on and replaces our faces with something funny like movie characters,' laughs Ozzie while rubbing his eye behind his greasy pair of glasses.

— 'What do you require to do all this?' asks Jay tentatively.

— 'A few spare computer towers, monitors and a couple of decent Chinese mobile phones.'

Jay takes his work credit card from his wallet and gives Ozzie the sixteen-digit code, expiration date, and CCV numbers.

— 'This is my gift to you. Don't go too crazy,' clarifies Jay, a big grin on his face.

Ozzie pumps his fist in the air in excitement.

— 'I know where to find the masks. There's the shop where I bought—' says Jay, catching himself mid-sentence before stopping abruptly. 'No! No!' he backpedals as he regrets his last sentences. 'We don't want to be seen. Let's shop online; the selection must be bigger,' he says before leaving Ozzie to watch over Amsterdam.

Jay's next meeting is with the 'Haka Girls', Andrea and Ed. Checking the time zone on his phone, he wants to call

Judy and, most importantly, talk to his kids. It's too early; mid-afternoon local time is better. Jay must stay patient.

At Oude Kerk, the twins again approach Jay. They're dressed as nuns: long dark dresses, white collars, clinical headpieces, pure face skin, and a minimalist golden crucifix dancing on their elevated chests.

— 'Peace be with us,' says Jay.

Looking around the public square, he tells the girls to secure a table on the first floor at 'Quartier Putain'. Andrea and Ed arrive a few minutes later; the three men shake hands. A few words are exchanged as they walk towards the establishment. This time around, their conversation seems civilised; although Jay is nervous, he can't stay still; his head is scanning left and right. As he enters the coffee shop, he notices one of the Haka Army girls posted near the coffee shop entry door. A split lip and a black eye give her undercover camouflage away. He makes his way up to the first floor and introduces Tia and Kora to the hypnotherapists. Ed is interested in spirituality but not religion and is curious to be invited to a meeting with two religious women. On the other side of the table, Andrea's sexual mind is well alive. His love hormones, oxytocin and dopamine, affect and expand his pupil size. Before being interrupted by the waiter, Jay does his best to introduce everyone and give a quick introduction on who is who and why they are all here. Jay lies about how he met Tia and Kora and goes straight to the point with the two men.

— 'Their mum is in a coma,' tells Jay, 'and I want her to be part of the medical trial. I'm asking you to make this happen.'

Andrea is lost for words, and his mind is equally lost in the girls' perfect golden skin and hypnotic eyes. His legendary smile becomes bigger by the second. The girls are silent, just like the entire floor of the coffee shop, where the bright red feature wall doesn't have much to say either; only the few picture frames are life stamps that only a few people acknowledge. The atmosphere feels slightly off, like in a movie scene. The consistent light that creates ephemeral shadows that dance across the room is interrupted when the male waiter checks on everyone, and another round of drinks is purchased.

— 'Are we all good?' clarifies Jay.

— 'Good for what?' replies Ed.

Andrea finally surfaces into reality and can't guarantee that additional participants can be added to the medical trial.

Kora takes a small bottle of eau de toilette from her formal outfit and sprays the back of her wrist while displaying a Māori tattoo on her forearm. After a few seconds, she passes her arm around the table and says,

— 'This is my mother's fragrance, the one I've known since we were kids. From my perspective, this smell is always associated with a generous smile, endless generosity, and the best attitude towards life that anybody can find. Her current health condition is the result of caring for her family — especially, my sister and me. My deepest wish is that one day she'll stand and smile before me and that her smell embraces and knots our hearts again.'

Another layer of silence has taken the air out of the room and wipes out Andrea's smile in no time. He lost his mother when he was a teenager, and since that day, he seeks his mum's love back in all types of relationships that always finish with an empty bed and a depleted heart. Andrea has a magnificent nature and equally a great mind; unfortunately for him, as he avoids the depth of his sadness and unfinished state of mourning, he cultivates a high volume of sexual-based relationships. His mum's love is an ongoing burden turned into an addiction and a collection of beautiful women that will never be the right fit or replacement. Andrea's partners are empty love containers as defined by his pain.

Feeling awkward around the girls' emotional burden, Andrea excuses himself from the table and disappears down the coffee shop's narrow staircase.

Jay looks at Ed and says,

— 'They're not nuns. Kora and Tia are businesswomen who make people happy, safe and entertained in no particular order. The three of us are having another meeting now, and I want a guarantee that their mum will be accounted for.'

— 'She will!' answers Ed. 'Knowing Andrea, he's already organising the logistics for your loved one. We'll be in touch later today,' Ed concludes before exiting.

After a quick toilet break and another interruption by the waiter, Jay and the twins regroup.

— 'I have a few things to clarify,' says Jay to the girls. 'You won't go to your friend's funeral this week or in the near future. Last night, while going through the diary, I found a pattern in the Polaroid photos. The killer or the person in charge of reporting on the killings always goes to the funerals; he or she annotates the photos and maybe targets more victims during the process. The disturbing fact is that the photos are taken at a very close range, and there are no zoom lenses on a Polaroid camera. Something else caught my attention that I'm unsure about; maybe I'm right or wrong, but I noticed that the pairs of shoes in some of the murder photos are always the same and have a feminine shape and petite size. They look like flamenco or tango dancer shoes.'

Tia replies,

— 'We had a quick look this morning too, and I must confess that it was painful to watch. We knew a few of the victims.'

Jay interrupts,

— 'In the diary, there's a funeral plan for tomorrow morning, and Ingrid's murder is scheduled for the day after. As mentioned yesterday, I have a little helper from Nebraska. He's a computer science student and a professional cybersecurity hacker with incredibly fast typing skills, a great liking for online borrowing and an amazing detective mind. He's tapped into the city CCTV network and its archives overnight. To save time and to protect each other's back, I need the residential and business addresses and phone numbers of all the ladies present yesterday at the cottage. I'll ask Ozzie, my helper, to run his scanning algorithm around the perimeter of each address and other places of interest, such as the cottage. Ozzie, I and anyone in danger should start wearing masks to conceal our identity. I saw some for sale at the fancy dress shop where I bought my clown outfit. I can't go back; I need your help!'

The girls nod in approval.

— 'How was your breakfast with Coco this morning?

What did you eat?' Kora asks with a grin that turns into a little girl giggle, which her sister embraces as they start bouncing their nun shoulder pads on each other. 'Did she serve you fresh sushi?'

Both are now hysterical.

— 'Who beats Abigail?' asks Jay sternly.

Like Andrea, who was stripped of his smile a half hour ago, the 'Haka Girls' look distraught now.

— 'I want an answer, and I want it now. The fucker deserves a visit and some free advertising, courtesy of The New York World News. Come on, girls, he's no secret to you; do you have any association or business with him?' clarifies Jay.

— 'His name is Paul Van Looke. He's a luxury car dealer here in Amsterdam. Like us, he services the celebrities, the 'A-listers' around town, but he also deals with the guys you shot forty-eight hours ago who had some money laundering business with him. He's well connected, very powerful, and somehow has remained untouchable,' replies Tia in a disgruntled voice.

— 'Where can I find him?' cuts Jay.

— 'His business is called A.L.D., short for 'Amsterdam Luxury Drive',' says Kora.

— 'Time to go!' says Jay. 'I must call my kids. They're twins and silly, just like you. I'll be in touch later today.'

In his hotel room, Jay tries to reach his sons through WhatsApp. No one picks up the call. He tries again. No answers. A few moments later, a message from Jack, one of Jay's sons, pops into the group chat. The message reads,

— 'Mum told us that you're not our father and forced us

to do a DNA test. Grandpa Roger is furious; he collected your stuff as Mum threw them into the bin. When are you coming back?'

Jay replies:

— 'This is okay, sons. Whatever my legal or parental status on paper, you are my boys, and I'm your father. Bloodline is not as important as we think. Today, we must commit to one another, and the three of us should love and embrace one another without questioning our origin. The same applies to your mum.'

Benjamin, Jay's other boy, comes online and comments,

— 'Uncle Lenny is our biological father, Mum said. Aunty Jeanne wants to divorce him.'

Jay adds,

— 'Let's keep our cool, boys. No silly business. I'm okay with the DNA results. I had doubts about our biological links a long time ago.'

Jack fires back,

— 'How can you be okay with the DNA results?'

Jay replies,

— 'It won't be easy, but humans like safety, comfort, and a sense of belonging. We all do!'

— 'Do you miss us?' queries Benjamin.

— 'Yes, I miss you! I miss you, and I love you. I don't know when I'll be back home. If I quit my assignment, I'll be out of work, and as of today, I can't afford it,' justifies Jay.

— 'Is our life a lie?' questions Benjamin.

— 'Are you okay, boys? Are you feeling mentally strong? I'm sorry that I'm not there for you,' clarifies Jay.

— 'Everything sucks!' Jack messages.

— 'Let me call Grandpa Roger! Let's catch up later!' concludes Jay.

Jay sits on the edge of his bed, overwhelmed by mixed feelings of joy, anger, resentment, lightness and guilt. He feels powerless, like the day he was forced to marry Judy.

— 'Better not to talk to anyone yet,' he mumbles as he opens his wallet and takes out a family picture of his boys, Judy and himself. Tears flow as he puts his thumbs on Judy's face, making her disappear.

Jay decides to call Juliana on his old office line. Jay quickly enquires about her time at the factory as she picks up the call. Their conversation doesn't flow well, but Jay asks Juliana to keep an eye on his boys, whatever it means. Listening to her silence, he hangs up on her. She calls him back a little bit later.

— 'I couldn't talk,' she says. 'I have bad news for you, Jay. Please don't interrupt me; I'm no good at delivering bad news,' her slightly masculine voice says. 'I'm in shock,' and the tone of her voice matches her seriousness. Jay is quiet and on edge but doesn't expect to hear that Natalia's body has been found at the airport this morning.

— 'She committed suicide the day you left. She shot herself in the back seat of a rental car with your gun,' Juliana says, her words breaking as she speaks before stopping, leaving the sentences unfinished. While sobbing, sniffing and gasping desperately for air, she continues,

— 'Natalia left a note for you on the car's dashboard. She had a very aggressive form of breast cancer and had days to live. She came to the airport to tell you about it but didn't find the courage to face you. She loved you, Jay, and I can assure you that her love is with you,' she adds.

Hearing Juliana crying uncontrollably on the line, Jay stops the call. His heart pumps with anger, and still, with great calmness, he grabs a chair, sits at the bay window, and looks around. He sees nothing, hears nothing, smells nothing, touches nothing, and only life's bitterness embraces his present moment. In a state of stillness or stiffness, Jay feels heavy, shallow, and empty of many things.

Early in the evening, a nagging text message from Bruno Lefevre brings Jay back to reality. Jay ignores the elitist Frenchman as he has no news to report. Andrea receives the same fate that evening.

Out of curiosity, Jay checks the value of a €500 note online and realises that some European countries are now refusing the eurozone banknotes. Whether the money has value or not, he proceeds with his plan to give it to the Sex Workers' Foundation. His knowledge increases when he realises that one million euros, made of purple banknotes, only weighs 2.2 kilograms. Jay packs €35 million into four mini suitcases he found in the hotel storeroom, and a total weight of eighty kilograms must be carried out of the building unsuspected. Before meeting Coco, Jay checks on Ozzie. He's nowhere to be seen, but his hacking quarters have doubled, and monitors are flooding his makeshift office.

Coco picks up Jay near his hotel; he displays poor baggage handler skills. He runs madly between the hotel door and the car boot, paranoid that the whole of Amsterdam is aware of his monetary transfer. Coco, sitting behind her steering wheel, laughs at the scene. When Jay makes it into the car, a white Porsche Panamera dressed in a refined Techart GrandGT body kit, Coco takes time to welcome him and sensually French kisses him as a teaser. Jay notices her fresh, gingery fragrance and takes time to enjoy his lover's presence by gently smelling her neck. Coco rubs his chest with her left hand and shows Jay that she has no ring adorning her fingers.

— 'I'm single and in love with you, Jay,' she says with a warm and seductive voice.

Jay is hypnotised, his shyness taking over. He'd never met a beautiful, forthright woman who gave her body as freely as she did this morning, showing interest and respect for him. During the trip, Jay can't stop feeling the leather pattern on his seat, the dashboard, and the door panels; he thinks the craftsmanship is first class as he runs his fingers along the stitching. His ears are also at the party whenever Coco pushes the finely tuned eight cylinders; the deep, grounded, legendary German noise is pure enjoyment, especially when the turbochargers join the celebration.

As they drive, Coco dreams of having a romantic evening with Jay, but sadly for her, as they agreed the night before, they are returning to the cottage.

Abigail and Zoetje can't make it tonight. Jay and Coco arrive first, followed by Ingrid and the Kiwi Girls. The greetings are less formal this time around. Middle Eastern and Indian food and a few bottles of champagne are carried through the door. Under the graceful darkness of the countryside and the glamour of a wintery sky displaying the endless location of lifeless planets, the €35 million is handled with more elegance inside the cottage.

As everyone looks peckish, the dinner is served immediately. All food containers are open in the middle of the dining table, and everyone is taking care of themselves except Coco, who assures Jay's plate is not missing delights from these other cultures. Middle Eastern and Indian cuisines are a first for Jay. He savours his meal, making noises of approval and comments as he eats. The Gobhi Pakora, cauliflower pieces dipped in salty and tangy chickpea flour batter and deep-fried, receive a five-star rating from Jay. Vegetable samosa and mango chicken are close seconds for the Indian dishes. Charred Eggplant Labneh, Lamb Kofta and Chicken Shawarma are the winners of his Middle Eastern sampling.

Tia and Kora can't resist teasing Jay and asking him if he had sushi for breakfast. Like this morning, they giggle like two schoolgirls.

Ingrid invites everyone for a toast and, without hesitation, addresses Jay with firmness,

— 'Using proceeds of crime to purchase real estate in the Netherlands is against the law. People will question where the funds come from, and links can be drawn from the incident,' putting her index towards Kora and Tia, 'along with the missing Mercedes and its content.'

— 'I thought about it!' replies Jay.

— 'So, what's your plan?' clamps back Ingrid.

Jay secures a piece of paper and a pen and says,

— 'Here are my thoughts; please challenge me if I'm

wrong,' as he draws circles and arrows to mission his idea. 'Ingrid and Ozzie go to the bank and convert the cash into a bank cheque. Subject to their success, Ozzie opens a legal entity in a tax haven country and a business bank account where he deposits the bank cheque. The overseas entity purchases Coco's business. On receipt of the money, Coco donates the funds to the charity organisation to complete the acquisition of Hotel L'Europa. At tax time, Coco gets a refund as her donation is tax-deductible and later purchases back Ozzie's shares for one dollar or less. With the balance of her tax refund, she can either invest back into her ice cream business or contribute more to your venture.'

Jay's phone rings; it's Ozzie, the cheerful. He wants to give an update on his arsenal. Jay cuts him short and asks,

— 'Out of curiosity, would you be interested in being a shareholder in a business for a limited time?'

— 'Nothing illegal that I can't control!' replies Ozzie.

— 'No, we're talking ice cream,' reassures Jay.

— 'If I can have free ice cream samples for the rest of my life, I'm in,' jokes Ozzie.

— 'Let's talk later,' replies Jay as he ends the call.

Everyone at the table is silent, but their inner computers process the potential for their dream to come true. Ingrid warns Coco again of possible legal repercussions if she breaches company and trading laws.

— 'We're already in a bad-flavoured ice cream tub,' replies Coco. 'We all know about the 'Clown of Amsterdam' identity, the diary, the money. We have no protection and no future if we don't act. Let me talk to my accountant and lawyer,' says Coco as she leaves. She rubs her soft hand on Jay's shoulder, blinking at him with a gorgeous and generous smile.

Kora and Tia notice Coco's gesture and tease Jay for the third time today.

— 'How was your day?' asks Ingrid to Jay.

The tone of her voice validates her need for power and control. Looking down at the table, Jay answers,

— 'A week ago, I was angry, rude and arrogant; now I'm fearful and stressed but hopeful that something positive will come out of my Amsterdam adventure.' With a cracked voice and teary eyes, he continues,

— 'This afternoon, I learned that my fifteen-year-old twins are not genetically my children, and to add to today's misery, I was made aware that my HR manager, who enrolled me in the job lottery, committed suicide the day of my departure from the US. From the little information shared with me, she had breast cancer and shot herself in the back seat of a rental car.'

The mood around the table is now flat and lifeless.

— 'For years, I wished for my life to turn around and did nothing about it. I made myself busy to avoid myself and my emotions. My fears and stresses today are linked to the new opportunities on offer. I often dreamed of a life reset, but I never expected it could be so radical,' he says quietly.

— 'Was Arizona a radical experience for David Swagg?' asks Ingrid, looking Jay straight in the eyes.

Jay's stunned face catches the attention of the Kiwi girls.

— 'Yes, it was! I never thought someone would call me

again, David Swagg. There's no need to open old scars. I had no choice but to kill my dear friend Polka. Losing him was extremely painful, and what happened here in Amsterdam is a reconnection and reminder of an awful, unsettling and unresolved past. I didn't want him to suffer any longer. There was enough suffering in our life then,' replies Jay.

— 'I watched the Arizona video,' tells Ingrid, 'and the one from Amsterdam too. In both footages, your body and its language are frozen for a fair amount of time, but in the two events, you took control of the situation. In Amsterdam, even under the thickness of your clown makeup and the pace of your footsteps, I—or everyone—can see your determination to take control of a desperate situation.'

— 'What happened in Arizona?' asks Kora.

— 'Before we go there and before I forget,' interrupts Ingrid, 'I'd like to clarify, for your safety and the sake of everyone sitting around this table tonight, that the Volvo and the Mercedes are two separate incidents and, to date, are not connected. The two guys that you gunned down to save the Japanese girl and her mum are both Dutch nationals with no criminal records and unknown to our justice system.'

With a victory smile on her face and clapping her hands like a joyful little girl, Coco returns. Jay looks at the twins and waits for another goofy reaction, but Kora repeats her question.

— 'What happened in Arizona?'

— 'Let's hear what Coco has to say,' Jay politely suggests. His last sentence is dismissed by Coco herself, who tells Jay,

— 'I want to know you. Please proceed!'

— 'In my early years of high school,' starts Jay with a dry, raspy voice, 'I had a friend, Andy 'Polka' Dots. He and I connected through his madness and his disconnected reality of the world. He lived in his creative mind. He was a great storyteller, and daily boredom was transformed into a supernatural, impossible, romantic, and unrealistic script. In his company, time flew quickly, and we were happy. He brought the pure joy of life to me and a few others. Around him, I discovered love, joy and happiness. There was no joy, love or happiness in my house or upbringing. It was depressing, and Polka gave me what I craved.'

Coco gently rubs Jay's shoulder blades as a sign of support.

— 'In the first two years of high school, Polka became a popular figure, and this alone wasn't appreciated by everyone, especially the older boys who started bullying him. Girls loved him, and the testosterone boys couldn't cope or comprehend that a boy full of facial acne and craziness could steer away or captivate the minds of all the princesses of the kingdom. Their jealousy took over, and Polka became the target of insults, bullying, and physical and verbal abuse. Whatever happened to him never changed his way of enjoying life, as he didn't see us as reality but as a pity mirror of our weakness or, on the other end of the spectrum, as breathing genius creating our matrix. He didn't retreat from the expectations of others; he was pure freedom. He was free. His interpretation of the insults, punches and kicks was hilarious. Whatever his mental or physical injuries, a rainbow was always crested over the horizon for everyone to enjoy. But as the weeks passed, his circle of friends narrowed. The bullies' anger made it unsafe for anyone around him. I had no plans to let go of Polka; he was my source of ongoing happiness, and I believe it was reciprocal. We were laughing at the simplicity of life, and life was unreal. From silly and dramatic interactions selflessly executed, he made me discover and enjoy my inner self.'

After taking a sip of water, Jay continues,

— 'A week before the school fair, there was an incident that became the trigger of the school shooting. The drama teacher chose Andy to perform an unscripted play as a solo artist; she wanted to bring a day of his life to the stage. His performance was the closing act of the school fair. The teacher's artistic choice became an instant controversy, as the last performance of the fair was usually given to the most talented student. Within a few hours of the fair program being finalised, a group of boys decided to tackle Andy to the ground and force dirty female underwear onto his head and rub his face in it; the knickers were soiled with dog poo and cat wee. The polka dot undergarment's print referenced Andy's acne. The boys took some photos and ran to the library to upload them on an online forum. The drama teacher came to the rescue, but she was too late. She helped Andy to clean himself up and drove him back home. I went along quietly, and the ride was an endless monologue addressed to Andy, the drama teacher begging him to be strong and to promise her he would perform at the school fair. While agreeing to her request, he informed her that he wouldn't be present at school before that as he wanted some time alone. With a funny voice, he told me he'd see me in a week.

I refused the teacher's offer to drop me back home. Anger and I were one. I wanted vengeance, and most importantly, I wanted to apologise to Polka for not finding any form of power to confront the situation. I skipped school for a week to be by his side in protest.'

Jay serves himself more water and commits to the end of his story,

— 'The fair's main stage was inside the school sports hall. On that day, it was packed from the edge of the laminated timber floor sports field to the last row of the seating area. Over a thousand people were gathered in the steel-structured building. Everyone had a great time, and it was mid-afternoon, around three o'clock, when Polka was announced through the PA system to join the centre stage. The hall's light was dimmed to a minimum, and only a directional spotlight hanging from the ceiling followed his entry. He was dressed as usual and held some masking tape in his hand, and with it, he marked a big circle in the middle of the sports arena.

He went to the microphone and started calling names of students forming his circle of friends in the early days. I was the first to join the circle, along with another twenty. So, we huddled around, and within seconds, we were back in the good days of freedom, mystical storylines and endless laughter. Hearing the stories coming out of Andy, the entire auditorium joined in on our laughter. Polka was alive; the world around us was one. As the show progressed, while talking and laughing, he started bashing the microphone against his head and making crosses on the floor with the paper tape. He removed one, two, or three friends from the initial circle for each cross designed. Twelve crosses were marked inside the circle, and I was the only one left.

He walked across the room and pushed two big trolleys past the circle. Now, for each microphone bang, he painted with dark lipstick black eyes on his face. Still doing his funny narratives, he applied bright red lipstick on his lips, chin, and shirt to simulate blood coming out of his mouth. He opened the bags on the trolley, took a big pot of peanut butter and a few bottles of orange lemonade, and started mixing them on the polished floor of the sports facility with both hands. The young kids in the audience were amused and giggled at the crazy mixing scene, and while doing his concoction, he started calling new names. It didn't sound good. The bullies were called inside the circle and forced to sit on the crosses. The public supported Andy's efforts to have them all in the circle. Some chickened out and left the sports hall. Ten boys were sitting on the crosses, some making funny gestures towards Polka; they wanted him dead. Polka grabbed me by the shirt with his peanut butter hands and dragged me to the opposite side of the trolley. He rolled me onto my left side and pushed and curled my body into a foetal position.

Andy, with a finger on his mouth, requested silence, and the atmosphere of the auditorium became eerie within seconds. He took a female polka dot underwear from his jacket, showed it around, pushed it into the peanut and lemonade mix, and put it on his head and face without hesitation. He massaged it until the peanut butter was dripping down onto his clothes. The crowd was nervously laughing at the vision they were seeing. Over the PA system and standing between the trolleys, he asked the crowd to be silent, and when silence reached its peak, he turned to the boys and asked with a gentle voice if they would like to apologise for their behaviour. A part of the crowd started booing, realising the turn in Andy's play.

— 'Silence!' shouted Andy. 'Would your parents like to apologise on your behalf?' he added cynically.

As some people in the crowd started to yell insults at him, he placed his fingers on his lips, requested silence again, and told the audience, 'It's just a play for you to remember, or not.'

Polka knelt between the trolleys and grabbed two loaded mini submachine guns from his bags, and while standing, effortlessly opened fire towards the boys first in a ninety-degree backwards and forwards rotating movement. A metallic rain of empty casings overtook the auditorium floor, instantly followed by awful screaming. Still, both were barely audible as the sound of the automatic weapons was the master of the ceremony.

I was locked to the ground. I froze. I couldn't move. I was petrified. Somehow, I understood that he protected me by placing me behind him. All I wanted at that moment was to save Polka, and when I could finally stand up, I realised it was too late to save him. The room was a massive, noisy cloud of smoke smelling of gunpowder, and its darkness was only illuminated by the orange halo of the overheated weapon barrels. The auditorium light came back, and through now the whiteness of the deadly cloud, I spotted one pistol of many in Polka's bag, grabbed it and fired it. The sound of the machine gun stopped, but its resonance echoed for a long time in the arena.

In the middle of this human carnage, I collapsed in a cold, rolling brass sea and lay down back in my foetal position, crying and holding a shaky .45 in my hand, perfectly knowing that a journey of regrets and pain had just started.

That afternoon, one hundred and forty-eight people of all ages lost their lives; nearly three hundred were injured and now had some form of disability. An entire community was destroyed.'

Ingrid puts a hand on Jay's shoulder and says,

— 'I just wanted to hear your story as part of my investigation. I had no intention to distress you.'

Coco dispenses a handful of tissues to Jay and gently rests her head on his other shoulder.

— 'Are you okay?' she asks, her voice filled with love, affection and compassion.

Tears were not only in Jay's eyes; everyone around the table also has a chaotic past, and all are aware of the emotional cost linked to their past trauma.

Kora and Tia make silly comments about their waterproof makeup to lift the mood and ask Coco for more tissues.

— 'How did you go?' Jay asks Coco.

— 'For a ten percent commission fee, I can have a bank cheque tomorrow through an angel investor,' says Coco, drying her eyes. 'About the paperwork and the transfer of shares, it needs to be done offshore, but the buyer needs to have serious business credentials. That's the point of view of my chief financial officer and legal team. I'll know more tomorrow morning,' she concludes.

— 'Talking of tomorrow, Ingrid's name is on the hit list. What are our plans to keep you safe?' questions Jay.

Kora jumps out of the table, rushes outside through the main entry, and comes back with a well-packed camo army bag that she throws down energetically onto her chair.

— 'Latex mask for everyone,' she squeals excitedly, stretching and fitting a horse head onto her head.

The room ignites in laughter. Ingrid taps the table loudly with a heavy hand and snorts at the same time. Everyone joins Kora's madness, tries a silly mask of their choice, and takes selfies of their funny and comical new selves.

— 'Time to go!' says Jay. 'It's been a long day, and I still have a few things to do tonight. Here is the money and the diary for Ingrid. Please keep the good vibes; don't open it tonight,' he adds.

Ingrid, who now wears a bald man's face, puts her thumbs up and says,

— 'Coco is the one to take care of the money and decide what's best for her first before committing to anything. She looks alive around you, Jay. I don't know what it is in you that makes her like that, but whatever it is, I sincerely ask you to be safe.'

Kora and Tia whistle madly, and Jay blushes instantly. To brush his feelings away, he hands the twins his mobile phone.

— 'Andrea and Ed's phone numbers for you,' he adds, 'Andrea left a voicemail early this evening. You need to contact him to organise your mum's treatment.'

Tia takes a piece of paper from her cord pants and gives it to Jay.

— 'Here is our homework!' she says while standing proud.

Jay now has all the names and addresses of all the women present last night at the cottage.

Back in the car, Coco apologises to Jay for being unable to keep their secret about the money.

— 'We're all good, I understand,' replies Jay. 'Let me introduce you to Ozzie if he's still awake, and maybe we can have a drink at the hotel where you can explain why you're so in love with me,' teases Jay.

Chapter eight

Peter Rudolf de Vries

In the morning, Ozzie knocks while yelling madly at Jay's bedroom door to invite him to look out the window. As Jay opens the door, he instantly notices Coco in Jay's bed, Ozzie mechanically apologising for the disruption.

— 'I'm not looking,' he adds when he realises Coco's nakedness seeking refuge under the bed sheets. 'Go to the bay window,' he pushes Jay back inside his room, 'there are hundreds of news reporters waiting for you outside. I'm sorry, this is awkward, I'm sorry,' repeats Ozzie.

Jay dresses himself enough to appear at the window. In an instant, hundreds of camera flashes bombard his eyesight.

— 'Good morning, Amsterdam! Let's check them out,' he says. 'No-one is allowed in, and we need to step up our building security access.'

Coco interrupts the boy's morning chaos and reads a text

message that she's just received from Ingrid.

— 'Your face is on the front page of The New York World News, and to make it worse for you, the diary's content has been published.'

Jay browses the news on his phone and discovers pictures of him in Las Vegas. The pictures weren't from the 'Swap your job with a stranger' convention but from Juliana's phone and her near grand final on his Hyatt's bathroom floor. Seeing Jay's face and body language, Coco can't resist checking the news. Laughingly, she says,

— 'Hey, you porn star, come here and welcome me into your day.'

Now, it's Ozzie's turn to check the news, and as soon as he flicks to Juliana's below-the-belt anatomy pictures, he questions Jay if he had sex with a guy dressed in women's clothing.

— 'I don't know,' replies Jay. 'She, Juliana, I should say, gave me the shits at the convention. She was excited to go to Lincoln and have my job. I was in misery and full of anger. She invited me for drinks to distil my bitterness, so I went off. A few hours later, I lost consciousness in a bathroom while trying to ejaculate in her cleavage. I didn't know Juliana was transgender or a cross-dresser until now. Visually, she's a woman—and a beautiful, annoying woman—but looking at the size of her oversized Lycra bulge now, I can only thank God for my loss of consciousness.'

— 'Were you a roasted chicken?' jokes Ozzie. 'Were you on the wrong side of the rotisserie shaft?'

— 'Good joke! Give me a high five, you little fucker,'

replies Jay.

As Ozzie lifts his right arm, Jay grabs him around the neck and gives him a headlock and a dry shampoo by vigorously rubbing his knuckles on his scalp. Ozzie slaps Jay's gut with the same vigour and tells him to stop and let go. The boyishness of Nebraska's country folks is good entertainment for Coco as she sits on the edge of the bed, wrapped in an itchy blanket. After the pair's fighting comes to a halt, Coco asks Ozzie to keep his eyes closed while she crawls down to the bay window to retrieve her silky undergarments, stockings, and last night's adventurous dress. Once dressed, she introduces herself to Ozzie, who looks puffed out. Jay is no better.

— 'I heard great things about you and your genius abilities.'

Ozzie's timidity makes it painful to keep eye contact with Coco. She hugs him and kisses Jay with great affection. Her presence, which lights any room she walks in, is one of the most valuable gifts God could offer to anyone alive today.

The three discuss the best way for Coco to leave the hotel. Through discreet visual and gestural clues, she reminds Jay that she needs to sort out the paperwork with the angel investor and load back the four suitcases in her car.

As the news reporters intensify their attempts to gain access by ringing the hotel bell more persistently, Jay asks Ozzie to check if all the hotel entries are closed and secure. Having more privacy to talk, Jay reaches out to Ingrid and the 'Haka Girls' for assistance via video call. Ingrid will organise a police cordon to create a diversion around the hotel. Tia will hire a van to collect Coco and the money, while Kora will retrieve her Panamera from the neighbourhood.

Ozzie returns to Jay's room, displaying his thumbs up and puffing out as he ran the hotel staircase.

— 'Last night,' he says, out of breath, 'I went to the university to borrow another few beauties to complete a mobile application. As an international student, I sought expert advice on the legal framework for conducting and testing illegal applications, telecom infringements, data breaches, and dark web mining as part of my university research papers and cybersecurity studies. I've received academic clearance to be a digital outlaw, subject to millions of terms and conditions. The outcome of this move is that I can now install a few helpful software onto your phone and offer you another layer of physical protection on the go.'

— 'He's a fucking genius, and he's also from Nebraska!' says Jay proudly to Coco.

— 'How do you do that?' she questions with genuine interest.

— 'Let me show you!' Ozzie replies, specifically addressing Jay. He continues,

— 'As you may remember, I scanned past CCTV footage and tracked back the journey of all six people killed by the 'Clown of Amsterdam'. The guys with the black Mercedes have another four accomplices in Amsterdam and have a residential address in Leidseplein. The guys in the Volvo aren't alone either. They have two business associates in Nieuwmarkt en Lastage. A week ago, four of them from both parties met in the Albert Heijn Van Baerlestraat car park. I saved the footage for you to check later. I've developed a real-time tracking application so we know where our potential threats are. Have a look!'

Coco and Jay are surprised by Ozzie's technological prowess. Now, Jay doubts the truth of Ingrid's statement related to the two men who had kidnapped the Japanese woman and her daughter.

As Ozzie flicks through his mobile scanning app, he clarifies,

— 'Each emoji on the map represents one of them. All are linked to the computer farm downstairs. As soon as CCTV footage comes alive, they're on the map. The two funny icons here are Jay and me. We're connected like the others through facial recognition plus our phone's GPS location.'

— 'Could you add more people, numbers and addresses to monitor?' Jay asks Ozzie while searching the pocket of the jacket he wore last night.

Tendering the folded paper to Coco for final approval, he asks Ozzie if he can process them as soon as possible. The computer boy is over the moon.

Jay's phone rings. It's Bruno Lefevre.

— 'Not now!' fires back Jay.

— 'Take a big breath in!' says Coco, putting her hand on his chest. 'Everything's okay. You're up to the challenge!'

Jay answers the call and, without any form of greeting,

— 'Why did you publish the diary without my permission as previously agreed?' asks Jay.

— 'We're in business to make money and to generate the best return on our investment for our shareholders,' answers Bruno. 'If you don't supply news articles, I simply create them and don't regret what I've done. I'm watching CNN and the Al Jazeera live streams now, and I can't wait to see you facing the press down at your hotel door.'

— 'You've compromised people's safety by publishing the diary in its entirety,' replies Jay quietly.

— 'They're prostitutes!' Bruno answers. 'And in the eyes of God, they have no value. They're the trash or the reject of our capitalist society, and we're profiting dearly from their petty stories,' he adds.

— 'What about my kids? What are their values? I'm not around to protect them,' replies Jay.

— 'What's your worth, Jay?' the cocky Frenchman enquires. 'Who wants a fraud as a father? Maybe they'll be better off without you. Bonne chance,' he concludes.

Realising his phone was on loudspeaker, Jay apologises to Coco and Ozzie.

— 'I don't share his views. Sex workers aren't rubbish,' says Jay as he sits on the edge of his bed.

Ozzie leaps, throws his unathletic body on Jay, and tackles him on the mattress to cheer him up. A pillow fight starts, and both roll out of the bed laughing like five-year-old boys. As another frenzied round of doorbell sounds reaches the second floor, Coco invites Jay to dress up and face the circus. She opens his wardrobe and chooses some of his shirts, pants, socks, and underwear to offer him the best colour combinations.

After a shave, shit, and shower combo, Jay makes his way to the hotel's lobby. He kisses Coco and begs her to be safe while he invites Ozzie to dig some dirt on Bruno Lefevre and promises to take him out for breakfast when he returns.

While walking down the most dangerous stairs in Amsterdam, he hears police car sirens taking over the neighbourhood. A line of police officers in uniform circle the reporters, and as per Ingrid's instructions, they're moved to the opposite side of the bridge at the corner of the street. The sole entry of Hotel Lucius is now free, facilitating Coco's escape and the money transfer. As he opens the hotel front door, hundreds of cameras and screams bless him in front of the canal coldness. None of the chaos makes sense. He turns away from the displaced crowd and locks the hotel's front door. Recalling Polka's fatal play, he walks slowly to the edge of the bridge, faces the press reporters, places his index finger on his mouth and waits for any form of silence to join the gathering. Now, he points at the cameras and wants them down and out of his face. Slowly, the reporters agree and finally, when a cohesive silence is alive—

— 'How can I help you?' asks Jay.

A tsunami of words, noises and screams hits him hard. Once again, Jay places his finger back on his lips and quietly says,

— 'One at a time, please.'

Like children in a schoolyard, the reporters put their hands up and are forced to wait their turn.

Jay invites the first question.

— 'Suzanne Gallagher for The London Blaze, did Juliana Susas suck your cock in Vegas?'

The question raises eyebrows and waves of laughter from the audience.

— 'I don't know!' says Jay. 'Let me ask her.'

Jay picks up his phone and dials her number.

— 'Hello Juliana, Jay here; sorry to wake you up, but I've got an impromptu press conference here in Amsterdam, and the first question is—Did you suck my cock in Vegas?'

After listening carefully to Juliana's answers, he concludes the call. Looking at the crowd and clearing his throat, Jay says,

— 'Yes, Suzanne, she sucked my cock when I was unconscious on the bathroom floor of my hotel room.'

Holding a hand up as a request for silence, he adds,

— 'This is sad. It was my second sexual encounter ever, and I wasn't even mentally present to remember or enjoy it. My first time around as a young adult, I wasn't even good enough to make them my children. My foster brother is their father. It took fifteen years for this fact to come to light and to bless my reality. Juliana's trademark gives me back freedom, and I wish her the best in Lincoln. So, Suzanne, I can't wait to read your headlines tomorrow but do me a favour, don't make them too cocky.'

Heavy laughter and joyful hand clapping inundate the bridge's surroundings.

— 'Next, please!' tells Jay.

— 'Florian Van Bruggel, De Dagblad. Are you the next Peter Rudolf de Vries? You've been in Amsterdam for less than a fortnight, and without fear, you publish the underworld life of our metropolis without any applied filters.'

— 'Florian, sorry for my ignorance; I don't know Peter Rudolf de Vries or his work,' replies Jay. 'By the way,' he adds, 'I want to tell you that I enjoyed the tone of your deep raspy voice and the clarity in your pronunciation. Man, the Dutch women must be in love with you.'

Here again, Jay's audience laughs and cheers the American countryman, who proceeds,

— 'Back to me, I'm no journalist—far from it. For those here who are unaware of my situation, against my will, I swapped my job with a stranger at a lottery in Vegas a week ago. My speciality is compiling user manuals for lawnmowers and chainsaws. I didn't write or publish the latest article in The New York World News. You made me aware of it when you pressed the hotel doorbell. Are there other things or matters I'm unaware of?' asks Jay.

Well, before anyone can answer his question, he clarifies with a comical French accent,

— 'Bruno Lefevre is the sole owner of the publication and has no interest in the newspaper's content. The New York World News' shareholders are his only focus!' Florian interrupts,

— 'What about your two first articles? They were full of grace, sensitivity, humour and very respectful. You did a great job!'

— 'Thank you, but no thanks, Florian,' tells Jay.

— 'My two first articles were the fruits of artificial intelligence. The reason I'm here is simple: I'm a fraud in the eyes of many. So, like many of you, I'm only here for the paycheque to pay my bills back home. I think we're done now,' concludes Jay.

— 'One more question,' screams a gentleman.

— 'Yes, go ahead!' replies Jay.

— 'Alexandru Bosalac, for Ecoul Liber, Romanian newspaper. When and where did you find the diary?'

— 'I didn't find the diary,' answers Jay.

Before another word comes out of his mouth, four undercover police officers yell and push Alexandru to the ground with great force, handcuffing and dragging him away. The bridge is now chaos and invaded by police sirens and barricades. The press gathering turns into a scramble for new information and livestreams. Jay makes his way back quietly into Hotel Lucius.

Ozzie waits for him on top of the stainless-steel protected stairs.

— 'It works! Did you see that? It works!' screams the cheerful nerd.

— 'What works?' enquires Jay.

— 'The guy they arrested is one of the emojis on my app that I installed on Coco's device. She noticed him and spoke to someone called Ingrid. Voila!' While hugging Ozzie, Jay thanks him and expresses his gratitude.

— 'I'm so happy to have you around,' Jay says. 'Let's go for breakfast; you deserve it.'

— 'Can we go to Omelegg?' asks Ozzie with a spark in his eyes. 'It's a thirty-minute walk from here, but on the way there, I can show you the location of the private massage parlours.'

— 'The hairdresser was enough!' teases Jay.

— 'Did you fuck her?' snaps Ozzie with a curious voice.

— 'None of your business, young man, and before we go, I've got something for you. Just wait!'

Jay returns with two latex masks and invites Ozzie to pick one.

— 'After this morning, we need to be prudent,' clarifies Jay.

Omelegg's theatrical white and red-brownish street windows that invite you inside are traded for yellow and white wall tiles and farmland artefacts that generate a warm countryside atmosphere inside the dining room. The oversized range hood and cooker are the visual pieces of resistance when you enter the establishment. In a big wooden basket, the croissants display their freshness and quietly invite any customer to place an order. The smell of cooked bacon, sausages and eggs celebrates the mid-morning coldness of Amsterdam and reminds Ozzie and Jay of their native American Midwest generous-size cuisine.

— 'A big bazaar, a farm boy, and two coffee lattes as a starter,' confirms Jay with the waitress.

She's a petite Filipina doll-like woman with naturally shiny charcoal wavy hair and golden-brown, butter-smooth skin. Her micro waistline and curvy bottom, which could have been manufactured out of a three-dimensional printer, are no competition against her beautiful smile and welcoming, glamorous facial expressions.

Ozzie's mask is a time travel to the eighties; he looks like a heavy metal band lead singer with long curly hair running over his shoulders and covering half his thick glasses frames. He's a chubby, intellectualised version of Nikki Sixx, the legendary songwriter of the heavy metal band Mötley Crüe. Jay is now a mid-fifty-year-old computer science teacher— short salt-and-pepper coloured beard and a well-combed hairstyle. Both men vacuum their food; only a few words are exchanged between the bites. Their eggs are cooked to perfection. Their silent chewing is interrupted when a young man taps the establishment's front window to get Ozzie's attention. He's a skinny guy with long dark hair, fully dressed in black leather. He waves a 'shaka' sign to Ozzie, stretches his pointy tongue out of his mouth, and starts a head-banging session while offering a rock-and-roll sign gesture. Ozzie stands up, pushes his chair aside, climbs on the dining table, mirrors the man's behaviour, and starts a crazy theatrical air guitar solo. The mad geek of Amsterdam is applauded and cheered by Omelegg's patrons. The show stops, the guy moves on, and Ozzie feels a little bit belly sick, but his eyes are filled with glee.

— 'Let's go there. I need to walk,' Ozzie says, pointing to Olof's Amsterdam, located across the road and housed in the Sint Olofskapel. 'I had a seminar there, and the building conversion is interesting and worth the walk,' he comments while massaging his guts.

The narrow brick-paved street, lined on either side by a blue stone kerb line, is Ozzie's digestive exercise. While inside, Jay instantly admires the fourteenth-century-era carpentry work.

— 'I have something to share with you,' tells Jay.

— 'I know what it is!' replies Ozzie.

— 'How can you?' mumbles Jay.

— 'Okay, let's type it on our phone and see who's right?' smiles Ozzie.

Reading Ozzie's message, Jay says,

— 'How did you know?'

— 'CCTV footage doesn't lie. I digitally traced back the steps of all the parties present at the shooting, including the 'Clown of Amsterdam'. His journey starts at Hotel Lucius, and you're our sole customer,' declares Ozzie. 'The day we met, you were very agitated. Your backwards and forwards trips between the rental car and your room were suspicious, especially when you refused assistance with the hotel's steep front entry staircase. At the Korean restaurant on our first night out, your fork couldn't find your mouth when you realised that you were the highlight of the news. Your anxiety had the best of you. Your red shoes were the only visual clue that gave you away in the CCTV footage.'

— 'You're fucking good and so bloody right!' answers Jay.

— 'For me, it's just a game,' replies Ozzie. 'You took me out of my mundane life. This is very exciting! I enjoy the thrill.'

— 'You probably saved my life this morning,' smiles Jay.

— 'Thank you for trusting me,' tells Ozzie, reaching out for a fist pump.

On returning to the hotel, the Nebraskan boys order coffee at Prins Heerlijk coffee shop. While seated outdoors, they enjoy Amsterdam's ever-moving, glamorous human landscape—particularly the spectacle on offer by the bra-less bicycle riders bouncing on the city's cobbled stones. All-size breasts and nipples, nicely tucked in shirts and T-shirts, rub and push proudly through the garment fabric to freely guarantee the boys' enjoyment. Between bursts of their eclectic pleasures, they discuss the money, the guns and ammunition, the hit list, who they need to add to Ozzie's live map app, and how to deal with all compromised CCTV footage. While leaving, and to Jay's astonishment, Ozzie decides to thank the barista for her craft with a funny one-line sentence,

— 'If you make love like you make coffee, where can I place an order?'

The redhead waitress with blue eyes, white teeth, and freckles on her face—who somehow looks related to Abigail—invites him to come back later as the special-order counter is not open yet and sends flying kisses as a 'see you later' gesture. Ozzie blushes at her offer.

As they arrive near the hotel, Jay spots Ingrid next to the bike rack on the opposite side of the road. He walks towards her and introduces Ozzie.

— 'I'm here for him, and I didn't expect such a look,' she says while laughing, snorting, and admiring Ozzie's mask. 'Let's get in! I want to see what he's up to,' she adds with an authoritarian voice.

On the first floor, Ozzie gives her a tour of his surveilling computer farm. Ingrid is impressed and tells the boys that, for their safety, she plans to relocate them and their lab into a safe house. The morning arrest is the reason behind the move.

Based on Ingrid's direction, Ozzie contemplates disassembling his digital kingdom. On the other hand, Jay grabs the locker dockets on top of his hotel bedroom wardrobe and makes his way to the storage outlet. 'Lockbox Luggage Storage Amsterdam Centraal' is the destination. On-site, Jay walks through the locker rows to find the ones matching his printed dockets. His nervousness makes him dyslexic. Reading the 'how to open, store and close a locker' instructions on the digital screen becomes a nightmare. As he's ready to commit to releasing the unknown content of the storage boxes, his anxiety takes over when he realises that he has only two options available with his bounty. His choices are to transfer and secure the content into new lockers or to carry everything back to Hotel Lucius. His hands and fingers shake madly and can't coordinate with his mind's instructions, and based on this self-observation, he aborts his retrieval mission. He walks the streets of Amsterdam and cries his anxieties out. Jay's mental health leaps backwards big time. Amsterdam fuels his unhealed Arizona mental state of sadness that sometimes invites him to drown himself in the numbness and harshness of alcoholic beverages. Jay resists his inner demons' offer and makes his way back slowly to Hotel Lucius.

As he approaches his accommodation, he notices red and blue lights flashing in the middle of the road in front of the hotel doors. He runs, passes the paramedics and climbs the narrow and steep staircase of the hotel. A young man lays on the floor in a pool of blood. Jay recognises him; he's the heavy metal head-banging guy who interrupted their breakfast at Omelegg. He's been shot in the buttock. The medical team push Jay aside, who can't resist asking questions.

— 'Why are you here?'

— 'I came here to find and invite the long-haired guy to make some YouTube and TikTok videos for my channels. I recorded his Omelegg moves this morning, and within a few hours of being posted online, I received over ten million views, shares and likes. I'm Sebastian Dubrick, a local influencer. I'm no bad guy!'

— 'How did you get in?' questions Jay.

— 'The entry door was open; I climbed the stairs and called for assistance. I heard some noises, turned around, and I got shot. It's all on my GoPro,' answers the influencer with a voice filled with pain and heavy breathing.

— 'Did you see Ozzie?' presses Jay.

— 'You mean the guy with the long hair? No! My mum needs assistance; I'm her carer; you must help her.'

As the paramedics take Sebastian down the stairs of hell, Jay follows with great caution and requests his action camera and a way to contact his mother. A few minutes later, the police take over the place. Ingrid is present and leads the operations. Jay runs through the building, searching for Ozzie, yelling and screaming his name. Having no answers, Jay calls him on his cell phone; he can hear his ringtone coming from the upper floor of the building staircase. Ingrid catches up with Jay and, while puffing heavily, grabs him by the arm and, as the paramedics did, pushes him against the wall—with the exception that she uses force and conviction to do it. She invites the tactical team to take the lead. They wear bulletproof jackets, helmets, and machine guns and climb the next level of the staircase like movie stars, moving their bodies and weapons with great synchronicity. Ingrid instructs Jay to call Ozzie's mobile. There are no answers—only the melodic sounds of his ringtone that fill the last set of steps that give access to the building's attic. One by one, the elite troops enter the roof space. Ingrid and Jay follow behind only when the clearance is approved. Ozzie is discovered alive on the roof. For safety reasons, he'd wedged himself between his homemade 'free internet' antenna and a decommissioned red brick chimney. Ozzie confesses to the officers that he'd been waiting for assistance for at least two hours and couldn't return to the skylight as his safety rope rolled down the roof's slippery slope. Ingrid pushes her head through the window and can't stop laughing and snorting as usual.

— 'Bloody Americans,' she says, shaking her round podgy head.

The fire brigade is called in, and the front street is cleared to allow the aerial ladder platform of the fire truck to take over the rescue. Hundreds of black bicycles are relocated in the process, and some, through the emergency chaos, fall into the canal. Like this morning, the corner bridge is the rally point for another press congregation, bundled with camera flashes and loud television crews. Jay then gives Ingrid the influencer's camera and makes her aware of his mother's health condition and her need for assistance. As he wants to find out who opened the main entry door of the hotel while he was away, he invites Ingrid to check the hotel CCTV footage on Ozzie's equipment. Both are surprised to see a member of the Haka Army skilfully unlocking the door and preparing the venue for a gunman. To Jay's astonishment, Ingrid tells him,

— 'Keep quiet and don't mention anything to anyone, including my colleagues.'

Jay's facial expression approves her stance visually as he receives more clarification.

— 'If anyone is aware of this incident, Tia and Kora will lose their government contracts, licensing, and accreditation.'

As she wants to inform the 'Haka Girls' first-hand, Ingrid runs into the female bathroom, her phone on her ear.

Back in Ozzie's spying lab, she faces her colleagues, who question his setup and activities.

— 'They work for us! They're contractors!' she shares with her entourage. 'Their relocation is organised, and we must transfer them now as we have plenty of distractions in the street.'

Ozzie joins the group; he's apologetic.

— 'You did what I asked you to do; I didn't evaluate the risks,' says Ingrid. 'It's my fault. I'm so sorry! Thank God you made it back safely. Now, you have thirty minutes to pack everything to the ground floor. I have a press conference to attend in less than two hours with our mayor,' then pointing at Jay, 'You must be there. Please dress sharply,' she adds before organising their transfers with her colleagues.

It's late afternoon; Jay is exhausted and checks Coco's progress. A few minutes later, he receives a text message from her. The message reads,

— 'Are you okay? I can't wait to see you. The paperwork is almost finished. We've been summoned to the cottage tonight by Ingrid.'

After a quick shower and dressing in his best formal wear, Jay packs his belongings and helps Ozzie unplug his digital arsenal. He instructs Ozzie to back up the hotel CCTV hard drives, erase their content, and reformat all devices afterwards. Ozzie shares with Jay that the computer farm setup is duplicated at his university lab and that he's looking to build a third data farm as soon as possible.

The hotel owner rings Ozzie and enquires about the shooting, the roof rescue, and why his property is negatively featured in the news twice in a single day. The conversation is painful for Ozzie as he doesn't like any form of confrontation. Meanwhile, Jay receives a text message from Bruno Lefevre stating that his assignment for The New York World News is suspended until further notice due to the unprofessional targeted comments during his press conference. The suspension also applies to The New York World News credit card. Based on this news, Jay reshuffles his belongings and splits the remaining €15 million notes into numerous bags and suitcases. He makes Ozzie aware of the news. Ozzie stops him, opens a few computer towers, and invites Jay to stash some of the cash inside the hardware.

— 'You're a fucking genius,' compliments Jay while throwing a high five to Ozzie.

The helpful geek is now responsible for transferring the goods as Jay makes his way to the press conference.

The press conference is related to Amsterdam's mayor's 'Erotic Centre' mega project and its impact on the red-light district. The New York World News' publication of the diary has flared up old wounds within Amsterdam's communities, its political landscape, and the sex work industry. The town leader must disclose the latest progress of her delusional project, including all potential locations. Ingrid wants Jay to familiarise himself with the mechanics of the council projects, the local political platform and landscape, and Coco's acquisition plan for Hotel L'Europa. The mayor's popularity is declining in the opinion polls; most of her female electorate voters are not in sync with her views and proposals. They believe that women, prostitutes or not, are ignored and sold cheaply for personal and short-term political gains.

The council chamber is packed to the rafters; the mood is far from friendly as everyone in the arena believes their opinions are the sole answer and resolution to the oldest trade in the world and its inclusion in the modern world. Jay enters the media section of the council chambers, and instantly, he's the target of insults and repulsive gestures. As he pushes and shoves himself to safety inside the media pack, one politician is forcefully expelled from the room for throwing a shoe targeting Jay. On the other side of the spectrum, Jay is applauded, and his name is chanted loudly over hand-clapping rhythmics; Jay is now a suspended representative of The New York World News who can't talk on their behalf.

Assisted by her aides and numerous legal and government representatives, the mayor of Amsterdam enters the stage and makes her way towards the microphone. As she addresses the community, Jay doesn't understand a single word, as her monologue is delivered in her native Dutch. He observes the facial expressions of the gallery members and tries to decode the content of their emotional interaction with the town leader. The words New York World News are pronounced, instantly catching his attention, which is short-lived as the assembly's chaos reaches new heights. Having no control over the rowdy crowd, the mayor invites Jay up on stage, but he doesn't understand the Dutch invitation.

His immobility intensifies the hostility in the room and the loudness of the cheering of the opposing parties. The local BBC news reporter translates the mayor's message to him, and with some hesitation, Jay makes his way to a set of microphones on the opposite side of the stage, where a flying chair lands next to him. The loud crash reminds Jay of the build-up of the Arizona incident, and he decides to leave the stage; his movement is stopped abruptly when he realises an individual dressed as a clown gains access to the main stage, roughly grabbing a microphone and putting a gun on Ingrid's head.

— 'I am the Clown of Amsterdam,' yells the intruder.

Everyone in the room is now on the same page. The situation is tense and serious. A stampede takes place as screaming and fearful attendees try ruthlessly to force their way out to safety. At the same time, Jay makes his way back to his set of microphones, grabs a loose one and walks at a fast pace toward the impostor, telling him over the chamber audio system that he's not the 'Clown of Amsterdam' as an attempt to divert his focus from Ingrid. A few cold camera flashes follow every one of his steps. Jay, now facing the man, whose gun turns in his direction, performs without hesitation a single elegant, forceful, deadly straight-leg martial arts high kick, striking the aggressor under the chin. The fake 'Clown of Amsterdam' collapses backwards like a wet dishcloth to the ground. As the blood runs down from his shattered mouth and nose, his inert body doesn't interact with the free light show generously offered by the representatives of the press. Jay takes possession of the gun, unloads it, and tenders it to Ingrid. Facing the room, Jay tells the crowd over the microphone that the situation is over and that anyone making their way home should thank Roger Smith, his foster father, for teaching him the art of self-defence basics. The impostor is pronounced dead at the scene, and the officials are frantically escorted out of the room by the Dutch police force. Ingrid is in shock; tears of fear fill her eyes, pearling along her rounded piggy face and disappearing at the edge of her chin into the fabric of her jumper. While cleaning the gooey snot coming out of her nose with the sleeve of her jacket, she thanks Jay and instinctively hugs him with great vigour, shivering in their embrace. After a quiet, brief chat, Jay receives her clearance to leave the scene.

Jay jumps in a taxi to escape the journalists and calls Kora and Tia through a video call. He begs them to meet him at the locker place. Understanding the urgency, both agree and hire an on-demand van. The cleaning contractors, an old Indian couple, welcome the trio inside the locker room. This time, Jay isn't suffering from dyslexia; he points out all lockers that need to be emptied. He swaps the paper dockets under the red laser light, and the sound of the door opening is the beginning of their manutention workout. Jay takes evidence photos of the well-packed lockers before emptying each of them to the ground and piling the bounty close to the entry door without hesitation. He tells the girls not to open anything, as the room is filled with surveillance cameras. Simultaneously, they realise that wearing silicone masks and overalls is a good idea. Jay then asks the cleaners if they know how to print a rental agreement receipt for his records. The cleaner calls someone, goes over the digital screen and processes the instructions received over the phone. Receiving the printed information, Jay thanks the couple for their assistance. Paul Van Looke is the name printed on the docket.

Back in the van, Jay scavenges through the bags and suitcases. The bounty includes tons of cash, guns, ammunition, another set of diaries, and a severe amount of child pornography. In panic mode, Jay calls Ingrid and asks for instructions on how to proceed with the lockers' content this time.

— 'Same as last time. You scan all the documents, distribute them to the right parties and give me back the original for records,' she clarifies with a shaken, terrified Dutch accent.

Coco calls Jay, asking how he is. She'd seen the town hall footage.

— 'We're not going to the cottage,' she says. 'Ingrid's cancelled her plans as she wants to be with her children. They need reassurance. I love you, Jay.'

— 'I love you too,' replies Jay.

Hearing these four magical words, the 'Haka Girls' whistle madly, teasing the young lovers while performing their usual shoulder-bouncing giggles. The mood in the van is uplifted. To spice up the story, Jay invites Coco for dinner. The twins are now going ballistic, and while drumming the dashboard of the van, they scream,

— 'Sushi, sushi, sushi!'

Jay passes the information to Kora and Tia that the meeting with Ingrid is cancelled; they look excited not to have another late night. They all look tired, and Jay isn't feeling better after today's chaos. Everyone had a big day.

— 'How did you go with your locksmith employee?' Jay asks the duo.

Kora, with a dry sense of humour, replies,

— 'I bought a blank diary and a Polaroid camera today. She, the fucking bitch, will be our first casualty. We need to step up our security and the security of our clients, and we don't know how to do it—we're not that smart. We're extremely good at physical protection and marketing our services to the market due to our UFC profiles, but when it comes to computer or IT solutions, we're knocked out before the fight starts,' comments Tia.

— 'Let me introduce you to Ozzie. Anything requiring digital expertise will be made easy for you to conquer,' says Jay. 'The first thing to do is include your entire team's visual and facial data and phone numbers in his scanning application. He'll then install his application on your devices, and you'll know instantly where anyone recorded on his platform is located in real time and check their doings by manipulating the city CCTV cameras and networks.'

As Ozzie did earlier with Jay and Coco, Jay shows and explains the emojis and who is on the maps.

— 'The 'Ballerina' is Coco, the 'Long hair' is Ozzie, the 'Police car' is Ingrid, and I'm the 'Clown'. You'll be the 'Sushi girls',' laughs Jay. 'Please follow the 'hairy' emoji on the map, and you'll have the pleasure of meeting this crazy but generous person.'

The safe house is located at the back of Amsterdam Police Headquarters and only a few blocks from Hotel Lucius. The post-war art deco building is made of pale, thin, greyish bricks laid in what appears to be a double Flemish bond pattern. Countless naturally washed blue stone sills and lintels highlight the door and window façade geometry. Well-positioned round, submarine-like openings animate and visually balance the monotony of the horizontal façades. The ugliness of the retrofitted electric blue sun-faded external roller blinds somehow diminishes all architectural features except for the Glory Day sculpture displaying three men and a teenage boy suspended on the northern façade. All are naked, and two of the subjects have their genitalia on display. The shape and size of their penis are in line with their age. The sculptor has been very generous with the middle-aged and the older men on the right side of the art display; both subjects don't have a beer belly and falling gut lines but a perfect single-pack flat abdomen. On the opposite side of the artwork, the boy and the man behind him appear to be related. This conclusion doesn't come from the fact that the teenage boy has his father's manhood stacked in his armpit but from the resemblance of his facial and physical attributes. Their well and deeply carved, athletic six-packs and rib cages are identical in look, size and proportion. Sadly, they missed the social media era and didn't monetise their bodybuilding hard work. The sculpture is a collection of sadnesses. The first one is to acknowledge that a barely formed man has reached his peak physicality well before his intellectual greatness or any form of emotional awareness and now has an impossible life goal to maintain his fading perfection. Secondly, the ensemble, which represents the law and, more pertinently, our freedom, is as rigid as death—except for the subjects' nakedness. All are men and no women; the four selected ones are normalised through the same body shapes, postures, and a poor-man-style haircut. All appear to be the puppets of a set of transgenerational corrupted societal values, which are poorly symbolised by a mighty dragon, a menacing lion, some hairy fairy wings on wheels and a funny-placed triangle with a vertical line inside, which alone can be translated, by the Pink Floyd controversy lovers, as the Netherlands is living on the dark side of the moon.

The primary access to the safe house is through a short and heavily armed gated driveway, directly connecting to an urbanistically designed open space defined by well-maintained garden beds and scattered parking spaces.

The safe house's top floor and roof terrace are perched on the cantilever part of a new yellow building extension; three of its façades are exposed to Amsterdam's openness and can be easily targeted by snipers. A dedicated set of stairs and lifts gives access to this unprotected haven.

Ozzie opens the door and didn't expect to see three ugly masked faces making their way in. After moving the bounty into his newly acquired residence, Jay introduces Ozzie to the Kiwi twins, who remove their latex masks and overalls. Ozzie is in awe as Tia and Kora are now in their training crop tops and tight boxing shorts. Their trademark six-packs and athletic bodies leave him lost for words, retreating to shyness. Feeling his inadequacy, Kora goes closer to Ozzie and invites him to poke her sculpted belly; as Ozzie commits to the invitation, Kora tells him,

— 'If your app fucks us up, this is what to expect.' Ozzie looks at Tia, goes towards her and without asking, pokes her six-pack. He looks back at Kora and tells her,

— 'She's harder.'

Before knowing it, Ozzie is locked to the ground, begging for air as Kora's legs are wrapped tightly around his neck.

— 'Who's the hardest?' asks Kora.

Tapping his hand madly on the carpet floor, Ozzie accepts defeat.

Jay inspects his new quarters; the place is luxurious, and the bed is firm. The views on Amsterdam's waterways fade away as the sunset's fiery orange colour smoothly engulfs the canal's darkness.

Ozzie installs his app onto the girls' handsets and diligently processes their employees' and contractors' data into his surveillance workstation. He asks them to review numerous footage extracted from his CCTV database. The first one is the afternoon locksmith incident.

— 'Veronica Delbursh,' Kora reacts when recognising her team member.

The second and third sets are diverse camera angles and time captures from the entire neighbourhood the day Jay saved the twins in the red-light district. The girls ask Ozzie to rewind and replay the footage before and after the shooting occurred. Their fingers touch the screen when they notice and validate the authenticity of the details Jay has shared with them at the cottage. They're surprised by his fearless body language and way of walking when he commits to saving the little Japanese girl.

As Jay is getting ready to meet Coco, he asks Ozzie to demonstrate the power of his system by finding out where and when Abigail was bashed two nights ago and who the suspect was. Ozzie punches his keywords into the CCTV search engine at a robotic speed; seconds later, Abigail's number plate is on the screen. Ozzie scrolls through the search results and selects the footage; he rewinds the tape to the moment she arrives and parks her van at her client's address, removing her wheelchair from the car before entering the property. He slowly forwards the footage to catch her exit and points to the girls, the cars, and people entering and exiting the surroundings. Two hours after her arrival, her client wheels her back to her car, passionately kisses her and returns to his property. She was attacked a few seconds later while manoeuvring her wheelchair back into her van. The video shows a dark Continental GT Bentley, with its emergency lights on, pulling beside her vehicle. In less than a second, Abigail was the recipient of some severe assaults and physical abuse. She was slapped, kicked, thrown to the ground, walked on, and her head was repeatedly bashed against the door of her utility vehicle by the driver of the luxury car. The horror scene is twenty-seven seconds long, as accounted for by the video player's time stamps. Ozzie notices the girls' moods and attitudes swinging as they mumble between themselves in Dutch. The Bentley belongs to Paul Van Looke.

Jay is ready to go and asks Ozzie and the 'Haka Girls' if they want to join him and Coco. Tia, poking Ozzie's belly, says that they'll take care of him. Jay informs Ozzie that the girls' emojis on the app should be a 'hard' and 'floppy' sushi. Kora gives Jay the middle finger.

Disguised under an old man mask and a hat, Jay enters Coco's Panamera. The softness of the leather seats is as good as the tenderness of her kisses and the smell of her gingery fragrance. Jay invites Coco to consider wearing masks and driving a rental car to hide her identity. She agrees. Gliding her right hand on Jay's inner thigh, she enquires with her gentle voice,

— 'Are you okay with us going to Ostend tonight? I want to introduce you to my Papa. He's my lifesaver. I want to do it before flying to the Dutch Caribbean.'

— 'Where is Ostend, and how do you pronounce it?' replies Jay.

— 'The city of Ostend is in Belgium, and in my view, it's a beautiful, romantic coastal town with very long beaches and a paved promenade. As a teenage girl and during the summer break, Ostend was my spiritual refuge and the best place away from my professional ballet dancing commitments. At the time, Papa had an apartment close to the seawall and the maritime port. The place is mine now, but at the time, and to offer me an adventurous spirit, he rented a little wooden cabin and a set of recliner chairs on the beach—as the Belgian holidaymakers do. It was our one-on-one vacation, no matter the weather.'

— 'It sounds great fun! I've never been to a beach; Nebraska has no sea beaches.'

— 'Are you okay to have breakfast with my Papa tomorrow

morning?' she enquires.

While enjoying Jay's smile as he agrees to breakfast, Coco tells him,

— 'Tonight is unhealthy dinner night. 't Pleintje frituur in Brecht is my weakness. They do amazing fried chips served with frikandel and andalouse sauce, and if we're lucky, we can have a fresh Lindemans Kriek.'

Jay tries to make sense of this foreign-language food terminology and once again smiles at Coco while appreciating her bright and peaceful persona.

Jay receives a text message from Roger, his foster father, who appreciates Jay's recognition at the press conference but is slightly puzzled by his reported behaviour in Las Vegas. To appease the situation, Jay replies,

— 'Fake news! Let me call you tomorrow.'

Jay lets his right hand glide on Coco's legs. He likes the smoothness of her dark, shiny stockings and tells her that being a passenger has profound benefits.

— 'Go higher, and you'll find my leather garter belt,' Coco replies while moving her dress up along her thighs. As she's starving and has Jay's full attention, she refrains from letting him check her crotchless panty and her cupless open bra.

The fried food dinner is electrically charged, sensually intimate and maskless for Jay's benefit. To fully enjoy Coco's spell and uneasy freedom, he turns his back to the television set to avoid watching himself in the news report. Back in the car, their sexual ardour is translated into the mighty roaring sound of the Porsche exhaust line. Their evening is short-lived. The Belgian highway police patrol puts a cold shower on their spicy plans. As foreigners, the speeding fine must be paid in full and on the spot at the local police station. A slow bureaucratic pace is now their evening, celebrated on uncomfortable plastic chairs and numerous body posture repositionings.

Chapter nine

Ostend

Coco and Jay reach Ostend just before sunrise and on time to join Papa for breakfast at the Patisserie Caruso. Both are exhausted. Coco's old man is a tall, skinny, seventy-year-old pale man. His presence is less glowing than Coco's, who shines and whose smile is infectious. She hugs her father passionately, rubs his back, and holds her hands on his ribs. They look into each other's eyes with great intensity, connecting to each other's deepest feelings and emotions. Finally, it is Jay's turn to be introduced, and the profoundness of the eye contact makes him uncomfortable. Holding Jay's right hand firmly,

— 'I'm Gaston,' says Coco's Papa.

— 'Nice to meet you,' replies Jay softly.

The old man takes Jay to the front window counter and invites him to appreciate the pastry chef's craftsmanship.

— 'I've savoured each one, and they are a delight for all the senses,' Gaston exclaims with joy, playfully nudging Jay's arm.

Jay acknowledges the sign of affection or acceptance with a smile and, at the same time, notices Gaston's mannerisms when talking, walking, and even breathing. He is a fragile living choreography, and his long-gone youthfulness is now only embedded in Coco. Some strange thoughts cross Jay's mind as he tries not to imagine Coco becoming, in a not-so-distant future, a slow-moving marionette mirroring the moves and progression of her Papa. He finds the pair so intriguing that he cannot appreciate the fineness of Caruso's pastry. Somehow, Jay feels challenged by the old man. 'Am I good enough?' pops into his cerebral party, making him instantly anxious, questioning his every move. Like the first night they met at the cottage, Coco puts her hand on his leg when she realises that her lover is drifting down into the rabbit hole of his imaginary and unhealed mental world, distancing himself from the present moment.

Noticing Coco's gesture, Gaston excuses himself from the table and walks towards the bathroom. She apologises to Jay for the mixed-language conversation and tells him she has shared the little she knows about him with her father and how she profoundly feels since they met. Jay, relieved, leans over and sensually kisses her neck. In the process, he notices a man taking pictures of them through the mirror affixed at the counter's end. He tells Coco to go to the bathroom and take care of her Papa until he returns. Jay calls the café's owner, grabs his wallet, pulls out a handful of euro notes, and requests to use another door to exit the establishment, discreetly pointing at the photographer. Like at the Hotel Lucius, the other exit door faces the main street; there is no 'plan B'. With great curiosity, the pastry chef asks Jay,

— 'Are you a celebrity? Is he a paparazzo?'

— 'I write lawnmower and chainsaw user manuals, and I'm good at it,' replies Jay.

— 'Is it a trendy occupation?' enquires the chef and adds, 'In the news last night and even in this morning's edition, the guy who saved the life of Amsterdam's mayor does the same thing. He writes papers for garden equipment.'

Standing up and putting the money in the business owner's hand, Jay says,

— 'I'm the guy on TV. Please look after my partner and her dad until I come back.'

Jay moves to the establishment's front door, and with no time for reaction, the photographer is thrown off his chair and lands heavily on the ground. Jay grabs his camera and, with no second thoughts, smashes it on the edge of the street gutter. He frisks the photographer's coat to retrieve his mobile phone and repeats the wreckage with the same intensity.

— 'Stop, Jay!' the photographer screams. 'I'm Florian Van Bruggel from De Dagblad. Please stop!' he begs, adding, 'I'm here to talk to you.'

Jay recognises Florian's voice, and now his attention shifts to the few patrons and bystanders who record the incident on their portable devices. As he doesn't want Coco or her Papa to be part of their digital capture, he helps Florian stand up, asks him to keep quiet, and waits for him as Jay picks up his jacket inside the tearoom. After securing the memory and SIM cards from the broken equipment, Jay invites Florian for a stroll. He texts Coco and tells her he'll return to Amsterdam with Florian. She replies by asking him to be safe and saying that she needs three and a half million euros tonight for the angel investor's transaction fee.

Jay Smith trends again on social media. After a ten-minute limping walk, Florian suggests stopping at 'L'Apero Ostend' on the Albert One Promenade. The establishment is open, and the waiter invites both men to make themselves at home under the west-facing beachfront glass pergola and to warm up under the infrared roof heater. Looking nervous, Jay refuses and tells the waiter that they need privacy. Florian helps to negotiate a table in a far corner inside the restaurant dining room. So far, not much conversation happens between the two men, as Florian moans about the soreness of his injuries. This is about to change very fast as he breaks the ice.

— 'I'm a news reporter for De Dagblad and a police informer. My assignments are for the police commissioner. Just the top gun, not the entire police force.'

— 'Amsterdam is full of surprises!' comments Jay.

— 'I do undercover and private investigations exclusively on the elite members of the police force and their ongoing professional integrity. Only the police commissioner and Evi, my editorial assistant, know my role in the justice system, and you've just been added to this tight circle. So, I'll ask you to keep it confidential for my safety and yours. Not everything must be published in newspapers or heard in news reports.'

Raising his hand to avoid any form of interrogation, Florian asks Jay if he'd be interested in becoming an informant for the Dutch police commissioner.

— 'Why?' clarifies Jay.

— 'At the moment, and even in the police quarters, you don't have any police protection. Ingrid doesn't have the power and the authority to secure it. This is why you can still move so freely; only the police commissioner can act and seek an outcome for your situation. Your safe house relocation has been done without following the legal protocol. This is a big concern for the commissioner. We suspect that Ingrid wants to monitor you and your techie collaborator closely.'

— 'What are her reasons?' questions Jay.

— 'She likes to control and does stupid things to have the upper hand in petty situations. She's now under investigation, and I'm the investigator.'

— 'I noticed her controlling behaviour at the cottage,' validates Jay with a soft and calm voice.

— 'I'm pleased you mention the cottage because it's under surveillance. I have an audio recording of your meetings. The police commissioner and I are aware of the 'Clown of Amsterdam's' identity, his life story, the diary, and the shelter disaster,' clarifies Florian.

The waiter stops the conversation, and both men scramble through the menu. With his warm, charming Dutch accent, Florian buys some time off the waiter while translating the menu to Jay. They settle for two croque monsieurs and two lemongrass and ginger teas.

— 'Why did you come to Ostend and spy on us? Why is the shelter a disaster?' enquires Jay.

— 'Last night was very intriguing for the police commissioner, the Dutch police force, the media, and the public. A lot of parties, including the political ones, would like to understand how a foreigner who's now the centre of the most brutal national crime stories kills someone in a public gathering with a brilliant self-defence move, then secures the aggressor's gun, talks like a superhero over the microphone, makes his way out through the media pack and disappears in a taxi. In the history of the Netherlands, it's never happened! I enjoyed every second of it,' shares the Dutchman, with a grin on his face.

Jay unlocks his phone and points to a business location on Google Maps.

— 'It's a luggage storeroom. The taxi took me there, and I secured some precious information.'

— 'What did you retrieve?' queries Florian with great interest.

— 'Cash, a lot of it, guns and ammunition, multiple diaries and an incredible amount of child pornography. I shared this information with Ingrid,' Jay clarifies.

— 'So, what is next?' demands Florian.

— 'She instructed me to scan the content, distribute it to the right parties, and give her back all originals when done. So today, Florian, you are the only appropriate party to receive and publish the new information. I won't share it with The New York World News; they suspended me,' says Jay.

— 'You're already a great informer!' replies Florian.

— 'There is one piece of information I can't disclose now,' emphasises Jay. 'I know the name of the person who paid for the lockers. He has a private debt to settle before he faces the justice system for his crimes. I'll keep you informed on this one.'

Their breakfast is served, and Jay is intrigued by the lemongrass and ginger tea's playful aroma.

— 'If you agree to be an informer, we need complete transparency and honesty between us,' highlights Florian. 'So based on this preamble, could you tell me what the old man, who had breakfast with you this morning, transferred out of Ms Carajuca's car into his vehicle while both of you were still sitting at the table. I took photos of it; they're on the memory card if you didn't break it.'

Jay is taken aback and has no answers to give Florian. To his knowledge, Papa went to the bathroom.

— 'How can an informant be not informed?' he thinks.

— 'Who paid for the lockers?' asks Florian.

— 'Let me know why Ingrid is under investigation, and you'll have an answer,' replies Jay.

— 'Gambling. Illegal gambling is the reason! She's addicted to gambling, and from time to time, she collects massive debts from the wrong people. We've bankrolled her numerous times. For over twenty years, she was a savvy undercover police officer and infiltrated, with the help of her gambling skills, the most sophisticated gangs harming the Netherlands today. So, if you want honest advice about your collected cash, please hide it, or she'll take over it.'

— 'What do you mean by you bankroll her?'

— 'That's a subject for another day!' answers Florian.

Jay is shocked and thanks Florian for the twist in his circle of new friends.

— 'Paul Van Looke is the guy who paid for the lockers,' he adds.

— 'Are you sure?' enquires Florian.

Jay opens his wallet and retrieves the proof of payments printed by the Indian man at the locker centre.

— 'This is no good!' comments Florian, scratching his scalp and breathing heavily. 'The rumours are that Paul is the love child of Jos Larbeck, a former Finance and Trade Minister, and Corinne Lagueule, the Director of the Customs Administration of the Netherlands. Back in the day and while in office, he was her senior, and she was a fifteen-year-old student doing some compulsory schoolwork experience. The controversy started when a staffer found an explicit ministerial memo addressed to Corinne.'

— 'What did the note say?' Jay queries, with a very intrigued voice.

— 'It was something along those lines: 'You are the type of woman that lights the carpet on fire and doesn't care. Only a bucket of ice can now extinguish the blood-fuelled parts of our anatomies," smiles Florian as he confesses that Corinne has a lot of sex appeal.

His hand gestures support his thoughts. Acknowledging his hand curving the air, he pauses to sip some of his lemongrass and ginger tea to clean the gawkiness of his last sentence. Florian continues,

— 'Paul was a premature baby, and consequently, Jos was forced, behind closed doors, to swear under oath that he didn't have sex with an underage girl and enter a nonpaternity agreement with Corinne. As a result, Paul has no father recorded on his birth certificate, Corinne is our unique Dutch Virgin Mary, and none of the parties could seek or enforce a paternity or DNA test.'

— 'Single mum at barely sixteen! How did she survive the political arena?' queries Jay.

— 'I interviewed her numerous times. She's a smart woman and a great leader. I feel awkward around her. Her story makes me stutter, and I sound like a lost college boy. The notion of time, the veracity of my content, and my assurance are gone in seconds,' comments Florian.

— 'Too much sex appeal!' teases Jay. 'Why Paul Van Looke and not Paul Larbeck or Paul Lagueule?'

— 'That's a great question! The rumour is that Paul Van Looke is the surgeon who saved Corinne's baby at birth, and as a thank you gesture, she named her boy after him,' clarifies Florian.

— 'What do you know about Paul, the luxury car dealer?' asks Jay.

— 'I know a little bit about him. A few years back, his mum was investigated by the Dutch police commissioner for corruption but came out of the investigation clean with a perfect ten. On the other hand, her son is a modern-day bad boy. Corporate hero from nine to five, making millions in the process, and an extravagant and flamboyant arsehole and money burner by night. He's a wheeler-dealer, a self-made millionaire who still likes his mum's roast dinner every Thursday night.'

Jay interrupts Florian,

— 'I have a video of him bashing a disabled woman. Some locals think that he's untouchable. Is it true?'

Florian laughs,

— 'He's very well connected across all layers of Dutch society, but he's not untouchable. Do you agree to be an informer?' asks Florian.

Jay avoids the question and repeats his question about the sex workers' shelter.

— 'Thank you for last night,' Florian starts. 'You gave the people of Amsterdam a voice, and a bloody good one, and your action will trigger a new outcome for the red-light district, the erotic centre, and the sex workers' shelter. Our local government representatives are selling the change of the location of the red-light district by telling us all about the nuisance, the drug dealing, the drunkenness, and the disorderly behaviour, only to hide, in plain daylight, the truth. They don't want anyone to realise that both projects are real estate megadeals and a pure money grab. The red-light district brothels are now paying top rent, and soon they can disappear from the centre of Amsterdam; some landlords will be forced to sell their property as they can't afford the repayment of their mortgage or the conversion cost of their property. With taxpayers' money, the city of Amsterdam is buying some property well above the market price. Rumours suggest that these properties have been onsold quietly—some at a loss—to our leader's political acquaintances and financial supporters. It also appears that our city administrative services rent these properties back, and all building renovation and maintenance costs are also funded through tax money and council levies.'

After another tea-sipping session, Florian proceeds,

— 'The erotic centre mega project is privately funded, developed and managed. High rents drive their development profit to guarantee the ongoing maintenance cost of their single-use asset. The losers are the sex workers, as the price of their services is linked directly to the 'offer and demand' of the local market. How much can someone charge for a blowjob when your direct competitors are less than three metres away from you? Someone's always ready to undercut their competition or work for nothing in any industry. That alone can trigger or encourage, behind closed doors, sex slavery, as some prostitutes will have difficulties meeting their employer's financial KPIs. The safety and moral issues are also appalling, but this is another conversation. The political parties will make tons of money from these deals. Unfortunately, my ties with the police commissioner don't allow me to bring this information to the people of Amsterdam. I need you!' tells Florian.

— 'What about the shelter?' replies Jay.

— 'Hearing your view not to turn Hotel L'Europa into a sex worker shelter and to consider a rebirth of their business model makes me happy and makes sense. The worst outcome for the property is the Eastern mafia's plans to convert the building into small fuck rooms and run dozens of privately owned brothels illegally and behind closed doors. All projects, from whatever parties, will force humans behind walls. The majority of sex workers are people who have no or little control over their destiny and who can, in the blink of an eye, lose their freedom to unknown parties.

History has repeatedly proven that building enclosures to solve self-created problems is pathetic and infringes on basic human rights. As a Dutch person, it's hard to believe that my city, Amsterdam, wants to add its name to the wall of shame. Narrow-minded people are in town, and I can't understand how our elected leaders can embrace, promote and value the idea of having their version of the West Bank wall, the Apartheid wall, the separation wall, the Berlin wall or the fucking Trumps' wall. How twisted are we to entertain this type of thoughts and rhetoric as a modern society? We're pushing our brothers and sisters into the shade or the darkness of our personal and societal delusional egos.

The Covid-19 pandemic has been a blessing for the local sex industry. Let's thank the pussies' gods; all the mad planning is now on the back burner, and as the city of Amsterdam is financially stretched, no funds can be allocated to the project. I'm ashamed,' concludes an out-of-breath Florian.

— 'In order of preference, would you prefer to help the Dutch police commissioner or the breadcrumb peoples of Amsterdam?' asks Jay.

— 'How can you call my neighbourhood breadcrumbs?' snaps Florian.

— 'Breadcrumbs feed the pigeons that shit everywhere and at every opportunity on offer,' replies Jay. 'One does not exist without the others. And to reassure yourself, a pigeon can also be another layer of breadcrumbs, and vice versa, in different contexts. Please answer the question, Florian, what's more important to you, the police commissioner's little secrets or your livelihood?'

— 'I can have the two if we join forces, and in the process, your safety's guaranteed,' answers Florian.

— 'Can you also guarantee the safety of Ozzie, my computer freak? It's a deal breaker for me,' clarifies Jay.

— 'Done! The four of us will meet soon!' concludes Florian, with a smile on his face.

The trip back to Amsterdam includes a stop at a camera and mobile phone store. Jay returns the memory and SIM cards to Florian and requests to view the pictures he took while spying on him.

Jay is in awe; every picture of Coco and him is sensually loaded, especially when she purposely wears an Andalouse sauce moustache when eating her frikandel. A profound level of intimacy and complicity is revealed in every composition. Jay realises that Florian had followed them all night, from Amsterdam to Ostend, and was present and unnoticed at the police station. Florian is correct; there are pictures of Papa transferring a brown, flattish parcel out of Coco's car. Jay asks the shop assistant to print a selected set of Florian's photos and purchase a few wooden picture frames.

Back at the safe house, Jay is surprised to see Ozzie and the Kiwi twins still reviewing footage of the CCTV archives and live streams. Every member of the Haka tribe is now under scrutiny. The three have formed an overnight bond and have a secret plan to build another monitoring farm.

Jay packs three and a half million euros in a bag and texts Coco that her bundle is ready for collection.

— 'Be ready by seven o'clock on the dot. We have an

appointment!' replies Coco. A few 'love heart' emojis soften the harshness of her direct instructions.

Jay reviews Florian's photographic prints and selects his preferred ones, which he frames with great care and skill. He then places a photo of Coco on his night-side table, facing his silky pillow. Lacking wrapping paper, he sacrifices his favourite T-shirt, bundling up a couple of framed pictures to give to Coco.

He calls his sons, and none of them picks up the call. He calls Juliana and learns that Natalia's funeral is in three days at the Lincoln Memorial Cemetery.

He inquires about the progress of Tia and Kora's mum's treatment. Their answer is positive; consequently, the twins will be out of action for three to four days. They reassure Jay that their business is as usual except for the three corrupted members, pointing to the CCTV screens, who will be expelled from the Haka Army before the business day closes.

— 'Do any of your fighters speak Japanese or happen to be Japanese?' asks Jay. 'I need to contact Yusomito Mitashino, the Japanese businessman, to return his wife's watch.'

— 'Yes and no,' replies Tia. 'We have a Japanese lady who trains with us and owns a Geisha service here in Amsterdam. Her day rate is twenty-five thousand euros, including a tea ceremony and, let's be clear, no sex. Geishas are not sex workers; Oirans are. We received a two-hour-long lecture on the subject when she joined our gym,' giggles Kora.

— 'What is an Oiran?' asks Ozzie.

— 'If I recall well,' starts Kora, 'a Geisha is a worker for the art. She is a highly trained artist and, through her chic appearance, will create a seductive atmosphere to entertain the man's mind and not his penis. Music, literature and meaningful conversation are their trade tools. Geishas are also great negotiators, as explained to us. Oiran can offer sex services but no entertainment of the mind or tea ceremony. Saying that, Oiran sex acts are primarily designed for the mind; the courtesans are also well trained on how to take possession and control of the needs and wants of their patrons. For the kimono to open, there is a build-up of intimate interaction through the power of grace, charm, sliding and rubbing.'

This sentence alone enacts frantic laughter, interactive hand gestures and high-pitched dolphin noises between the Kiwi Girls. Tia laughs, banging her forehead on Ozzie's shoulder, tears flowing down her face. Noticing the boys' stunned facial expressions, she explains with great pain and through laughter bursts that some girls at their gym like to masturbate in the shower cubicle after their training session, and one of them's made a ritual of rubbing her pussy on the cubicle door edge and producing very distinctive vocal marine-type moaning sounds.

— 'I don't get it,' says Ozzie.

Another round of madness embraces the CCTV spying room, sending Tia flying off her chair flat straight to the ground in a loud and ungraceful manner. Now everyone's laughing, and the more Tia tries to reclaim her sitting position, another and louder round of laughter kicks off. She begs everyone to stop as she's ready to piss her pants.

Florian calls, interrupting the madness. He invites Jay and

Ozzie to the lobby of the police station on the ground floor to meet with the police commissioner.

Agreeing, Jay tells Ozzie they must present themselves to the police station downstairs.

— 'We've no choices,' he adds, with a preoccupied look.

Tia makes her way to the bathroom, and Jay asks Kora to stay until their return and not to open the door to anyone, known or unknown. She agrees.

While walking down the stairs, Jay gives Ozzie a short version of last night's events and a quick debrief on Ingrid and their guaranteed protection. Jay puts his mobile phone on audio recording mode and pushes it back into his pocket, quietly inviting Ozzie to do the same. In the lobby area, a police officer in full uniform mechanically invites them to go outside into the gated carpark. He walks them toward a parked Skoda Superb station wagon, opens the back door, and tells Ozzie and Jay to proceed inside.

In the darkness of the car, Florian welcomes the pair with a handshake; the police commissioner does the same while introducing himself.

— 'I'm Ludo Middelkerk,' and without a second to lose, he tenders the back seaters a digital tablet and requests a few signatures. As he scrolls through the document pages, his words are basic and can be summarised by 'here, there, one more, done and congratulations.' With a joyful voice, Ludo confirms to Jay and Ozzie that they're now under his protection and the protection of the Dutch government.

— 'What do you expect from us?' asks Jay.

Ludo scrolls through his tablet and opens a memo full of

bullet points and keywords.

— 'Let's start with you, Ozzie,' Ludo clarifies as he reads the screen and embellishes each keynote's meaning. 'I need a computer farm to be operational within three days. The delivery location is still undecided, but it'll be in the centre of Amsterdam. The Dutch government will pay all expenses. Florian will drop a set of credit cards tomorrow to help you with all your purchases.'

— 'That is easy!' comments Ozzie.

— 'On a more serious note,' Ludo continues, 'You are, from now on, our hacking team leader and application developer. To help you succeed, I've teamed you up with Jiayi Jue, an out-of-this-world Chinese young woman who lives an extraordinary and lavish life from scamming the dark web. She's a modern-day pirate who scams the scammers on behalf of the Dutch government. She's digitally skilled, agile, and so fast that no one in our organisation is able to—or can—understand her manipulating tactics and deceiving strategies. As her manager, you must monitor her activities, and anything that doesn't benefit our government must be reported.'

Ozzie is quiet and accepts his new role silently.

— 'The last item is personal. Could you teach me how to prepare and cook the perfect fried chicken? I'm sorry, but I can't help myself. Your family recipes look delicious,' requests Ludo with a cheerful voice.

Everyone in the car has a good laugh, and a mutual feeling of trust is established.

— 'Onto Jay,' he transitions, 'To protect Ms Carajuca

within the guidelines of our legal and corporate systems, I strongly invite you to be the new owner and shareholder of her ice cream business. This move is included in our protection agreement and helps us to investigate the current action against her business and interests without putting her in the spotlight.'

Jay stays quiet and receives his next round of instructions.

— 'Please give all newly secured diaries and child pornography materials to Florian tomorrow. He'll scan everything, make digital copies, and return all items as soon as possible so you can follow Ingrid's orders.'

— 'Thank you for that!' says Ozzie, feeling relieved.

— 'We—Florian and I—believe the first published diary is not in Ingrid's or the National Police's hands. We know you gave it to her, but as of today, the document hasn't been recorded as evidence in her investigation.'

— 'Should I do something about it?' queries Jay.

— 'No! There's nothing you or we can do about it at this stage. As Florian suggested, please hide all cash, guns, and ammunition. She's a heavy gambler; now, you can be her automatic teller machine. No PINs or cards are required. Under any circumstances, please don't put yourself between her and the money. I'll let you decide where it's best to hide the money and, as a rule, keep it convenient and accessible for you around the clock. The cash can be your life insurance,' insists Ludo.

Jay quietly acknowledges the danger posed by Ingrid and is surprised to hear Ludo's position on his employment status,

— 'Your New York World News assignment is over!

Please email your letter of resignation as soon as possible. You're now a freelancer, and Florian will drop you an all-access National Press Card. Tomorrow morning, there's a press conference with the Mayor of Amsterdam, and as an independent news reporter, please feel free to challenge her egomaniac project. Florian is dying to hear your words. This alone gives us time to dig deeper into her personal and political motivation and establish a list of all potential beneficiaries of her actions. To give you time and space to manoeuvre your cash and artillery, I've sent Ingrid to Den Haag for a mental health assessment. Following any serious work-related incident, it's a compulsory safety practice, and last night was no laughing matter. She'll be back in Amsterdam late tomorrow evening, and your path won't cross before your return to Amsterdam,' Ludo insists, with a firmer voice.

— 'What do you mean our path won't cross?' questions Jay.

— 'Florian will book your flight for Lincoln later today, and you're leaving tomorrow night; you have a funeral to attend,' clarifies Ludo.

— 'How do you know?' asks Jay.

— 'I put a microphone into your jacket while you admired your beautiful self in my photos at the camera store. Please give it back to me now,' jokes Florian. 'Ludo has organised a lunch for tomorrow with Mr Yusomito Mitashino at the Wilshire Hotel on your behalf, and unfortunately, no geishas or oirans are required. I'll be your driver,' cheers up Florian.

— 'Thank you for everything, and thank you for Ozzie,' says Jay.

— 'To conclude, we have never met. All communications

of any form are through Florian, and if something happens to him, you'll receive new directions in due course. Thank you both in advance for your collaboration, and I look forward to our joint and individual successes. Time to go, gentlemen. You have a busy night ahead of you,' says Ludo while the car engine is switched on.

Jay jumps onto his computer in the safe house and emails Bruno Lefevre his termination letter. In the process, he copies the interim HR manager at the Nebraska Mowers and Chainsaws. This action triggers an instant phone call from Juliana. Jay informs her that he's returning to Lincoln tomorrow night and must catch up with her to collect his belongings from his former office. She agrees. Jay calls his sons, and again, they're not answering. Having no other option, he messages them his travel plans. His wife, Judy, has taken over their portable devices and invites Jay to make time to finalise their divorce while he's in Lincoln. Jay agrees not only to proceed with her divorce request but to consent to expediting the outcome. Bruno Lefevre's reply is another round of insults towards Jay and his family and a monologue on the French culture's superiority. Jay ignores the Frenchman's arrogance and focuses on his to-do list.

Ozzie interrupts Jay with celebratory cheers.

— 'It works,' yelling like a madman.

On his computer screen, two new icons are alive and symbolise Ludo and Florian navigating the streets of Amsterdam. Through a newly installed application sourced and customised from the dark web, he can now milk whatever he wants out of anyone's communication hardware when located in their proximity. In a silent assassin style, Tia and Kora are his next victims, and based on the conversation with Ludo and Florian, the ultimate target to get is Ingrid.

Jockey-less Trojan horses are now galloping the invisible Dutch capital's online cloud services and hurtling through data fields to compromise the integrity of unaware and unsophisticated targets. Ozzie's malware is seeding the tulip country to protect the freedom and life of the Nebraskan pair and a circle of women.

On his way out to meet Coco, Jay announces his trip back home to Nebraska to the 'Haka Girls', wishes them the best for the coming days, and tells them he looks forward to hearing great news about their mum's recovery. He receives instructions from Coco not to proceed to the main gate of the police headquarters but instead to wait along the canal edge where a taxi boat is waiting to pick him up. The ride on the canal is magical; all the buildings are telling their intimate evening stories. The combination of all indoor lights, street lighting, and their blurry reflection paint millions of illuminated moving shadows of the squared window facades on the waterways. The short boat ride stops at the Amsterdam National School of Dance, and Jay is invited by the smile of the captain of the vessel to proceed inside. When exiting the boat, the man in charge tenders him a plain golden ticket for tonight's event. Jay carries his bag full of money and proceeds to the ticket booth to validate his entry.

A gentleman comes along and invites Jay to follow him through the darkness of the building. Only the light of a hazy, narrow LED torch leads their steps into the artistic and unknown labyrinth. The guide stops, and the blemished light rests on an empty armchair. Jay pushes his bag under the chair and sits quietly, aware that other people are in his proximity. He can hear their breathing and their muffled conversation. A light beam hits Jay softly from above. With great synchronicity, a loud mandolin concerto takes over the space and inundates his inner senses through the instrument's vibration and resonance. Multiple soft lights join the drama, and Coco appears on the ground stage, swirling through the musicians. Her ballerina figure is well-sculpted in her white tutu. Her body expresses the nuance and the drama of the music. She moves as freely as a fish in the ocean. Her grace, elegance, softness, precision, and purity touch Jay.

The music becomes chaotic to mark the entry of a hag onto the stage, holding a rotten apple in her hand. The atmosphere in the room is now dark and heavy. The tone of the music adds some depth to the drama. The malefic fruit changes hands and, with little conviction and great innocence, is consumed. Jay's body becomes an instant container of pain when seeing Coco inert on the floor. Her status is mirrored by all cells of his being. A feeling of loss is now his identity. The old lady blesses the limitations of her world and leaves the stage, branding her hands maleficently towards the sky. Coco's lifeless body is now shining under the dimmed light. The hundreds of diamonds sewn on her dancewear are now the only life around, and the unmistakable sounds of the mandolins amplify her new reality.

As the music evolves, her glittery figure only breathes through the magic of the light show, and hundreds of ballerinas fill the stage with the same grace and elegance as Coco. They move freely like a school of fish, never questioning whether the water is wet. Their elastic bodies express the fluidity of the music, rolling one after another around Coco's body to perform a miracle. They swirl and swirl madly around the stage, arms fully stretched and surrounding Jay by surprise like a nest of hornets. He is in a hot seat; the spotlight is melting his skull.

As the light slowly fades away from Coco's body, the ballerina pack invites him gently out of his chair. As soon as he stands up, a mad three-layer dancing circle, Sufi whirling-like, navigates him through the concerto players towards his lover—the choreography changes to two human circles rotating at an incredible speed along both sides of his body. The moving ballerinas create an optical effect. Jay's vision is reduced to only a small triangle created by the fast-moving white silhouettes. The scene can be compared to hundreds of trees planted on each side of a narrow road and travelled at high speed. The tunnel effect suddenly stops when Jay reaches Coco. He is aware of the script. He must kiss the princess. A tiny ballerina grabs his arm and, through some sweet gestures, invites him to proceed.

Jay bends down slowly, rests on his hands and knees, and elegantly hovers over Coco's face. He admires her beauty and perfection. A tear leaves his eye and lands on her forehead. The scene is graceful, intense and authentic. Jay gently kisses Coco, who also has pearly eyes. He passes his arm around her and softly lifts her to bring her body close to his chest. The music duplicates their individual and collective emotions. Coco opens her eyes, and the auditorium bursts into a standing ovation. Both lovers are locked in each other's arms, acknowledging each other's heartbeat. The ballerina cohort invites Jay and Coco to embrace the crowd's clapping and cheering. As darkness gains back its authority in the space, the lovers kiss with great passion while their hands softly rub each other and, in the process, generously steal the self-created intimacy of their interlocked bodies.

Backstage, Coco confesses to Jay that she's refused to dance and perform tonight's choreography all her life as she had no prince in sight. She reassures Jay that tonight's performance was a one-off improvisation and a cherished dream that he made come true. With great emotion, she shares the moment she felt Jay slowly moving above her face and letting her entire self be free, trustful, and open to the unknown. Knowing little about her past, Jay understands the meaning of every word intimately shared with him in the comfort of her changing room. As no crafted words can validate Coco's beautiful inner self, Jay brings her into his arms and lets her settle her emotions at her own pace. He kisses her numerous times on her forehead to mark his presence and support. The same set of hands that were stealing intimacy a few moments ago are now building emotional comfort and support.

Coco is called to join her dance troupe back in the foyer to complete the end of their evening rehearsal. Another standing ovation occurs as she joins the gathering, mainly formed by an army of dancing angels of all ages wearing their ballerina bun hairstyle proudly. Coco tells the crowd that tonight's assembly was her best performance ever and the one she wants to be remembered for. Rounds of high fives and tears of many meanings are shared among the dancers and their loved ones. Another wave of emotions brings the crowd into a frenzy when Coco announces her retirement as a professional dancer. She requests a moment of silence and, with eyes loaded with heavy emotional content, unties the ribbons of her pointe shoes. The used suede leather and satin footwear are bundled into a single item and tendered as a gesture of good luck to the new troupe leader. Monica Arminastron is the chosen one, and to Jay's astonishment, she is a Coco Carajuca lookalike.

Back in the changing room, Coco seeks comfort in Jay's arm. Not knowing if it's the right moment to do so, he breaks the news about his trip back to Nebraska, and Coco enquires about his flight details. As he can't answer, Jay messages Florian. Multiple apologies fill Jay's mobile phone screen as Florian's booked the wrong flights. Coco jumps excitedly, grabs her mobile phone out of her locker, scrolls through her applications and, in no time, books a private jet for two through the ice cream business account. Jay shares the news with Florian, who replies with multiple two hands blessing emojis. The lovers will travel together; the pair are delighted! Florian communicates to Jay that it's beneficial to have Coco out of the country for the time being, as she's the next potential victim on the mafia's hit list.

Coco invites Jay to follow her through the back end of the building. They reach the garage, and she invites Jay to take possession of a cargo bike as she secures her bicycle.

As soon as the steel roller door releases them to the fresh air, Coco is unstoppable. She rides the city like a bovver boy. Jay can barely follow her; the weight of the money bag penalises him. As they ride along the canal, she points to a boathouse on the opposite side of the waterway.

—— 'It's ours!' she screams.

The pair reaches the vessel. Coco acquired it eight years ago under a life annuity purchase contract and finally took possession of her purchase a fortnight ago when her elderly vendor passed away.

—— 'The floating property has been fully refurbished and was used as an Airbnb most of the time,' Coco tells Jay. 'No one, including Papa, is aware of my acquisition. He only believes in brick-and-mortar investments.'

—— 'If you wish to stay under the radar, it makes sense to remove the SIM card from your electronic devices,' Jay tells Coco, who automatically switches off her mobile phone.

After a quick tour of the luxury barge, Jay approaches Ingrid's subjects, including the police commissioner, and their respective to-do list that needs to be acted upon before their departure tomorrow night. Jay shares with Coco that he'll finalise his divorce papers while he's in Lincoln. With that in mind, all burning matters are addressed quickly, and Coco invites Jay for a shower play. The Ostend trip needs to reach some conclusion. A wild kissing session takes place under the hot running water, and both are keen to experiment with the loose boundaries of their sexual relationship. Just having his hand on Coco's curvy hips and feeling her tiny waistline and her muscular, flat belly makes Jay excited. Coco instantly feels his stiff cock rubbing against her abdomen. She slowly strokes it and forms a tight ring with her fingers by squeezing the base of his penis to inflate his shaft and glans. Jay licks Coco's nipples and tiny underboobs. His fingers move slowly all over her body, doing uncoordinated circular movements starting on her athletic shoulders and navigating down her neck, chest, rib cage, abdomen, genitals, inner thighs, butt cheeks, lower back and way up her back to her shoulders where they started. The foreplay is well-paced, joyful, interactive, and steamy, and reaches various levels of intensity subject to the subtlety and pressure of their touches and the areas being touched. Coco's erogenous body energetically embraces the physical stimulation. Jay lowers himself down and kisses her tummy in the process before gently licking her labia, pushing the point of his tongue through the softness of her vagina and sucking with different intensity and rhythm her now enlarged clitoris. After gliding his fingers through her warm and tasty wetness, he pushes a pair of fingers into her well-lubricated vagina. He tries to synchronise the G-spot rubbing and clitoris vacuuming performance. His other hand joins the party by inviting her bottom into pendulum momentum. Jay can feel her anal sphincter muscles doing their squeezing gymnastics, and with the help of water running down her firm arse, he inserts his thumb, the one he used to hide Judy's face in his family photo, into her relaxed anus. Coco asks Jay to be gentle. She moans and manages the gravity of her body weight by resting her arms on Jay's shoulders and head. Her legs begin shaking and giving in. Her breathing is uncoordinated; she mumbles before cumming loudly, locking Jay's face into the deepness of her vagina. She asks to pause momentarily as the intensity of their sexual intercourse makes her feel light-headed. Jay complies with her request and paces himself by gently kissing her lower abdomen. After a few seconds, Coco turns around and invites Jay to kiss her beautiful ballerina derriere. She bends forwards, stretching her bum cheeks aside and pushes her anal rose onto his lips. Jay licks her butthole with great passion and pushes and rolls his tongue as deep as he can while she artistically moves and massages her arse on his face, seeking the perfect anal tickling pleasure. To hold her balance, she grabs his nipples and stretches them madly. As Jay feels another level of stimulation, he then inserts back two fingers in her pussy and, with the help of his thumbs, puts pressure on her shaved skin to stimulate her G-spot from both sides of her vaginal wall. Coco is receptive to the stimulation, and her short and quick breathing is a loyal testament to Jay's fingering accuracy. Jay finds intense pleasure in their sexual encounter, and the taste and smell of his partner have blessed his olfactory and gustatory senses. Jay's excitement makes him ejaculate on the shower floor. Coco compliments, with words unknown to him, the velocity of his thick white sperm getting blasted out of his hard knob. Both rejoin together, sensually holding one another and rinsing their bodies without much movement. The vessel bathroom cubicle is tight, and due to the lack of space, drying off and dressing become erotically loaded.

Coco tells Jay not to lie on the bed as she can fall asleep in his arms in no time. Their to-do list countdown has just started, and as a team, they agree to hide the money inside the boathouse; Jay to be the new owner of the ice cream business; after their stop in Lincoln, they'll go to the Dutch Antilles and back to Amsterdam as soon as convenient. More urgently, Coco will use the cargo bike to deliver the money and finalise the bank cheque transaction, and Jay must text her a picture of his passport. Coco gives him a set of keys to the floating residence, and while kissing him on the lips with great passion, she tells him that she has amended her will, that he's now the sole recipient of it and that her Papa has lost his privilege. Jay has no words to express his gratitude. He smiles and kisses her on her forehead as a loving thank-you gesture.

Barring any drama, the pair will meet again at Schiphol International Airport tomorrow evening. Coco disappears with her loaded bicycle at lightning speed while Jay returns to the safe house. Ozzie is asleep when he arrives, and Jay puts a note on his keyboard to insert the conditional geographic inclusion zone on the tracking maps. Coco's boat is the first one. Within an hour, all cash, guns and ammunition are hidden inside the Riviera cruiser hull. Jay packs the diaries and the child pornography for Florian to collect. As one missing diary is already enough, Jay places a second note on Ozzie's keyboard, inviting him to insert miniature tracking devices inside all diaries and other illegal documentation.

Jay texts Coco a copy of his passport and requests tomorrow's agenda from Florian. He contacts his kids in preparation for his short stay in Lincoln and seeks a copy of his divorce papers from Judy. Within seconds, she notifies him that she's already signed her part of the deed. Jay needs to present himself to the local family court to finalise the paperwork; as their divorce is amicable, he doesn't require legal assistance except if he disagrees with the settlement terms. Judy has taken possession of everything except his Dodge Challenger, and an additional clause has been added to the document:

— 'Jay Smith is not the biological father of my children - no financial child support is required.'

This sentence alone brings instant bitterness. He hopes to see the boys, whatever his parental status is, as they are no strangers to him. His following line of communication is with Juliana. He confirms his trip to Lincoln. She informs him that Natalia has a will, and he is the sole beneficiary of her estate. Her legal representative sent a notification to his work email account yesterday. Still, due to the change in his employment status, he's been unable to access it as his company credentials have been terminated. Juliana will forward the correspondence to his private email account.

While pacing the four walls of his bedroom, Jay realises that he forgot to bring Coco's present to their early meet-up. He calls her and invites her for a late dinner. She agrees with great excitement and tells him that their previous evening meet-up was too short and that her heart has so much love waiting to be experienced together. Jay feels awkward, as he doesn't know how to reciprocate her passionate statement, so he invites her to pick tonight's venue. Coco books a table at the Madras Diaries, a South Indian restaurant. Riding a bike with a loosely wrapped parcel under one arm is difficult for

Jay; every 'start' and 'stop' is full of wobbles and uncertainty, mainly when operating the front brake too harshly. A more significant dilemma faces him when parking his bike in a packed sea of parked bikes. In the city darkness, all bicycles look the same; they are all black with shiny bells mounted on shiny handlebars that reflect the busyness of the night sky. After assessing the surroundings, he rests and secures his bike against a street sign pole.

Jay's entrance into the restaurant is noticed. He glows like a five-year-old boy impatiently waiting to surprise a loved one. Coco is equally radiating, and when both meet between the blue and pink dining furniture, their love shines through the establishment. The restaurant patrons cannot ignore the intensity, warmth, and sensuality of their welcoming gestures. Jay notices little girls having their family dinner, looking at them like they are from a fairytale. They are in absolute awe, and because of being part of this instant of pure magic, the little girls innocently validate their early definition of love. Jay is Coco's prince for the second time tonight, and a sense of pride makes him glow. The waiter invites both to take a seat; Jay can't wait any longer to offer his present to his Dutch lover. As soon as the first frame leaves the softness of Jay's T-shirt, Coco's face is filled with emotions, and tears follow suit. Each frame is inspected with great meticulosity with her now luminous red eyes. She stretches her arms and locks her hands into Jay's; it is not enough; both stand up in synchronicity, and she seeks comfort on Jay's shoulders. They stay still for a very long time. The curious little girls notice Coco's reaction and add subtlety to their definition of love. Jay tells Coco that he's placed one of the pictures on his nightside table and, with stuttered words, expresses his feelings of love and connection. The waiter feels awkward, too, as he waits to present the menu. Having no chance of untangling the lovers, he capitulates, leaving the menus on the table alongside the picture frames, which catch his attention.

For the second time in Amsterdam, Jay enjoys the pleasure of Indian food. He shares one of his many passing thoughts with Coco, which dates back to his last year of high school and has haunted him since. He was forced to read, by his literature teacher, The Moviegoer by Walker Percy – winner of the 1962 National Book Award and named one of the Times' One Hundred Best English Language Novels. Percy's words have seeded the notion and reality of relationship malaise in Jay's head. The truthful words have become a never-ending nightmare as Jay's awareness starts to analyse and understand the value, authenticity and reality of his past and present relationships. With great ease, he shares with Coco that she is part of a narrow circle of individuals he feels free of unease around. Coco is flattered and curious to find out who the other individuals are.

— 'Ozzie, my kids, Polka and Natalia, before the prom night,' comments Jay.

— 'I wasn't always like this,' replies Coco. 'It took me years of building trust to be myself and feel free around people. Today is the epitome of my life. Our evening's performance, your kiss, and seeing myself with you in the photos is something I've deeply wished for a long time, and in a matter of a few days, you've turned the tables and fulfilled my deepest desire, which is being loved.'

— 'I feel loved too, and I suggest we add a stopover between Nebraska and the Dutch Antilles. Is a wedding in Las Vegas okay with you?' asks Jay.

The ringless proposal leaves Coco stoked and speechless.

— 'Will you marry me, Coco?' asks Jay with a voice full of light.

— 'Yes, I will,' replies Coco loudly, jumping out of her chair and kissing Jay wildly.

Showing their missing deciduous teeth, the little girls smile in admiration and validate, in their language, Coco and Jay's fairy tale by making pumping heart-shaped hand signs on their chests.

While riding their happiness away and returning their bikes to the dance school, Coco and Jay notice themselves highlighting the late Dutch news. The headlines read,

— 'The beauty and the beast!'

They stop and watch themselves performing on hundreds of television sets that make the front windows of the 'MediaMarkt Amsterdam Centrum'. Pointing her finger towards the screens,

— 'The best day of my life,' murmurs Coco. 'You should be a dancer; you're so elegant and natural, and what a beautiful tender kiss.'

— 'I was nervous,' laughs Jay. 'Very nervous indeed.'

OSTEND

Chapter ten

My father was a puppet full of madness

Well before the sunrise blesses Amsterdam, the lovers leave the boathouse with little sleep under their lover's wings. Coco returns to the dance school for her early coaching classes while Jay walks along the canal towards the safe house. He feels pumped and excited to tie the knot in Las Vegas with a person of his choice. Jay takes a shower and massages away the stiffness of his short night out of his muscles. His new sexual life has an impact on his beard growth, and a smooth look is required for the day ahead. As the triple shaving blades contour his face through the softness of the soapsuds, a light bulb moment hits him hard on how to negotiate, if the opportunity arises, Florian's cause for the red-light district. After dressing as sharp as a knife edge, he prepares his luggage for his trip back to somewhere he now loosely calls home. His new European wardrobe is neatly folded and organised like supermarket shelves into his suitcase. Pants with pants, shirts with shirts, socks with socks. His dirty laundry is rolled into a big ball and thrown into a travel bag, which will be addressed later on American soil. His night-side table photo begs him to be part of this adventure; unfortunately, due to the lack of space in his luggage, it doesn't receive VIP treatment and remains in the safe house, watching and holding down the fort.

Knocking on Ozzie's bedroom door, some muffled noises answer his call. Jay opens the door, and to his surprise, the Haka twins have had a sleepover. Their sports gear and tiny, funky triangular underwear scatter the floor. Their mid-tone chocolate skin colour contours the whiteness of the bed sheets, providing warmth and exotism to the plainness of the room décor. One love found an address in Amsterdam. With just one eye open and a small but sharp head move, Ozzie excuses Jay from the room and gives him a thumbs up, confirming his virginity status has been sent back to heaven, where our universal creator can reassign it to the next mortal joining our living garden called Earth. The fried chicken master and the nerd from Lincoln, Nebraska, have had a threesome with the sushi girls; this early morning news brings a cheerful smile to Jay's face. Their Nebraskan friendship is celebrated when Jay places a small 'Post-it' note in the middle of the CCTV monitor, the message reading,

— 'Working for the Dutch government has some serious benefits!'

Florian is also an early bird. He parks his massive and shiny Iveco Daily van close to the safe house's entry on the ground floor. Jay starts his day with painful manutention tasks and heavy lifting. He goes up and down the stairs with a heavy heart. His favourite motto is always:

— 'I put my heart in what I do!'

But today is tough. His morning joyfulness fades quickly as he feels the pain of hundreds, if not thousands, of victims of sexual abuse immortalised on glossy photographic papers. Every step, whether he ascends or descends them, is associated with ugly and barbaric visuals. He regrets checking the content of the latest diaries and child pornography materials. The shallowness of our civilisation makes no sense to him. The van is fitted like an office space where Jay and Florian sit around the curved table when the last bag is loaded. Jay takes out a Glock G43 X nine-millimetre pistol and two boxes of ammunition from his suit's inner jacket pocket and offers them to Florian.

— 'I don't want you to be the next Peter Rudolf de Vries,' he tells Florian. 'This one comes from the luggage storage, clean and loaded with ten rounds. Regarding the luggage storage, here is the latest content,' pointing towards all bags inside the van.

— 'Let's put all this aside for a moment,' replies Florian. 'I've set up a meeting with some of the residents of the red-light district. Not the prostitutes, the residents. The meeting is in fifteen minutes. Please inform yourself of their personal and collective futures, and from there, we are going to the press conference.'

— 'I forgot the watch,' shouts Jay, making his way out of the van.

Florian calls him back, handing him his national press reporter card and a set of credit cards for him and Ozzie.

After a short drive through the streets of Amsterdam, Florian parks his van near De Oude Kerk and tells Jay where to meet with the residents of the red-light district.

Nah Hoo, Gilles Lombard, and Sandra Halleb are neighbours and residents of the red-light district and have accepted Florian's invitation to meet with Jay. Their homes and units are part of the city's urban fabric and have brothels adjacent to their dwellings. Nah's house is located a few steps from 'Quartier Putain' and oppositely faces the northern façade of De Oude Kerk. She lives in an open museum, and her door welcomes anyone interested in their life stories, lifestyle choices and unusual arrangements. Photos and postcards fill the entry room, where a large table is filled with clean coffee cups, water jugs and delightful-looking pastries. Jay is welcomed with three sets of handshakes, which have different intensities, firmness, and, unfortunately, humidity. Sandra's hand is far from dry; her squeeze is a gooey, sweaty, acidic pond that needs to be absorbed as quickly as possible, and with great discretion, by the fabric of Jay's trousers' back pockets. This singular encounter is the catalyst for Jay's refusal of food offerings, igniting instantly some initial resentment toward Ms Halleb. As part of their small talk, everyone introduces themselves.

Nah Hoo is a quantum physicist who teaches at a local high school and is an avid canal landscape painter. She migrated from Indonesia over twenty-five years ago, and since then, she's vibrated spiritually by observing the red-light district's ongoing motion and evolution. She is fascinated by the surrealism of the daily simplicity of all human and commercial interactions sealed within this tiny sexual microcosm and its grandiose settings. She dreams as she talks.

Gilles Lombard serves everyone a cup of instant coffee; his mannerism has a touch of feminine elegance. His little levitated pinky measures the room's air temperature. He is a retired sailor, born and raised in New Caledonia. His parents were Dutch nationals touring the world looking for better weather. Four decades ago, he found a place called home above the red neon lights, where he now works as a locksmith all over Amsterdam, helping the locals with emergencies, whatever the time of day. He is a skinny guy with a pointy fox face who rubs at his crotch energetically when talking about his exotic commercial neighbours.

Sandra's blouse underarms are layered with unattractive circular pancake-shaped stains. Her wet, bushy armpits mirror her anxious persona. She is a refugee from Pakistan who escaped the death penalty for being accused, without supporting evidence, of having an extramarital affair with a tourist the day after her wedding celebration. The incident gained local and international attention from major news outlets and human rights support groups. As a result, her forced marriage was revoked under the pressure of the International Court of Justice. Charges have since been dropped, but potential retributions still exist. She has lived on the run for most of her life, fearing for her safety, and changed her name and identity whenever necessary. This included a few cosmetic surgeries to disguise her ethnicity.

Her current look is far from her Middle Eastern genetic heritage. Her Botox-filled lips, giraffe-style eyelashes, heavy makeup, vintage clothing, a green fluorescent pair of socks and thick-heeled Palladium boots are all let down by the magnificent darkness of her silky curled black hair. She is a nervous mid-thirty-year-old woman in a free city. Her acquired posh British accent is a proper camouflage and an 'all night' pass into the city's pompous drinking events. By day, she owns a cleaning business servicing her neighbourhood.

Gilles teases Jay when he tries to introduce himself.

— 'We know everything about you; we can see your face everywhere. Every day is a discovery,' jokes the locksmith.

— 'Last night was the best, what a beautiful kiss!' interrupts Nah.

Jay blushes, but as time is of the essence, he pushes his queries related to the future of the red-light district and its political direction back to the forefront of the conversation.

Gilles becomes nuclear in no time, validating Florian's views on the red-light district's current climate, commenting that Amsterdam's libertarian picture, promoted around the world as the perfect postcard for a unique tourist experience, is sinking fast into the depths of our canals. The town's visitor nuisances and rowdiness are used for political gain and societal correctness.

— 'Amsterdam is perfect as it is; we want all the sea liners, riverboats, trains, plane passengers, and all types of curious dreamers to experience the uniqueness of our city, its warmth, and love. Our multi-dimensional and layered society is a unique place to experience the self and act as a playground for all to break our individual and collective educational taboos,' gently comments Nah.

— "To be and to do' is a dilemma and a balance that needs to be inserted in our modern way of living,' interacts Sandra. "To do' is not sustainable if there is no 'to be', and currently, we're forced into so much doing. Like many places around the world, our existence is filled with compliance and expectations in all aspects of our lives. Freedom is a rarity for many of us. The red-light district is far from perfect, but it allows and offers the opportunity for many human relations of all types to see the light and value the existence of the individuals involved for a brief instant. We all seek love, care and attention, and here, maybe for a fifty-euro note exchange, givers and receivers coexist in the present moment to satisfy what is lacking in our lives.'

— 'Spiritual intimacy at its best,' dreams loudly Nah, 'Amsterdam is a healing place.'

Sandra interferes,

— 'Criticism and judgment are easy and cheap. Anyone walking the streets of Amsterdam should question themselves if they're on the right side of the windows. Any of the girls, boys, and those in between trading themselves behind these windows are skilled, and their resilience is well above that of most people footing and flooding the narrow streets of Amsterdam. As a solo entrepreneur, they're chameleons. Developing skills to adjust and adapt to the wants and needs of the ever-changing marketplace. They are masters of communication, able to juggle, within seconds, products or service presentations, address and overcome any forms of objections, convert sales without shame, collect their due and deliver pleasure for the mind, body and the soul.'

— 'Politicians are all talk, no delivery and suck from the day they gain power,' interrupts Gilles angrily.

Nah giggles silently and shares,

— 'Opening the doors of my house is a daily pleasure. Anyone who enters here has something to share which is unique and personal. Positive and negative balance each other in this room; all extremes are balanced in this house. We are an equilibrium. The energy around this table now is also an equilibrium; we balance and complement each other. I came to Amsterdam to experience my deepest desires as a young adult, and even before that, I didn't feel comfortable sharing or experiencing my true self with my partners, companions, or lovers. My sexual fantasies were not within the limitations of their values or the deepness of their sexual commitments. I was constantly concerned about how I'd be received and perceived and was scared to be rejected. So, I ran away. I didn't want to compromise my need for fantasies, my desire for kinkiness or my love for fetish. Amsterdam gave me all the answers I was looking for. There was no denial, refusal or judgment in the process. It was a gentle, transcendental human experience. It was healing at its best; I felt safe and valued. Countless selves, relationships or families have been saved behind and within the red neon lights. Our true selves can be found and experienced here. So, why change something that works magically.'

After receiving a phone call from Florian, Jay says he needs to move on and thanks everyone for their time, authenticity and valuable input. He avoids any physical contact. Gilles walks him to the front door, and as they reach the entry, Gilles' facial expression changes from foxy-friendly to vampirical, ready to suck someone's life away. He notices Jay's caught his shift in demeanour and says,

— 'Russian oligarch,' pointing his pointy hunter nose towards an older buffed-up-looking guy making his way out of a matte black Mercedes Maybach, 'Putin's ally and Amsterdam's mayor's best friend,' Gilles adds.

Back in the van, Florian's eager to show the viewfinder of his camera to Jay,

— 'This is what you missed,' he says, showing a few photoshoots of the Russian oligarch and Amsterdam's mayor. 'Every week, they meet here for half an hour to an hour. The property belongs to the city council.'

Swiping the screen on his mobile, he scrolls through his Dropbox archives, revealing pictures from last week and the weeks before. As Florian starts driving, Jay takes over the device and zooms through the photos. Every frame's captured feelings between the pair; their mirrored eye contact, smiles, and excited body postures are digitally saved.

— 'This is the best series,' Florian adds, showing pictures of Amsterdam's mayor undoing two buttons of her business cotton white shirt and exposing a fair share of her laced cleavage. Jay's sharp eyes spot something intriguing in numerous pictures. He presses the share button, copies the access link into a text message, and returns the device to Florian to approve the data transfer. Florian instantly complies with the request.

More than an hour later, the press conference venue is packed, and the police force appears in huge numbers. Their presence ratio is close to one to three, which is very impressive, knowing the national force is well understaffed. Anyone attending the conference of the Dutch's god is checked first by a docile pack of impressive and athletic Belgian Malinois, followed by the moving handheld body scanners and, finally, a good old hand strip search. Some of the sex workers in tiny outfits are complaining about the procedure, while others know how to play their cheeky and kinky games in these unusual contexts. Sandra's right; they are skilled negotiators. The room is noisy, and Jay goes to the media-allocated section. Florian is there too, and the two men do not interact. The mayor of Amsterdam is on stage surrounded by her team, legal advisors and security. Only Ingrid is missing.

She addresses the gathering in her native Dutch dialect and acknowledges and thanks Jay in English for his intervention at the last press conference. The room atmosphere is tense as the town's leader delivers a fifteen-minute monologue blasting the locals through the room speakers. She sounds like a short man with a square moustache, and her machine-gun voice's tone and punctuation cannot be interrupted. The modern dictator has full power, and wrongful history lessons are in the process of being repeated. Supporters and antagonists are on the edge of their seats and look out of sorts. Finally, silence regains the space, and questions and answers are invited.

The local BBC journalist, who helped Jay with translation

at the last council meeting, gives him an overview of the situation. In short, the mayor wants to proceed with the sex centre development and has entered a non-disclosure agreement with a private property developer.

Questions, answers, and reactions from all parties are now well alive. Jay raises his hand and receives the mayor's invitation to proceed. Jay introduces himself as a freelancer, a revelation that gathers ample attention in the room before proceeding with his queries.

— 'I have two questions. First one, do we know the identity of the man that put a gun on the police lady's head the other night?'

The question is off-subject with purpose. The mayor's response is vague and redirected to the police representatives, who currently have no comments.

— 'My second question is, could I share something privately with you now and have your approval to publish it?'

As the mayor agrees, Jay makes his way to the stage. Everyone in the room is sitting quietly on the edge of their chairs. Only the noise of the air travelling through the mechanical ventilation diffusers is audible. He takes his phone out, scrolls through the received pictures messaged by Florian, and, with a soft and quiet voice but loud enough to be picked up by the microphone, he says,

— 'Red here and white there.'

Now, it's the mayor's turn to be outraged. Her authoritarian body language decomposes in front of the auditorium. She places her hand on the microphone and nervously tries to find the off-switch button. Her administrative assistant comes to her rescue but is sharply pushed back to her seat. The scene is ugly, and Jay waits anxiously for the outcome. She must be the first one to talk. Camera flashes capture the moment as fear embodies the mayor's face with the growing pressure. She comes very close to Jay and tells him,

— 'The deal is, I resign now and, no publication, you keep quiet forever!'

Jay replies,

— 'No sex centre now or later, and we have a deal!' Thrusting his hand forward, Jay seals the historic moment with a handshake.

As Amsterdam's mayor addresses the room, the crowd loses it—some in disbelief, some in euphoric joy. Jay's name is again chanted, a bloody mayhem is brewing, and the police force is ready for whatever outcome. Jay walks out of the building and is followed by journalists and photographers. One of them tries to steal his mobile phone through a grab-and-run move. With no time to react, the thief receives a forceful double-eyed poke that blinds him instantly. As he tries to balance and search directions, he gets a straight kick to his testicles, followed by a swift and powerful open-hand slap to the face. The torsional force implied on his neck is too much and lands him hard on the ground. Jay checks the welfare of his attacker while inviting someone to get him medical assistance. Jay, once again, highlights the Dutch news.

To escape the pressure of the press gathering, Jay steals an unchained push bike and rides the cobbled street ungracefully. While waiting for Florian's instructions, he calls Coco and discovers that Abigail will accompany them to the US. Her current vulnerability is high on Coco's agenda. The next call he makes is to Ozzie, who rattles on crazily like a summer bird enjoying the first ray of morning light. The Nebraskan boys agree to meet swiftly before Jay's departure.

Café Van Leeuwen, located just a few steps from the Wilshire Hotel, reunites Jay and Florian. The latter is more than curious to understand how his newly recruited informer manages the resignation of the Amsterdam mayor just by flicking through a few photos on his phone. Jay keeps him on his toes by smiling and repeating,

— 'White and red is the answer.'

Florian now begs for knowledge and is flattened by Jay's sharpness when he becomes aware that the city leader had a change of underwear in last week's photos: a red glossy bra on arrival and a white one on departure. Jay texts Ozzie and seeks his expertise to access the establishment's security network and secure the data if available.

The cosiness of Café Van Leeuwen is traded for a dose of frivolous neoclassical and neo-Renaissance replicas at the Wilshire Hotel. Highly decorated ceilings, luminous hallways, large blue and brown Persian carpets, royal Calacatta marble and squared Corinthian columns welcome Jay through the entry glass box. The concierge guides him to the Opus Lounge, which is closed at this time of the day, and invites Jay to sit wherever he wants. The atmosphere feels artificial and complex to appreciate at this time of the day. Jay acknowledges the space's discomforting environment and turns on his mobile device's audio recorder. Jay has an eye on the wall clock, and after over thirty minutes of waiting, he can't resist the urge to use the bathroom. The male amenities section has the same building grandiosity but in darker hues. Jay checks himself in the mirror suspended above the refined golden taps elegantly mounted on the white porcelain basin. While his face is blessed with the rays of warm artificial lights, he notices that his morning shaving skills are far from perfect. Tiny patches of beard inside the crease of his neck require a second round of attention. He locks himself inside the toilet cubicle and releases his morning coffee loading. The airlock door of the male restroom compartment opens and shuts within a few seconds' intervals, and no footsteps or human movement can be heard. Jay's blood pumps instantly at a high-velocity rate; he's immediately concerned for his safety. As a precautionary move, he climbs the toilet bowl and peeks above the toilet partition. A 'Help me!' message is written with dark red lipstick on the mirror above the golden taps. Leaving the bathroom, he washes his hands and cleans the message with a few sheets of toilet paper.

Back in the lounge, a stern Mr Yusomito Mitashino stands beside the counter. He drinks a self-served Negroni. The handshake between the two men is formal, with Mr Mitashino thanking Jay for his heroic action and selflessness. It's Jay's turn to play the barman, and the Japanese businessman invites him to try a mixture of Martini Bianco with a generous drop of Angostura aromatic bitters served on ice with a thick slice of lime firmly squeezed. The men salute themselves with great pride by clinking their drinking vessels. Jay is delightfully surprised by the drink's complex aroma and flavour.

Mr Mitashino invites Jay to give him the watch back. Jay

reaches into his pocket and places the item on the counter.

— 'There is only one way to find out if the watch belongs to my wife,' says the Japanese man as he grabs a glass magnifier and a small jeweller's toolbox from his jacket. He carefully inspects the luxury good, flips it upside down, and releases the back casing. The inner side of the precious metal casing is engraved with microscopic Japanese calligraphy symbols. The validation of their authenticity generates a smile on the Asian businessman's face. 'I was trained as a watchmaker and customised this watch,' explains Yusomito joyfully. 'It was my engagement present to my wife.'

— 'Is your wife okay?' asks Jay.

— 'It's been a rough few weeks for all of us, so please take my silence as the best answer on offer!' replies the Nippon representative with a deep diaphragm voice.

— 'I didn't come here for the money,' says Jay.

— 'Why did you come, if it's not for the money?' questions Mitashino with an even more resounding voice.

— 'Silence is the best answer I can give you,' Jay replies, offering his counterpart a status quo fist pump.

The gesture is not accepted or reciprocated; the watchmaker is too busy sealing back his reclaimed treasure. Jay holds onto his thoughts, and in the process, he feels an air of awkwardness taking over the room. Jay scoffs down the end of his drink quietly.

— 'I'm not a good man when I'm disrespected,' Mr Mitashino tells Jay. 'Not accepting your part of the deal is disrespectful. Are you ready to face the consequences of your choice, Mr Clown? Maybe you should've minded your business in the first place.'

The discomfort is real, and Jay has no answers, and keeping his mouth shut is the best he can do now. For a fraction of a second, his mind recalls his friend Polka's final moment. The Japanese man's last words sounded precisely like the endless rounds of live ammunition that've abruptly stopped the lives of so many. Jay knows that his best next move is to leave before the rawness of his anger settles verbally—the difference in their emotional limitations with the boor man.

Walking back to the Wilshire lobby, Jay comes face to face with Mr Mitashino's older daughter and her grandmother, as introduced to him. They were waiting for Jay to exit. Little words are exchanged; their eyes do intense yet silent talking. Jay's anger is traded for compassion; another set of awkwardness is live now. Many cultural thanks are exchanged, but they physically lack affection, as no warm, comforting, and reassuring hugs or embraces are exchanged.

The painful goodbye session is interrupted when Mr Mitashino's daughter forcefully handshakes Jay. Her apologetic grandma tries to stop her in the process. The young, determined woman holds the handshake for a few seconds and, in the process, forcefully transfers a concealed lipstick tube into Jay's hand cavity. Feeling the object, he rounds his other hand around hers and bows nervously numerous times. His compassionate face masks with great pain his intrigue and inquisitiveness. After securing the makeup into his pocket, he gently reassures the older Japanese lady that healing has many forms or shapes and that maybe her granddaughter needs to express her feelings.

Jay knows he can't leave the property without acknowledging the young lady's welfare. After saying goodbye, Jay is back in the hotel male restroom. The lipstick's colour matches the one used to write the 'Help me!' message on the mirror. It doesn't take long before the male toilet's airlock door opens. Mr Mitashino's older daughter enters, undoes her dress and pushes her underwear down. She looks like Dora the Explorer after the war. Her exposed body is raw from layers of heavy-handed belt marks. Her genitals are the most affected and are bleeding at the surface, which explains the red marks on her underwear. She is a horror show on legs. She covers herself and, without a word, walks out of the male amenities. Jay tries to make sense of how to deal with the situation. He runs through the hotel corridor, trying to catch up with the wounded girl. She waits to enter the Opus Lounge, and as Jay is in her visual proximity, she proceeds. Jay follows her footsteps, and a firework of words blasts through the entertainment venue as she tells her father with a bitter and harsh voice her intentions to leave while making him aware that Jay has witnessed his atrocity. Her old man's reaction is both physical and verbal, as a decorative thick glass ashtray flies in her direction, just missing her before shattering to the ground.

— 'She is a whore,' he screams. 'She is a fucking whore. She should have been kidnapped like the others. The fucking whore had sex in the pool service room with the maintenance guy. She deserves her punishment. She disrespected me, and her punishment is far from finished,' the upset Japanese man yells.

— 'Her beating stops now, and I, Mr 'Clown of Amsterdam', take full responsibility for my choices. You felt disrespected because we don't share the same values, so be it. We are going to the police station now to report your animalistic behaviour,' shoots back Jay.

Jay believes Miss Mitashino's exit was well organised, as it took her no time to gather her belongings. As they run the streets of Amsterdam, pulling her heavy suitcases, Jay calls Florian, who seeks assistance from the police commissioner. A police car picks them up and drops them off at the police station located below the safe house, where Miss Mitashino reports the ordeal.

Happiness is void within Jay. He can't wait to leave Amsterdam and cuddle in Coco's arms. In the safe house, Ozzie cheers him up, with Jay returning the gesture, teasing him about his last night's adventure with the twins.

— 'We realised that we were all virgins and needed to do something about it, so we all committed,' self-justifies Ozzie.

Jay laughs and hugs his Nebraskan pal. A round of high-fives and fist pumps brings life to the harshness of the day.

More seriously, Jay debriefs his morning encounters with Ozzie, downloads the voice recordings onto his computer, and duplicates the data onto a USB stick for Florian. To have total privacy, Jay invites Ozzie onto the balcony, where he shares, very quietly and confidently, the location of Coco's houseboat, stating that that is where the money is stored and, more importantly, the fact that Ozzie owns the funds if something happens to both him and Coco.

Meanwhile, Florian drops back the child pornographic

material and countless diaries for Ingrid to collect. Later that evening, as instructed by Jay, Ozzie inserts microscopic satellite tracking devices into the covers and packaging.

Coco texts Jay that she's making her way to the airport with Abigail. Jay replies, asking Coco to add another passenger to the trip. Sakura Mitashino's safety is now Jay's priority.

Florian drops the pair at Schiphol airport and receives the USB audio stick. The duo becomes a quattro. Coco, Abigail, and Sakura introduce themselves before making their way to the airport chemist to secure the fundamentals of their first aid kit. Jay notices the presence of a few members of the Haka army blended into the crowd. Some familiar faces from the police station are also nearby.

The customs clearance for private jet customers is done in no time. The refinement of a Gulfstream G Seven Hundred welcomes Amsterdam's fugitives. Jay volunteers to carry Abigail onto the plane as her accessibility needs have been omitted, giving her a tour of the aircraft while letting her know he can move her around whenever needed. Jay is fascinated by the cabin décor and the refinement of its craftsmanship. He opens and closes all doors and drawers of the joinery fit-out. His fingers glide on all surfaces and textures with the same passion he exerts when he touches Coco's body. Leather, polished wood, carpet, and plastic receive the same attention. His pleasure is interrupted when he's in the process of putting his mobile phone on 'flight mode'; Florian has shared a link; the Japanese businessman has told the world that Jay is the 'Clown of Amsterdam.' The story reads that Jay tried to extort money from the

Japanese businessman and kidnapped his older daughter for a ransom. Pictures of Jay at the Opus Lounge tendering the watch back and drinking a fancy cocktail are plastered across the World Wide Web. 'Ambushed in Amsterdam' punches one of the many headlines.

The take-off is effortless, followed by a welcome round of drinks and a light gastronomic dinner. Coco is interested in hearing Sakura's story and situation, and Jay secretly records the audio in a precautionary manner. He's curious to acknowledge the consistency between what he already knows and the hurtful secrets of his protégé. It doesn't take long and much effort for Sakura to display her bruised body. Abigail, who sits next to her, requests permission to touch her body with a healing and caring hand. The first aid kit joins the pair, and a fair amount of soothing balm is applied where needed.

Jay and Coco let the duo care for themselves and retreat to the centrally located sofa. They're looking for intimacy and connection. Coco lies down on the luxurious leather cushions and rests her head on Jay's thighs. He glides his fingers slowly on her face and brushes her hair with smooth movement and significant inconsistency. Their imperfections are perfect.

— 'Are you okay?' queries Jay with a soft, loving voice.

— 'I am better now,' replies Coco.

— 'Your eyes are red and teary.'

— 'I know Sakura's pain well; I've experienced it numerous times before. I deeply feel for her.'

— 'I'm here for you.'

— 'I love you, Jay.'

— 'I love you too, Coco.'

Jay's hands offer comfort to his future wife as she sobs the pain of her former self.

— 'Is it something you want to share?' he asks.

— 'When we first met at the Egmond aan den Hoef cottage, I listened to your story attentively. I was moved and blessed at the same time. But back home, I cried, fearing the thoughts of losing you. I felt connected and wanted you more than my next breath of fresh air. I've never experienced this closeness or bond before. I am you; I am us without compromising any aspect of myself.'

— 'What's your relationship with Gaston? You looked unusually connected. Hypnotised, I should say.'

— 'Papa is my saviour. He saved me from another round of poor human treatment. As part of our journey together, he trained my brain to overcome past, present and future life obstacles and emotional hurdles and how to tap into my universal clarity and purity. He taught me to believe in myself, trust my judgement, develop a thought process that supports my wish, and, most importantly, design a life I can embody well before it becomes reality.'

— 'Sorry for sounding stupid; I don't understand the concept of life embodiment,' interrupts Jay.

— 'When Papa and I met for the first time, I couldn't hold any eye contact with anyone. I was scared; I was a self-created victim of my past life self and events. As a playful exercise, he trained me to hold eye contact with him until any fears, doubts and emotional glitches were converted into a sense of peace, purpose and an opportunity for love. Love for me first, I should clarify.'

— 'The way you both connected in Ostend made me very uncomfortable. It was intense.'

— 'It was truthful and authentic; I felt your discomfort. I like your weakness,' Coco adds with a tiny, sweet grin.

Their conversation is interrupted by the graceful smile of the cabin attendant, who requests Jay's assistance to take Abigail to the bathroom.

Jay kisses Coco on her forehead and makes his way towards the end of the plane to clear any obstacles off the path to the bedroom. He returns and offers Abigail a piggyback ride. She slides herself onto the edge of the seat; Jay squats down and pushes his lower back between her legs; with powerful arms, she locks her body weight around his neck. With strength and laughter, the duo moves carefully through the seating section of the plane. Her lower body and legs are dangling at the rhythm of their procession. Jay slows down to go through the entry door of the bedroom before carefully landing Abigail on the firm mattress.

'Sorry, Jay, but you'll need to remove my pants and knickers,' she says with a solid and joyful Irish accent.

— 'No mile high club,' cracks Jay.

— 'How do you plan to land me on the toilet seat?' queries the half-naked redhead.

— 'Due to the height restriction, a face-off's best,' Jay replies as he gently slides Abigail on the corner of the bed.

He carefully rests her legs on the thick and expensive carpet floor. As he positions himself, he spreads her legs around his waist. Abigail helps him to push her upper body and locks her arms around Jay's neck again. To have maximum strength and lock Abigail's legs into place, Jay tucks his hands in his pant pockets before gently lifting off both bodies.

— 'It's okay to have an erection; I can feel your manhood,' Abigail teases.

— 'Sorry, the toilet seat is the target! Watch your head.'

— 'My arse is wide open!'

— 'I know, I saw it in the mirror. Nice booty.'

— 'Did you feel my breast?'

— 'I'm too busy managing the perfect toilet seat landing.'

Abigail relieves herself in front of Jay, who is slightly uncomfortable at the scene.

Noticing his awkwardness, Abigail tells him that her OnlyFans followers will pay good money to be in his position and won't refuse a well-earned blowjob.

Jay kneels down in front of Abigail and holds powerful martial arts-style eye contact. Their heads are now approximately at the same height. The kinkiness of their dialogue evaporates quickly.

— 'I want more than a blowjob from you. I want you to be the new CEO of Coco's ice cream business. I trust you and have great faith in your business acumen.'

— 'I know nothing about ice creams,' replies Abigail with a soft, child-like voice.

— 'I'm not better; I know nothing about owning a business either. Your sex-worker shelter venture needs leaders.'

— 'I need to poop!'

— 'I'd pay heaps to see that, but no thanks,' laughs Jay,

turning his back to Abigail and leaving the bathroom. Sitting on the corner of the bed, he waits for Abigail to call him back.

— 'I need help; I can't clean myself,' calls the redhead.

— 'I'm here; how can I help you?'

— 'I can't stretch my arm around; it's too narrow here. I'm stuck and have a cramp in my lower back.'

— 'Just bend over; I have the toilet paper.'

— 'I'm sorry, Jay!'

— 'You're bleeding, the water is red.'

— 'It comes and goes since he kicked me.'

— 'Van Looke?' Jay questions harshly.

— 'Yes, Van Looke! The fucking bastard!'

— 'I'm no doctor, but I suggest that you check yourself during our stopover in Lincoln for any type of internal bleeding or blood clots.'

— 'I'm washed out. I need some rest. Can I sleep on the bed?'

— 'Let me give you a piggyback.'

— 'You're a good man, Jay; Coco is lucky!'

— 'Have a good night, and feel free to call me,' says Jay while switching off the lights in the plane bedroom.

Jay checks on Sakura and invites her to join Abigail if she wishes. Coco is well asleep and looks beautiful. Her facial expression invites world peace. Jay smiles, rubbing his chest as a sign of contentment. Jay joins the group and falls asleep without any form of resistance.

A few hours later, the flight attendant wakes him and tenders the cabin's portable handset.

— 'The FBI wants to talk to you,' she says quietly.

— 'Hi!' says Jay with significant discomfort and a sleepy voice.

— 'Juliana Susas, FBI. Welcome back to the United States of America.'

— 'What the fuck? You scared the shit out of me.'

— 'I'm no joke! I'm an undercover agent, and coming to Nebraska and taking over your job was no coincidence. It was pre-arranged! Your shit in Amsterdam is something else.'

— 'I've little to say,' Jay replies quietly.

— 'I gave instructions to your pilot. You and your entourage stay in the plane until you see my face.'

— 'Can I trust you? You're no joke.'

— 'Luckily for you, I'm no joke, Jay. I work for the FBI.'

— 'Two of the girls here need urgent medical attention. One has symptoms of internal bleeding, and the other's body is mutilated beyond belief. Please help them.'

— 'You've forty-eight hours to get out of Lincoln.'

— 'I'm here to finalise my divorce papers, Natalia's funeral, and looking to catch up with Roger, my foster father, and my kids.'

— 'As the sole beneficiary of Natalia's estate, her will's paperwork must be finalised only when your divorce is officially done.'

— 'I'm still surprised with her choice,' replies a teary Jay.

— 'I don't know what to say; she loved you. You're a lovable guy. I'm sorry for the mess you're in now. I'm profoundly sorry. Your assignment was supposed to be just a hocus-pocus medical assignment.'

— 'Is the medical trial real? I don't want to disappoint

my Kiwi friends.'

— 'Yes, the hypnosis coma therapy is legit. Let me help you with your schedule and secure your safety here. I'll see you soon.'

The call stops abruptly. Jay's mind, body and soul are instantly painted by the bittersweetness and guilt bleeding out from his unfinished relationship with Natalia. He recalls their times together through nauseous memories; his sorrows are expressed with shaky hands, stuttered breaths, and red, glossy eyes.

The cabin attendant notices his shaken mental state and brings him a pack of tissues, a cold bottle of sparkling water, and a glass filled with ice cubes. He thanks her with a short, shaky thumbs-up. His mucus joins the commotion and runs down as fast as the tears coming from his crying eyes. He rolls the icy glass across his forehead to dissipate the heat of his emotions. Silence is his best ally as he settles into the comfort of the luxury leather seat.

Detroit's turbulences signal Jay that he's in American airspace. He's ready to turn a few pages of his former life. Coco's words about designing and embodying life intrigue him.

Before landing, Abigail requests another round of toilet assistance. Her good humour and cheekiness cheer up Jay, and while peeing, she accepts Jay's job offer. He informs her that her medical assistance is organised for their arrival in Lincoln.

Coco and Jay are together for the landing, holding hands. Coco complains about her bad morning breath, but Jay is in love, smiling and kissing her on her forehead.

The pilot follows the FBI's instructions and parks the flying palace inside a dark commercial aviation hangar. The disembarkment is done behind closed doors. Juliana oversees the operation and is first on board for a formal meet and greet. No Las Vegas deep cleavage or bulging breasts. She wears a plain on-duty uniform. The customs officials are ready to process everyone's entry into the American sovereignty of the United States with great diligence. The crew is the first to leave the plane and is immediately escorted out of the building. Abigail is next; she is assisted out of the plane, and as soon as her passport is stamped, Coco is invited to follow suit. Jay is next. The smooth clearance operation turns into an immigration stunt when Sakura walks down the airstair naked and parades, with great dignity, her assaulted body. She seeks asylum when her bare feet touch the cold industrial concrete floor. The night turns into an administrative procedure. The paramedics help with the situation. Abigail is sent to CHI Health St. Elizabeth emergency department for her medical examination. Once again, Coco and Jay sit on uncomfortable, hard-shell plastic chairs while they wait to regain their freedom, taking turns resting their head on each other's shoulders. Juliana invites Jay to turn on his mobile and check the news updates.

Ozzie and Florian have left numerous messages. Ozzie's managed to secure hours of footage of the now former mayor of Amsterdam performing unregistered sex work for financial proceed. The footage shows the town leader wearing high heels and a whole-body red dominatrix leather outfit; her bare boobs have no support and poke through two circular openings of her corset, and a large-size strap-on dildo hangs down from her crotch area. Her curved tits bounce to the rhythm of her hips. She masters the art of submission with great ease. Her Russian friend is the receiver of deep and forceful anal sex. All footage has a common brutality theme, whether she engages in foot fetish practice, genital kicking, arse whipping or facial golden showers. All illegal sex-working sessions are concluded with passionate kisses, tender hugs and massive transfers of cash.

Florian's updates are less joyful. Mr Mitashino, before his arrest, placed a seven-digit American dollar bounty on Jay's head, and Zoetje Saar has been assassinated in a drive-by shooting in the heart of Amsterdam.

Jay messages Ozzie back and instructs him to share the videos with Julian and Ludo. He also invites him to trace Zoetje's movement on his CCTV setup. Ozzie replies instantly and informs Jay that Ingrid has collected all diaries and child pornographic materials and came back later to query about the money's location. In a second text message, Ozzie states that Ingrid became out of control and intimidating and fell flat on her lies when he told her that he was waiting to give a tour of his surveillance station to the Dutch police commissioner himself. On her way out, she mumbled something like,

— 'I should've followed the instructions and killed you all.'

— 'She was a strange bird with a creative big heart. I'll miss her dearly,' Coco reacts to Zoetje's passing. 'We are all shooting targets,' she adds, squeezing Jay's arm.

— 'You and I are not; we'll dance through life together.

I'm sure you didn't embody or picture yourself as a shooting target, so we don't need to project something that'll never happen in our minds. We need to be careful until everything falls back into place in Amsterdam.'

— 'I love you, Jay.'

— 'You are my anchor, Coco. I'm grounded when we're together. It feels good, I feel good.'

— 'I'll feel even better when your naked body spoons me. I hope it's soon! It's nearly three o'clock in the morning.'

— 'We are the lucky ones. Sakura's life is worth our back pain.'

Just before seven a.m., Sakura is escorted out of the building on an ambulance stretcher by a group of paramedics and Immigration and Border Force officers. No waving, no traditional Japanese salutations, no goodbye. She is now alone in her new steep journey.

Juliana, surrounded by a few colleagues, invites Coco and Jay to a meeting room at the front end of the hangar.

— 'Ken Dumbbells, your attorney from Dumbbells and Dumbbells,' Juliana points to a sharply dressed mid-forties man standing behind a table covered with legal papers.

She introduces Jay as 'Your client' to Ken and Coco as 'Jay's partner.'

— 'Here is the plan for the day, and you have no choice,' continues Juliana. 'You sign your amicable divorce papers now. Ken has a special hearing booked at nine o'clock with the Family Court. By nine-thirty, you should be declared divorced. Ken will return here and provide your divorce certificate and other legal documentation. At ten o'clock, you will assist, and I am sorry about this; you will attend remotely to Natalia's funeral. I am sorry, Jay.'

Seeing Jay's reaction,

— 'Our safety is at risk,' comments Juliana with her strong South American accent. 'That is not all! Ken will also finalise Natalia's will after the memorial service. You will receive the key to her house, where you will spend the rest of your day in Lincoln in our company.'

— 'No spooning,' Jay comments to Coco.

— 'Are you okay and ready to proceed?' queries Juliana.

— 'Give me the pen, I want my freedom back,' says Jay, squeezing Coco's left knee.

— 'Sign here, sign here, sign here, sign here, one more here, and we are done,' cheerfully claims Ken. 'I shall see you in an hour,' he adds, packing his stuff before being escorted out of the room.

— 'Any chance to meet Roger today or tomorrow?' softly asks Jay.

— 'He will be here before noon. So late tonight, we can all spoon together in Vegas,' replies Juliana.

Coco laughs loudly and tells Juliana she can't wait to see her in her stretched Lycra bulge, spooning Jay.

— 'I didn't suck his cock! He lied to the world at the press conference. It was a good move for his safety but not so much a great one for my undercover mission here in Lincoln,' blinks Juliana to Coco.

— 'I'm sorry for the inconvenience,' Jay replies sheepishly.

— 'Breakfast is on its way! Please feel free to use the showers and restrooms!' indicates Juliana.

The breakfast is from Cooks Cafe, and Jay can't resist sending Ozzie a few teasing pictures. The pair had a California omelette and fresh veggie benedict. Juliana and her colleagues opted for the classic breakfast.

Ozzie calls Jay. He cries over the phone,

— 'Something ugly happened,' he says.

— 'Talk to me,' shouts Jay, leaving the table.

— 'Kora and Tia's mum died. She was executed at the medical trial.'

— 'By whom?' yells Jay.

— 'Ingrid shot her.'

— 'Are you sure?'

— 'She also executed Zoetje. It's on the CCTV. Six bullets to her face.'

— 'Where are Kora and Tia now?'

— 'On my screen, they're still at the scene.'

— 'Let me call them. Wait! Wait! Where is Ingrid now? Please tell me.'

— 'In Belgium. She crossed the border an hour ago. She's taken the diaries with her.'

— 'Fuck, fuck, fuck me dead!'

— 'Fuck what, Jay?'

— 'Coco's father lives in Belgium on the seaside.'

— 'I'll keep an eye on her. Please warn Kora and Tia.'

— 'Okay, I'll do it now.'

Jay turns to Coco and, without much diplomacy, shares the content of Ozzie's latest phone call. He invites her to call her Papa now and strongly suggests he seek refuge at the nearest police station.

— 'There's no time to waste,' he insists. 'As quick as he can. He might be Ingrid's next victim.'

Jay manages to talk to Kora, but not much has been said. Her silence doesn't feel healthy. In a desperate act to avoid a bloodbath in the Dutch capital, Jay calls Florian and suggests that Ludo should arrest the entire Haka army, including Kora and Tia, as a preventative measure until Ingrid is found. Jay hangs up as Florian is speechless.

With no time to lose, Jay's anger turns to Juliana. He blames her for what's happening in Amsterdam.

— 'All this shit, it's all your fault!' Jay tells Juliana.

— 'You killed six men, Jay! I didn't! Maybe you should think and accept your life choices before helping the world.'

— 'I had no choice.'

— 'Everyone has a choice; you played the hero. So, keep on playing!'

— 'You came to Lincoln to be a hero.'

— 'The reason I'm in Lincoln is none of your business. I'm sorry about your situation. I'm sorry for all the helpless people that'll die as part of your story, but if you don't open your eyes and face your reality, you'll be dead in no time.'

— 'All this because I outsourced my work, purchased a few parts for my car, and watched some porn.'

— 'You should look at the upside, Jay.'

— 'There is no upside!'

— 'Turn around and tell Coco she's not the best upside. Tell her she's not the most beautiful, charismatic woman you could've met.'

Coco intervenes and pushes her hand on Jay's mouth to

silence him. Her skinny body frame is now a strong wall in front of him. Her facial expression is full of fear. Juliana backs off and gives them space to let things settle down. Jay also steps back, returns to the hangar, and goes back into the plane. Coco follows, catching up with him, and invites him to sit. She's unsettled and can't hold her words any longer.

— 'I spoke to Papa. He's waiting for Ingrid. He's not scared and doesn't need assistance,' shares Coco.

— 'Are you serious? It can't be true! What is wrong with people?' replies a defeated Jay. 'I'm flabbergasted, I am! Coco, what's important to you? Do you want to proceed with all our plans or make our way back to Amsterdam?'

— 'I'm lost, Jay. I don't want any bad things to happen to Papa. He's my only family, and I love him. I do.'

— 'No rash or reckless decisions,' says Jay as he rubs his tired eyes. 'We've no control over the situation. We're puppets and not immortal,' he carefully adds.

— 'In my right, I'm immortal! Biologically immortal,' smiles Coco.

— 'Are we now in the Matrix? I don't have any red pills to appreciate and understand our life's illusions.'

— 'The present moment's intentions should always mirror the life we design and embody. I clear my heart on the go so that no harmful emotions can become illnesses or diseases.'

— 'This is how you manage to glow and shine all the time.'

— 'You're so sweet, Jay. You make me blush; it's all positive emotions. They'll be cherished within. I love you.'

— 'How do you clean your heart?'

— 'Mine happened by accident. I went to a few Kundalini

sessions to align and connect myself to myself. I remember clearly one of the sessions. The music started, and I felt some strong energy tickling through my fingers; my inner voice invited me to massage my whole body with it. I did, and it became an instant, loud, powerful orgasm that lasted for over half an hour. It was a true cosmic gift; it was not sexual but awareness in its simplest and purest form. Suddenly, my inner voice shouted, 'Clean your heart.' From that, I started smacking the timber floor as hard as I could. I felt my Kundalini energy trapped within my chest; I had difficulties breathing, and I was gasping for air. The session facilitator helped me embrace my powerful energy by touching the inner side of my ankles. I burst into tears. My inner pressure bubble pops. It feels good, very good indeed.

— 'I suspect mine needs a big scrub.'

— 'We all do. I made mine an instant ritual. As soon as I feel off about something, I turn myself into air. Nothing can stack, grab, or pull air. Air is my mantra for my emotional freedom. It works well for me.'

— 'Last night on the plane, you looked distressed and affected.'

— 'It was last night! Since then, I've cleaned my heart numerous times. I don't let things build up; I process on the go.'

— 'I am still furious at Juliana,' Jay cuts in.

— 'You should thank her for bringing your unresolved emotional issues to the surface for you to address and work through. She is just a messenger like Ingrid, Abigail, Sakura, your friend Ozzie and my Papa. We are all messengers to someone's unpleasant reality that needs to be addressed.'

— 'I do not understand how Juliana, as an example, is beneficial to me.'

— 'The sole or the soul purpose of anyone who enters our life, consciously or not, is to make us grow emotionally. See it as human interaction at its best.'

— 'You mean that all Amsterdam's events are designed to make me a better person. How can a bounty on my head help me?'

— 'I know, this is hard to believe when you hear this stuff for the first time. The answer is simple: clean your heart.'

— 'Can I clean my heart through kissing?'

— 'As much as you want, I am a good kisser.'

— 'Coco, I like your kisses and passionate way of kissing. Come closer, let me feel you!'

— 'Just a kiss; we have a funeral to attend soon.'

— 'Do we?'

— 'Is your heart cleared of this past?'

— 'Sadly, for me, it is not, and it is far from it,' confesses Jay.

— 'Once I read a book by an Australian author, I cannot remember the title. I keep a copy at hand inside my nightside table as a refresher when things go out of hand mentally and emotionally. The first chapter of the book is about expiry dates. Like tins of tomatoes on our pantry shelf — things, events, people, relationships, and so on — we have an expiry date. Nothing is permanent! The only constant is an inevitable change. We hold onto our past and whatever its version is because it defines our identity for ourselves and our imaginary place in human society. We crave the love of others through our projected or fake identity.'

— 'I am honest with you, Coco.'

— 'I know you are! I wouldn't be here otherwise. To come back to my meditative experiences, the biggest life lesson, apart from cleaning my heart, is that I, we, or everyone must be very specific with our intention or universal request. We only receive what we wish for — good, bad, and anything in the middle. In that session, I intended to understand how to experience biological immortality. The outcome is now an ongoing life practice on the run.'

— 'How can you — or can we — be specific with the sex shelter, the transfer of your business, the Haka army, the police commissioner, and everything else?' queries Jay.

An FBI representative enters the plane, interrupting the conversation abruptly and invites Coco and Jay back into the meeting room. Ken Dumbbells is back. Jay receives his divorce certificate, a blokish handshake, and some serious, fervid congratulations from Ken. Juliana is on her way to the funeral, where she will pose as Natalia's colleague while her team monitors for suspicious activities. The meeting room is now silent; the television set is the centre of attention. Natalia has no relatives. Only a handful of wishful community members have turned up to face the coldness of the Lincoln Memorial Cemetery. The mood is far from joyful. The bodycam captures handshakes, pats on the shoulder, and heartful hugs. The screen motion picture stops over Natalia's casket. It is a plain white box, as plain as it can be. A small bronze engraving reads,

— 'I wish you the best.'

Jay's tears cascade along his face before running down onto his shirt. Like in the cottage, Coco squeezes his right knee as a sign of support. It's Jay's turn to release his mucus in the softness of aloe vera-scented paper tissues.

Natalia has opted for cremation, and the guests are now invited to give their final goodbye to her. There are no blessings, sermons, or benedictions. The memorial is just a last get-together or a subtle invitation to reflect on life as a meaningful concept or a painful reality. Jay recognises his colleagues from the factory. It seems so long, and their familiar faces bring a little bit of sunshine to his nostrils' drying activity. Coco rests her head on his shoulder and enquires if he's okay.

No incidents or news reporters are reported. It is a simple, uneventful community event. As the television set is turned off, Ken and a few FBI officers offer their condolences to Jay.

— 'Sorry for your loss' is their repeated sentence.

Everyone is emotional, but Coco maintains a brave face. Ken is not waiting for Jay's tears to dry up as another round of papers circulates on the table. He explains the process and procedure for Natalia's will documentation. He also invites Jay to set up a new bank account online and revoke Judy's access to his old accounts. Jay's bank account balance has not improved since his New York World News Headquarters trip. Jay signs without questioning. Another round of 'sign here, sign there' and the will allocation is done. Ken will act as Jay's attorney until he's back from abroad. An envelope containing sets of keys slides across the table and lands in Jay's hand. Ken gives a quick summary of the content of

Natalia's will that has been transferred to Jay.

— 'A house and its content, two cars and her bank account balance and savings. It'll take a few days to complete everything, and I'm available when needed,' Ken concludes, pushing his business card across the table. When leaving, he highlights that Juliana has paid all expenditures.

Everyone is tired, and Coco retreats into the plane to nap while Jay seeks permission to sit outside the hangar. He needs some fresh air; it's sunny outside, and the cold air blesses him unconditionally. The scenery comprises aircraft of all sizes landing, taking off, and rolling across the runways. He resists contacting Ozzie and the Haka Girls. He prefers to save his peace.

Roger's voice interrupts his daydreaming.

— 'Can I join you?' the martial arts master and foster father queries.

Jay jumps out of his chair and hugs his visitor with great strength and joy.

— 'Happy to see you,' Jay rattles with joy.

— 'I won't be long; Juliana has given me instructions.'

— 'She's a control freak; please take a seat.'

— 'Yes, she's forcing us to relocate to California until your story settles in the Netherlands.'

— 'Judy will like that. She always wanted to live in California. How are the boys?'

— 'Mixed feelings. Good days and bad days. They'll grow out of it. You've been a great father to them. I'm not worried. Time heals everything!'

— 'Being abroad makes me realise your impact on my life

and your choice to accept me into your family. I am and will always be grateful for your generosity towards me.'

— 'I'd like to apologise for forcing you to marry Judy. It was my mistake, and I'm deeply sorry about it.'

— 'Don't be silly! I've no resentment towards you or anyone. Nothing has changed between the two of us.'

— 'I appreciate your words. It helps with the situation.'

— 'Let's catch up when I return from Europe.'

— 'I'm sorry, Jay, it won't happen!' says Roger without much diplomacy. 'I came here to say goodbye and to wish you good luck. You must understand that I need to protect my family. Nobody else will do it.'

— 'We are family!' presses Jay.

— 'We've arrived at the end of our relationship, Jay! It's painful, and I'm not at ease. I need to protect my loved ones. Lincoln is a big city with a village mentality.'

— 'This is brutal; you can't be serious!'

— 'Everything has a life span. Today, you and I are at a crossroads and going in different directions. You're a free man! Make the most of it!'

— 'Dad, you're not serious. Please tell me that you don't believe what you just said.'

— 'I'm sorry, Jay,' says Roger. 'It's so painful, I can't even look you in the eyes,' he adds, pinching the skin of his hand.

— 'You're the second person today who has told me everything has a life span. It's awful.'

— 'Hug me, boy! It's hard, Jay! Give me one fucking last hug, please!' begs Roger as he stands up.

Jay does the same. Both men hug as never before. It is

intense, painful, and truthful.

— 'I love you, son!' says Roger.

— 'I love you, Dad!' replies Jay.

— 'Enjoy your freedom, you deserve it. All your belongings that I've been able to save are with Juliana.'

— 'Roger, I'm unsure if I can live or experience my freedom without you. You've been so good to me. I owe you my life.'

— 'I love you, son. All the best, and be safe,' repeats Roger, hugging Jay one more time with great affection.

— 'I love you, Dad. You can change your mind at any time. I'll be there for you. Like you did for me.'

Roger makes his way out of the hangar, walking unusually slowly. His shoulders are down; his posture mirrors his inner sorrow and dilemma. Jay wishes he would turn back and change his mind, but it doesn't happen! Roger is escorted out of the building.

Jay sits back. The Nebraska sun is his best ally and the only comfort available. Juliana interrupts his contemplation and takes over the chair Roger has previously inhabited. She is dressed in a dramatic and glamorous all-black outfit. Her style resembles the South American widows pictured in the gangster movies. Her presence has some similarities to Coco's. She cannot be ignored; anyone would feel her presence.

— 'How did you go with Roger?' she inquires, knowing the outcome of their rushed catch-up.

— 'I've not much to say! I'm gutted! I'm ruined!' replies Jay with a bitter voice.

— 'I know the feeling!'

— 'What feeling?'

— 'You've been kicked out of the nest, Jay. I've been kicked out, too.'

— 'How do you begin to cope with it?'

— 'There are different levels of healing for different levels of anger, frustration, resentments and so on.'

— 'What was the reason for you to be kicked out of your nest?' insists Jay.

— 'My sexual orientation. One day, as a teenager, I dressed up as a girl—a hot one. Full makeup, lingerie, a sexy short skirt and top, and high heels. I remember it was around dinner time. My father called two or three times for me to join everyone at the dining table. The guy was a macho man with no patience. He came to my room to force me to comply with his order. Seeing me dressed as a crossdresser, his first reaction was a beat-up—a full-fist, hard beat-up, Mike Tyson style. My mum was next. She was blamed for giving birth to a girl with a penis. He gave me fifteen minutes to pack and go. I was in shock. I'd never been in a fight before. My body was soaring. I walked out of the house dressed like a punched princess, wobbling on my high heels. My mum tried to stop me; she barraged my path as best as she could and begged me to stay. Her request didn't go well with my father. He grabbed her by the back of her neck and slid her on the ground like a potato bag. She screamed! She screamed not just for herself but for my safety, too. I don't know how, but that day, at that moment, I found my fists. I found the mighty power of my fists. I freed her and unleashed my anger on my father. The beating he received was nothing compared to the one he'd given me a few minutes before. I had the upper hand; he begged me to stop numerous times. I didn't want to stop. I had no reason to stop. I pushed and kicked as hard as I could until there was only human pulp staining the entry porch.'

— 'Were you and your mum okay?' queries Jay.

— 'The ambulance and the police came. We were all covered in blood. My two younger sisters were frantic. They didn't understand how life could flip in a quarter of an hour. I undressed, took a shower and went with Mum to the hospital. She was ashamed. She always lived in the shadows of others, and now she's in the spotlight.'

— 'What happened next?' asks Jay, with a voice full of interest.

— 'The police didn't press any charges. It wasn't the first domestic violence incident that occurred under our roof. The neighbours dobbed my parents in a few times to the police. My sisters and I knew nothing about it; it was an eye-opener. We didn't know that my father was a wife-beater or a fucking weak bastard. That day, I left school and found a job to care for my mum and sisters. The salary was pure misery, and I had no skills; I was a useless sissy boy! My only talent was twerking my arse in front of my bedroom mirror, so being an erotic dancer was my only option!'

— 'What happened next?' asks Jay.

— 'When your mind is on something, it can't let go. I wanted to experience my sexuality at any cost. I found a weekend job in a nightclub. My mind was aroused at the prospect of getting fucked or fucking someone. At the club, I was surrounded by go-go girls who were getting extremely well paid to entertain the crowd; I asked to join them as a showgirl.'

— 'And?' impatiently queries Jay.

— 'I made more money on weekends than during the week. I received offers for private gigs and tons of sexual offers from my many clients. Tons of cash changed hands in no time! My mother and I no longer got along; she became resentful and bitter. She invited me to pack my gear and leave the house. The harshness of her words had the same intensity and impact as my father's punches. She couldn't accept the fact that a sex worker subsidised her existence.'

— 'Were you okay with her request?' queries Jay inquisitively.

— 'We did a deal. I moved out and went on with my life; I still support her and my sisters financially. Surprisingly, it works! There's always a man who wants to explore their sexual deviations. The first-timers are the best; they act like lovers. They like the guidance. They like the balance between submission and dominance. They don't fuck like rabbits. In and out in no time. I want them to have value for money. I want them to enjoy the full experience both ways. Receiving and giving is the right recipe for recurring business. The dangerous ones are the ones who want to control you or take advantage of you. These guys picked the wrong sissy slut. I know how to fight, and I learnt to blackmail any cockheads that try to outsmart me. Blackmail makes me rich in no time but takes away the pleasure of living. So, I migrated to the US.'

— 'How did you manage a gig with the FBI?' questions Jay.

— 'I managed to enter the country on a clean passport

and had enough money to enjoy life for thirty years without moving a finger—a big thank you to my sexual demeanour. I went back to school. I enrolled in a negotiating skills class. I was the best at it. I could turn the tables in any situation. In role-play, my opponents were left disheartened. I always won!'

— 'I'm not surprised!' reaffirms Jay.

— 'The teacher introduced me to a guy who was an expert in hostage negotiations. We met in a coffee shop next to a police station in New York. The meeting was a set-up to evaluate the end of my spectrum in hectic and impromptu negotiation scenarios. In short, he wanted to know how I can negotiate without any bullets being fired!'

— 'Keep going!' tells Jay.

— 'So, we were chatting when a guy entered the coffee shop, yelled some shit, requested the money from the cash register and took the waitress hostage. Most coffee shop patrons ran out to safety, whereas I stayed with two others. The gunman was of South American descent, and I started the hard conversation. He'd lost his job and needed to feed the kids. I asked to count how much money was inside the register. He did, and I asked how long his family would survive with so little money. Two days was his answer. I made a deal with him; I told him that I could take him to the bank and give him three months of freedom without getting a criminal record. I let him think. Having no answer, I invited him to put his gun down and to follow me to the bank. I walked out of the coffee shop.'

— 'Are you serious?' comments Jay.

— 'He was next to me in no time. He acted like a pet

with a gun in his pocket. We entered the bank; he gave me a childish warning. I went to the counter, withdrew the money, and asked him to put it in his wallet; when he did, to his mistake, I knocked him out hard and put the money back in my bank account.'

— 'You've got some serious boxing skills,' compliments Jay.

— 'Yes, I do. The guy I knocked down at the bank is now my boss, and that's how I entered the FBI.'

— 'Wow! That is an amazing story! I'm grateful that you shared it with me. I sincerely am. Thank you!' tells Jay. His voice is filled with appreciation.

— 'You're a good guy, Jay. It's time to enjoy yourself and life.'

— 'What's your suggestion?' asks Jay.

— 'I have no suggestions. You came to Lincoln many years ago to seek and find your freedom. You went around the world and returned to where it all started, where freedom was buried like treasure in your garden. You're free.'

— 'The Alchemist by Paulo Coelho pops into my mind when you mentioned treasure in my garden,' laughs Jay.

— 'I've read the book. Do you want me to call you 'Santiago'? Just learn to appreciate your newfound wealth.'

— 'Knowing Roger's generosity, I'm surprised by his decision. That's no gold!' says Jay with a voice full of sadness.

— 'Your foster brother, Lenny, is the reason. You're a better son. Lenny is probably resentful towards you.'

— 'How do you know that?' snaps Jay.

— 'I don't need to know. It's obvious! Roger is protecting you by excluding you from their circle.'

— 'Why do you relocate them to California?'

— 'Your boys—Lenny's boys, I should say—are easy targets to make you bleed. I don't want to take any risks. They're kids, and I was their age when my life turned around.'

— 'Thank you. I feel better now!'

— 'I've been forced to pull Roger aside at the factory and disclose my federal identity to organise today's meeting and their interstate relocation.'

Seeing Jay's interest, she changes the subject and, with an energetic voice, says,

— 'This is from Roger!'

She smiles when tendering the keys of Jay's Dodge Challenger.

— 'My baby is here!' smiles Jay.

— 'No! She's at the FBI salvage yard.'

— 'Do you want it? I'm happy to give it to you. That's my way to say thank you!'

— 'I'm not allowed to accept gifts.'

— 'That's a good weapon to pick up first-timers off the street,' tells Jay, a grin on his face.

— 'Mister Smart, I checked your Pornhub history. You watched a fair amount of gay porn during business hours. How many times did you masturbate while watching men in leotards? Did the two Asian gay boys in their green and pink spandex outfits rubbing their stiffened cock make you hard?'

— 'That's none of your business!' replies Jay with a shallow voice.

— 'Did you masturbate?'

— 'I was bored and scrolled my life away!'

Jay's body language is all over the place. Juliana's negotiation style is cutthroat.

— 'My view on men is that they're all gays to some degree. They vary on the gay scale from zero percent to the full-on 'Village People' fantasy personas type. It's just a matter of finding the right triggers to stimulate the opening of their back door,' convincingly tells Juliana with her subtle male South American accent.

— 'I'm not gay!' replies a panicked Jay.

— 'How many times did you milk your prostate while watching gay porn? It's the best feeling ever! All these nerve endings getting stimulated. All these stacked energies returning to your head that make you feel pleasurably dizzy and great.'

— 'Keep the car!' answers Jay in an attempt to diffuse their conversation.

— 'Maybe you need it more than I do, leotard boy!' laughs Juliana.

— 'Keep it before I change my mind!' Jay snaps.

— 'I didn't suck your cock in Vegas. You sucked mine while wearing my silky panties. The shape of your hard dick in the stretched fabric excited you madly.'

— 'I was upset and drunk!' claps back Jay.

— 'Your ego sent you drunk, and as a result, you fell unconscious while I had a great time. That's the price you pay for telling me to pack my plastic tits away!'

— 'Did you make me swallow your cum?' asks Jay with a dishevelled facial expression.

— 'What happened in Vegas, stays in Vegas!'

— 'Answer?' unleashes Jay.

— 'I'll tell Coco to buy you some bodysuits and finger your ass!'

— 'Are you blackmailing me?'

— 'Would you like to be on the front cover of every newspaper? That's blackmail!'

— 'Give me the key, please!'

— 'I should fuck your ass; it would've made better headlines.'

— 'Okay, I'm taking responsibility for my drinking, my anger, and my bad behaviour in Vegas, but I'm also taking responsibility for getting sexually assaulted.'

— 'That wasn't abuse! It was consensual, Captain!' laughs Juliana, massaging her breast.

— 'My days as Captain are over! Everything's sinking!' capitulates Jay.

Spotting Coco making her way towards them, Juliana cheerfully tells her,

— 'Good timing. We're falling in love here. He's flirting with me. I'm not sure I can resist any longer. His attitude makes me horny.'

Coco laughs and lands a sweet kiss on Jay's lips.

— 'I'm starving!' says Coco, changing the conversation. 'Any chance to have some fried chicken from Ozzie's family restaurant? Everyone is raving about it,' she adds.

— 'We can buy some on our way to Natalia's house. Take your luggage, we're going soon!' replies Juliana.

— 'Any news from Abigail?' queries Jay.

— 'None, her mobile is switched off, or she has no network,' replies Coco with a sad face.

— 'Let's check on Ozzie, Tia and Kora later. I need space

and a lot of it. It's been an eventful morning, and fried chicken sounds good,' comments Jay.

— 'Lea's chicken for everyone!' confirms Juliana.

The transfer from the hangar to Natalia's house is done with a removalist truck half full of Jay's belongings. There's no view on offer. The fried chicken was slid under the back roller door. It's just plain fried chicken—no flavourful sauces. As the hard-shell freight hull hops over Lincoln's potholes, Jay and Coco hold to its side railings, Jay grabbing a removalist rope and tying himself to Coco in one corner. He passes his hand behind her head to protect her from any wall banging. Coco's arms are responsible for keeping them tight in the corner. The pair exchange neck and lip kisses when the truck stops at the red lights. Giggles, laughter, and body rubbing fill the rest of the trip.

The truck reverses and reaches its final stop. The roller shutter opens to display Natalia's cottage garage door, which opens in synchronicity. Only one step out, and the pair are in another safe house.

Juliana turns the double garage into another debriefing ground. Coco and Jay aren't allowed outside except on the back veranda. They'll have the house for themselves if they comply with the order. The whole neighbourhood is under surveillance. The fridge has been filled with a few meals, and departure time is around sunrise the following day. Both agreed with the request. Juliana tenders her business card to Coco before leaving, and the garage door closes behind her in no time. The house is theirs.

— 'Welcome home!' says Jay.

— 'Did you come here before?' asks Coco, who clings to Jay's arm.

— 'No, never. I am just as intrigued.'

— 'Did you love her?' asks Coco, standing before Jay to see his answer.

— 'Yes, I was platonically in love with Natalia as a young adult. She was everything! She is the one that converted emotionally this boy into a man!'

— 'And now, do you still love her?'

— 'Love is not the right word. I am grateful for our time together and our shared learning experiences. My understanding and meaning of love have evolved since our paths crossed.'

— 'What do you mean?'

— 'We fell in love because we were outcasts. I can say the same for my friend Polka. We are a weird bunch; our awkwardness attracted us, and sadly, our awkwardness becomes normality at some point.'

The garage light turns off, leaving Jay and Coco in total darkness.

— 'Do not move. Let's be silent!' instructs Jay.

Silence is in the basement. Seconds become minutes— quietness and suspense at its best. Jay turns on the torch on his phone and takes two quiet steps towards the garage door. The light sensor picks up his movements, and the artificial light of God returns.

— 'I did not like that one bit!' Coco whispers.

Jay notices cars under protective covers and the illuminated staircase, inviting them to leave the basement's plainness for the luxury of the ground floor.

— 'I need to wee badly! Says Coco, crossing her legs.

— 'Let's explore our home and find you a bathroom,' invites Jay.

The staircase landing opens to a gorgeous Shaker and Quaker timber batten high ceiling space comprising a lounge, dining area, an open plan kitchen on the left and office and amenities on the right side. All the roller blinds are down, courtesy of the FBI. The natural light is provided by the vertical ventilation windows located at the ridge of the roof. It is now late afternoon; the entire space has a moody and soft atmosphere. The space is furnished with a subtle country minimalistic elegance. The cushions are neatly placed on the couch, and a bouquet of fresh-cut flowers dress the dining room table.

— 'It is probably Juliana's gift,' thinks Jay.

The fragrance and the colour bring joy and life to the empty dwelling.

Coco overtakes Jay, running for the bathroom. Jay continues discovering and thanks Natalia mentally whenever an unusual sensory experience blesses his fingers or eyes. He walks through the kitchen and opens the fridge to check out what is available for dinner. A bottle of French Champagne, a few cans of beer, lots of fresh local produce and a pack of ribs fill the fridge. He opens the drawers and cupboards. There are forks and knives, plates and glasses to serve an army. Natalia's items are still there; only Natalia is missing.

The butler pantry is as big as the kitchen. The shelves are filled with kitchen utensils, culinary robots, and hundreds of labelled jars, which are the testimony of hard and dedicated labour. Each container has a little label telling the novice which treasure awaits to be cherished.

Jay opens the patio doors to discover a barbecue and a garden swing. Numerous candles decorate the edge of the timber deck, clearly defining the limit of his freedom. A free America is only a few steps away.

The house's first floor has three bedrooms, two full-size bathrooms and a room with a brass plaque on its door. The sign reads,

— 'Jay's room.'

The door is closed. Jay decides to venture into his room. As the door opens, hundreds of well-wrapped presents are Natalia's love testimony towards him. Again, labels and cards of all sizes and colours await reading. Every possible celebration or life milestone has been carefully selected, packaged, and secretly cherished from prom night to a few days ago.

Jay's astonishment is interrupted by Coco running and apologising simultaneously. She hugs him and repeats,

— 'I am sorry! I have been curious, and it was none of my business.'

— 'What are you talking about? You can be as curious as I am! Look, I just found Ali Baba's cave,' laughs Jay.

— 'In the office, all shelves are filled with letters addressed to you. Every envelope has your name on it. There are hundreds, if not thousands, of letters addressed to you. None of them have a stamp.'

— 'All these are signs of a past that only existed in someone's head. It is strange and somehow challenging. I do not know what to say, so we have three options: open a letter, a present or a bottle of Champagne. The presents and the letters can wait, but you and I need to settle down, breathe the fresh air of Nebraska and have some serious quality time together.'

— 'I love you, Jay!' Coco says, rubbing Jay's chest under his shirt.

— 'We have some serious talking to do about our next move,' replies Jay, smiling.

He excuses himself to go to the bathroom. To have privacy, he walks downstairs and passes the office door. The light in the room is warm and inviting. A desk, a chair, and metres of filled shelves witness Jay's indecisiveness to satisfy his curiosity. Like Coco, the white opened envelope resting on the furniture top has his full attention. He slowly enters the room, grabs the letter, and heads to the bathroom. Sitting on the toilet, he reads Natalia's words.

Dear Jay, My Jay,

This is my last letter to you. The pen is not running out of ink; I'm running out of life. I want to celebrate you one more time. I am making my way to the airport to see you leaving. I hope that our arms will join one more time. Whatever happens, I am at peace. I have accepted my destiny and, most importantly, embraced ours. My body is hurting; I cannot find the strength to carry myself around any longer. I had a beautiful life with you and without you. My wish did not come true, but my heart and soul are filled with my endless love towards you.

More than ever, I love you!

Natalia

P.S. Please disperse my ashes around the flowers in your garden.

Jay folds the letter back into the envelope and meticulously places it on the windowsill. He grabs the toilet paper, dries his eyes, cleans his arse and, with a juvenile boy's voice, says,

— 'I'm sorry! I'm very sorry! I always loved you!'

Coco scavenges through the fridge.

— 'I'm starving!' she yells out to Jay.

Jay reunites with her in the kitchen, and for the first time, they prepare a meal together and do some basic house chores. Coco and Jay's phone messages and alerts ring in synchronicity. The message reads,

— 'Ingrid is dead! She has been shot. It is not us! Tia.'

Coco checks the Dutch news online, and Jay messages Ozzie to check his welfare and health.

— 'I'll call you later. I'm having dinner with Jiayi Jue, my new colleague. She's cute and crazy!' is Ozzie's reply.

Jay gives him a 'thumbs up' emoji.

The news is far from human; Ingrid shot dead her parents, husband and children before killing Tia and Kora's mother. Holland is in disbelief! The police force spokeswoman said that the investigation is ongoing. She invites the Dutch people not to speculate and strongly advises the press representatives to be respectful in their publications. The news keeps on rolling; Ingrid has also executed the three excluded members of the Haka Army. One of them is the daylight locksmith.

Jay calls Florian. He also declines the call and gives a short update via text message.

— 'In Belgium with Ludo!'

— 'If you have access to Ingrid's stuff, please keep an eye out for a GoPro camera. Ingrid took it away from the injured Dutch influencer. I want to know who tried to kill me the day we were forced to move out of the Hotel Lucius,' replies Jay.

— 'I'll seek clearance from Ludo.'

— 'The girl who opened the door to the gunman won't talk; she just signed for free rent in heaven,' adds Jay to the conversation while Coco sings cheerfully,

— 'Let's celebrate our existence, Champagne for you, Champagne for me?'

— 'Is one bottle enough, or should I ask the FBI for more?' comments Jay.

— 'I won't be able to give you a family; I can't have babies,' mumbles Coco.

— 'Where did this come from? Are you okay? Until now, I didn't have time to think of us having a family. I just lost mine today.'

— 'Did you see Roger today? How did you go?'

— 'Yes, he came, and lucky for you, you were asleep in the plane. Our life path came to an end this morning. This is not a first-world problem but a bloody painful one! Let's sit on the couch and discuss why two foster kids with no or little family can't have a family of their own?'

— 'I didn't think that way!'

— 'I told my story at the cottage when we met; now, I want to know you as much as I know myself. Cheers,' says Jay, smiling and lifting his glass.

Coco starts making herself cosy in Jay's arm.

— 'I was born and raised in Ukraine. My parents were from Kyiv. My mum was a factory worker in an automobile plant.

She worked night shifts to have extra money and benefits. My father was a corner shop owner, a drinker and a gambler. The earnings of a full trading day were lost in lousy poker hands. We had a room between the back of the shop and the hallway of the house, where he played with anyone who could entertain him and put a few coins on the table. My mum dropped me off at school in the morning; she slept during the day, prepared dinner and did the house chores before returning to the factory. That is as much as I saw her. Like all little girls, I wanted to be a ballet dancer, and my mum made it happen. After school and from an early age, I was the shopkeeper. Dad was either playing or drinking somewhere or bringing strange guys home. One night, there was a dispute about money he did not have. Their noise and commotion woke me up; I went down from my bedroom to check on him. As soon as I appeared in the room, a guy grabbed me by my pyjamas, forced his hand onto my bare chest, rubbed it and started pulling my tiny nipples. He told my father that I would pay his debts from now on. My father, having little lucidity, tried to intervene but was knocked down cold in the middle of the gambling room. The men left; I rushed to the kitchen, grabbed a cooking pot, filled it with cold water and threw it on my father's face. I screamed. I cried. I shook him madly. He gained back consciousness and warned me to keep quiet about what happened.

— 'That is our secret!' he added.

The following day, I could not look my mother in her eyes. I cried into her arms when she left me at the school gate. A few days later, the gamblers returned to collect their money;

they dragged me out of my bed in the middle of the night. They stripped me naked and forced me to perform oral sex on one of them while another one was on his knees, stretching my bum cheeks and licking my ass. The guy I sucked did not have an erection; It was all about showing his bravado to my father, who was restrained and begged for the horror to stop; the more he pleaded for them to abort their doings; the quicker my head was forcefully moved backwards and forwards. My hair was used as handles; I had no control over the situation or myself. My tears did not stop anything; only the test of sperm in my throat put an end to my oscillating motion. My father received a massive punch in the liver and collapsed to the floor. I screamed; I was hysterical. After that evening, the shop was closed nights and days. My father lied to my mum; he pretended to be sick. Whenever he and I made eye contact, he reminded me of our secret; I became fearful of him. The others forced their way into our house one evening; they grabbed me, stripped me naked, landed me on the gambling table, and fuck me as hard as they could. The cocks were hard and were moving hectically like pistons into a too-small cylinder chamber. The plastic tablecloth helped them to slide me at a faster pace and contributed to their pleasure and, unfortunately, to my pain. My body momentum was scary fast; They muffled my screams by pushing a towel in my mouth. It was painful! I could feel myself bleeding. My skin was burning, and having no power or strength, I kept focusing on the lampshade's light bulb and prayed for help. Surprisingly, my mum returned early that night; the factory had a power outage. She came to my rescue as she entered the room, but unfortunately, she finished next to me. As an unfortunate duo, we were raped in synchronicity as hard as they could. They flipped me on the edge of the table, fucked my ass, and forced me to look at my mum. A pillow also muffled her screams. She fought back and partially freed herself through kicks, punches, hand slaps, and dozens of uncoordinated movements. One of the attackers tried to force her to suck his manhood; she bit him as hard as she could. The guy yelled all sorts of profanities and begged his pack of friends to stop; his injury put an end to our torture. The men left and warned my father that his debt was still unpaid. The plastic tablecloth was a swimming pool filled with poop, blood, unwanted semen, spit, and urine that I could not control. My father was a puppet full of madness. He was jumping up and down, holding his head, and giving us lectures. My mother ignored him and grabbed me, running to the kitchen to clean herself and assess my injuries. An argument broke out between my parents; my mum screamed and slapped my father for his stupidity, and in return, he grabbed a cast iron frying pan and smacked her hard at the back of her head. She fell, hitting and displacing the stove top grates and collapsing like a heavy mass. Her eyes were upside down; she looked like a dead dog that had been run over by a car. She was bleeding heavily, and her legs and arms were twitching. Her face was not hers. She had that silly dead dog face and died next to me. I passed out. My father ran away, and I was found two days later by my ballet teacher. I was unconscious; my genitalia and my bottom were damaged, and I needed reconstruction. I spent a long year in a Kyiv hospital and was put up for adoption on the day of my ninth birthday. Through a charity organisation, a Belgian family adopted me. Papa had something to do with the organisation. He was fluent in Ukrainian and many other languages. We took the long bus trip from Kyiv to Brussels together. I stretched and danced all the ballet moves I knew at every stop. He complimented me and gave me tips on how to improve my posture and some of my choreographies. He told me he was a dancer but did not attend the national dance company. In Belgium, he drove me to my new family. We said goodbye. He left, and I felt instant sadness,' Coco cries profusely.

— 'Let me find some tissues and get you a glass of water!' says an emotional Jay, who, until now, did not want to interrupt his lover's horror story.

After blowing her nose and drying her eyes, Coco continues,

— 'Within fifteen minutes in my new family, I was beaten up by the lady and raped by her husband. They chained me naked to the leg of their kitchen table. In no time, I needed medical attention and another round of surgery. I received no food and no water. They took hundreds of photos of me; I begged them to stop. She beats me and beat me and beat me. I had black eyes and broken ribs. All kinds of sex toys were pushed beyond the limits of all my orifices. They were taking photo rolls after photo rolls. Like my mum, I kicked, punched and slammed them, but I was powerless, and as retribution for my resistance, he fucked me like a dog. The doorbell rang. Panic had the best of them. The doorbell did not stop ringing; knowing they were trapped or had no choice, she finally opened the door. It was Papa doing a routine inspection. Our eyes met, and before anyone could say a word, both were shot dead. He fired a gun through the pocket of his duffle coat. The gun did not make any noise. It only smelled terrible. Both looked like my mum, but they did not have silly eyes or faces that did not belong to them. They were swimming in their warm blood. Papa told me to trust him and that he was a doctor in a previous life. He took me back somewhere in Ostend and performed surgery on his kitchen bench.

— 'You mean your Papa is a surgeon?' queries Jay.

— 'Yes, and a great one. He doesn't want to talk about it. I made a pinky promise with him not to share what happened to me or us on that night.'

— 'What do you mean, a pinky promise?'

— 'For over nine months, he healed me, addressed my every need, and did his best to be home. He trained me to dance. He was often on the phone doing business with Ukraine and other Eastern countries. One day, when I was able to walk, urinate, defecate, jump and dance without pain, he told me that we were going back to Ukraine as he had two surprises for me.'

— 'What were the surprises?' Jay queries, trying to put a positive note on Coco's story.

— 'We did another long bus trip together, except I was nearly ten years old. We danced together at every bus stop and service station. Papa is an amazing dancer. In Kyiv, we moved into a small unit. The next morning, he asked me to sit at the kitchen table and to listen carefully. I did. He told me that through friends and colleagues, they'd manipulated my adoption papers. What happened in Belgium didn't look good for the charity agency, and to counteract this matter, he adopted me. I cried, laughed, thanked, hugged, and kissed his cheeks as much as I could. I danced for him. Next were good and bad news. He enrolled me in a private ballet school that prepares dancers for national and international ballet companies. That was the good news! The bad news was that it was a boarding school, and we could only see each other during the school holidays and summer breaks. To be sure I wasn't missing out on anything, he pre-paid for my full tuition.'

— 'I understand now you were meeting in Ostend for the summer break,' comments Jay.

— 'I accepted the boarding school on the condition that he calls me every night to wish me a good night. He did and still sometimes does.'

— 'Papa and I have something in common.'

— 'What is it?' asks Coco while drying her eyes and cleaning her nose.

— 'We've killed people for a good cause. I'm unsure if we can be proud of it, but we did it!'

— 'Could you promise me never to share our conversation with anyone? I don't want anything to happen to Papa for forging my adoption papers. I owe him my life.'

— 'I promise! Pinky promise, if you want. When did you learn that you can't have children?'

— 'When recovering at Papa's place in Belgium, he told

me that I'd be able to have normal sex later on in life, that lubrication wouldn't be a problem, but having babies wouldn't happen!'

— 'How, as a nine-year-old girl, did you react to the news?'

— 'At the time, I was simply content to be alive. As a nine-year-old girl, my head didn't think about sex or the future. My thoughts were with my mother. I still remember her face that didn't belong to her, bleeding on the kitchen floor.'

— 'Did you manage to heal this part of your life?'

— 'Yes, I did through dancing and training. All practice sessions or performances are dedicated to my mother. When I endured pain, setbacks or physical and mental breakdowns, it was nothing compared to the pain of losing her. She blesses me every day.'

— 'I love you, Coco! I'll call you every night to wish you a good night's sleep.'

— 'In my dreams, I can see my mother with Papa as her husband. They are my heroes!'

— 'That's a beautiful thought!'

— 'What else do you want to know?'

— 'Why an ice cream business?'

— 'After the bad guys came to my place and touched my breast. My father closed the shop for a good hour to buy my silence and took me to an ice cream parlour on the other side of town. For the first time in his life, he held my hand! As young as I was, I knew something was wrong. Sadly, I played along.'

— 'I don't understand!'

— 'I should've told my mum about getting touched by a

stranger. She would probably still be alive.'

— 'You mean that a single ice cream was the catalyst of your business.'

— 'Yes, the place was buzzing, the atmosphere was relaxed and friendly, and anyone eating ice cream didn't look worried. Everyone took the time to enjoy their gelato. Enjoying an ice cream is a time-stopper. Time stops when we indulge ourselves. That memory drove me to join the ice cream industry.'

— 'If you let go of your business, do you have another time-stopper to make you live in the present?'

— 'Yes, I have something in mind,' replies Coco with an energetic smile.

— 'What is it? Please share it with me!'

— 'I want to be the next Sabine Schmitz. I want to be a professional touring car driver. I want to lap the Nürburgring in record time.'

— 'Where is the Burgring? How do you say that?'

— 'Nürburgring. It's a circuit in Germany where my Panamera and I passed our lonely weekend trying to achieve faster lap time after faster lap time.'

— 'I noticed that you like to push all the gears, all the way, to the red line when you drive!'

— 'I'll take you there! It's great fun and good discipline!'

— 'I'm looking forward to it. Are we following our plans or returning to Amsterdam?' queries Jay.

— 'I want to marry you, Jay! So, if you agree, let's go to Las Vegas, and from there, we can decide what's best for us as husband and wife,' replies Coco.

— 'The marriage office bureau opens at 8.00 a.m. Do you want a wedding in a chapel or a civil ceremony? If we get there early enough, we can have our validated wedding certificate on the same day.'

— 'You did your research!'

— 'Google has all the answers. I don't have rings.'

— 'Maybe you should remove the one you're wearing first.'

— 'Give me two seconds; I'm going to check if there are any tools in the garage,' says Jay while leaving the living room.

A few seconds later, Coco can hear Jay yelling and screaming.

— 'Come, come down, quick!'

Coco rushed down the stairs to find Jay in awe in front of a fully spec dark grey Dodge Challenger.

— 'How did we miss that?' cheerfully says Jay.

— 'Maybe it was in the rear mirror of my Panamera,' says Coco, quickly running back up the stairs, knowing well that Jay won't take any shit on his American pride.

— 'Where are the keys? Please give me the keys; I want to hear this baby roaring. Please, Natalia, where did you hide the keys?' yells Jay.

Unfortunately for Jay, no keys can be found. He sat for minutes in front of his gift, moving from time to time to enjoy a different angle of his new pride and joy.

It's Coco's turn to call out for Jay. The online news portrays Ingrid as Amsterdam's most vicious underworld executioner and a debt collector for different mafia syndicates. The source of this information is currently undisclosed but supported by a few Polaroid photos.

— 'Who takes all these photos?' queries Coco.

Jay ignores her question and can't resist calling Ozzie. As the call goes unanswered, he texts,

— 'Did you manage to track the diaries?'

— 'I can't talk right now. Yes, I have a location. They are in Ostend. The approximate address is Kapucijnenstraat 58. The location is also an entry of a public carpark.'

Jay replies,

— 'Keep this information confidential until my return.'

— 'Cutie and I will keep an eye on it. Thumbs up!' replies Ozzie.

Jay's curiosity is on all alerts. In his mind, he needs to play the detective and find out where Papa's address is. Only Coco can answer this question, so he decides to wait until tomorrow, when life choices will be made as husband and wife.

— 'Any updates on Abigail?' asks Jay.

— 'Nothing at all,' replies Coco.

— 'Let me text Juliana and have some food. We need to be in good shape for our wedding tomorrow! Oh shit, I still need to remove my wedding ring,' says Jay, going back to the garage.

Juliana's answer blows Jay away. He can't contain his excitement.

— 'Coco, Coco!' he screams while running back to the ground floor. 'Finally, there is good news!' he says, out of breath. 'The President of the Cervical Spine Research Society has examined Abigail today. He ran some tests, MRIs and scans. He concluded that the loss of feelings in her lower body was caused by reactive behaviour in her nervous system. There are no fractures or major spine structural damage. She enrolled in an experimental spine surgeon training program based on the doctor's recommendation. Her bleeding is also linked to her nervous system dysfunction.'

— 'That is fantastic! That is great news!' cheers up Coco.

— 'Imagine if she could walk again!' says Jay with wild open eyes.

— 'That would be great! So, she won't need to ride your cock again to go to the bathroom, Mr Jay! I heard her joyful teasing!'

— 'I was helping!'

— 'I need to go to the bathroom, take me there. I want to ride you!'

— 'Abigail didn't wear any panties; I want to check your beautiful arse in the mirror!'

— 'You'll have plenty of my arse on your face. For safety reasons in our anal intercourse, my bottom will only accept your kinky tongue or a slow-moving and well-lubricated finger. Nothing bigger, as I don't need or want a third rectum reconstruction. On the other hand, if you fancy some anal sex, I'll be a willing participant.'

— 'Did Juliana blackmail me?'

— 'What do you mean?'

— 'Nothing! Our conversation in the hangar went badly out of hand.'

— 'Okay, drop me to the bathroom, Mr Blackmail! Let me ride you! I want to feel my husband-to-be,' Coco says while flicking her underwear in Jay's face.

— 'Let me have a shower first!' begs Jay.

After a few minutes, Coco joins her future husband in the

bathroom. She has a grin on her face and is ready to have some fun. Under the shower head, she rubs her tummy on Jay's belly. It doesn't take long for Jay's penis to get excited; she plays along but can't contain herself and bursts into laughter.

— 'You look suspicious! Are you looking to play a trick on me?' queries Jay.

Coco can't find her words. She laughs, holding onto Jay. He doesn't understand, but after a few deep breaths, Coco manages to get a half-sentence out.

— 'You like men in leotards rubbing their cocks together!'

— 'Juliana, fucking bitch! What else did she say?'

— 'What happened in Vegas stays in Vegas!'

— 'Did she blackmail me?'

— 'No, she didn't! I asked her!' answers Coco while bursting into more laughter.

Jay is upset; his resentment towards Juliana deflates his penis. He dries himself and leaves the bathroom. Coco laughs loudly at the scene and repeats,

— 'I can't breathe! It's too much!'

To put aside his frustration, Jay cuts his wedding ring and puts what's left of it on Natalia's office desk.

Coco joins him and cuddles him.

— 'Let's cheer up, let's open some of your presents.'

Jay offers a piggyback to Coco and enters the treasure trove.

— 'Help me! I'm not a present person!' he says.

— 'Get used to it! You must receive as much as you give. Life is an equilibrium; a healthy life is.'

— 'Talking of equilibrium, I listened to your story, Juliana's story, Abigail's, and Tia and Kora's too, and I'm happy that somewhere in the world, there are people who are living without trauma or at least not the ones we've got or experienced.'

— 'Cleaning our hearts on the go is vital to the equilibrium. It restores the balance in the everyday chaos!'

— 'Roger said to enjoy my freedom! I don't feel free at all. When you mentioned embodying the life I desire or cleaning my heart, I don't get it; if I do, I won't know where to start.'

— 'The first step is to silence the mind and to give back some power to your body. The aim is to free up the emotional content within our cells and deeper.'

— 'How do you do it?'

— 'Lie down on the floor, close your eyes, open your arms, open your hands; the only activity allowed for your mind is to scan your entire body, from head to toes, for cellular memories that need to be shifted or recycled. Your system will purge itself automatically. The more you practise, the more you are freeing yourself!'

— 'That's all!'

— 'Life is simple; we make it hard! Lie down, and I'll do the present opening. I'll tell you the content of each wrapping and see how you react to them without losing focus on your body!'

— 'I'm ready,' says Jay, lying on the floor with his arms open and palms directed to the sky.

— 'A lovely hand-knitted jumper, a vintage copy of Muscle Car magazine, three pairs of comfy socks, a Mopar five-hundred-dollar voucher, a pair of jeans, a beautiful pair of hiking boots, a three-year-old calendar full of girls in micro bikini rubbing their assets on car bonnets, another knitted jumper, a set of overdue Red Hot Chili Peppers concert tickets, American muscle car memorabilia, a Dodge Challenger set of keys.'

Jay jumps out of his relaxation and says,

— 'Show me!'

Coco can't stop laughing,

— 'There are no keys! You failed the test! You were supposed to focus on yourself.'

— 'I'm exhausted but felt my body for the first time. It was tingling!'

— 'I'm also exhausted! Do you want to continue? I think that you should do it before our wedding ceremony. So, the past won't consume you!'

— 'I'm done. I'm thankful for Natalia's gesture. She was and is a beautiful lady, and unfortunately, the universe didn't roll its dice in our favour. Seeing the content of this house, I feel proud that someone dedicated their life to worshipping me. I'm sad that the same person didn't let go and write a different life story for herself. If she did, we wouldn't be here tonight, but most likely, she would have a family of her own and be alive today. My stupidity breaks my heart, and I'll never be able to bring Natalia back here to enjoy her destiny.'

— 'Please lie down again, close your eyes, open your arms and hands, observe your body's inner language regarding what you just said, and let your body do the cleaning. Your head won't. Good night, Jay! I love you!'

Coco leaves the room and can instantly hear Jay sobbing profusely. She falls asleep on the couch; she doesn't want to sleep in Natalia's energy.

Chapter eleven

Kapucijnenstraat

Jay did not leave the room and was awakened by Juliana's instructions to move on. It is 5:30 a.m. Coco and Jay shower, dry and clothe themselves, tidy up the kitchen, and in no time ride the street of Lincoln inside the back of a Pantech truck. Their bodies are bumping through the streets of Lincoln.

'Good morning!' is shared in synchronicity! They smile at each other. Jay again puts his hand behind Coco's head, and morning kisses are exchanged. Her gingery fragrance hooks Jay's attention.

Back in the hangar, Juliana is on fire, giving another round of instructions,

— I applied online for a marriage licence in Vegas on your behalf. Once landed, an FBI crew will take you to the Clark County Marriage Licence Bureau to collect your licence, and a civil ceremony is organised at two o'clock after lunch at the County Clerk's office. Your breakfast will be served on the plane, and lunch and dinner will be provided at a safe location. You must leave American soil before six o'clock in the morning tomorrow. We need to know your next destination as soon as possible as we need to confirm your private jet booking.

— 'How do you know about our wedding plans?' queries Coco.

— 'Walls have ears. Is it part of the procedure? Thank God you were asleep early last night,' tells Juliana.

— 'To answer your questions, it'll be done after our wedding as a husband-and-wife decision,' says Coco softly.

— 'It is no news to me! I heard it last night too!' replies Juliana with a bitchy attitude before addressing Coco, 'Would you like me to organise a wedding dress, shoes, floral arrangement and a suit for Jay?'

— 'No, thank you. I prefer our wedding to be as simple as possible. No frills!' answers Coco.

— 'What about you, Jay?' presses Juliana.

— 'No-frills is good, but my dirty laundry needs to be addressed!' answers Jay.

— 'No sissy boy leotard or bodysuit?' teases Juliana.

— 'The joke stops here,' interrupts Coco with a voice and a posture that Jay had not experienced before.

Coco has had enough of Juliana's diminishing attitude and bullying personality. Before Juliana could answer, she bolds her following sentence with a firmer voice,

— 'As a wedding gift, Jay'll receive his fair share of whatever he wants to wear. I've no problem with my husband-to-be watching gay porn! On the other hand, I'd like to thank you for your help and protection.'

— 'I did not mean' replies Juliana before being interrupted again by Coco's stance,

— 'No one means, we all laugh before someone gets hurt. We're looking forward to having you as a close friend. If you're interested in our offer, please put your controlling and blackmailing personality aside.'

— 'You want me as a friend?' a stunned Juliana questions.

— 'Not only as a friend! I appreciate your quality. You've organised our stay here meticulously and went out of your way to make it like clockwork. I appreciate your passion, pride, and ethical attitude.'

— 'I'm touched! No one's ever complimented me on anything except when I fuck them! Sorry, I'm a little bit emotional now. That's no good for my makeup,' a humble Juliana answers.

— 'You've skills, presence, a great-looking body, and a glowing face. Have you ever considered working for a private company? You can triple, if not quadruple, your income for just being yourself.'

— 'How do I do that?'

— 'That's simple! If you listened to our conversation last night, you know by now that cleaning your heart is the first step, and secondly, call me! I always have a job for talented people. You're better than I am!'

— 'Better at what?'

— 'Selling ice cream to Eskimos!' Coco smiles as she tenders her business card.

— 'Are you serious?' a shaky Juliana replies.

— 'The American market is humongous, and together, you can achieve the perfect American dream! Enough, for now—Vegas is waiting! Are we good to go?'

— 'Yes, yes! You take care, we'll be in touch!' mumbles Juliana.

Jay is surprised; he's just discovered another side of Coco. The glamorous, glowing beauty is not just a soft, pretty face. She can hide her iron fist very well inside her velvet glove. Her firmness is couched and channelled through her respectful, feminine gentleness.

The trip to Vegas is filled with online duties, from answering emails to keeping updated with all the latest Dutch news. Something brews in Jay's head; he can't come to terms with the fact that Paul Van Looke booked the lockers, and their contents are now in Ostend. A dark thought about Papa crosses his mind; if the guy killed two paedophiles to save Coco's life, is he linked to the content of the diaries? And if he is, why is Coco, his protégé, on the execution list? As he doesn't want to ruin his wedding day, he pushes aside his wild conspiracy theories, texts Ozzie, and asks him to secure and process the video footage of the locker place as far back in time as he can. He wants to know with great certitude when Van Looke secured the diaries and the child pornographic materials.

Jay is so deep in his thoughts as he watches the clouds through the plane windows that he doesn't notice Coco has had a change of clothes. She stands tall next to him, waiting for his tick of approval. Her no-frills wedding is symbolised with a white silk spaghetti strap slip dress, a pair of white mid-heels and a white pearl three-piece jewellery set. Her hairdo is perfect for ballerina standards. Her red-manicured fingers and toenails match the captivating colour of her lipstick. The dress moulds her body to perfection, especially the protruding and defined geometry of her sculpted pelvic bones and the curvature of her small breasts. As she can't wait any longer for Jay to notice her, she rubs herself gently against his shoulder. As he turns around, he smiles and glides his hands on the softness of the white silk.

— 'It's your turn to dress up!' Coco says, pointing towards the back of the plane.

— 'Did you buy me an outfit?' says Jay with great astonishment.

— 'It's waiting for you on the bed!'

Jay stands up like a steel spring. He smiles and makes his way to the improvised change room. A few minutes later, he appears, matching Coco's grace and elegance. He radiates and takes a few pictures of Coco and himself. Both are getting extremely excited. The pilot alerts them to be ready for landing.

Like in Lincoln, their plane terminates its journey in a hangar, and the representatives of the FBI are ready for action. A convoy of black cars with heavy dark tinted windows is parked inside the shelter. The transfer is done in no time, and thirty minutes later, Coco and Jay have crossed the city, and its architectural merit only appears as grey ghostly silhouettes. They are escorted inside the Las Vegas marriage licence bureau, and as per Coco's predictions, they jump the queue. The venue has been cleared out of any other wedding aspirants. Four bodyguards block their visual surroundings. For security measures, their protectors push them as close as possible to the service counter. There is no chance for Coco and Jay to appreciate the flamboyant reddish copper texture of the terrazzo floor or the honey colour of the maple wooden wall panelling. Juliana's homework is predictable; everything is synchronised to perfection. Coco and Jay confirm their identity; the duty officer drums his computer keyboard at lightning speed. The final 'Enter' key sends the invisible data to the printer, inviting Coco and Jay to a wedding commitment ceremony. All fees have been pre-paid. The certificate reaches Coco's hand through the counter glass opening. The Dutch fugitives smile and kiss each other. The Clark County Clerk's officer gives them two thumbs up as a gesture of good luck and goodbye. Coco and Jay are hushed away in their government-owned limousine. This move is not going as planned; some wedding certificate applicants pushed outside the venue are now scrambling with the FBI forces to get a glimpse of the protected couple. One man screams,

— 'It's Jay Smith! He's the 'Clown of Amsterdam'! He's the guy on TV!'

Coco and Jay are invited to proceed to move quickly.

The man shouts again,

— 'Fuck this wedding, come here, little prick, the bounty's mine! I'll fuck your wife to have that money!'

Jay surprises the FBI representatives and, in no time, with a swift move, grabs the man's testicles and unleashes,

— 'To fuck my wife, you need a big fat dick! I don't think that you've been blessed on that front — all talk, no balls, little bitch!'

Jay has no intention of letting go. He has the same type of posture and energy that he displayed when he killed the intruder at the council chamber in Holland. The guy begs him to let it go and becomes the centre of laughter and humiliation. The tension escalates, the FBI intervenes and gives a warning, and a set of handcuffs joins the party. The man finishes his parade face down on the ground. His movements are restricted, and the social media content inflames in a heartbeat. The world knows the 'Clown of Amsterdam' is getting married in Vegas!

Back in the car, a local FBI agent asks the couple-to-be if they'd like a little more celebration for their wedding day.

— 'For safety reasons, your pre-wedding lunch is scheduled in your jet. The catering is organised. My colleagues and I assessed the risks of taking you somewhere slightly more romantic outside the main strip. Is it something that you would consider?'

Coco is the first to answer,

— 'No, thank you. Thank you for offering. It's lovely of you!'

— 'Let's stick to Juliana's plan! Our wedding is our priority for now! I don't want to fight with another idiot!' comments Jay.

In the hangar, Love Paradise Sushi's catering service melts Coco and Jay's hearts with a sublime tempura combination bento box and their signature Las Vegas sushi mixes. Bite after bite, tastes and textures are enjoyed; the pair complements the discovered pleasures and the forcefulness of the wasabi with strange noises.

Ozzie interrupts their munching with a silly text message that reads,

— 'Check the meme of yourself in Vegas! It's hilarious!'

Jay replies

— 'It was only the pre-wedding warm-up! Another hour and Coco and I will be married.'

— 'Send me some pictures!'

— 'I'll do! Just thinking crazy here, could you retrace Ingrid's last trip to Belgium? Are you able to tap into the Belgian camera network? I want to know if she was executed or committed suicide.'

— 'Cutie and I are on it.'

— 'How is Cutie? I'm looking forward to meeting her.'

— 'She is the one! I want to propose to her!'

— 'What are you waiting for? Today is a wonderful day! We can share the date!'

— 'Give me two seconds, let me ask her; she's next to me.'

Jay's phone rings — it's Ozzie! As the video call transfers, Ozzie and Cutie emerge, laughing, cheering, and yelling. Cutie accepted the proposal. Both are over the moon; they are glowing. Ozzie is right; Jiayi is a cutie. Jay shares the screen with Coco. Everyone is excited and emotional. Ozzie terminates the call by saying they want to share their first kiss in privacy.

Jay texts him,

— 'Go for it, little fucker! You've been punching well

above your weight!'

Seeing Jay going down the melancholic road, Coco holds his hands.

— 'He's a good kid! I'm grateful to have him as a friend and family!' says Jay with glistening eyes.

Coco smiles and invites him for a cuddle. Their bodies become one, their hands glide on each other, and meaningful kisses are exchanged.

— 'Are you naked under your dress?' queries Jay as he can't feel any underwear lines.

— 'Yes, I am. It is my wedding, and I did not want Pippa Middleton to come and steal the show with her glamourous derriere.'

— 'Who is Pippa?

— 'A smart woman!'

— 'Just like you! I like your sharp mind as much as I like the way your nipples stand atop your delightful breasts. I also like how you turned the tables with Juliana. You did it without diminishing anyone.'

— 'Thinking of you in a leotard excites me! Throughout my ballerina career, I had my fair share of male dancers parading their anatomy in their dancewear. I always secretly like how their rip cages, bums, chests, bellies, and genitals turn them into graceful erotic performers. You have everything to fulfil my fantasies. My clitoris cannot wait to rub against the soft fabric of your moulded, hard cock. It will make you cum!'

— 'I cannot wait to titillate your body either! Your words make me horny; I am hard; feel my erection.'

— 'I am aroused and wet just thinking of our oncoming

naughty games. I cannot wait to suck and lick your nipples through the fabric like you did to me.'

— 'Feel them! They are electric!' says Jay while undoing his shirt buttons.

— 'Sorry, Jay! We do not have time for a quick one! We need to go! We cannot be late!'

— 'I have a special request to ask before our wedding?'

— 'Oh! Last minute special request! What is it?' asks Coco with a surprised look.

— 'After our wedding, can I wear your name? Can I be 'Jay Carajuca'?'

— 'This is the best wedding present ever! It is so sweet and so thoughtful! I love you, Jay! I sincerely love you! Let me marry 'Mr Carajuca-to-be',' says Coco, kissing and hugging her lover with great affection.

330 S 3rd St, Las Vegas, is the Clark County Civil Marriage Office. The internet did its job, and the world knows about it. The press representatives and bystanders are in numbers. The FBI agents are not intimidated; they make their way through the crowd, protecting Coco and Jay to the best of their abilities. The lobby is secured, and within no time, the level 6 ceremony room is in sight. The paperwork changes hands, and after some control and identity verification, Coco and Jay are invited to enter the civil chapel, which is simply an all-white wall, white ceiling tiles, and grey carpet office fit-out. Only a floral arch backdrop softens the room's atmosphere and creates an artificial, easy-going, no-frills wedding mood. The deputy marriage commissioner introduces herself as 'Jana' and asks if they have any preferences for their vows.

Coco and Jay look at each other and hold hands. Surprised by Jana's request, their body language takes over their awkwardness, and they do some 'I do not know' shrugging.

Having no answer, Jana asks,

— 'What are you trying to achieve through this union?'

— 'Be there for Jay, whatever the weather!' says Coco, a glowing smile on her face.

— 'That is beautiful!' comments Jana, 'and for you, Jay, what is the symbolism behind this union?' presses Jana.

— 'Be Coco's sun whatever the weather!' Jay replies softly and clearly.

— 'Let's proceed!' declares Jana. 'Dean is your witness. Come in front of the lectern.'

Coco interrupts and asks if one of the FBI representatives can take some photos. She unlocks her iPhone and passes it to one of her assigned bodyguards. Jay does the same!

The camera's flashes embrace Jana's words; Coco and Jay are declared husband and wife. They kiss. Coco dries Jay's pearly eyes.

Jana congratulates them with a firm handshake. The paperwork follows. Coco and Jay review their photos. They are thrilled with their 'no frills' wedding. The FBI's express service secures Coco and Jay's wedding certificate.

In the street, a circus of news reporters and curious bystanders waits with great impatience. As soon as the newlywed's silhouette embraces the Clark County ground floor entry lobby, the camera flashes erupt with no mercy. The FBI agents give strict instructions to Coco and Jay. Their words are,

— 'We walk as one, head down, back to the car, no silly business!'

Both agreed. Jay tells the officers' leader to invite the journalists and photographers for a press conference tomorrow in the early afternoon.

Coco interrupts,

— 'We are leaving at six.'

Jay, a grin on his face, replies,

— 'It will be a pre-recorded message to have a time advantage wherever we decide to go!'

The officer faces the media outlets outside the Clark County lobby. The message is received with mixed reactions. He does not care and ensures his forces secure a clear path of egress for the newlyweds. From the lobby entry door to the car, a strong police line waits for Coco and Jay to be shuffled to safety. The newlyweds' walk of fame is received with mixed reactions ranging from wishful words to verbal abuse directed towards the pair and most probably to test Jay's temper. Hundreds of camera lights highlight a Nevadan sunny afternoon. The convoy speeds off like in a movie. Most of the Las Vegas roads are closed off, and the city is barely acknowledged due to the darkness of the luxury sedan-tinted windows. Jay and Coco cuddle on the leather backseat while returning to the hangar.

Coco noticed that she received a message from her Papa on her cell phone,

— 'Congratulations! Let's celebrate when you get back. Nice photos!'

Coco replies,

— 'Thank you, Papa. Jay and I are looking forward to catch up with you soon.'

She shows the Dutch written message to Jay, who tries to pronounce the sentence mimicking Amsterdam's accent by emphasising the letter 'R' in every word; he notices that the message was sent before they exited the Clark County wedding venue. The photos Papa refers to are not from the Paparazzi or the big World Wide Web thrashers. They are from Coco's phone. This is a mystery that he prefers to keep quiet about.

— 'Is Papa in Vegas?' self-questions Jay.

This thought alone keeps him on the edge, knowing now that the frail man has killed two child molesters to protect his ballet dancer protégé. Jay asks Coco to share Papa's contact details so he can expand his new family to a third member. She does, and Jay quietly forwards the information to Ozzie for him to add to his surveillance system.

Juliana calls the newlyweds, congratulating them and has a friendship present for the new couple. They will spend their nuptial night in another aircraft hangar.

The FBI organises the transfer to a Cheyenne Air storage facility. The hangar is in darkness. Only the illuminated exit lights give a hint of its dimensions. Jay and Coco are speechless when hundreds of dimmed garden lantern lights illuminate a rose petal path that guides them towards a glamping teepee tent erected close to the hangar's massive scissor lift door. The teepee comes alive; rugs, carpets, and animal skins cover the ground, and a sofa and a dining table are outside the tent. A large-sized bed with white satin sheets will comfort the couple for their nuptial night. A paper note indicates that the amenities are located on the opposite end of the building.

The sound of a handbell interrupts their fairy tale discovery. It comes from the opposite side of the hangar, where a food and drink tray waits to be collected. A collection of flickering candles dance inside their glass holders, providing a romantic and charismatic mood.

Jay is eager to have answers to some of his internal questions. He knows he must pace himself to receive valuable information for his inner jigsaw puzzle.

He collects the tray and invites Coco for a drink and some nibbles. They cuddle and kiss with great passion. Their hands and lips are the main actors of their foreplay. Coco slides down her shoulder straps, and her wedding dress falls off. She invites Jay to massage her entire body. While maintaining their kissing activities, his arms and hands are stretched as far as they can reach on Coco's body. He lightly touches her nipples one at a time and rubs her muscular belly with the back of his hand. He draws big and small circles around her belly button and pubic area as he ventures towards her clitoris with a soft and light backwards and forwards motion. Coco's heart pumps faster, and the rhythm of her breathing entertains it. Jay's hands move down to her inner thighs and return towards her face, hair, and skull, which embraces a light-pressure massage. Coco grabs and plays with her breasts with great vigour, her eyes rolling backwards. Their waists move in motion. Jay's hands now trail down her spine, one vertebra at a time. He traces little circle after little circle until he reaches the curvature of her bottom. He ventures towards her anus, where he applies numerous times some gentle stimulating pressure. Coco's hands are now divided between her nipples and redirecting Jay's hand towards her vagina. She selects the fingers that will rub her G-spot. Jay notices that the inner skin of her pleasure hole is abundantly lubricated. Motion, pressure, 'stop' and 'go' interactions bring Coco's feet to perform some ballerina's pointe, her legs naturally moving apart as she lowers her body, forming an inverted 'U' shape muscular bridge. Jay follows her movement and rests on his knees. His fingers adjust the pulsing to Coco's motion as the orgasmic epiphany builds its momentum. Coco's grand plie pointe positions sculpt her muscle mass; every part of her athletic body is visually well-defined. She stretches and massages her arm to the sky. While maintaining the perfect position, she climaxes loudly when Jay ventures his tongue around and within her smooth and tasty labia; through heavy body spasms, loud noises and deep breaths, she holds her posture and begs Jay not to stop. Her hands press Jay's head against her clitoris as hard as she can before her body strength finally gives up. Jay's face is wet, and his cock's pre-ejaculation lubricant has already stained his underwear. While Coco undoes his shirt and sucks at his nipples, Jay removes his pants and underwear. Coco invites Jay to lie down on the animal skin and offers him a reverse cowgirl. Her fingers secure Jay's nipples, and part of their motion, she stretches them as far as she can. Jay's balls cannot hold their content anymore; it is his turn to beg for more as he ejaculates loudly. Coco slides out and places her filled pussy quickly on Jay's mouth to transfer his warm load back to him, and in the process, Coco's anus drums Jay's third eyes, and at every bounce, Jay visually cannot ignore her Papa's craftsmanship.

Coco is the first one to reach the food trolley. She serves herself a glass of sparkling water and offers one to Jay.

— 'I am hungry,' she says.

— 'Me too,' replies Jay.

— 'Steamed dim sims and dumplings, they look yummy!'

— 'Let's move the trolley next to the bed so we can eat naked!'

Jay lies on the bed and places a few drops of hot red chilli oil sauce on his tummy for Coco to enjoy. He cannot move, or the white bed sheet will be exotically stained. Coco laughs, pretends to ignore him, and eats her fair share without assistance.

— 'Come on, Coco, that is not fair play!' says Jay.

— 'It is so delicious; You are missing out on a good feed. Oh, sorry, do you want me to dip my dumpling in your belly button? says Coco with a strong Dutch accent while giggling madly.

— 'Sorry for being creative!' tells Jay.

— 'My naked man wants to be creative,' teases Coco, gently hovering slowly and sensually over Jay. She sucks the red condiment off Jay's navel and invites him to sit on the edge of the bed. With a smile on her face, she displays outstanding chopstick skills. In a deviant Nyotaimori style, the dumplings now travel from the bamboo tray to Jay's mouth via her stretched-open vagina lips, where she rolls and lubricates them slowly. Jay enjoys the service so much that he cannot resist stroking his manhood. Coco invites him to cum as she waits with a set of two Siu Mai next to his penis. In no time, Jay's white cream glazes the Chinese meatballs shared between the pair as a salty homemade delicatessen. A loud burp comes out of Coco's mouth, and the meal finishes with crazy laughs and another round of 'I cannot breathe!' statement from Coco.

Next, the pair locks themselves inside the bathroom cubicle, ready to shower. Coco cleans the toilet seat, sits, and urinates. Except for Abigail on the plane, Jay has never had a partner who freely releases themselves in front of him. Seeing Jay's awkwardness, Coco invites him to do the same while she waits for him to join her for a shower.

— 'I am sorry, I need privacy,' says Jay.

— 'Privacy for what?' teases Coco, sensing his awkwardness.

— 'I cannot do it in front of you.'

— 'We have only each other to take care of ourselves. In our older years, I will clean your bottom, and I hope you will be there for me. Everybody poops! Why do you need to hide?'

— 'Not today! We can make it a goal for later, but it is a 'No' for now! I am not taking a shit in front of you. I am sorry!'

— 'Let's be clear here: if a day I need to take care of you and I need to clean you, there will be no drama!'

— 'I promise. I need to poo, please!'

— 'What is the difference between you poking your tongue in my butt hole and me seeing you sitting there doing your job?'

— 'The red chilli sauce is the difference; I had too much of it!' says Jay as he capitulates, sits and defecates in front of Coco, hiding his head in his hands. His pride is ashamed when a noisy fart echoes in the room. Coco laughs at the scene. She cannot hold back, becomes hysterical, kneels down and slaps the vanity benchtop as part of her enjoyment and release mechanism. As always, she begs for more air.

Back in the hangar, Coco diffuses the atmosphere, serving Jay a drink and telling him that he has experienced his freedom like never before. Jay is silent; he slowly sips his drink. Having no answer, Coco breaks the ice.

— 'What are we doing now?'

— 'I need to change my residential address at some stage,' replies Jay, 'Natalia's address is the easy option for now, and when it is done, I can change my name to 'Carajuca'.'

— 'What are your thoughts on the ice cream business and Hotel L'Europa? Zoetje and Ingrid are out of the picture, Abigail is away, and Tia and Kora are mourning their mother. It is just you and me!'

— 'We need to consider your Papa too, what is your plan for him? He is getting old, and someone at some stage needs to clean his bottom, too. Where do you want to live?'

— 'Papa is in Ostend only a few days a week; he is still active and travels around Europe frequently. I never thought about him being dependent on me.'

— 'To help us, to help me, as I am unfamiliar with the European geography, could we tag all addresses on Google Maps? So, we can evaluate the travel time and best place to enjoy ourselves.'

— 'Where do you want to start?'

— 'I saved Natalia's house in Lincoln, the safe house at the Police Station in Amsterdam, Hotel Lucius, which is prepaid for another two months. For you, I added Hotel L'Europa. What else do you want to add?'

— 'The barge, the cottage in Egmond aan den Hoef, my house in Ostend, and Papa's one, across the road.'

— 'I need help with the spelling. The Dutch language and I are not friends.'

Coco sits next to Jay and browses through Google Street View.

— ''56 is my house, which, as you can see, needs renovation. Papa's house is across the main road on Van Iseghemlaam.'

Another screenshot is saved on Jay's phone.

— 'Van Olderborghweg, Egmond aan den Hoef is the cottage. Sorry, I cannot find the street number. Look how beautiful the street looks. In Spring, the colour of the tulip fields melts your heart. It is so unreal, especially when the morning mist and the sunrise frame the flowers.'

— 'We can visit it on our return,' replies Jay, a gentle smile on his face. 'The daytime pictures are more impressive than the dark driveway I am used to.'

— 'I always wanted to have long walks in the tulip fields. I cannot wait to hold your hand while splashing paddles in our gumboots,' says Coco, leaning on Jay's shoulder.

— 'Perhaps we should share our time between the cottage and the barge. Both are peaceful environments, and we can always escape to Ostend, Nebraska or anywhere else when we feel like it. What is the travel distance between the centre of Amsterdam and the cottage? What is the address where the barge is anchored?'

— '51 Amstel across the road from the HartMuseum' types Coco on his phone keyboard.

— 'Amsterdam looks better at night,' comments Jay. 'It is more romantic! I enjoyed our late-night bicycle ride. It was magical!'

'If you like romanticism, we should go to Kyiv. I will be delighted to show you around.'

— 'Show me where you lived and danced in Kyiv.'

Jay's mobile phone changes hands again, and Coco types 'Volodymyrska St, 51/53, Kyiv, Ukraine, 01034.'

— 'Papa's unit is just opposite to the National Opera of Ukraine,' she comments.

— 'What about your parent's shop?' asks Jay as he saves all information on his device.

— 'There is nothing to see, Jay! I never went back. I do not know what happened to our belongings, especially my mum's ones. As a little girl, she showed me her wedding dress and promised to give it to me for my wedding day! Today, on my wedding day, I have nothing—not her, not the dress,' says Coco in a deflated little girl's voice.

— 'I am sorry! My curiosity got the best of me. It is the first time since we met that we have taken time to get to know each other under the surface. I had no intention to offend you or to be hurtful!' Jay says, rubbing gently Coco's back.

The apologetic gesture is not well received.

— 'I am okay!' says Coco, leaving and making her way

towards the bathroom with pearly eyes.

Jay gives her some space but cannot resist texting Ozzie all the addresses and screenshots to learn more about each property's ownership. He wants to know why the diaries are hidden at Coco's place in Ostend.

Ozzie is quick to answer. His reply reads,

— 'This is Cutie's forteit; she will be delighted to help you. We traced Ingrid's final moments across the border, and there were two cars with Dutch number plates at the crime scene. One is the green Bentley we picked in Abigail's footage, and the second is a white Audi A7. Sadly, its registration numbers were blurry and could not be read on our screens.'

— 'Great job! Please send me the footage. I have a press conference soon,' replies Jay with great excitement.

— 'Cutie would like to know how much cash you are ready to spend to get the info.'

— 'Be the judge; you know our financial limitation,' answers Jay.

A 'thumbs up' emoji concludes the exchange.

Another bell resonates through the warehouse; fruits, desserts, tea, and coffee await their collection. As Jay makes his way towards the trolley, Coco enters back the hangar and races him. She wins and runs mad with her treasure on wheels inside the warehouse. Jay chases her to secure his share of sweetness. Laughter joins their game as she takes sharp turns to avoid his physical barrage; g-force-induced pastries, cups, and saucers are invited to experience instant gravity and crash loudly on the concrete floor. The game and the waves of laughter stop immediately.

— 'Kintsugi is the only way the tea set can find its way back to the trolley,' says Coco.

— 'What is Kintsugi?' queries Jay.

— 'Kintsugi is a Japanese art of repairing broken pottery by highlighting the repair with urushi lacquer that is dusted or mixed with powdered gold.'

— 'Sakura left us too early; she could give us a craft lesson.'

— 'I think that she is too busy mending herself.'

— 'She is not alone; when we mend ourselves, there is no gold.'

— 'Invisible, individual or collective, stitches keep the world together,' replies Coco in a slightly high-pitched voice.

— 'What keeps your world together?'

— 'You, you are my world!' tells Coco with extraordinary assertion.

— 'How do you see ourselves evolving as a couple or individuals?'

— 'Since you entered my life, I acknowledge quietly my ignorance and naivety in so many areas of my life. Ingrid is the epitome of it. I trust and trusted unquestioningly.'

— 'Ingrid was a trained poker player. She knew how to manipulate or have the upper hand on anyone.'

— 'We all roll the dice of life. I rolled mine badly and with a blindfold on. Consequently, my business suffers, the shelter is in jeopardy, and Zoetje and my friend's mother are no longer with us.'

— 'You are too harsh with yourself!' comments Jay, inviting Coco onto the couch.

— 'I introduced Ingrid to the group, and now I suspect

she joined us to make me or us all fail. Her, or someone else's agenda is unfolding in my head.'

— 'Could you elaborate on that?'

— 'I do not know; it is a big mess! I try to comprehend what went wrong or out of hand. I can only say that things went backwards after she joined us. I suspect that she contributed to having us on the hit list. Even if she did, I cannot grasp the fact that she is on it, too. Things do not add up. Was she a debt collector for the mafia as reported in the press?'

— 'She did not commit suicide; Paul Van Looke executed her. Ozzie retrieved the crime scene footage; Van Looke did not act alone. He had an associate or an accomplice that has not been identified yet.'

— 'Did she work for Paul Van Looke? If so, why did she kill her children and family? Did Zoetje know something compromising about her? If so, why did she not surrender to the authorities and ask for protection.'

— 'Maybe, and this is speculation, she failed to stop you from acquiring Hotel L'Europa. And maybe, and this is even more speculation, Paul Van Looke wanted to slaughter her family, so she did it herself to avoid additional suffering for her loved ones.'

— 'Are you the guy who disrupted her plans to make us fall?'

— 'That is a possibility. Ozzie must take credit for all recovered evidence and the evidence to come.'

— 'Thinking back, she did not offer any assistance to Abigail. Did she consciously protect Van Looke?'

— 'Maybe he was her boss! The future will tell us!'

— 'Without you tracking back Kora and Tia, we would

have failed to secure the money and be dead by now.'

— 'Talking aloud here, is the money I stole from the bad guys belonging to Paul Van Looke?

— 'Holy fuck! Shouts Coco. 'That is winning the lottery in a war game!'

— 'Again, this is all speculation; Zoetje was probably killed because she knew everything and everyone that works in the red-light district. Losing fifty million euros in plain daylight feeds the rumour mill very quickly. Equivalent to the Haka Army, the Red-light district power brokers have a well-trained army, and we do not know who is in charge and what their strategy is. Let's not forget that Zoetje was also Amsterdam's mayor's vocal public enemy.'

— 'For most of the representatives of the Dutch society, Zoetje had immense powerplay. Maybe too much for some people; She was an outstanding woman with a beautiful heart.'

— 'My speculation about the Haka Girls is that Ingrid targets their mum, not Tia and Kora, for only one reason.'

— 'Which is?'

— 'She knew that by killing their mum, the girls would seek hard-blooded vengeance. This is the only way Ingrid could seek some form of idealistic revenge for killing her loved ones.'

— 'We should warn the girls to stay under the radar.'

— 'We will after the broadcast at my press conference tomorrow. I do not want to risk my plans against Van Looke.'

— 'Are you going for Paul Van Looke?'

— 'Yes, and for his associates.'

— 'I do not want you to die, Jay.'

— 'Kora, Tia, Abigail and yourself are still on the hit list. I am not good with funerals!'

— 'As mentioned before, I have amended my will. Like Natalia's, you are the sole beneficiary!'

— 'I do not want another room full of presents. I only want to be with you. So, when we return to Amsterdam, you must stay at the police station safe house with me.'

— 'I will, but first I need to check on Papa and introduce you as my husband.'

— 'Could we fly to Ostend and hire a rental car to drive back to Amsterdam? Does the city of Ostend have an airstrip?'

— 'Detective Poirot, no more lawnmower user manual for you. You should write fiction novels; I like how your imaginative mind works.'

— 'Who is Poirot?'

— 'A brilliant mind just like you!'

— 'I just want to keep us alive.'

— 'Do I need to buy Hotel L'Europa after all? If Paul Van Looke is out of action, his threats and sabotage will disappear, and at some stage, the business will flourish again.'

— 'The same logic applies to your ice cream production facility; it will bounce back.'

— 'We can go back to Amsterdam, wait and see the outcome of Paul Van Looke's arrest.'

— 'What are we doing with the bank check?'

— 'You will need to cash it up.'

— 'Are we going to the Dutch Antilles to finalise the business transfer? if so, my press conference strategy needs to be amended.'

— 'I prefer to return to Amsterdam. I want to be with Kora and Tia.'

— 'On our way to Lincoln, I offered Abigail the position of CEO of the ice cream business. I could not see myself acting in that role. She accepted the offer.'

— 'Did you ask her before or after you saw her Irish moon in the bathroom mirror?' says Coco, laughing out loud.

— 'I simply offered some assistance and did not know my offer would be rewarded with unexpected perks and bonuses.'

— 'I love you, Jay. I feel accomplished! Abigail is a good choice; I have faith in her. What can go wrong? I hope my naivety will not bite me back.'

— 'Let's reassess her choice when she gives us an update on her wellbeing. Let's hope a miracle happens!'

Coco informs Juliana that they plan to leave Las Vegas as soon as possible to go to Ostend airport. She also requests a rental car upon arrival. Coco informs Papa of their plans and books a table for lunch at Caruso.

The flight activities were shared between Jay's presentation for his media release, Coco's yoga stretches and ballet postures, light refreshments and catching up on some much-needed sleep. Ozzie helps Jay to schedule his pre-recorded press conference. Jay informs Florian of his strategy and lets him decide whether to notify the Dutch commissioner. Florian is thankful for the heads up and invites Jay not to proceed with a press conference but instead to let him deal with the scoop through a special edition of his newspaper. Florian reiterates that Paul Van Looke's mother has substantial power and plenty of political connections, and Amsterdam is still in shock with the mayor's forced resignation. Jay accepts the offer as Florian has secured his safety on Dutch soil. Jay then informs Ozzie of the strategy change and agrees to email all evidence to Florian. Ozzie then invites Jay to check his email. Cutie has been digging critical information through the dark web, and the true bombshell is that all properties located in Ostend, Kyiv and the cottage on the Dutch seaside are owned by Paul Van Looke. Jay is shocked and asks Ozzie to keep this information confidential again, as Coco is at risk. Jay also invites Cutie and him to browse Paul Van Looke's luxury car dealership website to secure any information and phone numbers that could help locate the next most wanted person in the Netherlands. A 'thumbs up' emoji from Ozzie concludes their exchange.

Jay and Coco are forced to take a detour to the city of Brugge to pick up their rental car. Jay is in awe as he travels through the city. The medieval settlement, made of Gothic architecture, which had defined the commercial metropolis of the North for centuries, retains its appeal for new visitors. Having no spare time, Brugge is left behind in favour of an Ostend comeback.

Caruso's front window is as attractive as ever. The pastry chef's art is on display, inviting anyone to consume its indulgence. Like the first time, Papa and Coco's locked eye contact is out of this world. Both smile and hug each other. Coco receives her father's blessing; Jay receives a floppy handshake. As a response, he passes his arm around Coco's waist with tremendous sensuality. Coco's saviour notices and dismisses the move when he drags his protégé with great elegance to the front of the main pastry counter. The well-dressed puppet and the glowing ballerina dance and swirl while selecting their pastries. Their hips, legs, chests, shoulders and fingers extend in synchronicity. Jay feels sorry for Papa for missing out on his ballet dance career; he can see the passion, elegance, time and effort invested in an activity that cannot even be a hobby now. Papa has no audience except Coco. Seeing the grace and precision in his movements, Jay acknowledges that the old man has everything a dancer requires to succeed on a big stage; he cannot ignore the love and affection he displays towards Coco while they move in unison.

Back at the table, Gaston enquires about the wedding ceremony and the plans for the newlyweds. Jay avoids the question and replies,

— 'Coco was concerned about your welfare when we were abroad, especially when Ingrid passed the Belgian border.'

Coco nods her head as a sign of approval. By the same subtility, Papa diverts the question and answers,

— 'Coco spoke about Ingrid and some of the other members of her circle of friends. Coco's call surprised me when she invited me to seek refuge in a police station. I am an old man; I am not James Bond.'

Gaston's tone and facial expressions have changed slightly to bitterness, and Jay feels his hostility.

— 'I love you, Papa! Maybe I am overprotective,' says Coco while rubbing Gaston's forearm.

— 'You were part of our conversation in Vegas. Coco spoke highly of you, and as part of us deciding where to move or to live, we questioned how you would like to be assisted or cared for in the years to come. Please do not be offended by the question; I am aware of your high level of fitness and mental sharpness; we want to include you in our plans if you wish to do so,' tells Jay.

Papa snaps and rudely tells Coco in Dutch that both should mind their business. Coco is shocked; it is the first time in her life that Papa raises his voice on her. Tears pearl and roll down her face as she tries to amend the situation. There is little that can be done to reshape the moment; Papa has had enough and walks out of Caruso with the body language of an angry man. Jay runs after him and tries his best to overturn the situation, but things become worse when Jay says,

— 'We are family, we do care for you!'

— 'We are not family, Jay. We have got nothing in common!' bites back Gaston.

— 'Yes, we have!'

— 'Please explain!'

— 'I cannot tell you; I promised Coco not to repeat it.'

— 'Everywhere you go, trouble comes with you!'

— 'You went through big troubles to save Coco and give her the true gift of life,' tells Jay with an affirmative voice.

Seeing things getting out of hand, Coco rejoins Gaston and Jay in the middle of the street and, in no time, receives another angry blast. Papa clarifies that she broke his trust by sharing their stories and does not want to see Jay again!

Gaston jumps in his car and drives off like an eighteen-year-old hooligan. Coco is more than distressed and bursts into tears and cries in Jay's arms.

— 'It is a nightmare! It is all my fault! I should have kept it quiet,' childishly says Coco.

— 'It is not your fault; I broke our promise not to repeat how Papa saved you from the child molesters in Belgium. I am the only one to blame. Let's try to salvage the situation before it escalates.'

— 'I do not know if he wants to see me again!' cries Coco.

— 'Let's drive to his place. You can talk from your heart to win his love back. I will wait outside; my heart is with you.'

Coco and Jay arrive in proximity to Papa's house. As Jay parks the car, Coco points her index finger on the windshield and says,

— 'He parks his car at my place, wait for me here. He will cross the road soon.'

Coco runs like a child, and Jay observes her as she meets her Papa. His gestures are not loaded with grace and perfection, and his anger has gotten the best of him; Jay knows the feeling well. Coco puts her hands together as signs of prayer, drops to her knees, and begs for her pardon while holding her father's leg. Jay cries, seeing his wife desperate to save her childhood golden hero.

Papa bends down over her, puts his hands under her armpits, and lifts her back on her feet. He pulls a tissue out of his pocket and dries her eyes with great care. Seeing his protégé's distress, he squeezes her against his chest. More tears flow for Coco as Gaston invites her to cross the road. He holds her hand like he probably did a few years back during the summer breaks. Both enter Papa's home.

Jay walks the neighbourhood, waiting for Coco to emerge

back, hopefully with a smile on her face. He is now at the corner street where Coco and Gaston met a few seconds ago. On his left side, Jay is surprised by the beauty of Papa's well-crafted art nouveau house. The masterpiece was erected in 1904 and survived two bloody long wars. The façade and its articulations and detailing are the work of the Malines-born architect Jacques de Weerdt. On his right side, Coco's dilapidated dwelling is a post-war constructed building in which the front door has been bricked up, and the only access to the building is through the brown garage roller door. A 'no parking' sign keeps the kerb access free all day. The symmetrical façade starts and stretches three levels above the ground floor; its geometry is made of rows of horizontal tiles and narrow vertical windows spanning across the curved features of the façade. Meanwhile, her real estate is squeezed between a high-rise apartment building and the abandoned remains of a four-storey art deco hotel poorly defined by its blue-painted chipped perimeter walls, curved balconies, and a leaking roof. Jay imagines how he could reach the hotel's upper floor and cut an opening in the partition wall to access Coco's building. He is eager to solve the location of the missing diaries. As mentioned by Ozzie, a public carpark entry is only metres away from the building.

Jay makes his way back to the rental car; he does not want anyone to become suspicious of his outing. He informs Ozzie and Florian of his location and his plan to return to Amsterdam by mid-afternoon. Florian is the first to answer. His message reads,

— 'The scoop is ready to be published, and Ludo wants

you back in the safe house as soon as you are back in the country. Based on the evidence, Paul Van Looke is no joke. A police operation has been activated.'

Jay thanks Florian for the update and calls Ozzie, as he wants his protégé to be safe, too. The larrikin quickly answers the call; he cannot wait to see his pals back. The data digging on Paul Van Looke reveals multiple identities in different countries. Cutie checked middle names and date of birth to narrow down her search. The conversation is cut short as Coco returns to the car. Over three hours had passed. She looks sad; her trademark glow is missing.

— How did you go?' queries Jay.

— 'It was tough! He is upset! He thinks that you see or judge him as a lifeless man who should be in a nursing home.'

— 'Anything else?'

— 'I answered his question about our wedding ceremony in Las Vegas. Our magical night in a plane hangar. I clarified the fact that we both shared our life stories and informed you that I cannot have babies. I told him that it was a simple harmless prenuptial honesty gift.'

— 'Is he still angry? At you or me?'

— 'I explained our current situation and our decisions while overseas!'

— 'How much did you share? What does he know?' presses Jay.

'Papa has been a good business advisor for me through the years. I have little secrets for him. I asked him his opinion on the ice cream business, Hotel L'Europa acquisition, my life after ballet, my debut as a competitive race car driver and so on!'

— 'That is all!'

— 'Yes, that is it! Why? You sound and look confronting.'

— 'Did you mention the press release or Paul Van Looke?'

— 'Yes, I did! I told him we must return to Amsterdam as you have some business commitments. I did not want to tell him we must seek refuge to guarantee our safety!'

— 'I am serious here, Coco. Did you mention Paul Van Looke's involvement in the Ingrid assassination, the CCTV lockers, or Abigail's bashing?'

— 'Yes, I did! I am proud of you and wanted Papa to appreciate you as you are, the real you and not his perception of you. I wanted Papa to see and appreciate the good man that you are!'

— 'That is nice of you! Thank you, but we have a bigger problem! Please put your seatbelt on; we need to go!

— 'What is the problem, Jay?' queries Coco with a distressed voice.

While rolling the car slowly, Jay points his finger towards Papa's house and Coco's building and tells her with a broken voice,

— 'The owner of both buildings is Paul Van Looke and the stolen diaries are here in Ostend.'

— 'What are you talking about?'

— 'I am sorry, Coco, the same applies to the cottage. Everything belongs to Van Looke.'

— 'What makes you say that?' replies Coco with the same voice intonation that she used with Juliana.

— 'Ingrid collected the diaries from the police station

before her shooting spree and crossed the Belgian border with them. She did not know that Ozzie hid geotag locators in them. The day of her assassination, Van Looke or his associate moved them from the crime scene to the building that is not yours!'

— 'Papa has nothing to do with that!'

— 'I never said that your Papa has something to do with Paul Van Looke, Ingrid or the diaries. Maybe he is renting the house or sold it to Van Looke without your knowledge. I do not know! Or, he has been manipulated without him knowing. I am puzzled and surprised as much as you are. I try extremely hard to figure out how all these people are entangled together!'

— 'Let me call Papa, I need to know!'

— 'For everyone's safety, please do not call anyone! We need to stay under the radar. Florian will release the scoop anytime soon, and we can become shooting targets in no time. I did a rough estimation of how many people lost their lives just by adding all the diaries together. It is over a thousand people, from underage kids to adults.'

— 'Papa has no blood on his hands. He is a good man!'

— 'Coco, your Papa killed two people. Did he come back to save you because he had remorse? Did he drop you at the slaughterhouse in the first place?

— 'Are you mad? How can you think that way about the only person who loved me, cared for me and did his utmost to give me a decent life.'

— 'Why did he perform secret surgeries and hide you for months? He could have sought assistance from the police like a normal person would.'

— 'Are you fucking mad? What is going on?' yells Coco.

— 'This is speculation, Coco! None of what I said is true. I want to open your eyes to alternative scenarios and want you to consider if your naivety has been secretly abused.'

— 'When did you know about the property ownership?'

— 'While we were in the US. Ozzie told me.'

— 'Why did you keep it for yourself? Did I also trust you blindly? Am I that naive?'

Jay stops the car on the side of the highway and calmly reassures Coco.

— 'No, you are not naive. I have been truthful to you since we met. I did not want to damage or distract us from our speedy wedding. I wanted a romantic celebration for you, me and, most importantly, us. I love you, but I fear Paul Van Looke is aware of our return to Amsterdam, and our names are on his hit list. I do not know if Papa has something to do with all that. I hope not. Seeing you crying, praying, and begging for his love today was painful to watch, and I am well aware that if Papa rejects you at some point in his life, you will not be able to cope with it. He is your universe, and I sincerely hope from the bottom of my heart that everything stays that way.'

— 'Is Papa in danger?'

— 'In all honesty, I do not know! Paul Van Looke is in Amsterdam, and if he is on the move, Ozzie will let us know. His profile is locked on the CCTV camera. As a loving and caring partner, could you promise me to follow the safety procedures as directed by the police commissioner?'

— 'As my loving and caring husband, will you do the same?'

— 'Yes, I will! When we arrive in Amsterdam, can we quickly stop at the barge? As a precautionary measure, I want to pick up a gun or two and some ammunition. While I do this, you return the rental car to the nearest drop-off station, book an Uber or taxi, transfer our luggage, and return safely to the police station headquarters. I have no superpowers! I am just a country boy who opened a bad can of worms. The only upside of my story is I fell in love with a beautiful ballerina, and my deepest wish is to have a long and happy life together.'

— 'Is there anything else that I need to know? What else are you hiding from me?

— 'Nothing! You know as much as I do! Are you okay to proceed to safety? If so, please guide me to the barge.'

The rest of the trip is quiet. Coco cries profusely. She is in disbelief and shocked by Jay's ugly speculations.

When they arrive in Amsterdam, Jay parks within walking distance of the barge, and Coco takes over the steering wheel. They kiss without passion, and Jay reassures his wife that everything will be okay soon. He begs her to reach safety as quickly as possible. She agrees.

Jay walks along the canal and realises how wide the waterway is. Seeing it during daylight is a different experience. As he approaches the vessel, he realises that a curtain edge flaps in the wind and that a sliding window is slightly open. He tries to remember if he or Coco left it open the night they came here to hide things away from Ingrid. His heartbeat increases substantially as he climbs the narrow concourse of the boat. A pair of scissors is in front of the entry door; he is one hundred percent sure these items were not there a few days ago, and as a safe move, he walks around the barge to inspect the boat. On the canal side, another window is also slightly open. His heartbeat is now in overdrive. He yells things through the window gap and hides as low as possible on the concourse as a safety measure. Nothing happens. He repeats the yelling two or three times. The wind on the canal muffles his call. Having no answer, he slides slowly and, with great care, opens the window to have enough space to pass his head through it. As he does, terror gains his whole body and mind. Four hand grenades inserted in glassware are placed on the edge of the table. Their safety pins are removed. A fishing line links them to either the entry door or the boat windows. Jay realises that he has no room for error and that his only option is to retrieve and seek assistance as quickly as possible!

Jay leaves the boat and calls Coco. She does not answer. Her Papa called her a few seconds earlier. Jay leaves voicemail after voicemail and text message after text message to warn her of the danger. He runs as quickly as he can to reach the police headquarters.

Coco acknowledges the message, but the conversation with Papa is her priority. As the online scoop is live, Papa enquires if she has yet returned to Amsterdam. Through heavy tears, Coco tells Gaston that she is driving the car back to 'Avis Autoverhuur' and wants to refuel the vehicle beforehand. Papa queries why is she crying; Coco decides to press the hard button and asks Papa why his and her property are under Paul Van Looke's name. Papa laughs aloud and replies,

— 'To minimise my taxes'

— 'Why Paul Van Looke, why him?' she asks

— 'My financial planner introduced me to different parties, and Paul Van Looke was one of them. Who told you this information?' queries Gaston.

— 'Jay did. He fished for information on Van Looke and disclosed it to me when we left Ostend. I do not know what to think. I am dizzy; my head is spinning!'

— 'I can hear your blinker. Where are you?'

— 'At the Total petrol station on Tweede van der Helststraat. I am scared, Papa.'

— 'Please stop the car, take a break and do some breathing exercises. It will not be long before all this arrives to an end.'

— 'I am stopped. Let me find a tissue!'

— 'Take your time, breathe in and out. What car do you drive?'

— 'A white rental BMW.'

— 'That is good. Relax yourself, dry your eyes and breathe deeply. Forget about what Jay said. It is not important! Let me put you on hold for a few seconds; I have another call to answer.'

Seconds become minutes, and when Papa joins back the conversation, Coco cannot hold her words,

— 'Paul Van Looke is not a good man. He is a woman-basher, he deals with child pornography, and he killed Ingrid.'

— 'That is okay! He is not the worst one of all! Jay and yourself should mind your business; if you did, you will not be distressed and fearing for your life.'

— 'If he is not the worst one, who can be worse than him?'

— 'His father!'

— 'Who is his father?'

— 'Paul Van Looke'

— 'Who is he?'

— 'Just ask Paul when you meet him.'

— 'That makes no sense!'

— 'It will, I guarantee you!'

After a fifteen-minute mad run through the cobble street of Amsterdam, Jay arrives at the Police station headquarters. He is out of breath and can barely talk. He explains the barge situation and how the grenades can detonate at any moment. The entire police station is on high alert. Police officers and police cars hood out of the main gate while the duty officer orders him to proceed to the safe house. Jay calls Coco; her phone rings and diverts to her voicemail service. Through text messages, he begs her to call back. Jay is stressed out. He calls Florian; he is also forced to leave a voicemail. Running out of options, Jay makes his way to the safe house. As he enters, Ozzie screams.

— 'Fuck! Fuck! Oh no! Coco and Paul Van Looke are close to each other. The two dots on the tracking device are still. Nothing is moving.'

Ozzie bashes his keyboard frantically to gain live access to the petrol station camera and instructs Cutie to upload any CCTV footage from the area.

Within seconds, Jay realises that Coco has been executed and Paul Van Looke is dead. Only a Polaroid camera with a processed photo attached to it stands between the two bodies.

Jay is wordless. His eyes cannot leave the screens. Ozzie smashes his keyboard on the edge of the desk and punches his screen monitors like a madman. He tearfully apologises to Jay. Both men hug silently in tears while an unemotional Cutie reviews the petrol station carnage.

She rewinds the footage, and her monitors reveal the truth as Coco enters the petrol station while talking on her phone. She stops the car in the driveway and appears highly distressed. She goes through her handbag, secures a tissue, talks and takes deep breaths. She repeatedly dries her eyes and blows her nose. Her arms and hands are mad when she talks. She bashes her door window numerous times. The conversation seems intense and goes on for a few long minutes. While texting, her head turns when she notices a luxury green car entering the petrol station refuelling area. Still talking on the phone, she recognises Van Looke coming for her out of his car. She mentally and physically freezes. Fear is written all over her face. He walks straight towards her with an assault weapon in his hand and, without hesitation, fires huge rounds of ammunition through the side window and front windshield. Coco's blood and flesh are splashed all around the car interior and well beyond that. Not much is left of her head and upper body. Without wasting time, Van Looke rests his automatic weapon on the car bonnet, takes a camera out of his jacket and snaps his latest victim. On his way back to the green Bentley, a small truck strikes him with full force. His head smashes the truck windshield, his body collapses and rolls on the ground, and an instant paddle of blood circles his head. As a last attempt to survive, Van Looke tries to secure a gun out of his jacket's inner pocket; the truck driver forcefully stops him, takes over the weapon and, without hesitation, shoots him dead with a single bullet to his chest. The truck driver drops the gun and asks for help. A few minutes later, the police swarm and barricade the crime scene.

Florian frantically calls Jay's mobile. All his calls are ignored, as Jay is still locked in Ozzie's arms. The graphic news spreads worldwide; within seconds, condolences, sorries, and sorrows, and online trolls acknowledge Coco Carajuca's passing.

Hours of silence pass for Jay and Ozzie. Cutie offers them water and a box of tissues. Jay introduces himself, and Cutie gives him a silent hug before returning in front of the monitoring equipment.

Florian calls repeatedly as he tries to establish contact with Jay, who checks his mobile and notices an unread message from Coco. The message reads:

— 'Paul's father!!!'

Jay jumps out of his seat and asks Cutie to play the footage. Coco texted well before Van Looke arrived at the petrol station.

Abigail, Tia and Kora call Jay to express their sorrows. The phone calls are painful and tearful, but Jay tells them that it is not over yet and that everyone should be cautious! Kora and Tia want to regroup; Jay reluctantly agrees.

When he enters his bedroom, he grabs the framed picture of himself and Coco, running his finger over her face. Heavy tears splash onto the glass as he cries out in distress.

Hearing Jay's pain, Ozzie joins him, passes an arm around him, and rests his head on Jay's shoulder. The two friends are in agony. There are not enough tissues to dry their eyes and their bleeding hearts.

Juliana interrupts them and is next to offer her condolences. The call is short and filled with silence and heavy cries.

Amsterdam is in shock. The news swirls madly. Ingrid and Coco's assassinations are only the top of the Dutch iceberg. Paul Van Looke's life of crimes is no secret anymore as evidence and revelations come to light. Paul's mum is followed in the streets of Amsterdam by camera crews and news reporters. Her face is also filled with tears and pain. The single Dutch mum lost her adult baby boy. The online trolls have little sympathy for her loss. She is vindicated as the worst mother in the world, and she is blamed for her son's actions.

Ludo and Florian join Ozzie and Jay at the safe house. Both present their condolences to Jay and check up on his mental state. Florian sees the picture frame on Jay's bed, and as a way to break the ice, he says,

— 'Lovely photo.'

— 'Thank you,' nods Jay.

— 'I have plenty more if you want. I can email them to you.'

Jay's eyes fill again with heavy tears, and a heavy silence amplifies the awkwardness. Ludo is less diplomatic and wants explanations and answers. Jay listens to his monologue without physical, intellectual, or emotional interactions. Ozzie interrupts the commissioner and gives an update on their progress. He discloses the location of the missing diaries and child pornographic materials and clarifies Paul Van Looke's property ownership and identity.

Jay is forced to share his last hours with Coco to Ludo. The commissioner requests as many details as possible. He does not take notes; he listens with careful attention. Florian does the same, maybe for commercial reasons. Jay starts with the messy meeting with Papa and the truth about the Ostend property's ownership. In a broken voice, he narrates his painful conversation with Coco on their way back to Amsterdam. He concludes with the stop at the barge and the instructions she was supposed to follow when driving the rental car to the depot. He shares the last text message from Coco. Florian asks Jay if he recalls the conversation they had in Ostend.

— 'Yes, I do, it is spinning in my head! From Coco's perspective, no one knew about the barge except myself and Ozzie, as I told him before leaving that if something happened to Coco and me. He must take care of the content in the barge.'

— 'When you say no one, there is still a vendor, financier maybe, and some conveyancers for sure,' clarifies Ludo.

— 'No one from her family or circle of friends knew about her acquisition. She aimed to have a private retreat in the centre of Amsterdam.'

— 'When did the purchase happen?'

— 'A few years back, she bought it from an old lady who passed away recently. The day I hid things from Ingrid was the day I received a copy of the key to her floating asset.'

— 'Anything else I need to know,' asks Ludo.

— 'Only a few people knew about our trip from Ostend back to Amsterdam, Coco's Papa, Ozzie, Cutie, Florian, the rental car outlet. None of them knew our exact itinerary. Only Ozzie and Cutie could follow us on the map.'

— 'Who is Cutie?' asks Ludo.

— 'Jiayi Jue. She is Cutie!' Ozzie clarifies with a shy voice while pointing to his lover.

— 'How sweet,' adds Florian.

— 'When I watched the footage of Coco's execution, it looks like she has been slowed down to a standstill,' says Ludo.

— 'Let me track back Van Looke's trip to the petrol station,' says Ozzie while leaving the conversation.

— 'Any idea who was talking to her?' asks Ludo.

— 'Most likely her Papa!' says Jay, looking down at the ground.

— 'Do you think or suggest that he gives her to Van Looke?' Florian queries.

— 'I do not know!'

— 'What do you know about Gaston?' insists Ludo.

— 'He is a man of many talents!'

— 'Could you be more specific?' snaps Florian.

— 'Coco told me her life story and her Papa is or was her god. From her point of view, she owes him everything. Even in her last breath, he has been celebrated! He raised his voice on her for the first time today, and I am most likely the reason. 'We are not family!' was his last sentence to me.'

— 'Why?' asks Ludo.

— 'Maybe he lost his control or his God-worshipping status. I must confess that the guy did his utmost for his protégé.'

— 'Why do you call Coco his protégé?'

— 'She was adopted at the age of nine through unusual circumstances. Both are ballet experts. Sorry, today is not the day to share her story. She deserves the truth, so her life was not wasted.'

— 'I understand! Do not try to fix things by yourself. Vengeance is a double-edged sword that will kill you in the end. No stupid things, please! We,' pointing to everyone in the room, 'are smart enough to solve the unknown and today's challenges,' clarifies Ludo with a firm bureaucratic voice.

— 'Did you retrieve the Go Pro from Ingrid?' asks Jay.

— 'Yes, we did, and Ingrid shot the influencer. There was no one else on the footage.'

— 'How is the guy? Did he recover?'

— 'Yes, he is back on social media and home caring for his mum. We offered him assistance and access to the carer's funding scheme. He is a good kid!' smiles Ludo.

— 'Thank God for some good news! Out of the box here, can you organise a DNA sample on Van Looke?' queries Jay.

— 'For you, I will; you must provide me with the other sample. Without evidence, I cannot force anyone to do so. You need to be creative!'

— 'I or we will. Ozzie is keen for this type of mission,' painfully smiles Jay.

— 'Me too!' shouts Cutie and adds, 'Jay, do you know Coco's email login credentials and passwords for her phone and computer?'

— 'I have her business card in my wallet, why?'

— 'Let's secure her accounts; we do not want to lose

important information or evidence.'

Jay tenders the business card, Cutie types on her laptop keyboard and instantly shares,

— 'She has three devices logged in to this email address. Their IP addresses are hidden behind VPN curtains, and server locations are pinned in Holland, Belgium, and Ukraine. She has two phone handsets; all devices are backed up on Cloud platforms. Here are her account passwords.'

Jay is invited behind the screen to acknowledge the access code of his lover's computer. '#IMissYouMama#' reads the unencrypted data. Jay leaves the room and bursts into tears as he feels Coco's lifetime pain. A few minutes later, Ozzie checks on him. Both finished again in each other's arms. The Nebraskan boys have a challenging time coping with their harsh reality. When their emotions settle down, Ozzie invites Jay to change the online access keys, as Cutie's process cannot be exposed. Jay writes with no hesitation,

— '#ILoveYouCoco#'

Cutie forced a log-in cancellation on all devices and cloud service accesses.

— 'We are now protected! I can link your credentials to her accounts so you can access whatever information you need!' Cutie tells Jay in a voice simulating Siri's voice.

— 'Can we do it later?' asks Jay, who managed a slight grin with Cutie's antics.

— 'And here, while doing hundreds of screenshots, this is all her passwords and passcodes for her mobile devices and computers, as well as security codes for some alarm systems, apps, software, and subscriptions. Where do I send the bill?' jokes Cutie while emailing Jay.

Florian is astonished. Seeing his face, Cutie asks him,

— 'Florian, give me your first and last names, birthplace and just your day of birth,' she teases.

— 'Florian Van Bruggel, Harlem, 8th.'

In no time, Cutie says,

— 'Your last online purchase was for an amount of €49.50. You purchased books on Napoleon and Julius Caesar. One book is on backorder. Your bookstore password is weak.'

Jiayi Jue's technical prowess also puts a smile on Ludo's face as he tells Florian they need to move on. At the same time, Ozzie calls everyone behind his screen monitors. He plays Paul Van Looke's ride to the petrol station. It is fast-paced before a lengthy tactical stop at the barge. The time of the footage coincides with Jay and Coco's departure time from Ostend. As usual, all footage is far from perfect, and the camera angles and locations could be better. The monitoring devices did an excellent job anyway as they captured Van Looke forcing his way into the barge with a travel bag on his shoulder and tapping the end of the fishing lines around the door and windows of the vessel. After receiving a phone call, he aborted the deadly mission and packed his handyman gear quickly before running and tripping. Things fall out of his bag; he collects most of them while running back frantically to his car.

— 'Is it the moment that Van Looke has been informed of the press release?' asks Ozzie, pausing the recording.

Ludo tells Ozzie to press the play button as he is curious to know what is coming next.

On the screen, Van Looke drives at crazy speeds, burning red light after red light and using the tramway lines to overtake the slow traffic. It appears that the now most wanted person in Holland tried to make a run back to his dealership. Two blocks from his destination, he makes a 'U' turn and slides the Bentley with outstanding driving skills. For approximately eight more minutes, his driving style gets worse. He flashes his light and pushes his Bentley as fast as he can. Heavy drifting tyre marks are left at every intersection and on pedestrian crossings. He cuts fearlessly through the traffic, to nearly miss the entry of the petrol station. A big blue cloud of burned rubber is the testimony of the braking power of the Continental GT. The car plunges into the driveway and stops abruptly, and merciless warhead bullets fly.

Jay turns to Cutie, asks if she can tap into Van Looke's mobile, and retrieves his log calls and messages. Ludo intervenes and validates Jay's request with the condition that all findings must be disclosed and discussed, and potential actions must be approved beforehand. With a firm voice, Ludo reminds everyone that Cutie and Ozzie's underground activities are a well-protected secret from the public and within the police force. Any of their actions can not interfere with or compromise any official investigations in any way. To avoid misunderstandings, he checks if everyone is in agreement. The Chinese and the Nebraskan geniuses nod silently and fist-pump their secret boss.

Ludo and Florian offer Jay one more time their condolences. On their way out, Ludo invites Jay not to go to the crime scene and to keep only the good memories alive.

— 'Let me know when I can retrieve things from the barge, our suitcases from the rental car, and most importantly, the Polaroid photo taken by Van Looke!' asks Jay.

— 'I will organise clearance for the barge. I will do my best for your luggage, but I cannot guarantee anything for the Polaroid photo,' replies Ludo, offering a solid goodbye handshake.

— 'My wedding certificate and a thirty-five million euros bank check are in the suitcases,' says Jay.

As the safe house door closes, Jay apologises to Cutie, as he does not remember if they introduced themselves early on before he announces to Ozzie that he needs some space and will spend the night at the Hotel Lucius. Ozzie offers to walk him there, but Jay refuses. He thanks both of them for their generous support and the Nebraskan boys hug with great intensity. Hidden under a latex mask and a hoodie, Jay protects his identity.

At Hotel Lucius, the steep staircase welcomes him and adds to his pain. As he reaches the second floor and sits at the bay window millions of emotions of every possible nature join him. Jay is broken, and the abundance of his warm tears can fill the city canal in no time. His mental state is similar to the one he experienced after the shooting in Arizona as a teenage boy. The reality of life is painful to accept with open arms. He cries profusely like Coco did in the car returning to Amsterdam. He feels sorry for the harshness of their last conversation. As the hours pass, the darker his thoughts are. Suicide is his best option, but he has doubts about how the heavens work. He has no clue if he will see Coco on the other side or if their love will be the same. Jay's mental discomfort is mirrored by his body's elevated temperature, extensive sweating, and the vast amount of mucus coming out of his nose. He takes a cold shower to ease his mind, body and soul. His immobility is joined by the softness of Coco's voice, which invites him to clear his heart. The clarity of the message makes his legs instantly shaky and forces him to sit down his naked bum touching the cold water of the shower floor. Another wave of heartfelt tears embraces the cold flow of the shower.

The water stops abruptly; Jay looks up and sees his friend Ozzie offering him a hand to stand up. Both cry; Ozzie uses all his muscle power to lift Jay out of the shower tub and brings him back to the bedroom. Ozzie helps Jay dry himself, opens the bed sheets, and forces him to rest. Jay complies with no resistance. It is now Ozzie's turn to sit at the bay window and embrace the sadness and melancholy of Amsterdam. He checks the online news on his mobile; raw emotions instantly fill his gentle heart and load his eyes with heavy tears.

As the sun rises over Amsterdam, the worldwide ballet community celebrates the highlights and the tragic passing of one of their all-time icons. Floral displays and messages of love celebrate the charismatic superstar. No charges have been laid against the truck driver that killed Van Looke. Amsterdam sees him as a man of courage. The accuracy of Florian's article and its respectfulness towards Coco beats his competitor hands down.

Chapter twelve

A red mushroom light

Early in the morning, Ozzie wakes Jay as he receives news from Cutie. Gaston is heading towards Amsterdam; he is a good hour away from the centre. Jay dresses rapidly, checking his mobile phone for the time, and notices dozens of messages and unanswered calls. Most of the phone numbers are unknown. He listens to his voicemail. To his surprise, there's a voice message from Roger, who is very emotional as he presents his condolences. The unexpected voicemail from his foster father shocks Jay, but it also reassures him that their relationship is not yet over. Next, Florian invites him, as suggested by Ludo, to contact Coco's legal team as soon as possible. Florian has attached the lawyer's details, a few photos of Coco and Jay, and a Dropbox link to download the complete set in high resolution. The other voicemails are from newspaper outlets offering crazy types of money for an exclusive interview.

— 'Where is he going?' questions Ozzie.

— 'I don't know! Let's inform Florian and receive the green light to monitor him.'

As Ozzie reaches Florian, Jay browses the photos he received. Coco is simply stunning! Every picture captures her beauty, natural smile, and womanly elegance, evoking deep admiration and love in Jay's heart. He zooms through the images taken that night at the Belgian police station during their maiden voyage to Ostend, recalling her cheekiness as she disclosed that she was wearing an open-cage bra and crotchless underwear under her dress. The next set of photos were taken at Caruso, and the intriguing sequence of Papa taking something out of Coco's Panamera and hiding it in his car.

— 'Florian is our driver for the day,' confirms Ozzie.

Jay asks him to review Papa's pictures and seeks his opinion.

— 'Without hesitation, I'm happy to bet five thousand US dollars that this is the first missing diary. I raise my bet to twenty-five thousand US dollars and suggest that Ingrid used Coco as her mule for her dirty delivery business. You were fortunate that the Belgian police didn't search the car. I'm not sure if you'd be here today.'

— 'Coco would be alive if we were arrested. That is the irony of the situation!'

— 'Show me the picture again, the next one and the one after. Hold on a second!'

While waiting for Florian to arrive at Hotel Lucius, Ozzie calls Cutie and asks her to check the Dutch registration number of Papa's car.

— 'Paul Van Looke owns the car,' says Ozzie a few seconds later.

— 'What made you check the number plates?' queries Jay.

— 'Belgian and Dutch plates are different, and when you look closely at the surrounding of the dealer advertising plate holder, it reads, 'A.L.D. – Amsterdam Luxury Drive', which belongs to Paul Van Looke.'

Ozzie messages Cutie to tag the car in the CCTV tracking system. She agrees and informs Ozzie that she has exciting results on Paul Van Looke's identity scan here and abroad. Ozzie calls her and puts her on speakerphone.

— 'Paul Van Looke's full name is Paul Gaston Lars Van Looke, and running online searches on their full names and variations, the guy who died yesterday is very wealthy. He has a portfolio of properties all over Europe and Eastern Europe. His automotive business is a money laundering machine wildly used by the Eastern European and Middle East markets. In the early days, he sold and bought the same cars repeatedly through what seemed like a pyramid scheme of fake buyers. The cars never crossed the border or made a round trip on the Dutch highway on the back of a transporter. The formula is always the same: he sells the cars for a high price and repurchases them for not much. The profit of the transaction is split among the vendor and buyers. Some cars change hands two to four times a day; however, car registrations never change ownership. Recently, the business formula changed; the principle is the same except that there are no sales at all, just hefty deposits are taken, and partial refunds are processed when the transaction is cancelled. The revised model has numerous advantages. There is never a commercial transaction; no stock is required. Paul Van Looke duplicated his core business and developed a very profitable luxury rental car business by renting luxury cars at an overrated price and offering a huge cash handout on completion of the rental period. As a matter of urgency, and before my colleagues did, I took over his cryptocurrency accounts and wallets; it was a delight to do business with him,' laughs Cutie.

— 'Was it worth it?' asks Ozzie.

— 'Eight digits on the high side!' brags the Chinese genius.

— 'Fried chicken celebration!' tells Ozzie.

— 'As much as you want! The other, Paul Gaston Lars Van Looke, started his career in Holland as a gynaecologist and retrained in the Philippines as a genital reconstruction, sphincteroplasty and gender realignment surgeon. After graduation, he moved to Ukraine and changed his name to Gaston Lars after gaining Ukrainian citizenship. He represented a non-profit organisation and did serious travelling on their behalf. His flying rewards programs don't lie. His flight booking has an unusual pattern: two passengers on the way out and only one for the return trip. He also flies regularly to Las Vegas and Tokyo. His organisation supports, through scholarships, ballet dancers, ballet companies, major dance events and touring programs!' tells an out-of-breath Cutie before leaving the call.

— 'Why do the two guys have the same name?' queries Ozzie.

— 'Florian told me that the gynaecologist dramatically delivered Paul Van Looke, and as a gesture of thanks, the baby was named after him,' replies Jay.

— 'Why and how did they reconnect?'

— 'That's a mystery! Even if they don't look alike, a DNA sampling will answer many questions.'

Florian is waiting across the bridge. Ozzie and Jay, hidden under latex masks, make their way to the van. Florian suggests they go on the highway and wait in the rest area until Papa overtakes them. Having no plans, both agree.

The trio is out of the city and drives towards the Belgian border. Ozzie monitors Papa's progress, and they are a few kilometres apart. Florian takes the first exit and drives slowly back towards Amsterdam. A cat-and-mouse game starts as soon as Papa's car is visually acquired. Florian hides the white mass of his van behind and between semi-trailers.

They enter and navigate the heart of Amsterdam. Papa enters the 'Q-Park Amsterdam Centraal' parking station; due to the height restrictions, Florian is forced to drive away and cannot find a space ample enough to park his van in proximity. Florian tells Jay to jump out, run to the car park, and keep them informed. Jay finds Gaston's BMW, but Papa is not in sight. Jay walks the full car park and checks all the ramps, staircases and fire egresses. Gaston is nowhere to be seen. Jay returns to the car and performs a closer inspection. He notices that Papa has left his mobile phone on the lower section of the central console next to a garage door remote control.

The car park and train station are busy. Hundreds of people

walk in all directions. Jay has difficulty moving around at a fast pace, and he has no clue where to go. Ozzie calls Jay; the locating dots have disappeared from his tracking apps. There is nothing the trio can do except wait for Papa's reappearance. Ozzie contacts Cutie to fire up the train station and car park CCTV network for information.

— 'Is he hiding in a car?' queries Florian.

As they have little visual on the car park entry from their location, Jay decides to go back and check the car park and the train station entry again. Only human chaos welcomes him. Defeated, he regroups with Florian and Ozzie to brainstorm. There's nothing they can do except wait next to Papa's car. Cutie is on a mission to solve the daylight mystery; she reviews the CCTV footage of the car park exit and Gaston swapped cars in the basement. He now drives an old white Volkswagen Caddy heavily branded with the city's triple red crosses logo. Everyone is in disbelief; Gaston is a man of many talents. Florian relays the information to Ludo. The utility vehicle belongs to Paul Van Looke. Police surveillance is activated. Florian and Jay walk back to the car park and wait for Gaston to return. Ozzie decides to join Cutie at the safe house to assist her. Under his latex mask, Jay waits at the entry gate, and Florian is further away inside the car park, wearing his heavy professional camera around his neck. He's committed to publishing some exclusive material. The police report no wrongdoing, and Papa finally enters the car park driveway, takes a ticket at the boom gate and proceeds through the parking station. Florian receives a go-ahead signal from Jay, and now he's on the hunt for capturing the best possible photos. Gaston parks his vehicle at the first available spot, jumps out of the car, and retrieves a small two-wheel trolley in front of the passenger seat. He locks the car and, at a fast pace, strolls his way through the car park. Jay has both men in visual contact as he moves and hides between the stationary cars. Florian takes unnecessary risks to capture the content of his next editorial. Gaston notices him and makes his way towards him. His walking pace is crazy; he doesn't look like a frail dancer anymore. Florian doesn't hide and makes himself visible; they are only a few steps apart. As the two men's postures are not an invitation for peace, Jay moves closer and uses his mobile phone to video record the exchange. Florian speaks and extends an honest handshake, but the gesture quickly shifts into a severe and threatened position. Papa seems to be carrying a weapon; Jay can't see it. Supported by dramatic hand gestures, Gaston requests Florian's camera. The verbal exchange is tense. With some hesitation, Florian complies and, through the process, keeps an open hand acting as a shield in front of his chest. The camera is dropped with no care into the trolley. Having no choice, Florian takes the opportunity to secure the upper hand in the awkward situation. He kicks Gaston in the shin in an attempt to destabilise his opponent's balance. It nearly worked; unfortunately for Florian, his self-defence move didn't have enough power. Gaston barely wobbles and, in retribution, fires twice with his silent massive calibre gun. Florian's head and chest are pulverised, and his body inertia brings him down to the ground. With no spare second to waste and like Paul Van Looke did with Coco, Papa grabs a

Polaroid camera from his trolley and takes a gory glory shot. The scene is unreal. Jay races madly towards Gaston and forcefully disarms and immobilises him. Another Polaroid camera finishes on the ground. Gaston tries to fight back, but he's no opponent to Jay, who uses Papa's trouser belt to restrain his opponent. Gaston is now face down on a parked car bonnet. His body is locked, but his mouth delivers rounds of insults and threats. Jay tells him,

— 'Sorry, we are not family.'

As a safety measure, Jay empties all of Gaston's pockets, which are filled with car and house keys, ammunition, a Polaroid snap of another female victim, a wallet, bands of cash and a small loaded automatic pistol also mounted with a silencer. Jay decides to steal Gaston's set of keys as he knows this is his only chance to access the Ostend properties. Within seconds, the police force swarms the car park; Ludo is present and, in no time, sprays his anger at Jay and invites him to leave the scene before all news reporters and photographers invade the crime scene. Jay walks through the car park to reach Papa's BMW, taking the opportunity to quickly secure the garage door remote and Gaston's mobile phone.

Jay shares the tragic news at the safe house with Ozzie and Cutie. Both already knew the outcome as they were glued behind their monitoring screens. Cutie informs Jay that she can delete or amend some video captures of him stealing evidence from the crime scene if required. The Chinese spy has eagle eyes, thinks Jay. Ozzie, reading his pal's mind, asks him,

— 'When would you like to go to Ostend?'

— 'I had great respect for Florian. He is a fantastic guy who went out of his way to protect us. Based on this fact alone, I'll ask Ludo's permission before proceeding.'

— 'Ludo will accept,' cuts Cutie.

— 'How can you be so sure?' clarifies Jay

— 'He doesn't want to share his success with the Belgian police force. They'll work under his instructions and not the other way around. It's all about credits, political and personal gains!'

— 'What made you say that?'

— 'Ask your friend Florian; his need for stardom or recognition killed him today. There's no need to rush to a conclusion! Patience is a virtue. What was the difference between getting Gaston today and tomorrow?

— 'Maybe he spared some lives!'

— 'Giving his life away makes no sense, I'm sorry! Yes, he'll receive the honour, the blessings of the country and some posthumous journalism awards, but he's not there to enjoy the glory. He is a waste!'

— 'Why are you mad at Florian?' snaps Jay.

— 'She is not!' interferes Ozzie.

— 'So what? I'm getting confused here.'

— 'She just asks you not to rush and to act with prudence and care.'

— 'My message to you, Jay, is that my boyfriend will not cope if you die. You are his brother, his friend, the respect and recognition he never received. Take it with humility; you are his world! You are probably more than I am,' says

Cutie, with a straight face.

— 'Your words have similarities to the ones I spoke to Coco about her Papa. Our last conversation hurt so badly; it destroyed her and her view of her world. I wish she never heard my speculation about Gaston and died full of naivety.'

— 'Reality, truth and honesty are never welcomed with an open heart!' comments Cutie.

— 'With Coco, it was speculation!' replies Jay

— 'There is no speculation today! Gaston Lars's naivety is over.'

— 'So, if there's no speculation, are you getting married,' smiles Jay, attempting to dissipate the tension.

— 'Jay, would you accept to be my best man?' queries Ozzie nervously.

— 'Before Cutie's speech on our friendship, the answer was a plain flat 'No'. But since this beautiful, attractive, young, smart lady described me as the pillar or the anchor of your life, I'll be honoured to be there for you. I'd be delighted to be your friend for the rest of our life; you are my world too, Ozzie,' cheerfully answers Jay.

The trio hug madly with great tenderness. Jay asks Cutie to operate with care, as he considers her role or job equal to a funambulism act with little margin for error. To reassure Jay, Cutie tells him that mining the dark web is not for everyone and that the benefits are worth the risk, her time and energy.

From one day to another, the Amsterdam news gets worse. Paul Van Looke's mum has been executed. The identity of her killer has not been disclosed to the public. The safe house trio have tracked Gaston in and out of the Amsterdam

Centraal station car park on their computer screens and are well aware that he is the killer. The police commissioner authentifies Corinne Lagueule on the Polaroid print. The instant print's rawness is extreme. Paul's mum was thrown down a set of stairs, hung from the side balustrade and shot numerous times at close range with a big calibre. A third of her body is missing.

Late afternoon, Ludo joins the trio at the safe house. His body language and presence display his loss. He wants to hear Jay's version of the event. Jay quietly shows him the footage taken from his phone.

— 'Thirty seconds! He took the bastard thirty seconds to kill a lifetime friendship,' growls Ludo.

— 'I'm sorry!' replies quietly Jay.

— 'I'll kill the bastard myself, and I won't be sorry!'

— 'Before doing it, we need to collect more evidence.'

— 'He'll die in jail. No need to worry about that!'

Jay puts Gaston's key sets and garage door remote control in front of Ludo.

— 'If you allow me, I'd like to inspect his houses in Ostend. I need to know exactly what type of man or father he was for Coco. I need to know if there was sincerity in their relation or pure abuse of her naivety.'

— 'Your luck is that we haven't released Lars' identity to the media. He'll be officially charged with both murders tomorrow. The prosecutor has approved a request for a DNA test to establish the biological paternity of Paul Van Looke Junior. If Gaston is Paul's father, he'll be subsequently charged for having sex with an underage girl a few decades ago.'

— 'Can we go to Ostend? We'll video-record the content of the properties. We won't take anything away. Just collecting evidence and peace of mind for Coco.'

— 'Who is we?' clarifies Ludo.

— 'The three of us. We trust each other!'

— 'I want you all back by ten o'clock tomorrow morning. If you have any concerns, here's my direct mobile number. I'll call you around eight; your input can be vital for my press conference tomorrow at lunchtime.'

— 'Thank you!' says Jay.

— 'Please don't take any unnecessary risks!' insists Ludo while leaving.

As soon as the door closes, Cutie secretly takes possession of Papa's mobile phone while Jay is calling the Haka girls.

Kora and Tia will join them even though their mum's funeral is scheduled for tomorrow late in the afternoon. The 'Haka Girls' will bring torches, plastic gloves, and overalls. Ozzie and Cutie oversee the technology. As a camouflage strategy, Jay books a hotel night for five in Ostend and buys tickets at the Kursaal for the 'Black Swan' ballet event interpreted by the Szeged Contemporary Dance Company and choreographed by Tamás Juronics.

Jay's reunion with the 'Haka Girls' is emotionally loaded; tears and meaningful hugs are shared. Everyone has lost a loved one. On the other hand, they're surprised to see Ozzie in a relationship. He is now the receiver of their giggles and childish jokes. Cutie plays along. The trip to Ostend is a long and painful summary of the last few days. Jay is proud to show his wedding pictures, and in return, Tia and Kora share their family's childhood photos of their mum.

After a quick check-in at Hotel Louise, the five make it to the 'Black Swan' performance. They miss a good third of it, grab some refreshments, and discuss their action plan at the interval. For safety reasons, Tia and Ozzie are one team, and Cutie and Kora are paired, Jay floating between. Their camera batteries are fully recharged, and the SD cards are ready to capture. Patrons are called back for the second part of the show. Jay prefers to wait outside. It's too close for comfort; he can feel the grace of the ballerinas taking over his heart and steering his emotions. He misses Coco and scrolls through the picture he received from Florian. He realises how glowing and proud he was and how caring and loving Coco was. One of his wedding photos is now his mobile phone screensaver.

— 'Life sucks!' he says out loud to himself.

The five drive a few hundred metres to Papa's properties. They'll start at Kapucijnenstraat. Jay prays that the brown roller door works when he presses the remote-control button. A streetlight attached to the building beams on them directly, and the darkness of the night doesn't offer them any camouflage. Tia gives protective equipment to everyone. A double layer of latex gloves and plastic slippers are used to avoid evidence contamination, and she invites everyone to wear a breathing mask. Their Mercedes Vito, parked in front of the garage door, becomes a change room. Within seconds, everyone starts to get hot and sweaty. The moment of truth arrives when the roller door opens before them. Kora puts two magnetic signs on the side doors of the car.

They're now a cleaning business!

As the roller closes behind them, the battery-operated torches take over. The double-parking space is empty and connects to a set of stairs and a tiny laundry. The staircase wraps around a wall; the three upper floors and a basement are ready to be scrutinised. The five make their way to the first floor. Jay goes through the set of keys and finds the right one to open the only door on the stair landing. The whole floor is a single apartment. The light coming out of the torches creates an apocalyptic atmosphere. The lounge–dining room and the kitchen are located on the street side. The two bedrooms are at the back of the building, and the bathroom is centrally located and faces the entry door. The entire front of the unit is filled with metallic shelving, heavily filled with folders on the top section and closed cardboard boxes at the bottom. Each folder has a white label with black calligraphy on it. Ozzie takes one out; the information inside belongs to Elena Popa, a six-year-old girl from Romania, as mentioned on her adoption paperwork. She was adopted on the 16th of May nineteen, eighty-four and passed away on the 20th of the same month. Her adoptive family were Mr and Mrs Francois Dupont from Biarritz. The first part of the folder includes her birth certificate, orphanage logbook, some medical and educational information and a handful of pictures of her at the orphanage. The middle section of the folder contains processed photographic negative rolls cut that are neatly packed into paper sleeves, and a thick brown envelope marks the end of the folder. It is filled with pictures of a paedophile's party in a hotel room. Elena dies from strangulation after being raped and beaten savagely.

Ozzie is in pain when taking pictures with his camera; he looks unwell even in the darkness. The mood in the room is far from happy; Tia opens the following folder. It belongs to Ariana Litsvich, an eleven-year-old girl from Poland. Her story is not better; she died three days after her adoption in a hotel room in the company of two paedophiles, one of whom sucked the air out of her lungs using a vacuum cleaner. The pipe was shafted in her mouth, and her airwaves were blocked while being raped in synchronicity by both men. Her adoptive family was Mr and Mrs Karl Wingshout from Stuttgart in Germany; It does not appear Ariana ever met Mrs Wingshout.

All the folders on the shelves contain the same atrocities, underage orphan girls raped and killed by what seems to be an organised paedophile group. The post-Chernobyl era looks very prolific. It was the same for the post-Yugoslav War.

Four hundred and fifty folders are roughly accounted for, three decades of insanity printed on glossy paper. Cutie points out that photographic recording has evolved over the years. It went from numeric to digital, and their recording media evolved from negative rolls and papers and moved on to CDs, DVDs and USB sticks. Not all folders have photographic evidence of their victim's passing or cause of death, but all adoption sheets have a recorded date of a child's end of life. Cutie points out an awful detail on the back of the adoption sheet. Each girl is a commercial transaction. Four accounting lines show their acquisition cost to the orphanage, the orphanage director's commission, the sales price and the profit. Twenty-five thousand American dollars is the average profit recorded in the early years of the operation, and the more recent folders indicate a sum of nearly half a million US dollars.

The photos indicate that paedophiles acting alone or in groups are very wealthy and educated people living in affluent and modern societies. They wear the latest fashionable clothes, refined jewellery and expensive watches. A full spectrum of nationalities, races, ages, and genders have made their way to the underage slaughterhouse or the butchery store, which came to them as an on-demand service.

Jay browses through the white-label folders as he wants to find Coco's adoption papers, but he has no success. As the group spread to leverage time, Tia noticed that each shelving row had a different labelling system on the folder. The yellow and the red stickers are sex trafficking files. The yellow tags are for teenage girls and young women, and the red ones are for older women. All recorded girls' and women's facial expressions are painted with pure fear; only its intensity varies. All have lost their natural beauty and glow. The themes of the folders are different, too—bondage, orgy, gang rapes, deprivation, starvation, mutilations and many combinations. Men are not the only perpetrators; women are, too. Photographic evidence illustrates the intensity of their anger, force, conviction, pleasure and orgasm when abusing or taking advantage of their victims.

The blue-labelled folders are the worst ones to navigate through. Forced abortion is the theme of the folders. The pictures are taken with some artistry attached to them. The composition and light are perfect. On the other hand, the content is revolting. Girls and women are tied up with legs open to a medical examination chair. They are forced to drink through a plastic funnel huge amount of murky water, which is most likely crushed Mifepristone and Misoprostol pills. Visual and physical pain, belly contraction, vomiting, heavy bleeding and stretched vagina are recorded. Unborn babies are pushed out and fall to the ground or hang to their mothers by their umbilical cords. The end of the abortion process is sickening and cruel beyond belief. Expandable foam is sprayed out of its canister into the mouth of the trapped victim. The chemical reaction grows exponentially within seconds, closing and sealing the victim's respiratory system. At the same time, the industrial mixture overflows, coming out of their nostrils and overstretched mouths. The brutal end-of-life facial expressions and pictures are too much for Ozzie. He takes a break and reconvenes in the hallway with Cutie.

Kora and Tia open one of the boxes stored in the lower shelving section. There are Japanese books filled with similar cruelty. The majority are underage girls dressed in their blue polyester school swimming costume. Their sizes and measurements promote explicit pictures of their moulded body anatomies. The girls are hypnotised; pendulums balance in front of their faces. Jay notices that their look or gaze are similar to Coco's one when meeting with Gaston. The storyline of the book varies from child pornography to bloody underage MMA cage fights. The girls are hypnotised to fight and to kill their opponents. Under the spell, the kids are transformed into instant weapons and killing machines. The hypnosis script triggers their basic primal survival instincts; there are no combat rules except taking the life of the other. Extreme graphical evidence is simply the testimony of free violence for others to enjoy. Broken teeth, arms, ribs and fingers, bitten ears, and poked eyes cannot hide in the final pools of blood. The winner has no better faith as she has been programmed to commit a 'hara-kiri' to seal off her decisive and ultimate victory. Jay is so intrigued by the girl's gaze that he opens numerous boxes to comprehend that Coco may have been hypnotised all her life by her Papa.

The first bedroom is filled with all sorts of sex toys, lingerie, skimpy underwear, strap-ons, and strange apparatus, and it looks like a sex shop without the funky dark lighting. The second bedroom is less joyful; there are lots of guns and ammunition, and another set of shelving filled, this time with a dozen execution diaries, including the missing one recovered from Coco's car by Gaston, which remains wrapped like in Florian's photos. Jay's intuition is getting rewarded. Due to the brutality and rawness of their discovery so far, the group check on one another's mental state. It's heavy for everyone.

The second-floor apartment has little furniture. There's only a chair, a coffee table, a digital projector and a white stretched fabric sheet on one of the walls. A few external hard drives and USB sticks are on the carpet floor. The two back rooms were converted a while ago into a fully operational surgery theatre and a patient recovery room. Both rooms are immaculate and spotless, and their atmosphere is eerie. Jay is eager to know if the kitchen benchtop that Coco referred to is indeed the theatre used for the deadly abortions.

Ozzie and Cutie visit the basement, and only three locked large-size key-operated safes are discovered.

The top floor is a mixed surprise for Jay. It's the apartment where Coco and Gaston lived many years ago. The furniture is minimal and looks like a rental place from the seventies. Jay is surprised to see Coco's bedroom when she was nine. The room is decorated in a girly style with Walt Disney princesses printed in a repetitive pattern on the wallpaper. Her bed has a big woolly blanket and a tiny silky pillow. There's a red mushroom light on her night side table and many ballerina drawings and artefacts. Her wardrobe is filled with ballet dancewear and girly clothing. A little desk, where she probably did some homework, still has old schoolbooks and a pencil case. A set of photos of her and Papa are affixed to the wall. Jay is now able to put a visual to Coco's words. He can see her enjoying the Ostend beach wooden cabin during summer breaks. There's also a picture of her eating ice cream with Gaston, and both have a big fat chocolate moustache under their nose. They look happy. Jay notices her natural glow and presence in every photo. He loves what he sees, but unfortunately, he can't take anything away with him to treasure.

Chapter thirteen

Stardust

After midnight, the group leaves the property, and the garage door rolls back behind them. They take a much-needed break in the van and drive closer to the canal to feel and breathe the freshness of the Belgian seaside. Tia is hungry, and a short trip to 'Ruby frituur' on the other side of town will bring some cheerfulness to the quintet's hearts. Boulet sauce lapin and hot chips are winners for the girls; frikandel, hot chips and andalouse sauce bless Ozzie and Jay's tummies.

Ozzie and Cutie are not wasting time securing the video recordings. All data is transferred to the cloud to save and acknowledge the fact that over a thousand women of all ages have lost their lives by fulfilling someone else crazed fantasies, addictions and ugly lifestyles.

When the after-meal toilet round is accomplished, they all return to the van and drive to Papa's glorious and elegant dwelling. The entry door key works perfectly. The flashlights do not embellish the experience; everything is neat, clean and well-presented. All decorations and furniture are in their right places. The bay window on the upper ground floor directly views Coco's old apartment. Gaston picked the location very well; it is perfect for a sniper. To save time again, the five spread to speed up the search. Ozzie inspects the ground floor. Having enough horror in his head, Tia stays with him. They open and close all cabinetry doors and drawers in the kitchen. There is nothing hidden. Cutie and Kora venture into the first-floor bedrooms, ensuite, wardrobe and bathroom. Everything is perfect, and like on the ground floor, there is nothing to report.

Jay visits the attic. Two rooms are located on top of a beautifully carved staircase and handrail. The biggest room is filled with two sets of bookshelves. One section is specialised medical literature related to Gaston's profession and, on the opposite side, hypnosis. Hundreds of books, programs, DVD sets, and tapes fill the cavity of the storage furniture. All genres are meticulously organised on both sides. Jay is curious, and his appetite for hypnosis is well alive. Gaston's collection includes literature on traditional hypnosis, clinical hypnosis, Ericksonian hypnosis, cognitive hypnosis, stage hypnosis, erotic hypnosis, behavioural hypnosis, and self-hypnosis. The top of the bookshelves and the side walls of the room are filled with Gaston's diplomas and professional memberships in either field. Group photos at hypnosis training in Las Vegas and Tokyo. In each image, he holds a new certificate or diploma. Again, Jay understands Coco when she mentioned that she and her Papa held eye contact to boost her confidence in humanity.

— 'Hundreds of books to create a single master hypnotist or simply a deceptive person,' mumbles Jay quietly.

The second room in the attic is Gaston's office. Nothing is out of the ordinary. On Gaston's desk, a picture of Coco and Paul Van Looke is placed on either side.

— 'The old man has a heart,' grumbles Jay.

Gaston's paperwork is well organised. Like across the road, there is a folder for everything: health, insurance, property, will, bills, accounting and so on. Jay cannot resist checking the Ostend property ownership. Gaston Lars owns both properties, and the land title certificate has never been updated since he changed his name. The accounting folder has no business papers inside; only a set of three long keys is secured through the metallic rings of the folder and a cutout of an unfinished sudoku game with only three numbers written on it. Intrigued, Jay calls the others and asks their opinion on the unusual findings.

— 'They are the keys of the safes across the road; they are Russian-made, and plenty of them are for sale on the dark web,' says Cutie.

After uploading a sudoku creator application from the app store on her mobile, Cutie types the numerical digits as per the printout and requests the app to finalise the game on her behalf. As the result pops on her screen, she performs a screenshot and displays the results to the others.

— 'There is only one way to find out; it is to cross the road,' she says.

— 'What are the combinations?' asks Tia with great intrigue.

— 'The only thing of interest for us tonight is the three-by-three nine-digit squares around the centrally located number from the folder. Each safe has three dial-in wheels; the middle number in the square is the second wheel on the safe, and the numbers on either side are the first and the third wheels. In total, we have eight possible combinations in all directions around the central digit.'

— 'Let's go back! And see if it works! It should not take long between the five of us!' says Ozzie.

The group leaves Papa's house, jumps in the van, drives fifty metres across the street intersection, and parks again in front of the brown roller door. Inside the basement, they share the safe keys and the potential lock combination one digit at a time. On the sixth combination attempt, the first safe opens. The second one releases its content on the second numerical attempt, and the third safe opens on the first attempt and is, unfortunately, empty. Folders inside the first safe contain the names of all associates and business partners related to Lars-Van Looke's business ventures. Each country has its classification. Ozzie and Cutie take photos but cannot capture the full content. All information is handwritten, and even the more recent records are not the beneficiaries of our modern technological advancements. The volume and quantity of the pen and paper paperwork produced and archived to date is close to or equal to a librarian or accountant's lifetime commitment.

The second safe content is all about clients' names and contact details. Some sub-classifications match the colour of the folder located on the first floor. Browsing quickly through the records to secure enough evidence, some account statements are painful to read. A quick extract highlights that Francisco Pizarro, a Spanish national, purchased thirty-two underage girls between nineteen eighty-six and nineteen ninety-eight. Two of the victims had some form of disability. Francisco's tally is near nothing compared to the one hundred and ninety-eight women who were forced into prostitution by a German mobster called Franz Goebbels between the years two thousand and two thousand and ten. Jay hopes that the three decades of unethical accounting will trap the future and destiny of many men and women. He also wishes that some families will find closure in their findings.

Ostend wakes up; it is nearly six o'clock in the morning. No one expected the recovery mission to take so much time and effort. Only one thing is left: they must return the safe's keys to Papa's office. Unfortunately for Jay, when Ozzie parks their van across the street to Gaston's house, the group notices an old lady with a broom, a cleaner's kit, and a vacuum cleaner entering the property.

— 'She must be Gaston's cleaner,' says Jay in a frustrated tone.

— 'She looks like our mum,' says Tia.

— 'I hope that she has a strong heart, her life will turn around soon!' comments Cutie.

Having no option, Jay secures the safe's keys to the house and the car's set.

— 'It will be to Ludo to sort things out,' he thinks out loud.

Back at Hotel Louise, the group splits for a quick shower

before meeting again for breakfast. Tia and Kora tease Ozzie in the lift, asking him if he has enough time for a quickie. The 'Haka girls' are childishly giggling until Cutie surprises them and says,

—— 'I am bisexual and a swinger; if you come along, we can save a fair amount of water. Eating your dark-skinned pussies is on my bucket list!'

Ozzie does not know what to do with himself except rubbing at his crotch unconsciously.

—— 'My curiosity is tempted to accept your offer, but today is unfortunately not the day. We do not want quickies! Ozzie showed us his power of endurance and slow release,' replies Kora.

—— 'It cannot wait to witness the three of you in action! Please keep my offer as an open invitation, either for a threesome or a foursome,' smiles Cutie.

Jay exits the lift and teases the 'Haka Girls' by telling them,

—— 'The sushi battle is on! Let Cutie decide which one of you has the softest and hardest one. I cannot wait for the result.'

At breakfast, everyone's mood is warm, friendly and slightly sexually charged between the girls. The buffet counter is a typical Belgian hotel buffet filled with bread, croissants, pain au chocolat, salami, ham, cheese, tea and coffee. Like children, a race takes place to be served first - even if it is a self-service.

With the food overload, everyone is tired, and Ozzie volunteers to drive the trip back to Amsterdam, with Jay keeping him company to ensure he does not fall asleep. The girls in the back seat are asleep in no time. As planned and near Amsterdam, Ludo contacts Jay; he is curious about their findings. His questions are particular about who and what is recorded in the Ostend archives. He also mentions that he prefers to delay the release of the information to the press by a week as he needs time to organise himself. Later, Ozzie and Cutie receive instructions by text message to transfer their data to a dedicated server. Cutie does not look too impressed by the request; she has issues with the proposed storage drives. As she shares her view with Ozzie, she loses her poker face.

Ozzie and Cutie announce they cannot attend Kora and Tia's mum's funeral. They are sorry, but they need to deal with an emergency. Jay confirms his attendance.

Something is brewing between Cutie and Ozzie; both now look upset. Jay breaks the ice and queries about their change of mood.

— 'We are going back to Ostend to install hidden surveillance cameras in both buildings,' says Cutie.

— 'Why?' asks Jay.

— 'Ludo's delay makes no sense. A lot can happen in a week, and we do not want to lose pieces of evidence. It will be disastrous for Coco, Florian and the others if things start to disappear,' presses Ozzie.

— 'Are you okay? Are you safe? I am worried for you!' replies Jay.

— 'The best time to do it is now; we still have the keys. All chaos and attention will be at the press conference when Gaston's charges will be made public,' comments Cutie.

— 'Sorry, we need to go and pick up some hardware. I will keep you informed!' says Ozzie.

— 'You should go to the press conference and show your journalist pass and make Florian proud; Ozzie will help you with the editing!' revs up Cutie.

— 'After the funeral, I will transfer the barge's content back to Hotel Lucius,' replies Jay.

Jay has the place for himself at the safe house and sits on his bed. He grabs Coco's picture and glides his fingers on it. Sadness and tiredness are not a good combination. Tears and sorrows embrace his face, and he misses Coco's presence, joyfulness, sharpness of mind, and laughter. He wishes that he could touch one more time the softness of her skin and fill the entirety of his lungs with the distinctive sensual smell of her gingery fragrance. Based on the night discovery, Jay is convinced that Coco was sent to a slaughterhouse the day she arrived in Belgium many years ago. He tries to comprehend why Gaston had a change of heart.

Having little to wear, Jay borrows some of Ozzie's clean clothes. Everything is oversized, and Jay looks like a baggy old man. The situation makes him laugh as he reverts to his three-piece wardrobe. The Press conference is at the exact location where he kicked the fake 'Clown of Amsterdam' to his death. He borrows an unchained bike from the police station and rides along the canal unmasked.

The media pack is the biggest ever seen, and Jay makes his way into it and automatically becomes the centre of attention. Flashes and questions bombard him, and photographers and news reporters push each other around to secure their day's paycheck. Jay stays silent. His lips are sealed tight even when the hard questions related to Coco's death blast through his heart. The police force intervenes and invites Jay to move to a secure spot alongside the stage curtains. Jay has prime vision on the gathering and the Police commissioner, who thanks the media for their attendance, and Jay for finding the courage to honour his wife and the loss of his new friend, Florian.

With an affirmative voice, similar to Ingrid's, Ludo gives an overview of the past day's events and the potential links between Kora and Tia's mum, Zoetje, Ingrid, Coco, Mrs Lagueule and Florian's executions, Paul Van Looke's involvements, and the arrest of one of his accomplices or associates at the Amsterdam Centraal station carpark yesterday afternoon. Papa's identity is not disclosed. Ludo confirms that the suspect is silent, does not want to cooperate with the investigators and refuses legal assistance. Due to the complexity of the events, the police prosecutors are still working on the charges. Ludo briefly confirms that the investigation will extend to numerous European countries as new evidence came to light recently. The commissioner plans to brief his overseas counterparts in the coming days. He also thanks and values the Belgian police force for their collaborative work.

Surprisingly for Jay, Ludo does not show any emotions during his monologue. His stoney façade works well, or has the harshness of his duties built a man with a hard shell over the years?

As the press conference comes to an end, Ludo checks

on Jay. Jay returns the gesture.

— 'How are you? Are you okay?' asks Jay.

— 'Florian was a great guy! An honest piece of a man.'

— 'Any kids or family left behind?'

— 'No. His job was everything! He was single as long as I knew him. The love of his life was his cat; the fur on his clothes was the testament of their relationship.'

— 'Has someone taken care of the cat since yesterday?'

— 'Honestly, I do not know!'

— 'If that helps, I am happy to do it. It will brighten my day; I am attending a funeral now.'

— 'He has no relatives; I am probably his next of kin.'

— 'Are you serious?' asks Jay.

— 'No, just kidding! That is my sense of humour for you,' laughs Ludo loudly before proceeding, 'If it does not bother you and brings you happiness, I will organise for someone to drop his keys and address at the safe house.'

— 'Any luck with my belongings and Coco's?'

— 'We are in the process of cleaning and making your stuff look and smell as humanly possible, and before you ask, the barge is secured to access, but you need to move all your stuff out of it. Sooner or later, it will not be a secret anymore.'

— 'That is my plan for the evening!'

— 'Taking about a plan, you need to check if your wife has life insurance or a funeral plan.'

— 'Florian informed me to call her lawyer. I will do it after today's funeral.'

— 'Wearing a mask is still a good idea! Is there anything

else I can help you with?'

— 'Coco and I were looking to live in Amsterdam; I want to stay with her. Is there a legal way to gain Dutch citizenship under my circumstances?'

— 'I cannot answer; I am not an immigration lawyer, but I will find out. I promise!'

Ludo and Jay shake hands and part ways. The media pack has dissolved. Jay jumps on his bicycle and goes to the city centre to purchase an outfit for the Haka Girls' Mum's last ceremony.

Jay arrives just in time at the twins' gym studio; it is a private gathering. Their sparring ring becomes a platform for love and a venue for a last goodbye. Tia and Kora have dressed elegantly out of their performance sporting outfits. The Haka Army is present; each member watches the white satin lacquered coffin. Friends and acquaintances attend, including a few family members who flew from overseas. Andrea and Ed are there, too; Jay joins them. There is no celebrant or priest, only the powerful voice of nearly two hundred women ready to express the authenticity of life.

The warriors' chorus transforms the room into a testament of love, a gateway to the afterlife and an endless blessing to an immortal soul. Fearful postures, scary facial expressions, intense body slaps, tongue wagging and killing eyes protect Kora and Tia's mum into her new life cycle—a better one, where presence and authenticity matter. The Kiwi Girls embrace their letting-go process as part of their powerful and meaningful cultural value; without exception, their mum is now everyone's mum. Everyone present connects to their perception of their new spiritual mother. The amplified ritual sounds coming out of the celebrating circle mean that the world suffers a little bit more when a woman dies, and tons of unconditional love dissolves when she expulses her last breath.

Jay has witnessed two Haka ceremonies since he first landed in Amsterdam. Both had a different meaning; the first one was more in the tune of 'Do not fuck with us,' and today, the warriors soothe the stretch marks and the blemishes of life. His thoughts drift on Coco; he quietly and without motion soothes her life story to fill his reality with imperfect perfection, comfort and a sense of belonging. His heart is empty, not because he cleaned it, as he acknowledges that his impossible dream will never be realised. Sadly, Coco is only a memory to be appreciated like a sweet and sour delicatessen, a small bite at the time. Jay must prepare himself to tango between the bitterness and sweetness of the coming months. He acknowledges that the Kiwi girls and himself have no path available for vengeance or justice as Ingrid, Lars and Van Looke are out of action.

The ceremony comes to an end. After a few hugs, kisses and handshakes, Jay is invited by Andrea and Ed for a drink at a nearby pub. Their medical trial is on standby for another three weeks as a dozen families need reassurance until a new secured venue is found. The three men check on each other. Jay receives words of support. They order their drinks; Jay opts for a Lindemans Kriek as a memory of his night trip to the frituur with Coco. The taste and the aroma of the cherry beer are worth his pain. Jay has a burning question for Andrea and Ed; he cannot resist asking it.

— 'Is it possible to interrogate someone who refuses to talk under hypnosis?' he queries with a broken voice.

— 'As a short answer, it depends on the person's level of suggestibility and willingness to be hypnotised,' replies Andrea.

— 'The person is a skilled hypnotist and a certified hypnotherapist who attended dozens of trainings in Las Vegas and with hundreds of hours of practice?'

— 'Who is your target?' asks Ed.

— 'The guy who killed the journalist Florian Van Bruggel from De Dagblad yesterday at the Amsterdam Centraal station?'

— 'What do you know about him or his hypnosis journey?'

— 'I saw pictures of him on stage in Las Vegas with diplomas and certificates. To add to the drama and confidentially, he is my wife's foster father!'

— 'Amsterdam is a small world.'

— 'I cannot talk about the details; I would like to know if he had a change of heart when he saved my wife from her predators when she was a nine-year-old girl.'

— 'How would you like us to do that or be involved?'

— 'He will not talk; I am one hundred percent sure this will not change. I will plant a seed in the police commissioner's head to have you on board. I will pay for your service. I have the money!'

— 'If the request comes from the Police force, I have no problem. I am up to the challenge,' laughs Andrea.

On his way back to the safe house, Jay stops at a frituur. He purchases a portion of hot chips, andalouse sauce, frikandel, and another Lindemans Kriek. As he sits to eat, Roger's voice passes through his head.

— 'Enjoy your freedom!' the voice says.

He smiles, and as he does now, Coco's voice interrupts him.

— 'Clean your heart!' she says with a smiling voice.

The food is served on a plastic tray; Jay takes time to appreciate his unhealthy snack. Everything tastes good!

Back at the safe house, his belongings, including Coco's, were returned. There is also an envelope with Florian's house keys, his address, a pack of cat food and a bag of litter pebbles. Ozzie and Cutie have returned from Ostend, and a few monitoring screens have been added to their arsenal. Everyone is exhausted but happy to see each other. Jay asks Ozzie if they should organise a copy of the set of keys before returning them. The Nebraskan boy quietly answers that it is already done, offering a fist pump simultaneously. Jay suggests he will return Gaston's properties to Ludo with a seeding note related to Lars' silence.

Coco and Jay's bags have been chemically cleaned from Coco's blood stains. The luggage stinks so badly that Jay is forced to open his bedroom window. Jay recalls the vision of her car's windows getting smashed and her body getting thrown around by the impact of the ammunition. Coco's set of keys is returned, and Jay realises he must pick up her Porsche Panamera at the Vallet carpark at Schiphol airport. This creates a new problem as he does not know where to park her car afterwards.

— 'Maybe someone at Hotel L'Europa will know,' he mumbles.

His priority for now is to take care of Florian's cat. Van Breestraat 52, is the address. An elegant manor house is displayed on Google Maps. Florian's van keys are also part of the set. Jay checks the Amsterdam Centraal station surrounding and after a fair amount of cycling through Amsterdam, he secures Florian's van alongside a substantial amount of photographic equipment. The GPS helps him make his way around the Amsterdam suburbs.

Stardust, as per its name tag, is at home waiting for his servant to return. The cat litter's overpowering smells diminish the first impression of Florian's home. All lights on, Jay makes his way to the tiny green kitchen, cleans and refills the cat water bowl, and puts some fresh milk in a cup found on the kitchen rack. He empties a tin can and sprinkles some granules on top of it. All smells combined offend Jay's olfactory system and make him vomit. Having no time to react, the kitchen sink receives a warm, sticky, gooey mix of his last meal. With the help of some hot water, his fingers mash his discharge through the sink drain. After drinking a few glasses of cold water, he tackles the cat litter. His offering of help is not heavenly rewarded.

Jay inspects Florian's house, a floor level at the time. He climbs the narrow grey staircase and realises that the house's upper floors have not been used for a while. He made his way to the attic bedroom and bathroom. The rooms are lifeless except for the clean cotton sheets on the bed. Jay finds Florian's temple in the basement. His office, bedroom and bathroom are connected. The laundry is converted into a professional photography processing laboratory.

The makeshift darkroom looks operational. A heavy-filled bookshelf and an enormous set of wardrobes make this section of the house autonomous. Numerous well-framed photographs sitting on the long office desk bring warmth to the space. Florian's intellectual persona is reflected through his book collection, neatly marked and tagged with notes and yellow Post-it. A collection of vinyl records and a turn table offer another perspective on the deceased journalist; He was a disco lover. Disco Inferno by the Trammps is on the turntable platter.

Jay switches all the basement lights off and sits on the ground-floor sofa to converse with Stardust. Jay's petting is converted into heavy purring and leg and paw stretchings. The intensity of their conversation exhausts Jay, who falls asleep in no time.

Early in the morning, Jay wakes up when Florian's entry door opens and shuts, and someone runs down the basement stairs. Jay has not been noticed. Intrigued, he pops up like a puppet, quietly moving towards the top of the staircase, and decides to wait for the intruder to make his way back. Stardust follows and makes his way down to the office, where a sweet, joyful female Dutch voice greets him. Jay feels relieved and announces himself out loud from his perched position. He tells the reason why he is there and how he entered. Silence follows!

— 'Are you Evi? Florian mentioned you in one of our conversations,' he queries.

A defiant young lady appears in the cloakroom at the bottom of the staircase, armed with a pepper spray can aimed at Jay.

— 'I came here to care for the cat and to change my mind; I was exhausted and fell asleep on the couch. I do not plan to harm anyone. I just needed a little peace,' explains Jay, putting his hand up.

— 'Yes, I am Evi.' says the fearful young lady. 'Nothing bad is going to happen?'

— 'No, not at all! I am Jay Smith! I am here for the cat, but now, knowing you are here, you can take over!'

— 'Sorry, but I cannot! Florian was my client, my only client and my first client, I should say! I helped him with his editorials and publications. I just came to pick up some paperwork and my computer.'

— 'Are you out of work?'

— 'Yes, I am! I returned from Ibiza overnight when I learnt of his passing.'

— 'What were you doing in Ibiza? Where is Ibiza?'

— 'Clubbing. I went clubbing! Ibiza is in Spain.'

— 'Are you looking for work?'

— 'Yes, this is why I am here to secure my computer and other things. Florian did not pay my last invoices, and I am running out of money.'

— 'Would you like to work for me? I need help. I must care for many things, but my head is not there. To simplify things, I will pay you all outstanding invoices and pre-pay your first six months. I can only do cash now.'

— 'Is it a serious offer? No dirty tricks?'

— 'I have an ice cream business to take care of, which has a few dozen employees waiting for me to appear, a funeral plan to be sorted, and a few legal issues requiring a trusted person to help me navigate the Dutch legal system. I am clueless about where to start!'

— 'Why me?'

— 'The way you have greeted Stardust was heartwarming.'

— 'He is a good source of inspiration!'

— 'He can be yours now.'

— 'That is a serious commitment.'

— 'Think about it. Shelter is next for Stardust!'

— 'I will think about it, I promise'

— 'Okay, if you want to get paid, let's jump in Florian's van, and I give you your money. So we can start working. Handshake deal, cash in hand until the paperwork is done.'

— 'Are you sure?'

— 'One hundred percent! You need money, I need help! I do not ask you to be perfect; just be yourself and be honest!'

Jay stops at the barge. As a precautionary measure, he walks around the boat first and gives Evi a clearance sign to proceed inside. Jay retrieves a bag full of cash and asks Evi to take out what Florian owns her. Evi diligently counts the notes and shows Jay her pay after a few seconds.

— 'When working for Florian, how much money did you earn?' he asks her.

— '€2500 a month on average and sometimes a little bit more as a contractor.'

— 'How long did you work for Florian?'

— 'Over twelve months!'

— 'Was your salary enough to enjoy life?'

— 'Financially, it was tough, and I appreciate the back payment gesture.'

— 'I am not done yet; €5,000 per month is your salary now. Take €30,000 out of the bag, and you are worry-free for at least six months.'

— 'Are you sure? That is very generous of you; I never expected to earn €5,000 a month.'

— 'Your first job is to contact my wife's lawyer and book a meeting with them. Next is the ice cream business; I know nothing about it except the business card given to me by my wife. I do not even know who is in charged while she is away. We need to organise a site visit to discuss a transition period.'

— 'What about the funeral plan?'

— 'Let's check with the lawyers if my wife, Coco, had any insurance. Here are their names and numbers. These are my contact details. I will take care of the cat tonight; we can meet again later. I need your mobile number! Are you okay to return home from here on your own? I have some maintenance work to do here. Welcome on board!'

— 'That is funny that you say that. We are on a boat!' laughs Evi.

As soon as Evi leaves, Jay gathers all guns, pistols, ammunition and bags filled with cash. A bag at the time, he transfers everything into Florian's van and makes his way to Hotel Lucius. Where the reversed logistic applies except for the staircase of hell, he brings Florian's van to the secured safe house carpark for safety reasons. He then makes his way to Schiphol airport to retrieve Coco's Panamera from the valet service and finish his trip back in town at Hotel L'Europa, where Eef, the head concierge, offers him assistance to gain access to Coco's apartment. Jay falls again in love with the charm of the carpentry work, the bathroom's elegance and the canal's magical views. Like a thief, he opens all doors and draws to find Coco's funeral insurance papers. No paper is to be seen, no invoices, no tax bills, no car registration, nothing. The kitchen cabinets are filled with kitchen stuff; the wardrobes are filled with clothes. Jay goes to the bathroom and perfumes himself with Coco's gingery fragrance. He feels at home in his heart for an instant before his mind reminds him that his dirty laundry needs to be addressed sooner rather than later.

Back at the safe house, he seeks help from Ozzie and Cutie to fire up Coco's computer. They show him how to search into her email accounts. Jay asks the pair to review the CCTV footage of the ice cream manufacturing plant as he needs to stop the financial bleeding. Before meeting the managing team, he must know who and how the sabotage occurred. Cutie accesses Coco's secured password list and, in no time, logs in to the factory system and links all the streets and surrounding cameras to the search. It is just a matter of time before the culprit can be identified. Jay realises that his life just slowed down to a standstill. There is not much for him to do except wait on Gaston's faith, do his laundry, and feed the cat.

The evening meeting with Evi is fruitful. She organised a meeting with Coco's legal team for tomorrow morning, and they already informed her that Jay is allowed to take over the ice cream factory management as per the condition of his late wife's will. The conversation turns to Florian's activities and how much he knows about Jay.

— 'He was fascinated by your personality.' says Evi, laughing loudly.

— 'What do you mean? I am just a country boy.'

— 'You were, for him, a modern-day Bruce Lee or Chuck Norris. The mayor's resignation was probably the highlight of his life. He has so many pictures of you. He liked to process and print his photos.'

— 'I am interested in seeing what I look like in someone else's eyes.'

— 'Come with me; it is all with his notes and journals in the wardrobe.'

— 'It is not just me! All of Amsterdam is in there!' acknowledges Jay.

— 'There are great pictures of you! He was proud of your collaboration. He likes it when you smashed his camera; he felt like an actor in a gangster movie,' laughs Evi.

— 'Was his life boring?'

— 'I think so; reporting on murder scenes and bad people is not an action movie. It is time-consuming, and when you catch something, it goes as quickly as it came!'

— 'Was he a well-respected journalist?'

— 'His forteit was to be at the right place at the right time or vice versa. He had a sixth sense for predicting things that will happen.'

— 'Or was he informed to be at the right place at the right time?'

— 'I can't answer! His best quality was to outsource his weaknesses. He could not write; he was a terrible writer. That is why we worked together.'

— 'Was he a great photographer? After smashing his camera, I received some of his photographs, which are fantastic artwork.'

— 'There are also plenty of beautiful Dutch stories in the wardrobe. To my knowledge and as instructed by Florian, they are confidential information that should never be seen in the outside world!'

— 'Could I have a look?'

— 'All yours. Let your curiosity make your spine shiver. I must go now; thank you again for my paycheck today. I will await you at the lawyer's office tomorrow morning.'

Jay secures the front door and dives back into Florian's office to quickly peep at another potential Amsterdam mystery. All notes and journals are in Dutch and manually written. Jay's folder is on top of the pile and filled with hundreds of photos of him and Coco. The other records make no sense to him except when Ludo's name appears on one of the files. Jay flicks through it. Ludo was still a young lad when the pictures were taken, and in some of the shots, he looked like a boxer who could scare anyone in a dark alley after a fight. The backs of all photos have handwritten annotations, dates, locations, and small sketches outlining the human content of the respective photographs. Each person in the composition has their name written within their drawn silhouette. Jay goes backwards and forwards between the files and Ludo's photos to check if any names match. A few similarities surface, but Jay has no clue. It is late, and Stardust needs attention. Jay falls asleep again on the green sofa.

Chapter fourteen

The spanner in the wheel

Early in the morning, back at the safe house, Jay realises that the washing machine is not a dryer, and Jay is forced to wear the same clothes again for another few hours. He meets Evi at the solicitor's office. She is a morning girl full of energy and ready for action. The session with Coco's lawyers is similar to Jay's with Ken Dumbbells in Lincoln, Nebraska. There are a lot of 'sign here' and 'sign there' and translations in the middle. The firm founder, Net Vanderlaard, comes and introduces himself. He is as old as Gaston; he is well-dressed and speaks English with a charming accent, like Florian. He offers condolences and speaks with great pride about Coco and Gaston and how outstanding the individuals were and are. Through Net's monologue, Jay realises that Gaston's identity has not yet been revealed to the media; if so, the words towards him would not be so kind.

Net invites Jay to establish contact with Coco's accountant as there are rumours that her business is on the brink of collapse as some creditors are waiting to get paid. Jay asks Net if he is aware of the Hotel L'Europa acquisition and the deposit made by Coco towards its purchase. Net is more than aware of it; his body language dobs him in, and he is surprised when Jay announces that he will not proceed with the building purchase as he wants the deposit back, a decision that surprises everyone in the room.

— 'Gaston will be delighted with the news,' comments Net.

— 'Why Gaston?' asks Jay.

Net unveils a secret,

— 'Coco and Gaston were secretly competing with each other for the acquisition of Hotel L'Europa. As their representative, it was challenging for my team and me to keep a straight face, especially with Coco. Both were struggling to bring the cash to the table. Gaston claimed a clown stole his money, and Coco was in the process of securing a bank guarantee to complete the purchase.'

— 'Is there anything else they were competing for?'

— 'Except for their pride, no!'

— 'Does Coco have debt with you? Good accounts make good friends.'

— 'No! All her accounts are pre-paid; she did not like debts. Her business cashflow crisis was unexpected and put her under strain big time.'

— 'What do you mean all her accounts?'

— 'Hers, Gaston and the foundation ones.'

— 'She paid for everything and everyone. Was she the

'naivety bank'?'

— 'Sadly, her naivety and generosity were her enemy.'

— 'Keeping her naivety and generosity aside, by paying all the bills for everyone, she was the client.'

— 'Yes! Technically, yes!'

— 'Could you bring Gaston's paperwork, please!'

— 'No, I cannot; his matters are confidential!'

— 'A few minutes ago, I signed a ton of paperwork giving me authority and ownership of my late wife's business and assets. So, as your client, I want to know where my money or company resources were used for.'

— 'It does not work that way!'

— 'Maybe not in your world, but in mine, we are not talking bullshit.'

— 'Only Mr. Lars can approve your request.'

— 'Could we have a two-second chat with just the two of us?'

Evi and Net's staff give privacy and vacate the boardroom.

— 'I understand your privacy concerns; I am not opposed to it. In all confidentiality, Gaston will never make it back to your office; soon, he will be charged with murders and other more serious offences. We are not talking pity crimes; we are talking about the killing of my wife and hundreds of people.'

— 'That is ridiculous! I cannot imagine Gaston as a fraudulent person or killing Coco.'

— 'Let me call the police commissioner; he will validate my words.'

— 'Let me call him, I know Ludo. I have his number; we

are both members of the Rotary Club.'

Net wanders between the four walls of the boardroom. His face shade becomes whiter and whiter with the intensity of the information he needs to process. His foot pace catches up with his increased heart rate. The water jug stops his demented psychotic pacing; he drinks its entirety with shaky hands. The end of the call brings Net back to a sombre reality that should never existed.

— 'Mr. Lars papers, please!' requests Jay.

— 'Okay!' replies a dishevelled Net.

The boardroom table is not big enough to contain Gaston's matters. He is selling his entire real estate empire. From the Ukrainian-Russian border to the feet of the Chapel of Santiago de Compostela in Spain, everything Papa owns is on the market. A pretty portfolio made of little cottages and country farms where, most likely, innocent underage children were abused and killed with no mercy.

With Evi's help, Jay records all addresses and information related to the properties and informs Net that the sale cannot proceed.

Net cooperation starts to deteriorate, and Jay verbally resists him before he can show the true nature of his personality.

— 'Please transfer the deposit Coco made on Hotel L'Europa into the business bank account before close of business day.'

— 'That is impossible!'

— 'I give you twenty-four hours to do so, or Amsterdam will know all about your unethical personality. I also want a refund on the transaction fees charged to Coco.'

— 'Coco was more amicable to do business with.'

— 'She was naïve, and you disgracefully abused her naivety. Do not wait for the news to come live to decide whose amiability is best. I am your concerns now and your client.' Jay presses while offering a solid manly handshake to Net.

— 'That is not how it works!' replies a bitter Net.

— 'Preserving your legacy should be your priority! Based on today's evidence, you sabotaged Coco's acquisition deal to favourite Gaston's sex trafficking venture, and this alone makes you an accomplice.'

— 'Are you blackmailing me?'

— 'Over a thousand people, mostly children and women, lost their lives because of little dirty deals. Ludo is only a phone call away. You have his number, and I give you the privilege of calling him.'

Back in the street, Evi is shocked by the little she heard. Jay explains, with little detail, the diaries, all files and folders found in Ostend, as well as the relationship between Gaston and Coco.

Evi informs Jay that Coco's accountant will meet them at the ice cream factory. Their meeting is scheduled for the early afternoon, and the factory is located an hour away on the outskirts of Amsterdam. Jay suggests they regroup around lunchtime; he wants to dress up for the occasion.

Back at the safe house, Ozzie is alone. He welcomes Jay and checks on his mental health at the same time. Both men hug quietly. It is a tricky question that does not have an answer. The Nebraskan pair plan to catch up for dinner and have some Korean fried chicken and a solid round of cold beers. The washing machine and the clothes dryer refill Jay's wardrobe for a limited time.

Jay is surprised when the Uber driver pulls over the factory driveway. The ice cream production facility is massive. The executive leadership team is in the lobby, waiting for Jay to enter. A round of condolences and formal handshakes are exchanged. Jay does not memorise a single name and introduces Evi as his assistant.

— 'Welcome home!' says Akanksha Mahindra, an older lady of Indian descent. Her hand salutation, head bow movement and generous smile caught Jay's soft spot. He returns the gesture, a tear in his eyes. Akanksha was Coco's assistant.

— 'Where would you like to start?' she adds.

— 'Coco's office, a factory tour to get my head around things and meet our workforce simultaneously and the boardroom where we can all sit together and go through the prickly bits.'

— 'Follow me! It is my privilege to take you there.'

After climbing the lobby set of stairs and walking through an open space office, Jay enters Coco's business temple; Akanksha gives him privacy. The first-floor office is strategically located. Coco had a full view of the production area, the loading docks, the employee and visitor's carpark, and the factory's entry from her desk. The space is overglazed and has a beautiful natural light. Jay spots a few framed newspaper cutouts on Coco's desk. He smiles as he massages her office chair headrest like he did with her shoulder. The stitching of the leather chair reminds him of his first ride in Coco's Panamera. After a few minutes, Akanksha checks on Jay and one more time repeats,

— 'Welcome home!'

Jay smiles and replies,

— 'Let's meet the family, Coco's family!'

— 'What title would you like on your business card?' queries the Indian lady.

— 'Akanksha's assistant is my first option or ice cream tester if I have no other choice,' laughs Jay.

— 'If you are my assistant, Sir, please follow me to meet everyone.'

— 'Akanksha, I am no Sir, I am Jay. You and I are equal.' Adding a white lie to the conversation, Jay tells her that Coco mentioned her numerous times in their chats and that Coco was blessed to have her as a personal assistant and a confidant.

— 'That is very nice of you, Sir', I mean, 'Mr Jay.'

— 'Jay, just Jay. No, mister.'

— 'Jay, for sure, Sir, Mr. Jay! Sorry, I am teasing you, Jay. On a serious note, it was a privilege to work alongside your wife, and with the same passion, I am delighted to help you in your journey.'

Akanksha and Jay rejoin the leadership group; everyone wears white protective equipment, safety shoes, and a headpiece to cover their hair. Having no clue about Jay's shoe sizes, ten pairs of steel caps boots wait for him to be tried on. Looking like a team member, Jay's ice cream world unfolds in front of him. He shakes hands with every employee of every department. Occasionally, he shares another white lie with the workers by telling them his late wife appreciated and valued them. In no time, his manufacturing knowledge grows. He learns the entire production cycle from raw material delivery and storage, scaling and weighting, mixing, homogenisation and pasteurisation, ageing, flavour addition and freezing, packaging, cartoning, hardening and anything and everything linked to the logistics that will deliver thousands of ice cream cones and tubs all around the Netherlands and the European market. The place runs like clockwork; most operating stations are fully automated. Quality control is manually done through the entire process.

Back in the boardroom, Jay is invited to sample some of the products that are ready for delivery. More knowledge is shared about the cone composition, the flavouring process, the packaging and printing requirements, graphic design and marketing.

Jay thanks everyone for their hospitality, generosity and enthusiasm. He shares his background, life in Nebraska, the 'Swap your job with a stranger' lottery, his short life with Coco, his fabulous wedding in Las Vegas, and everyday news content. He highlights the genuine pleasure he had in meeting everyone. Most importantly, he can now appreciate Coco's passion for her business, entrepreneurship skills, leadership talents, and fantastic trust in everyone working here. But now Jay must address the elephant in the room as he did at the solicitor's office,

— 'I heard some gossip and rumours suggesting that we are experiencing some serious manufacturing and financial problems poisoning the daily performances of the business and its reputation in the marketplace. Before answering, as I did not remember everyone's name, could we place a name tag in front of ourselves? I want to take the opportunity to introduce Evi as my administrative assistant, who is helping me to navigate the Dutch legal system and many other things. Evi will also work alongside all of us in the organisation. One person at the time, could we list all matters that require instant actions.'

— 'Hi, I am Cedric Lafkoof, Chief Financial Officer. Our pressing issues include our cash flow and revenue, the ongoing production sabotage, our current positioning in the marketplace, all legal proceedings, and the potential compensation scheme.

— 'The people who wanted the business to fall are either dead or arrested. I cannot disclose information on these individuals; I can tell you that the sabotage is over. We will find out who is responsible for the physical tempering of the goods and make them accountable for their actions. In addition to this information, I would like to add that this morning, I was made aware that serious financial sabotage was against the business and Coco's interests. Evi and I are working with her legal team to have the funds returned by tomorrow lunchtime, and I will supplement any shortfalls, if necessary, to the limit of my possibilities.'

— 'Hi, Sophie Natje, head of the in-house legal team; how would you like us to deal with the legal proceedings?'

— 'A settlement behind closed doors is our best option. We need to finalise this matter as soon as possible to minimise the business branding disruption.'

— 'The plaintiffs are very vocal on social media and are

represented by the law firm Aiken & Siken. All complaints are solely in Amsterdam,' adds Sophie.

— 'Are the complaints legitimate? Does anyone produce their proof of purchase?' queries Jay.

— 'Aiken & Siken are weirdos! Sorry, I am Arthur Delevigne, waffle cone production manager. Their reputation is questionable; everyone in Amsterdam is aware of their dirty tactics to make people pay. We should investigate their connections.'

— 'Could you tell us more?' snaps Jay with a voice filled with interest.

— 'Shards of glass or milled glass fibres in cone or ice cream mixes cannot be missed through our rigorous quality control processes and procedures. We ran contaminated batches to assess the claims; the foreign objects were easily detected, and this alone made me think that their claims were false and that the food tempering never existed. It is a smear campaign against the business or its owner.' suggests Arthur, with stern body language that supports his opinion.

— 'Could I receive the list of all plaintiffs and the contact details of Aiken & Siken?' seeks Jay.

— 'They do bad and lengthy advertisement campaigns late at night on national TV channels. They are not hard to miss; they look like cokeheads flashing their expensive jewellery and fancy Rolex watches in front of their luxury cars,' adds Sophie.

— 'Let me find out if the claims are fabricated. If so, I will take care of it personally!' comments Jay.

— 'We are all aware that you are used to making every

news outlet's front cover. Could we be reassured that your move, if any, against Aiken & Siken, will be executed within the guidelines of the business code of conduct?' interferes Simone Reynders, head of Human Resources.

— 'I will do my best to make you proud; please do not bet any money on how clean it will be,' replies Jay.

— 'We lost a great leader! One is enough!' Akanksha comments.

— 'Do we have better options?' asks Jay respectfully.

— 'You made it home safely so far! Let's do our best to keep it that way!' Akanksha concludes with a peaceful smile on her face.

— 'We will succeed together! Let's take a break! I need to go to the bathroom,' says Jay, leaving the board room.

As soon as he reaches the toilet cubicle, Jay searches Aiken & Siken on his phone. As described accurately by Sophie, they like to flash their wealth. Their supercars were purchased from Paul Van Looke's business; the advertising surrounding the car registration number plates is identical to Papa's. Jay texts Ozzie and seeks Cutie's help to scavage through Van Looke's email to find evidence linking the parties. Jay suggests that Cutie also use her skills to penalise Aiken & Siken financially as they accept cryptocurrencies as a form of payment.

Ozzie's answer is a collection of 'thumbs up and dollar sign' emojis.

Jay rejoins the executive leadership team; the outcome of the financial meeting is simple: Jay must cash up the bank check as soon as possible to salvage Coco's business.

Some creditors are ninety days overdue and are themselves in an untenable financial situation. Jay realises that the ice cream industry has a minimal chain of suppliers for quality ingredients. Coco's naivety, optimism and generosity may have gotten the better of her. Nico Spielberg, her accountant, and the CFO have difficulty explaining some commercial decisions. A product, market, and profit analysis must be conducted to return to profitability immediately.

Back in his new office, Jay invites Akanksha for a chat as he wants to know more about the charismatic and intriguing woman. Coco and Akanksha have been together for a lifetime; she managed Coco's professional ballet dancing career and was invited to join the ice cream venture from its inception. They were close friends. Jay forgot to ask the accountant for Coco's insurance paper; his only option for the day is Akanksha. There will be no funeral as Coco opted for a body donor program. Due to the circumstances of her death, Jay cannot comprehend how it will work.

— 'How do you feel about it?' asks Jay to Akanksha.

— 'She is alive!' replies with a smile, the charismatic Indian lady.

— 'How do you feel about not having a funeral?'

— 'She is not the type of woman we can put in a box and walk away. She is free! Everywhere we go, she is there too! She is free and knowing that makes me happy!'

— 'I would be happier if she was here now.'

— 'Your happiness should not be subject to others entering or exiting your existence. Clean your heart if that is the case.'

— 'Did you teach her that mantra?'

— 'No, she's the one who taught me how to make my life easier.'

— 'What was your relationship with Gaston?'

— 'In the beginning, it was both simple and complex at the same time. I was recommended to him; we had a phone conversation on the old landline. I received a cheque every year to take care of Coco's career. He was harsh with me to ensure she attains his vision and wishes. You made me so happy when you joined her on stage and danced elegantly with her. It was the best way to finish out her dancing career. I would pay big money to see it again. She loved you, Jay. I will pay even more money to see her glowing since the night she met you. We passed the day just dreaming of your fairy tale.'

— 'I felt something too that night.'

— 'Do you still feel it?'

— 'In a painful way, yes!'

— 'Go and clean your heart. She does not want you to suffer. You are a free man. It is your turn to show us the way!'

— 'And what is your relationship with Gaston now? Is it still simple and complicated?'

— 'Over the years, we became good friends; very good friends indeed, as Coco's interest was our priority.'

— 'Do you know why she was killed?'

— 'I think so!'

— 'Could you expand a little bit?'

— 'Her involvement in the sex worker shelter is when things start to go downhill for us. Very fast. Very quick.'

— 'Do you know who is behind her killing?'

— 'The rich boy of Amsterdam as seen on TV. Sorry! It sounds like bad TV commercial advertising. The truth is as seen on TV.'

'The truth is Paul Van Looke executed his father's orders! Gaston is Van Looke's dad. Both are responsible for her killing, and it is not yet in the news. Gaston has been arrested for the murder of Paul's mum and the journalist gunned down at the train station carpark.'

— 'Why would Gaston do such a thing? He did everything he could for his daughter's success and wellbeing.'

— 'I am the spanner in the wheel. I disrupted his plans and probably expedited Coco's execution.'

— 'You sound guilty!' quickly replies Akanksha.

— 'I am guilty, and I feel guilty. I am responsible for what happened to Coco.'

— 'Coco and I had conversations when she discovered her name and her friends' names were on a hit list. It did not phase her at all; she had faced more difficult challenges in her life. Trust me on that one!'

— 'What do you know about her life?'

— 'Dance and ballet, as hard as they can be to perfect, were the best therapies to heal her trauma.'

— 'Did you feel like her Mum?'

— 'I felt more than that. I felt loved and appreciated whatever the challenges put upon us. The feeling was also reciprocated!'

— 'Are you looking to stay and help me?

— 'I am only seventy-two. I have no hurry to leave. She is alive! You have no responsibility in her passing; she enters your life to make you grow emotionally.'

— 'Did you teach her that?'

— 'No, she did; it was her weapon to face any life obstacle.'

— 'What is your take on it?'

— 'My take on it is simple: You are now the 'Captain' of the big ice cream boat. Keep your eyes on the horizon, and do not anchor or tangle yourself in fishing nets.'

— 'Is there a better word than 'Captain'? I have grown out of it.'

— 'Enjoy your freedom! The place is yours, and this is your access pass to the building. Tomorrow, we will do your onboarding, secure your IT credentials, and put a picture of Coco on your desk. Life is great, Jay! Make it even greater, Captain!'

Evi patiently waited in the lobby for Jay to return. He thanks her for her support and patience, and they discuss tomorrow's agenda while travelling back to Amsterdam. He checks on Abigail's health via a text message.

Ozzie, Cutie and Jay meet at the Gangnam restaurant. Everyone looks exhausted but happy to gather. Jay apologises to Ozzie for not bringing him any ice cream samples to try. The trio warms up to joyfulness when the fried chicken dishes and the cold tap beers land on their table. They toast to their friendship and discuss their day. Jay is fixated on the television screen like the first time around. Gaston's name has not yet been released to the public. Later in the evening, the trio meet with Stardust at Florian's place. The evening is playful until Ozzie and Cutie's phone alert them simultaneously to the fact that Ludo is making his way towards Ostend. In no time, the pair disappears and goes back behind their control tower at the safe house.

Jay feeds Stardust, cleans his tray, and makes his way into Florian's office to take another look at Ludo's file among all the other files. The entire wardrobe is now on the floor; he takes hundreds of photos of archived pictures and carefully focuses on all hand-drawn sketches holding the identities of unknown individuals. Jay makes his way back to safety, ready to search the internet. Ludo is not far from Ostend, so it is just a matter of time before the trio knows his intentions. Jay set up Coco's laptop next to Ozzie, and the names of all individuals collected earlier at Florian's place are being processed. His primary focus is on those photographed in the company of Ludo. The search confirms that most men in the pictures are wealthy locals and professionals. Some of them have ugly, severe truths attached to their profiles. They are linked to crime, prostitution, sex trafficking, paedophilic networks, tax evasion and many more. Some of them are wanted, some are dead, some are jailed, and some remain living an everyday life in the Dutch capital. Jay types diligently the addresses where the photos were taken. It is all over Europe, and he realises quickly that some of the village names match Gaston's property location. Cutie and Ozzie are shocked by the news and are now on the edge of their seats to find Ludo's reason for being in Ostend.

Cutie's secret camera installation works perfectly at Kapucijnenstraat. Her luck is that the building is still connected to the power and that someone has invented remote internet access. Ludo enters the building through the garage door and makes his way to the upper floors via the central staircase. He brands a large-sized automatic weapon in front of his body as he moves along. On the first-floor landing, he adjusts his beanie and dark plastic gloves before opening the unit door. When in, he pushes a bag from which he retrieves a set of tactical flashlights that he strategically positions to navigate easily through the rows of shelving. He opens and closes folders and makes himself familiar with the classification methodology. He quickly moves to a section, filling his bag with some of the folder's content. He appears to be targeting specific dates or crime categories. He is in no rush; he moves back and forth between the different shelving sections and packs a substantial amount of evidence away. Ninety minutes into his mission, he decides to visit the other floors. He takes all the USB sticks left next to the projector on the second floor. He checks his watch a few times to keep track of time. The third floor is of no interest to him, and he makes his way out of the building.

The trio has been silent for the duration of their monitoring duties. Cutie and Ozzie now follow Ludo's movements on their tracking apps. He moves and stops through the town of Ostend.

— 'What did he collect?' asks Jay, 'It appears he knew what to look for.'

— 'Do you think this is linked to your findings at Florian's place!' queries Cutie.

— 'Why were you so upset with Ludo after our trip to Ostend? Why did you decide to install a CCTV network,' asks Jay.

— 'The server, he referred to, is a trash can. Any information transferred or tagged to it is immediately deleted. I already lost information and evidence that way. He teamed us up to check on each other. He did not expect or think it would benefit us.'

Ludo's driving pattern is strange. He drives for ten minutes and stops for five, drives another fifteen, and stops for another five. He circles Ostend's suburbs for over two hours before returning to Kapucijnenstraat.

The CCTV footage is concerning. Ludo brings loaded fuel jerry cans into the building. There are probably twenty of them. His driving pattern makes sense. He drove to all petrol stations to secure and purchase the plastic tanks and fill them.

The trio becomes aware of what will happen next. Cutie jumps on the internet search engine and calls the police and fire brigade in Ostend. Her Dutch accent is perfect, and her directive words sound harsh. The petite Asian beauty knows exactly how to distribute clear and concise information.

Ludo splashes the fuel across the room and on some of the shelving. Having no physical way to stop the destruction of the crime evidence, Jay calls him. Ludo freezes, looks at his phone, and ignores the call. Jay tries again, and as his call is not answered, he sends a text message to Ludo telling him that the police are on their way and that he needs to surrender. Jay calls again, and Ludo picks up the call.

— 'Stop, please! I beg you! We need this information to bring peace and closure to hundreds of families,' yells Jay.

— 'There is nothing you can do; I need to erase this

chapter of my life. I have no choice,' replies a distressed and erratic Ludo.

— 'Did you rape or kill anyone?'

— 'As an undercover cop, I infiltrated paedophile networks. My job was to clean crime scenes. I raped, killed and made victims disappear. I was forced into it to blend in.'

— 'How many times did you rape and kill?'

— 'A lot, it grew on me! I found a real pleasure to rape, mutilate and kill defenceless people, especially young flat-chested teenage girls. Just talking about it makes me euphoric about the prospect of raping the next one.' Ludo says, resting the fuel can on the floor and pacing through the rows of shelving.

— 'Did you seek assistance from the police force? When did you rape or kill last?'

— 'By becoming the Police Commissioner, I lost my travelling freedom, so now I drug, touch and rape my daughters in their sleep. It happens at least twice a week. I love them, but I can't control my impulses. I have great pleasure in seeing others suffer. It gets me hard, real hard. Female survival fears are my sexual stimulations!'

Ludo's voice is all over the shop as he realises that his lifetime webs of lies are exposed, as he self-confesses his past actions bluntly.

— 'Surrender. It is over! This is your best outcome. Give yourself to the police and seek help, please! This is my best advice to you!' says Jay frantically.

— 'Are you in Ostend?'

— 'No, I have set up cameras all over the building. I can

see you and our conversations are recorded. Surrender and do not destroy anything.'

— 'Ingrid never liked you! Your luck was that she found about her execution date in the diary.'

— 'What is the reason for her execution?'

— 'Ingrid learned that Gaston and Paul Van Looke offloaded their businesses to another mobster for big bucks. It did not sit well with her as we became obsolete overnight. Her financial situation inflames everyone's relationships. Bitterness settled in as he took us all out of the picture.'

As Ludo can hear the sirens taking over the neighbourhood, he runs down the staircase in an attempt to escape. The police force bashes the garage roller door to enter the building. He soon realises that he is trapped within the building. Ludo panics and does the unthinkable. He pours a jerry can full of petrol over himself and sets it alight. On the monitoring screens, a human ball of fire dances in agony in the garage before collapsing to the ground. The sound coming through the CCTV network is untenable. Police officers and firefighters manage their way through the building and take over Ludo's charred, moving body with fire extinguishers. They are too late.

Cutie is still on the phone giving directions to her Belgian counterparts. The fire brigade secures the first floor, removing unused fuel jerry cans and spray-absorbing foam around the room. She is informed that they manage to secure Ludo's bag from the trunk of his car. She receives photos of stolen archives inside Ludo's travel bag per her request. Ludo did not lie. He was a serial rapist and a lifetime paedophile.

The trio is thrilled that all evidence has been saved and equally shocked by the twist of events.

To prevent Ozzie and Cutie from getting into the spotlight and preserve their anonymity, Jay informs them that he takes full responsibility for installing and controlling the CCTV network in Ostend. Both agree. Cutie secures a few USB sticks and copies Ludo's two sessions. Everyone receives at least three copies. Jay goes down to the Police headquarters to give a set to the duty officer with clear instructions on how to proceed.

OSTEND

Chapter fifteen

To Florian

As Gaston's identity has still not been released to the press, Jay contacts De Dagblad newspaper. It is nearly three o'clock in the morning. Over the phone, he introduces himself to the night receptionist and requests to talk to Florian Van Bruggel's manager. With an adrenaline-fuelled voice, he makes it clear that the information he's ready to share is related to Florian's killing and other unthinkable matters.

Omar Luchtbrood, the night newspaper editor, takes the call. Hearing the veracity and complexity of the story, he immediately invites Jay to come to the Dutch Media headquarters. The communication flows between the pair, and by six o'clock in the morning, De Dagblad's scoop is online, and their headlines blast their competitors away. Hundreds of people around the world are now on notice. As a police informer, Jay does not want to be named or receive credit for the story. His only request is that the article is dedicated to Florian Van Bruggel.

Jay refuses a lift back to the police headquarters; he walks through Amsterdam and along its canals. His thoughts are with Coco and Florian. His sadness and melancholy bless the lives of two outstanding individuals. He acknowledges that Natalia's invitation to swap his job with a stranger is, in many ways, a blessing that has generated equal pleasure and emotional growth he never thought existed. As painful as it was then, Polka's loss seems insignificant today. He humbly comes to the fact that watching porn and buying car parts for his Dodge Challenger were band-aids or coping mechanisms to hide some of his unhealthy internalised sufferings. Outsourcing his job at the lawnmower factory was a waste of time and energy. As his head is spinning in all directions, he realises that Coco and Florian dedicated their entire life to the meaning of creation, and maybe they even received, without their acknowledgement, God's blessing for the perfect pirouette or a well-published article.

—— 'Is there a blessing in disguise for the one who overviewed the thousands of ice creams leaving the factory chillers every day while the delivery trucks counterbalance the ins and outs of the accounting sheets? Where is the joy of being the 'Captain' of a mega confectionery factory?' mumbles Jay as he recalls Coco's words about how time stops when we enjoy ice cream.

His steps take him to Omelegg by accident, where a generous-sized hot breakfast boosts his spirit.

Through text messages, Evi reminds Jay of his duties for

the day and asks him to take his passport along so he can cash the bank cheque. Net has informed her that Coco's deposit for the acquisition of Hotel L'Europa has been instrumented and refunded into the company account. Net has also offered a letter of apology to Jay.

Behind his spying computer farm, Ozzie, who has had no sleep, watches the online news. The Belgian police's public relations machine takes the credit for the Ostend bust. To cope with the online setback, the Dutch police release an extensive list of Van Looke's collaborators, business partners and perpetrators. Jay's face is back on everyone's screens worldwide. Cutie went for a voluntary debrief. On her return, she informs Jay that Coco's body has been transferred, as per her wish, to the anatomical institute of the Amsterdam UMC and that she has successfully downloaded and printed a stack of Paul Van Looke's emails inviting Aiken & Siken to disrupt Coco's business. She also proudly announces that she successfully targeted and emptied their online crypto wallets. Around two hundred million euros have changed hands early this morning. The trio high-five each other madly. Cutie wants to know where Jay wants his share of the money transferred. Without hesitation, the ice cream business account is his choice. Ozzie is stoked, knowing he also receives a third of the funds.

By midday, the ice cream factory bank account is replenished, and all suppliers have been paid. Jay passes the rest of the day walking through the production lines, meeting and talking to his employees, quietly celebrating the fact that their employment is now safe.

Evi secures a mediation meeting with Aiken & Siken and their represented parties. She sells them the idea of settling all compensation cases behind closed doors. The date, time and venue are still to be confirmed. Jay is excited and wants fun; Aiken & Siken will have a humiliating party. He calls Tia and Kora. He wants the Haka army to make a surprise appearance at the meeting.

Jay passes the evening with Stardust and Amsterdam is quiet. He packs all of Florian's files neatly on the floor; he does not want to lose evidence against Ludo and the other suspects. As a matter of due diligence, he checks every cupboard, cabinet and drawer he can find from the house's attic to Florian's office. Everything is in the basement, and Jay questions who is best to receive the information — the Dutch police force or De Dagblad. After his feed, Stardust finds his friend lying on the green couch. They fall asleep, cuddling each other.

Chapter sixteen

The librarian

Early in the morning, Jay's mobile ringtone wakes him up. Standing up, he realises he can't find his handset. The phone rings again, and the ringtone is muffled. He looks around him, checking Florian's basement, the kitchen and the ground-floor living room. He comes back and rechecks the couch, removes the pillows, and notices his phone stuck within the back frame of the sofa. He goes around, down to his knees, and runs his fingers alongside the bottom of the fabric. He can't do anything, as there is no space to put his head through. He runs down the stairs to Florian's office to pick up a pile of books and magazines and jack up the furniture. After a thirty-minute battle with the heavy green sofa, he retrieves his handset. There is a voicemail from the police headquarters, and Jay has been invited to give his version of the Ostend events.

Putting the books and magazines back on Florian's shelf with little care, a storage docket falls on the desk. Jay immediately knows its provenance — 'Lockbox Luggage Storage Amsterdam Centraal'. Jay pulls everything out of the shelves and, within seconds, retrieves another five hidden in a book titled The Thursday Murder Club by Richard Osman.

— 'Happy Birthday, Florian. Thursday only for them, full-time job for us. Your partner in crime. Ludo,' reads an annotation written adjacent to the book preface.

The book is three years old, and the locker facility access cards were issued ten days ago. Jay's head is spinning madly. He checks again the bookshelves' contents. He shakes every book and publication; nothing is added to his first finding. The only add-ons are his thoughts on Ludo and Florian; he doubts the honesty of their relationship.

— 'Was Florian an informer or a partner in crime?' thinks Jay.

— 'Is Amsterdam that fucked?' he mumbles to himself.

He secures the six dockets in his wallet and returns to the police headquarters, where he plans to use Florian's van to retrieve the lockers' contents. He calls Ozzie for help. Sadly, Jay realises he locked himself out of Florian's place. He left the house keys on the kitchen benchtop with Stardust's food pack. Cutie organises a locksmith who never shows up and, as a desperate manoeuvre, Jay contacts Gilles Lombard to the rescue. The door opens instantly, but the thank-you rounds of cold beers with the foxy Dutchman postpone the locker's retrieval mission to the following day.

Suffering a massive hangover, Ozzie and Jay drive to the centre of Amsterdam. This time, Jay doesn't take any precautions to hide his identity. Every locker opens at lightning speed, and Jay secures all proof of payment. Paul Van Looke paid for the storage ten days ago. All contents are transferred rapidly into the back of the van. Jay's handling skills have improved. He is in shock while acknowledging the volume of information retrieved. Ozzie drives the van back to Florian's place. They sort out the contents of the lockers inside the back of the utility vehicle: cash, photographic records, negative rolls, USB sticks and dozens of hard drives. All photographic evidence goes to Florian's basement for Jay to review. Ozzie takes care of returning the van and hiding the cash. When approaching Hotel Lucius, he doesn't look forward to climbing its hellish stairs.

It is near lunchtime. Jay texts Akanksha that he won't make it to the office today. He calls Evi to meet at Hotel L'Europa to book a function room and plan the meeting with Aiken & Siken.

The pair meets with Eef, who helps them with their enquiries and suggests the Weerspiegelkamer room as his preferred option. The room is as beautiful as Coco's apartment but in a different style altogether. The high ceiling, the natural light, the colour of the handmade wallpaper, the furniture, and the curtain selection make it the perfect room for negotiation.

Jay insists that all rare decorations and valuable items be removed from the room. The meeting setup is a square table with seating for sixteen people centred in the middle of the space. He makes sure the perimeter walls are free of obstacles. Eef is also informed that a few video cameras will be installed before the meeting, and an HDMI cable and a projector are required.

On a side note, Eef inquires if Jay wants to maintain the floral arrangement in Coco's apartment, as no one currently lives there. Jay breaks Eef's heart when he announces that he is considering selling the place as he doesn't have the time or financial resources to enjoy it. Eef informs Jay that management has received numerous queries about the property since Coco's passing.

Evi confirms with Jay that the meeting with Aiken & Siken is scheduled and confirmed for Monday afternoon. Eef accepts the booking. Jay informs the 'Haka Girls', Omar Luchtbrood and seeks Ozzie and Cutie's assistance for the video setup.

It is late Friday afternoon; Jay walks to Florian's place and stops at a frituur. His nostalgia pushes him to order another unhealthy round of hot chips, frikandel, andalouse sauce and a Lindemans Kriek. He eats slowly and quietly and hopes to solve Gaston, Ludo and Florian's mystery. He realises he doesn't have a computer to check the USB sticks and the portable hard drives. He returns to the safe house and visits the duty officer at the reception counter at the police headquarters. He wants to know who called him and when he needs to make himself available for his witness statement. As no one is available, he is invited to return tomorrow mid-afternoon.

Ozzie and Cutie are on the move. She has been invited to Ostend to help her Belgian counterparts, and Ozzie needs to update his monitoring farm at the University and provide an academic update to his lecturers. As the lovers cuddle before their short separation, Jay grabs Coco's laptop and prepares for his weekend with Stardust.

Back at Florian's place, Jay starts with the hard-printed materials first. Like in Ostend, he is surprised at how everything is well catalogued. Most of the pictures are of men of all ages abusing women and girls of all ages. In a short amount of time, Jay assumes that Florian is the hidden photographer touring Gaston's farms and cottages to take pictures of paedophiles in action.

— 'Was Gaston preparing pornographic material to blackmail his client if things didn't go as planned?' thinks Jay.

The room and camera angles are always the same, just different bastards exploring and embracing their sexual, physical and mental deviances.

Ludo's face appears in a photo set dated mid-August 2008. Sixteen graphic frames summarise his brutality. The still shots depict how he beats and kicks with no mercy an already bloody and bruised teenage girl. Collapsed on the ground, the girl's life was terminated by strangulation. Ludo twisted the bed sheets around her throat while resting his body weight on her lungs. The most disturbing frames of Ludo's set are him positioning the corpse on the edge of the bed, spreading its legs and raping it, and concealing the victim's body in a plastic bag inside a hard-shell suitcase that has been tampered with — tiny holes to facilitate its sinking.

— 'They are not ventilation holes,' acknowledges Jay vocally as he speculates that the victim's body was dumped in a lake or waterway afterwards.

The rest of the printed materials are not better. Ludo

reappears numerous times. His killing methods are getting more barbaric as he rapes his victim before ending their life. The result is always the same: an out-of-life body is bagged away in a suitcase.

On Coco's computer, Jay visualises all USBs and portable hard drives. After hours of gruelling data review, he locates a folder named 'Parties'. His curiosity gets the better of him, and he can't wait to have his optimism crushed. He is right! The first pictures depict Gaston dining with Akanksha. Both look relaxed and intimate. Gaston has his hands on Akanksha's thigh. A few clicks down the picture folder, a frame shows Gaston, Ludo, Florian and Akanksha drinking cocktails at a bar; all look like tourists wearing polos, shorts and sandals. Based on the logo embroidered on the bath towel, the next set of frames is taken in Chamonix in the French Alps. Gaston and Akanksha drink champagne naked in a hot tub. As the set evolves, Akanksha looks tipsy. She drinks from the bottle, pushing her puffy nipples in Gaston's face. In the last frame, Akanksha performs an inversion yoga pose; her legs are wide open, and Gaston pushes the champagne bottle annulus into her vagina.

Another folder titled 'Work' delivers the true professional relationship between Gaston and Akanksha. She is the librarian. She is the one who has recorded years of gory business manually. Her hand calligraphy is everywhere. Every page of every folder located in Ostend is a testimony of her working life. The most troubling picture of the series is when Jay recognises her wearing the female pair of flamenco heels spotted in numerous Polaroid snaps inside the diaries.

— 'Is she part of the execution team or the executioner?' questions Jay loudly.

His mind spins on his naivety and how easily he was controlled by Florian, Ludo and now Akanksha by simply trusting their words and embracing their playful and fake personas. Jay feels for Coco and how easy it was for her to fall for Papa's plan.

The set of pictures that seals Jay's night behind the computer is taken at a swingers' party or a nudist camp in Cap d'Agde, France. Paul Van Looke, Akanksha, and Gaston are snapped having a threesome in front of a mirror, which reflects a near-naked Florian wearing some stockings and a garter belt. Van Looke is the receiver of Akanksha's blow job while she rides Gaston's cock. Both Van Looke and Gaston are wearing high heels.

Jay copies and saves some of the records on a USB stick. He wants to print a few frames to put on his office desk. Akanksha will have a few questions to answer, and the most pressing one is 'Where is Coco's adoption file?'. Jay left Stardust behind and made his way back to the safe house. He needs a good night's sleep. While walking along the canal, he texts Omar. He wants to catch up early in the morning, and the meeting is accepted within seconds.

Chapter seventeen

He is in your care

Omar is punctual. As he arrives at Florian's place, he is surprised that Jay has access to the property. His concern vanishes when he faces the gruelling task of reviewing and acknowledging the hidden life of his colleague and the monstrosity generated and recorded over the years. Flicking through the photos, Jay clarifies that Akanksha is the only member of Gaston's circle still walking freely in Amsterdam today, and he hopes that he can corner her in his office early next week before the police force arrests her. As Omar is overwhelmed, Jay asks him to decide how he wants to secure the material before the police take possession of it. To take Omar out of his brain freeze, Jay invites him to buy big external hard drives to transfer the maximum amount of information, making him aware that he's got limited time to do so before the authorities take over Florian's place.

While Omar shops for data storage units, Jay calls the police station to follow up on their request to meet, which turns into an invitation to collect Florian's atrocities. His next call is Cedric Lafkoof, Coco's chief financial officer. Jay profusely apologises for calling on a weekend and orders him, as a matter of urgency, to freeze and cancel all business bank account accesses immediately. The Dutchman is surprised by the request and questions the motive for such actions. Jay diffuses the queries and invites Cedric not to talk to anyone or colleagues until further notice, as ordered by the police.

Omar is not a man of action; he only purchased two sixty-four gigabyte USB sticks. Less than a hundredth of the information can be transferred onto them. Jay acknowledges that Omar is on the verge of missing out on a big scoop. Omar is a lost cause who can't be helped. At the same time, Jay remembers how he was feeling when he abandoned his first visit to the luggage locker room because of his anxiety. As a form of compassion, he helps Omar to transfer a little bit of everything and hopes for the best.

The two Dutch police officers are as punctual as Omar. They're also surprised to hear that Ludo gave him access to Florian's home. Trying to put together a very complex jigsaw puzzle, they invite Jay to tell his story and the sequence of events since he arrived in Amsterdam over a fortnight ago. To facilitate their understanding, Jay goes to the basement, grabs a few sheets of paper from Florian's printer, and assembles them with some sticky tape found in a drawer. He invites the officers to move from the green sofa to the dining table so he can elaborate on his short time in Amsterdam. He draws a long line across his handmade canvas, and his strategy is good as it helps to break down any language barrier. A thick vertical black line on the timeline acknowledges each word or event. The first line is his landing in Amsterdam, followed by the meeting with the hypnotherapists, the purchase of the clown outfit, being the 'Clown of Amsterdam' and killing six people and saving four, discovering the first diary, contacting Tia and Kora, meetings with Ingrid, Coco, Zoetje, Abigail at the cottage, the sex worker shelter, meeting with Gaston Lars, Florian, and consequently Ludo. Becomes a police informer, the safe house, his wedding, Coco's assassination, Paul Van Looke and Florian's deaths, Gaston's arrest, tracking the diaries, trip to Ostend, Ludo's death in Ostend, Akanksha, Stardust, the sofa, the luggage lockers.

Jay writes 'Yesterday' on the timeline, followed by 'Now' and 'Tomorrow'. The officers are perplexed that Jay can predict the future.

— 'Yesterday, I discovered some valuable information for this investigation, and now it's your turn,' showing the written 'Now' word on the paper, 'to take possession of it,' tells Jay.

He invites the two police officers to the basement, where Jay explains and displays his findings. Like Omar a few hours ago, they're surprised by the intensity and cruelty on display. Jay starts with the hard-printed materials and goes through the digital media afterwards. He asks for the officers' attention by showing a picture of Ludo, Florian, Gaston, and Akanksha drinking cocktails in their shorts, polos, and sandals.

— 'They're dead!' Jay says, pointing to Ludo and Florian.

'He is in your care,' showing Gaston and moving his finger on the computer screen to Akanksha's head, 'She's free and in Amsterdam.'

Jay brings the officers back to the dining table and over the timeline of events. Indicating the word 'Tomorrow' with his index finger,

— 'I want you to arrest her on Monday morning at her workplace, which is my factory. I learned she managed my late wife's professional dancing career a few days ago. I suspect she's also responsible for organising her placement from a Ukrainian orphanage to a slaughterhouse in Belgium. I want her to answer a few of my questions about my wife's upbringing and how she was sex trafficked and to whom.'

As part of the procedure, and unable to provide a positive answer or commitment to Jay, the officers request assistance and need their superior to guide them through the process.

A few hours later, Jay is free to leave Florian's place with the agreement that he can still feed Stardust if he wishes to do so.

As he crosses the road, Jan Libbrecht, the inspector supervisor, calls him back and asks,

— 'Why is it so important for you to meet with Miss Mahindra on Monday morning when she can be arrested and interrogated now?'

— 'I need closure! I need to know how much of my wife's naivety has been abused. I'm curious to understand how Coco reinvented herself, knowing how much trauma has shaped her existence. I'm empty without her! I miss her dearly; I do! She was a pleasure to be around. She was my joy! The first joy I ever experienced,' tells Jay.

His facial expression and hand gestures mirror his sorrows.

— 'I understand your feelings, but I can't embrace them. I want to inform you that surveillance is organised to monitor Mrs Mahindra's movement. Her phone will be tapped soon. We appreciate your collaboration, but we don't want any interference. We don't want you in the news for the wrong reasons. This is our job, not yours!' clarifies the senior officer.

— 'How about Gaston Lars? Will you make him talk?' questions Jay.

— 'We can't force anyone to talk even if this person or individual has committed atrocities.'

— 'Would you be open to considering an elegant and smart way to do it?'

— 'I'm not Ludo; I'm not here to play games! Tell me how you'd like to proceed with Mr Lars.'

— 'Gaston is a trained hypnotist and certified hypnotherapist. You can play with his mind. The hypnotherapists leading the coma medical trial are interested in giving it a go!'

— 'As a matter of fact, not long ago, my wife and I were on a cruise ship on holiday, and as part of the entertainment package, there was an adult hypnosis show. Best laughs ever!'

— 'Your face radiates with the good memories!'

— 'Hundred percent! It was good fun! Let me see if the police can go off the beaten track to secure Lars' conviction!'

Jay returns to Florian's early evening to feed Stardust before going to Hotel L'Europa. Eef is at the main reception counter and welcomes Jay with a human touch; Jay returns the greeting and requests Coco's car keys.

— 'She'll be happy to know that you're taking her Porsche for a drive,' comments Eef.

— 'I'm taking her baby to the Nürburgring; it was her place to go when things were not so good! Both deserve a celebration.'

— 'Yes, she showed me her racing driving licence once. She is, or was, I should say, a big petrolhead! I miss her profoundly.'

— 'Are you okay?' Jay asks, seeing the melancholy taking over Eef's facial expressions.

— 'I'm okay, but I'm sad. I'm sorry!'

— 'Don't be sorry! I appreciate your authenticity. It's heartwarming!'

— 'Did you make up your mind about her residence?'

— 'Yes, it'll be for sale soon. Same for the Porsche and her other assets. I need to organise the removalists first.'

— 'Let me know if I can be of any assistance.'

— 'Let's talk about it next week!'

Chapter eighteen

The roaring ballerina

Jay receives the key to the Panamera and makes his way towards the German border. He needs a short break out of Amsterdam to allow some inner reconciliation work. The Porsche sounds like Stardust purring through the night. Jay drives well under the speed limit as he doesn't have the cash at hand to pay for any cross-border fines. His fingers glide on the edge of the leather seats the whole trip, admiring their perfect craftsmanship; as much as he is appreciative of the experience, he'd prefer gliding his hands on Coco's legs and pantyhose. Midnight knocks the dashboard clock, and the city of Nürburg is already in proximity. Jay books a hotel room for what's left of the night through his mobile device. The car park is full of head-turner cars ready to loop the ring after sunrise.

The night concierge informs Jay to buy some track credits

online and that breakfast is available from five o'clock in the morning.

Jay wakes up mid-morning, missing the breakfast cut-off time by a few minutes. He's not fazed as he dreamt that the best way to celebrate Coco's life is to buy bunches of flowers and give them to each petrolhead lining up at the Nürburgring entry gate, getting ready for the twenty-kilometre adrenaline rush. Florists in Nürburg are rare, and Jay bought what he could find at a petrol station. As he reaches the car park area, he's excited and asks everyone and anyone ready to loop the Nordschleife to take a flower in memory of his late wife.

Everyone is willing to participate, and hugs and tears are shared. Coco Carajuca is well known here. Jay gets introduced to some locals who are delighted to share photos of the roaring ballerina. Everyone speaks highly of her and expresses their deepest sorrows. Jay meets with the team at Ringtaxi. Coco was a regular customer and liked picking their expert brains to improve her track performance. Their receptionist emails Jay a few pictures of the glowing racer. Running out of flowers to give out and tissues to dry his eyes, it's Jay's turn to discover the world's most famous racing track. As much as his emotional state is uplifted by the beautiful words and memories he received, it's not an invitation to push the Panamera. While his flashing blinkers keep him on the slow side of the track, Coco's end-of-life celebration is now blessed by angry horn noises, flashing beaming lights, boxing air fists and tons of middle fingers. Five laps down, Jay has had enough of the abuse and returns to Amsterdam through the beauty of the country road. The police inspector's supervisor calls him. They must meet at the ice cream factory as soon as possible to discuss tomorrow's action and logistic plans.

Jay makes it back to Amsterdam just before nine o'clock at night and uses his entry pass for the first time. The production team is ready to start the night shift, and employees come and go through the car park. Two unmarked police vans enter the complex. Jay facilitates their entry to the building and into his office, where the confrontation with Akanksha will occur. A strategy is agreed upon, and a few wireless cameras will be installed in Jay's office. The police will monitor the meeting inside their vans, and four officers will pretend to be painters and interior designers preparing Coco's office for its new look. Jay texts Evi to come early to the factory. As it's too late to go home, he spends the rest of the night learning from the factory workers and testing ice cream samples.

Chapter nineteen

Karma is around the corner

The night shift is over, with the morning crew taking over their duties. Jay manages to wash his face and brush his teeth with his fingers. Having two hours to spare, he decides to check Akanksha's office. Her desk's drawers and filing cabinets are locked. Compared to other employees, her desk is neatly organised, and no personal items are left visible.

Evi arrives bright and early and is greeted by Jay's colour consultants and painters. She is briefed on the matter of the day and invited to seek safety when indicated or when she feels under threat. The police team, in a meticulous display of preparation, fits her with a set of wireless earphones to maintain their line of communication and a bulletproof jacket to wear under her shirt as a safety measure. Jay receives the same treatment.

It is showtime when Akanksha arrives and walks through

the carpark, greeting her colleagues with her charismatic smile. Jay and Evi are next for her morning blessings. She notices the painters placing masking tape around the ceiling. She enters her office and sets herself up for a day's work. Jay waits to call her until he can hear her drawers and filing cabinets opening. After a fifteen-minute wait, the moment finally arrives. Jay knocks at her office door and invites her to meet him with Cedric Lafkoof, the Chief Financial Officer, whom the police officers have briefed to run the meeting as long as possible until clearance is given. While the meeting proceeds, the painting team thoroughly searches Akanksha's office. A pair of flamenco shoes are found in the bottom drawer of the filing cabinets, and two concealed small-calibre handguns are spotted inside her desk. The officers unload the weapons and replace her ammunition with blanks.

Cedric receives a phone call from one of the officers and invites everyone to reschedule the meeting as he needs to address an urgent quality control matter.

On their way out of Cedric's office, the interior designers request Jay's attention for a few seconds. Jay excuses himself and pretends to sign a fake work order. He is now aware that his safety is guaranteed.

Jay invites Akanksha and Evi to his office. The painters are in the room.

— 'Please take a seat; I've got burning questions for you,' Jay starts.

— 'So early in the morning. It must be serious,' replies Akanksha. 'I'm listening and here to help!'

— 'It's about Coco and you. Since we met last, my head

has been spinning at the fact that you know her more than anybody else. I want to know more about her life, her dancing career, how she evolved as a woman, your evolution as an individual and your close-knit partnership.'

— 'I'd like to answer, but it's not the time or the place to do it. Look at all these people around. I prefer a face-to-face, intimate meeting with a glass of wine or French champagne in my hand.'

— 'I can ask everyone to leave, but my questions need answers.'

— 'I've prepared my resignation letter. It's my last day. I made up my mind over the weekend, and I waited for you to take over the business. Evi can take over my duties.'

— 'I didn't expect that! Are you all right? Did I upset you?' Jay replies, taking a piece of paper and a pencil from his desk.

— 'As my Dutch is poor and hard to understand, please write the name of a good bar or restaurant where we can meet to discuss Coco's life. Evi will book a table for lunchtime,' continues Jay as he passes the pen and paper to Akanksha.

— 'Restaurant De Utrechtsedwarstafel,' she says and writes in a flash.

— '4.6 stars rating on Google with a surprise menu,' she adds.

— 'Very nice and unusual rounded calligraphy,' comments Jay.

— 'Thank you for the compliment.'

— 'Let's talk about your resignation letter; you're not serious!'

— 'I've got it in my handbag and am ready to give it to

you. We've got a 'Captain'! I can sail away now. I'm free!' laughs Akanksha.

— 'Let's have a little privacy first. Evi, could you take the tradesmen out? I'd prefer to have this conversation one-on-one with Akanksha. Please close the door behind you,' says Jay with a formal corporate voice.

— 'Let me give you the letter now,' insists the Indian lady.

— 'No, wait! I've got a surprise for your last day. I knew this moment was coming; I can read people. I may be naïve, but I'm not one hundred percent stupid. I've got a surprise for you to celebrate the end of your busy professional life. Let me connect my computer to the big screen. If you wish, you can close your eyes for a moment. I've got a few photos to show you. Surprise! That's you with Gaston, Florian, and Van Looke having a great time together; here's your best calligraphy work stored in Ostend. You must realise I didn't plan to take you to the Restaurant De Utrechtsedwarstafel. I just needed evidence in front of witnesses, which were the painters and Evi, to validate your handwriting. This isn't finished yet; please sit down. In this photo, you're wearing flamenco shoes, which were snapped at numerous crime scenes and cemetery gatherings. Gaston is in custody, and Ingrid, Florian and Ludo are dead. It's just you now, and you've got nowhere to go.'

Akanksha's poker face hasn't changed. Jay flicks through the pictures to push her buttons. He comments on how the beauty of her gold bracelets and waist chains highlights the shape of her naked body and how the colour of her puffy nipples excites him. Putting a hand on Akanksha's arm, Jay says:

— 'You can leave the room free if you give me or tell me where I can find Coco's adoption folder. I want to know about her suffering and how Gaston set her up for sex trafficking.'

— 'I've got it here! Let me grab it!'

Akanksha crosses Jay's office, enters hers, makes some drawer noise, comes back, flicks the file on the table and points a set of guns at Jay's head.

— 'You're free! Just go! There's no need to kill me! I've got what I want! You can enjoy your freedom! I've got some reading to do.'

Akanksha does not budge; she is now a woman of steel. Her graceful Indian mannerisms are gone. The cobra is out of the woven basket, ready to strike.

— 'You walk me down to my car and follow my instructions to the letter, or I shoot you,' snaps Akanksha back.

— 'Okay, let me secure Coco's file. Please hide your weapons when crossing the office space. I don't want anyone to get hurt. I'll walk before you so you can act normally,' plays along Jay.

The office space is empty. The tactical team didn't want to take any risks. Everyone has been quietly evacuated. Jay walks in front of her, takes the stairs to the entry lobby, and walks towards her car in the car park. He opens the driver's door and starts the engine; Akanksha forces him to drive her car and sits behind him in the back seat. Jay slowly reverses out of the car space, hoping for the police force to intervene. Nothing happens. Jay drives through the entire parking lot, and now he is a few metres away from the gate, ready to exit the car park. There are cars in front of him waiting to pass the boom gate. Jay reaches a standstill, nervously waiting to know what will happen next. His nervousness makes his head spin, wishing for a miracle to happen. He checks left and right, and as he is ready to move on, he notices a forklift approaching the car at full speed. As a reflex, he leans his body towards the passenger seat. The forklift smashes the side of the car with full force; the impact is violent and extremely noisy. Glass projectiles spray across the cabin. The steel forks went through the rear body of the car, impaling and squashing Akanksha; her throat is slit, and her head is collapsed and rests on her upper body. Jay manages to escape the wreckage unharmed and discovers that Evi is the author of the dangerous manoeuvre, and her body has been catapulted out of the forklift cab enclosure. She requires instant medical attention; her face and hands are bloodied. Jay screams for help. He secures her gently and begs her not to move until the paramedics arrive. At the same time, plainclothes officers jump out of the two cars blocking the exit gate. They were unmarked police cars waiting for Jay to reach the other side of the boom gate. Everyone is shocked by the outcome. A toothless Evi smiles her pain at Jay as he takes care of her. He has an inner jubilation that he can't share with anyone; he is grateful for Evi's action. The ambulance is on her way! Akanksha is proclaimed dead at the scene, firmly holding two powerless guns in her hands.

The paramedic crew takes over, and Jay frantically returns to his office to grab Coco's computer. He accompanies Evi to the hospital. Her life is not in danger; she was lucky to be wearing the bulletproof jacket. Jay is invited to wait for her in the waiting room at the emergency department. He knows the feeling of the hard-shell plastic seat well. A discomforting bum dance is ready to start, but this time around, there are no shoulders to rest on. His red, blood-stained clothes give him plenty of attention. The television crews unveil the news to the world, with the Amsterdam drama reaching new heights.

The nurse informs Jay that Evi reminds him of his meeting at Hotel L'Europa early in the afternoon. Receiving the green light to go, Jay catches an Uber. He is running late.

Eef is in shock when Jay appears in the revolving entry doors. Jay apologises for his lack of glamour, and Eef confirms that Aiken & Siken and their guests have arrived and are waiting in the Weerspiegelkamer room. Jay spots Kora and Tia and gives them a visual thumbs-up. Eef informs that Net is waiting for him at the bar, and the IT set-up was done this morning.

— 'Was the IT girl pretty?' asks Jay to Eef as a way to relax a bit.

— 'Not only pretty, but she is sharp as a knife, and sadly for me, she is in love with the big guy.'

— 'He's my best friend! He has a big heart!'

— 'Good for him!' replies Eef.

Net joins Jay at the reception. He is dressed like a million dollars. Jay looks like the Pirate of the Caribbean after a night of adventure on the Calypso. He is proud of his appearance. Net is instructed to keep his mouth shut. As they enter the Weerspiegelkamer room, Jay introduces himself loudly and proudly, showing his stained shirt. He tells the gathering that he just settled a claim amicably with some wankers.

Sitting on the opposite side of the table, the Aiken & Siken teams introduce themselves and their clients. Luuk Aiken and Finn Siken are the first to do it. They, like Net, look sharp and do their best to display their bling. Eight of the twelve claimants are surrounding them. Each of them feels amused when introducing themselves. Jay introduces Net as his legal representative.

— 'I'm the chairman of the meeting; I'll record the meeting audio on my phone so I can easily produce the minutes afterwards. Does anyone have an objection?'

Receiving no answer, Jay proceeds and gives an overview of the agenda. Most importantly, he wants to know, from a customer experience, what happened. He requests Aiken & Siken's approval to question their clients. The request is reluctantly granted.

— 'Hi, I'm Jay Smith. I'm the new business owner, and the incident you have experienced is well before my time. So, I'd like to hear your story and, more importantly, your customer satisfaction experience. I'm sorry, but I don't speak Dutch, so if you don't speak or understand English, Net will translate our conversation.'

Finn Siken intervenes; he is not interested in Jay's strategy,

— 'These men are here for a fair and square compensation. We didn't come to bargain! No one around this table is interested to know how they lick their ice cream cone or where they purchased your badly manufactured products. Each man wants one million euros in compensation and

Luuk and myself five million euros each.'

Jay reminds Net not to intervene.

— 'Before I sign away a twenty-two million euros cheque. Let me connect my computer to the HDMI cable. I want to show you some of my research on the matter,' says Jay.

Pointing to the screen, he continues,

— 'Here is an email from Paul Van Looke to Luuk asking Aiken & Siken to disrupt my late wife's business. Now is your answer to Van Looke's email. One hundred thousand euros as a deposit, and you'll organise twelve plaintiffs to provide fake claims.'

The parties sitting in front of Jay start to get very agitated. Jay is the recipient of some insults.

— 'On Van Looke's approval, Luuk emailed the list of all plaintiffs. As per my research, all are little Dutch shits well known by the police force. Armed robbery, car hijack, rape, pub fights, shoplifting and so on. Each of you has received five thousand euros to sit your dirty fat arses in front of me today,' yells Jay!

Two of the plaintiffs make their way to exit the room; Jay stops them verbally,

— 'If you pass this door, I wish you good luck. Karma is around the corner!'

As the man proceeds, Luuk and Finn's faces are green. Their game is exposed.

— 'This is your last day as lawyers. The room is fitted with video cameras, and the feed is recorded at the police headquarters. Charges are coming your way. How do you want to deal with that matter now?'

Having no answer, Jay invites another two plaintiffs to leave the room.

— 'Remember, karma is around the corner,' he says.

Two more are invited to leave a few minutes later; the same is true for the last two.

— 'To conclude, I have more bad news for you. You should never accept cryptocurrencies as a mode of payment. This thing is so vulnerable! I hope that you can afford a lawyer now. It is your turn to meet your karma, showing them the exit door.'

Like the previous eight plaintiffs, Luuk and Finn are walked to the service staircase by a human corridor of two hundred hooded female MMA fighters. Kora and Tia give them personal heavy blessings in the darkness of the staircase. The ten men have been stripped to their underwear; their hands are zipped tight behind their backs. Their foreheads and chests are now billboards where the words 'liars and criminals' are written with bright red lipstick. Jay gives Cutie the green light to organise the fraudsters' collection. The Haka Army pushes them into the street and disappears like a flock of birds in the Dutch human landscape. Net is flabbergasted by the scene.

— 'Are you on my side?' questions Jay.

— 'Yes, oh yes! I need a drink!' replies Net with shaky hands.

— 'I want to acquire Dutch citizenship. Could you help me? My visa allows me to stay here for ninety days only.'

— 'After a drink and a little cash, everything is possible! There's no guarantee, but I can look into it. I owe you big time!'

Ozzie links Omar to the meeting video feed, and Amsterdam's news is getting surreal!

Jay calls Evi for an update on her medical condition. She does not answer. At the safe house, Ozzie, Cutie, Kora, Tia and Jay regroup for a light mid-afternoon celebratory drink. The conversation centres on Gaston and his future.

Tia and Kora are taking a short time off to New Zealand; they want to honour their mum's wishes and return her ashes to their homeland. Ozzie, Cutie and Jay decide to leave the safe house for good. Everyone feels free and safer now. The trio is moving back to Hotel Lucius as there are still over sixty days of pre-paid rent to be enjoyed. Florian's van is available, and everyone's belongings can be moved freely.

Later in the evening, Jay feeds Stardust and goes to the hospital. Evi is in good spirits despite having a broken hand and arm, and needing facial reconstructive surgery and a new set of teeth. Jay reassures her that he'll pay for her medical expenses, thanking her for her bravery.

The medical team pulls Jay aside; they want to know if her relatives live in the country.

— 'I will find out and, for the moment, put me as her next of kin; I will take care of the bills,' he answers.

Jay returns to the factory; the production lines are busy, and trucks loaded with thousands of flavoured ice creams make their way out of the dispatch centre. In his office, Jay grabs Coco's adoption file; he sits at his desk and reads slowly every detail about her younger recorded life. The first pages are glamorous, filled with big smiles and good-posture pictures to enable potential chances for adoption. Coco's birth name is Nikolina Koval. Her file also shows a photo of her and Gaston. She wears a cute summer dress, white socks and dark polished shoes. Gaston is business-dressed; he wears a brown suit and shoes, a white shirt and a pocket handkerchief. Both have a medium-sized suitcase next to them. Coco's one is brand new and probably contains, at the time, her life's belongings. Her medical report has distressed photos of her pre-orphanage medical intervention. Jay cannot comprehend how a little girl's body can be so damaged and brutalised. She is one big yellow, blue or purple puffed bruise. Tears flow along Jay's cheekbones. The post-orphanage pictures are taken in Ostend after Gaston rescues her from her fake adoption family. Her tiny body, or what is left of it, is the testimony of a night of horror. From her genitalia to her feet is a river of blood and excrement. Her face is swollen; her teeth are red; her lips are split, and her chest and arms are lacerated. Her tiny nipples are blue. Seeing the horror, he understands why Coco is so thankful towards her Papa. He gave her back the life that he voluntarily stole from her. There are plenty of photos of her reconstructive surgery, taken by Gaston while performing his craft. Jay has no words; his thoughts are focused on how much pain a ten-year-old girl can endure. There are also a few shots of her recovery in Ostend; she is either lying in bed or sitting by the bay window, having a glimpse at the greyish North Sea. Her facial expressions show no anger, resentment or frustration; only the glow of life can be found. Jay questions how a skinny, tiny, contused little orphan girl has so much trust in life and willpower towards it. Instant anger embraces Jay when he acknowledges that Jacqueline and Henry Wouters were the applicants on Nikolina's adoption papers. He recalls seeing their names in Florian's files but cannot put a face on them.

— 'Fucking bastards!' he yells while hammering his desk.

Another complex and painful thought pops into Jay's head about the circumstances of how he met his lover and how she and others avoided the hit list but still died due to his actions or interference with Gaston's plan. He is frustrated at the fact that Ingrid was never under investigation by Ludo or Florian. He realises that their camouflaged operation was well orchestrated and so deceptive, as he is forced to acknowledge that their condolences for Coco's passing were fake, manipulative and well-orchestrated. Jay also suspects that targeting the Mayor of Amsterdam was designed to deflect his attention from their plans. His awareness of his naivety consumes him badly, his head spinning like a washing machine drum as he flicks back and forth into Coco's adoption papers. He is equally taken aback by the horror produced by Gaston and his ability to operate on life-threatening injuries on a kitchen benchtop. Only battlefield surgeons have this type of skill and talent.

Chapter twenty

We are not expired

The following days, a routine takes place for Jay. He is out of the news spotlight. He's a nine-to-five ice cream maker, a cat feeder in the evening and a nighttime carer. Amsterdam is quiet, and somehow, it has become ever more boring. He plans the sale of Coco's place in his head, having already received an offer for the Panamera. Jay has a dilemma about what to do with Coco's belongings and adoption report. He puts an adoption notice for Stardust at the factory. Jay is falling off the cliff mentally. Every day is a struggle to cope with his powerless emotional state. Just seeing Ozzie happy is a burden. He's well aware that motion is the only thing that will put him out of his misery. During a night talk at the hospital with Evi, she invites him to surrender Coco's file to the police investigators.

Later in the week, Eef informs Jay that wealthy Qatari

clients are now in Amsterdam to purchase numerous luxury properties. Eef seeks Jay's permission to give them a private tour. Jay agrees, and within just a few hours, the property is sold on the condition that Coco's dancing memorabilia and art collection are part of the deal. The buyer, clearly moved by Coco's legacy, is eager to preserve and continue it. Net is invited to expedite the paperwork as the buyer wants a quick settlement. Jay visits Coco's place for the last time. The craftsmanship of the carpentry work still has the same impact on him. His morale is boosted. He lies on the bed for a few seconds; as the silky sheets have lost their sensual softness, he sits on the edge of the bed and admires Amsterdam's greatness. Out of curiosity, he opens the night side table. Coco's favourite book, What to Do When Our Emotions Hurt by Lionel Kools, is there. Post-it notes filled with comments pour out of the small publication, grab his attention, and, in the process, invite him to read the beginning of a chapter.

Everything has an expiry date

Just go to your pantry and pick up a tin of tomatoes, turn it around and read the expiry date. The can of tuna next to it is the same; it has an expiry date too! Now look around; everything has an expiry date: you, me, the dog, the cat, the flowers. Everything is falling under the same rule; the same principle applies to emotional healing. Our thoughts have an expiry date. Even when we repeat the same thoughts again and again, a day, this thought will die. Something new will enter our brain circuitry and years of beliefs will disappear without acknowledgement or a departure notice.

Any form of actions and reactions also have expiry dates. A lot of us, if not all of us, are or have been subject to single or numerous traumatic experiences during our life cycle. Whatever the severity, the frequency or the harshness of our past and present traumas; a day they will reach their expiry days. It sounds maybe hard to hear or to accept, but everything has a lifetime. 'Side effects' of any traumatic experiences such as anxiety, heartbreak, distress, agony fall under the same principle and have an expiry date too.

Nothing on this earth is here forever!

— 'This is bullshit! This is fucking bullshit! Coco, we are not expired! We are far from being expired; our love is alive!' says Jay loudly as he springs up off the bed, throwing the book back in the nightside table drawer savagely.

He grabs the picture frames of him and Coco and walks to Hotel Lucius to announce to Ozzie that he'll return to Nebraska when his Dutch visa expires.

— 'Good news! We're getting married in Lincoln. We're having a big fried chicken wedding! As my best man, I can't wait for you to walk me down the aisle,' teases Ozzie.

The Nebraskan boys hug as hard as they can; both are overwhelmed and emotional. Tears, high fives, and hugs are not enough to describe the intensity of their joy. Cutie is invited into their embrace.

Later that day, Jay meets with the police supervisor, and he surrenders a photocopy of Coco's adoption file as he can't yet relinquish the original.

— 'Thank you for dropping it in. We appreciate your collaboration! How are you?' asks Jan.

— 'I'm okay! I won't lie to you; it's tough!' replies Jay.

— 'I have something to cheer you up.'

— 'What is it? Today, I just want good news.'

— 'As an institution, we followed your recommendation and invited your hypnotist acquaintances to help us with Gaston Lars' interrogation. It's unusual, interesting, funny, and rewarding beyond belief. We're not done yet.'

— 'Did he talk?' swiftly asks Jay.

— 'Once on stage, he can't stop! Our luck is that he talks without filters!'

— 'What did he say?'

— 'We learnt that his team of executioners must provide a processed Polaroid of their crime to get paid. He sees Polaroid as a safe proof to allow payment as it's technically near impossible to tamper with the technology. He was unhappy when Polaroid closed their factory worldwide in 2008; he became mad when 'The Impossible Project' took over their manufacturing plant in Enschede, here in Holland. The Polaroid quality wasn't there, and all photos looked like funky abstract art or faded away over time.'

— 'Anything else?' asks Jay.

— 'While in the Philippines, he met Akanksha. They fell in love, and she invited him to come to Ukraine to live with her.'

— 'What's next for Gaston?'

— 'It's not up to me to decide. Based on his ongoing confessions, life behind bars is his trajectory.'

— 'Am I good to go?'

— 'Yes and no! As we need to run some ballistic tests to produce and secure crime scene evidence, we want all guns and ammunition that you've acquired from different parties back into our safety and custody as soon as possible. Also, your informant role, including your friend Ozzie's, ends now. As a thank you for your contribution to the safety of our nation, you'll both be awarded Dutch citizenship. To everyone's surprise, Ludo made the recommendation.'

— 'How twisted is that?'

— 'That's nothing! We assessed and reviewed the footage inside the action camera belonging to the influencer shot at Hotel Lucius. I apologise for the bad news and the disappointment, but Florian Van Bruggle is the gunman in the footage.'

Jay's facial expression acknowledges that his naïvety has been well abused since he landed in Amsterdam. Jan doesn't give him much time for inner reflection and proceeds with his next bombshell,

— 'With my Belgian and European counterparts, we're in the process of finalising a wanted list for all Lars and Mahindra's collaborators, paedophiles, and human and sex traffickers. We know that some of them are fugitives, and substantial bounties will soon be placed on their heads.'

— 'Why Lars-Mahindra?'

— 'Out of Lars' confession, we tend to believe that she is equally the mastermind behind their operations and most likely the catalyst of Gaston's involvement with the charity organisation as she needed someone who talks and presents well.'

— 'Nothing was missing in Akanksha's appearance or elocution.'

— 'Her origin and skin colour needed the support of a white salesman who could infiltrate without much effort their wealthy European target market.'

— 'A salesman!'

— 'That's how Gaston describes himself under hypnosis; she was a talent acquisition agent.'

— 'That's unbelievable! Innocent young girls weren't sent away to their deaths because of their talents. That's fucking bullshit!'

— 'The anecdote that should interest you is that Coco was saved because of her talent!' tells Jan.

— 'Could you repeat your last sentence?' asks Jay with wide open eyes.

— 'Gaston did save her because of her dancing abilities and,' pauses Jan.

— 'And what?' begs Jay.

— 'Nikolina was the perfect replica of a nine-year-old girl who was Gaston's ballet dancing partner when he was ten. The girl died in a car accident, and Gaston lost the love of his life and his passion for ballet.'

— 'His selfishness spares Coco's life — just!'

— 'She's the only one who was spared, Jay, and the only one who had a chance to make the bus trip back to Ukraine.'

— 'The only one!'

— 'If you guess how deep Gaston's selfishness is, I can guarantee 'no limit' is the answer. The name of the little girl killed in the car accident was Coco Carajuca. He wanted her back badly, and he did!'

— 'Was he in love with my Coco?'

— 'I can't answer your question! He told us under hypnosis that she was a dream embodied in his every cell and that he designed the life he wanted to live with her. He talks a lot about manifestation. I don't understand what that means,' says Jan with a dishevelled look.

— 'Gaston is a sick man!'

— 'The guy is seriously fucked up, but his acquaintances and clientele are worse than him! They're ruined to the bone beyond belief. All European countries are ready to spend big money to get them arrested and behind bars.'

— 'In Holland, does a bounty hunter require a licence to track down this type of person?'

— 'I don't know about bounty hunter licensing, but I can guarantee that cleaners don't require one.'

— 'Where and when will the wanted list be available?'

— 'You'll be the first to know about it. I'll give you the heads-up in due time!'

— 'Thanks a lot!'

— 'Make Amsterdam your home. You're a good citizen. We're pleased to have you around,' concludes Jan.

Jay informs Ozzie and Net of their citizenship status. It's another fried chicken celebration for the Dutch boys tonight.

Thinking of the expiry date in a relationship, Jay calls Abigail. She picks up the phone and apologises profusely for not giving signs of life. She expresses her sorrow for Coco and her infinite joy for the death of Paul Van Looke.

Jay learns she can stand up on her legs and painfully walk unassisted a few steps. She is hysterical and thanks him for taking her to America. Jay gives her a quick rundown on the latest news in Amsterdam, specifically the ice cream business. He checks if she's still interested in taking the top job. Abigail is zealous about the position but can only do it remotely for the next six months or until her treatment is completed. Both agree on her terms of employment, KPIs, and the need for Evi as her assistant. They decide to meet in Lincoln in a few weeks at Ozzie's wedding.

Later in the afternoon, Evi is discharged from the hospital. Her temporary set of teeth looks okay. Jay catches up with her and ensures she can manage independently. She laughs, thinking that Jay is funny and paternal. On a more serious note, he shares his plan for the ice cream business and her full-time role as personal assistant of the new chief executive officer. Evi is surprised that Jay won't be part of the venture. Like what was done earlier with Abigail, Jay negotiates her salary package. She is delighted to secure a company car as part of the deal. They high-five with great gentleness. Evi thanks Jay and gives him a one-arm, affectionate, tender hug. Jay acknowledges her gesture with a tear in his eyes. She is invited to join Ozzie and Cutie for beers and fried chicken. As she is not allowed to drink, she refuses the invitation. On the other end of the spectrum, Ozzie had no limitations. Beers and fried chicken are served in excess, and Cutie receives her engagement ring.

The following day, Jay has a massive hangover. Evi goes through her induction training, gets her access pass and takes over Akanksha's office. She emails all employees quickly, inviting them to a 'get together' function on Friday night. Based on Jay's recommendation, she organises the catering and invites Ed to be their DJ for the night. Everyone is on edge but curious about the invitation. Jay and Evi's lips are sealed, and within a few hours, over eighty-five per cent of the workforce have accepted the invite. Stardust has found a new house in the process. Jay extends the invitation to all the suppliers—Omar, Andrea, Cutie, Ozzie, and the Kiwi girls who've just returned from New Zealand.

The week is full of settlements. Net has made an offer to purchase the barge. Based on his online research, Jay agrees and proceeds with the sale.

Friday night arrives in no time; Jay dresses up for the occasion. As the weather forecast suggests evening rain, the festivities occur in the warehouse and the dispatch area. For safety measures, all equipment and machinery are fenced off. Garden lights hang from the warehouse's ceiling, providing a soft, intimate atmosphere. All tables and chairs are ready for their guests to arrive. Jay expects around five hundred people tonight. Ed's DJ booth is massive. Disco lights, smoke machines, lasers, tracers, and mirror balls receive their last pre-party checks. Heineken has provided mobile bars and kegs for an army to drink. The catering crew are in numbers. The buffet looks sensational and generous.

Employees and their relatives are welcomed into the venue by the leadership executive team, who have no clue what'll happen next. The music's pumping, the glasses are clinking, the laughs are coming, and the ambient noise is building up.

Before the dinner, Jay takes over the microphone.

— 'Hello, everyone; please accept my apologies for not addressing you in your native language. Thank you for coming tonight and for your generosity in accepting me as the new business owner. Before we go into why we're here tonight, I'd like to propose a minute of silence to remember my late wife, Coco Carajuca, the founder of the business. I invite you to remember her the way you wish; for me, I remember her glow, smile, generosity, laughter and gingery fragrance. Let's remember her.'

The minute of silence goes over time, and the room becomes emotionally loaded.

— 'Thank you. She's with us tonight, and I can guarantee you that she's happy to be here,' says Jay, a smile on his face. 'As you're aware, I've been on global news for a while now, and it was never my plan. My journey in Amsterdam's been an eye-opener to both the beauty and ugliness of our world and its offering. I can reassure you that my rollercoaster journey was worth it. We—because I'm not alone—take the credit for the actions and successes that exposed and took down probably the most significant and oldest sex trafficking and paedophile network on this continent. One of their young victims was Coco; she was sex trafficked at the age of nine. She shared her story with me, and I had the unfortunate privilege of accessing her photographic records. That alone makes me realise that we're living in a world made of smoke and mirrors, a world full of deception. Akanksha's death is linked to Coco's sex trafficking; she was a significant player in a criminal network and is responsible for the death and sex slavery crimes of a thousand women. That's not all; she's responsible for the sabotage of this business. As reported in the news, you did nothing wrong; your products are and were first-class. The reason why you were targeted is that Coco and a few friends are members of a non-profit organisation that had the ambition to open a shelter for sex workers. As Coco supplied the funds to the charity organisation, it didn't sit well with Akanksha and her accomplices. As retribution, the business's cash flow and reputation were targeted.

Tonight, I draw a line in the sand. Your past troubles are over. Our suppliers have been paid, and stolen funds have returned to our bank accounts. Today is a new beginning; your jobs are secured.'

A loud round of applause bursts from the crowd.

— 'Tonight, I'd like to acknowledge the bravery of Evi, who put her life on the line for the justice and welfare of thousands of women. She suffered severe injuries in the process and still has some rehabilitation to do. Evi's now part of this business full-time, and I invite you to help her in her journey and, most importantly, to enrol her in a forklift operator course. She deserves her licence.'

A round of laughter and applause takes over the warehouse. Evi smiles, her new teeth on show.

— 'You have a new CEO coming on board. It won't be me,' says Jay. 'I'm leaving the business, and the person taking over Coco's leadership role is Abigail Ashton. For those who don't know her, she's the 'Dutch Woman of the Year' and the 'Dutch Women Entrepreneur of the Year'. I've negotiated her contract, and for the next few weeks, she'll operate remotely as she's also undergoing rehabilitation in the United States. Abigail is excited to be part of the journey, and here again, your support is welcome!'

After taking a sip of water, Jay continues,

— 'The next two items will greatly impact you. The business is going to be publicly listed on the stock market. The private ownership is over.'

Jay marks a silence before committing to the core of his speech and builds some tension in the process.

— 'The second news is that you'll be the shareholders of the business. In the coming days, the employees will control the company. It's now your baby! I don't know where this journey will take you, but please keep your heart on what you're doing. You're doing well.'

The room explodes with cheering, clapping, laughter, and tears. The employees start drumming the table and clapping their hands to the rhythm of Queen's song 'We Will Rock You'. Jay smiles at the scene and takes over the microphone after a nearly solid five-minute corporate madness.

— 'I shouldn't stop you! You're in charge! For the past few weeks, I've had the privilege of being with you on the floor, and your passion and commitment to the business have been phenomenal. You deserve to be in charge! Your work, love, intelligence, and problem-solving capabilities deserve a reward. Today is the day! Before you jump into the next moment of euphoria, I'd like to thank all suppliers who had their fair share of stresses in our venture, and we'd like to enter a five-year agreement with you to secure our future together. Cash is now in the bank. We're ready to see our partnership succeed. To conclude, your new journey will be full of challenges, new learnings, investments, and, most importantly, human management, both at personal and corporate levels. When dealing with people, please remember how Coco treated us all; she did it with respect and humility. So, let's plea tonight to embrace her humane way of doing business and that your collective interests should prevail over your personal needs and wants. Please accept my congratulations on your achievements. The place is now yours. Thank you. It's time to party!'

'We Will Rock You' table drumming takes over the warehouse again. The factory workers surround Jay, lift him off the ground, and parade him over their shoulders. A night of madness starts, and Ed adds fuel to the fire with his techno beats.

Jay finally lands on his feet and manages to have a drink with Cutie, Ozzie, Kora, and Tia.

— 'What's next for you, Jay?' asks Kora.

— 'What's next for us? Should be the question,' he answers.

— 'Okay, what's next for us?' giggles Tia, bouncing her shoulder on her sister.

— 'The five of us should ally and work together.'

— 'Since we came back from our express trip to New Zealand, we've questioned our career direction, the Haka Army, our UFC trajectory, and everything else, to be honest. What do you have in mind?' queries Tia.

— 'We should become bounty hunters and bring to justice all associates, perpetrators and successors connected to Gaston and Akanksha. There's substantial money to be collected in the process.'

— 'The five of us, right?' clarifies Kora.

— 'Yes! The five outcasts! We, and our skills, complement each other well,' replies Jay, a big smile on his face.

— 'Who is in it?' screams Ozzie, pushing an open hand in the middle of the pack.

— 'We're all in!' replies Tia, putting her hand on Ozzie's one. Kora, Jay and Cutie follow.

Showing her engagement ring on top of the hand pile, Cutie tells Kora and Tia,

— 'We're getting married! I'd like the two of you to be my bridesmaids and, most importantly, my friends. My other offer still stands; maybe we can have a pre-nuptial gift!'

Ozzie is stunned by his wife-to-be's bridal invitation, and he diffuses the offer by proposing a toast to their alliance.

The end of the party and the following days are pure euphoria at the manufacturing plant. Productivity soars, waste is reduced, and job vacancies are filled quickly. Omar's publication boosts the company profile, and the fairy tale story captures the heart of the Dutch public and overseas buyers. Sales are on the rise. Abigail is on board, and Evi keeps things in check.

Eleven days after the announcement of the change of ownership, the legal hurdles are solved, and the business transfer is completed. Net informs Jay that he can return his access pass to the Human Resources Manager, and without a minute to spare, he informs Evi that his time has come. They hug tightly, and both share their thank you to the other.

Jay shakes many hands on his way out, and a line of honour takes him to his Uber ride.

Back at Hotel Lucius, Cutie has a surprise for Jay and Ozzie, inviting them to finalise and sign their citizenship papers. The Nebraskan boys are excited about the prospect of getting an European passport. Another beer and fried chicken celebration takes place.

Later that evening, Jay receives a phone call from Juliana. The conversation goes into overdrive in no time.

— 'Hello, Jay! How are you?'

— 'I'm returning to Lincoln soon; I'm excited! Is that okay with you?'

— 'When are you back?'

— 'Soon! I don't have a date yet. I still need to address my laundry!' laughs Jay.

— 'I need you here,' says Juliana with a distressed voice.

— 'Why? What's the urgency?'

— 'Sakura's been kidnapped today when leaving the immigration centre!'

— 'I thought she was under protection.'

— 'She managed to be part of an insertion program through her lawyer.'

— 'Are you sure that she was kidnapped? Maybe she ran away.'

— 'She was forced into a car. We've got witnesses at the scene.'

— 'Why do you need me?'

— 'I want her back, alive and in good health. I fucked up! The insertion program was my idea, and I don't have much sympathy or support from my organisation to find her.'

— 'Okay! Let me make some arrangements here, and we'll go to Lincoln soon!'

— 'Who is 'we'?'

— 'Surprise! Please send me the time and location where Sakura vanished so we can prepare ourselves.'

— 'Who is 'we'?' repeats Juliana with a controlling voice.

Jay laughs and terminates the call without answering her question. A few minutes later, he receives a text message from her that reads,

— '850 S St, Lincoln, NE 68508. Around nine o'clock in the morning.'

Jay forwards the message to Ozzie. Lincoln's surveillance infrastructure will be hijacked in no time as Cutie recruited a seclusive group of dark web users.

With Omar's assistance, Jay makes the front page of De Dagblad. He offers substantial financial rewards to anyone who supplies information on Nikolina Koval's rape twenty-four years ago in Kyiv. The crucial information included in the publication is that one aggressor had his penis injured and most likely required medical attention at the time.

Later in the evening, Eef notifies Jay that a parcel addressed to him has been delivered to Hotel L'Europa. After walking the few blocks separating the two hotels, Jay collects the goods but can't contain his curiosity. Back in the street and along the canal, he opens the packaging. To his surprise, sexy male bodysuits fill the box alongside an invoice dated the day he and Coco left Las Vegas for Ostend and a note that reads,

'Jay, when we met, I was turned on. Now, as I'm discovering your care, love and gentleness, my sexual desires are pulsing madly. I'm aroused and wet, and my kinky thoughts towards you are secretly ordering our wedding gift. I can't wait to lick your electric nipples and taste your spunk. I love you. Your wife. Coco.'

ACKNOWLEDGEMENTS

A special note of gratitude to:

Chris, Annie, Glen, Eef, Louis, Lila 'Chicken' and Nikki.

A big thank you to:

Frank.

ABOUT THE AUTHOR

Maxsense Maximus is a Belgian-born writer, born in Tongeren and raised in the Ardennes, whose formative environment cultivated a deep sensitivity to human behaviour, narrative nuance, and cultural subtext. In 1996, he migrated to Australia, where he encountered the complexities of cultural displacement—an experience that continues to inform the thematic architecture of his work.

His literary and psychological development was shaped by an acute perceptiveness from an early age: attuned to the moods, silences, and fractures of those around him, as well as to life events he experienced prematurely. A defining moment in his intellectual trajectory occurred during adolescence with the discovery of Ernest Hemingway's The Old Man and the Sea, which catalysed his interest in minimalist prose, internal conflict, and the intricacies of psychological realism.

Maximus's debut novel, Ostend, emerged from over two years of immersive observation and instinctive character construction. Composed largely in fragments during everyday life, the work reflects a creative process that prioritises authenticity over refinement, resulting in a narrative that is both emotionally resonant and formally raw. His writing style fuses cinematic detail with introspective depth, inviting the reader into a liminal space between memory, imagination, and emotional brilliance.

The pseudonym Maxsense Maximus is both an act of personal reclamation and symbolic transformation. Maxsense honours his mother's original wish to name him Maxence, while simultaneously articulating a literary philosophy that privileges perception as a pathway to creative and emotional abundance. Maximus, derived from Latin, situates his voice within a classical tradition of expressive depth and intentional precision. Maximus writes not to entertain, but to remember, to bear witness, and to engage with the emotional truths that often go unspoken.

www.ingramcontent.com/pod-product-compliance
Lightning Source LLC
Chambersburg PA
CBHW010255100726
47904CB00011B/2601